Ted Willis was born in London in 1918 and he makes no mystery of the fact that Rosie Carr is based on the character of his own mother.

He joined the Royal Fusiliers during World War II and worked as a writer of War Office films and Ministry of Information documentaries. Since then his distinguished career has been as a writer – playwright, screenwriter and novelist.

He was created a life Peer in 1963.

Spring at
The Winged Horse

The First Season of Rosie Carr

TED WILLIS

Futura

A Futura Book

First published in Great Britain in 1983 by
Macmillan London Limited

This edition published in 1989 by
Futura Publications, a Division of
Macdonald & Co (Publishers) Ltd
London & Sydney

ISBN 0 7088 4227 5

Typeset in Plantin by Fleet Graphics, Enfield, Middlesex

Printed in Great Britain by Cox & Wyman Ltd, Reading

Futura Publications
A Division of
Macdonald & Co (Publishers) Ltd
66-73 Shoe Lane
London EC4P 4AB
A member of Maxwell Pergamon Publishing Corporation plc

Dedicated with love to my wife, Audrey,
and to the memory of my mother,
Maria Harriet Willis

ACKNOWLEDGEMENTS

The author and publishers are grateful to EMI Music Publishing Limited for permission to reproduce verses from 'Knees Up Mother Brown' (© 1958 Peter Maurice Music Co. Ltd., 138-140 Charing Cross Road, London W.1.), 'Comrades' (© 1890 Francis Day & Hunter Ltd., 138-140 Charing Cross Road, London W.1.) and 'Honeysuckle and the Bee' (© 1901 Sol Bloom, U.S.A. and Francis Day & Hunter Ltd., 138-140 Charing Cross Road, London W.1.).

CHAPTER ONE

1

When Rosie Carr was thirteen years of age, her Aunt May died. The date was May 23, 1906 the day on which Henrik Ibsen also went to his maker. It must be said, however, that the death of the great Norwegian dramatist passed unnoticed by Rosie, or indeed by anyone else in Victoria Road, Tottenham. Their local theatre was the Wood Green Empire, a music-hall where Ibsen was unknown, Marie Lloyd reigned as queen, and her song 'Don't Dilly-dally on the Way' was like a second national anthem.

The doctor said that Aunt May had succumbed to pneumonia but Rosie was certain that her aunt had been killed by other people's washing. For as long as she could remember, Aunt May had lived out her days, (and part of the nights too) behind the clouds of hot steam that billowed up from the stone copper in the scullery where she boiled the clothes. Other people's clothes. There was the washing from the Misses Brown in Bruce Grove, from Mrs Waterson in Green Lane (her husband was a bank manager and a magistrate), from Major and Mrs Pauley who lived next door to Mrs Waterson, from Mr and Mrs Burgess who owned the big emporium in the High Road and – oh, from a dozen other fairly well-to-do families.

Rosie knew them all, for it was her job to collect the soiled laundry from the customers each Monday and to deliver the crisp, freshly-ironed bundles back to them on Saturday mornings. For this purpose she would use the ancient perambulator her aunt kept in a corner of the backyard under a worn waterproof sheet, and twice each week she trundled this tired old contraption, with its tyre-less wheels and squeaking axles, loaded down with laundry, around the streets of Tottenham on a circuit of six or seven miles, defying the worst that the weather could send against her.

There were times when Rosie allowed herself to wonder why all these good people could not do their own washing and ironing. The women looked strong and healthy enough, a good deal fitter certainly than her thin and weary aunt. Was it sheer laziness on their part? But then the practical side of her nature – never far from the surface – asserted itself as she realised that there was some profit in their idleness for without the income provided by Aunt May's labours the situation at Number 49, Victoria Road would have been even worse than it was. The few shillings brought in by the laundry helped to maintain a precarious equilibrium, a delicate balance between plain ordinary poverty and abject destitution. The distinction was a fine one, not to be recognised by the likes of Aunt May's clients, but well understood by the poor themselves.

Not that the clients were rich, although Rosie thought them so. They were, for the most part, members of the solid middle class, petit-bourgeois who lived in a sort of hinterland between the wealthy and the poor, driven on by the hope of rising into one rank and fear of falling into the other. And in anticipation of their ascent in the social scale they tended, with few exceptions, to adopt what they imagined to be the airs and graces of a superior class.

Thus the Misses Brown affected a twittering kindly gentility whenever they saw Rosie, asking always about the welfare of her aunt. But Rosie noted that they never appeared to listen to her answer and that their concern for Aunt May did not extend to paying the weekly laundry bill with any degree of promptness. They would often let it run up for three or four weeks at a time and then, when politely pressed to pay, express indignation at such bad manners and shock at the size of the accumulated amount.

Mrs Waterson, on the other hand, could always be relied upon to pay up on the dot but, being the wife of a bank manager, she invariably knocked something off the bill. She had a passion for what she called 'rounding-up': in practice this meant that if the bill came to one shilling and a penny, she would hand over a shilling, as if she were doing Rosie a great kindness, and announce with a motherly smile:

'There we are, my dear. I'll give you a shilling. A nice round figure.'

Rosie observed that the rounding-up process never operated in the other direction. If the bill came to elevenpence ha'penny, it would be reduced to elevenpence, never raised to a shilling. Aunt May knew the trick of it, however, and on the principle that it would be selfish to deprive Mrs Waterson of her pleasure, she always took care to add the odd copper to the bill, thus satisfying both parties.

Of Major and Mrs Pauley, Rosie had no complaint. The Major, long retired, was a quietly cheerful man, in appearance and manner quite unlike Rosie's notion of a military gentleman. At his house she could always be assured of prompt payment and a bonus in the shape of a ha'penny for herself or a piece of cake. And in the summer the Major would often send her off with a cabbage, a bag of potatoes or some other gift from the long garden that he tended so lovingly.

On one occasion, he had presented Rosie with a single red rose, bowing to her in grand style and saying with a smile:

'A rose for a Rose.'

The rose was so beautiful, its scent so delicate, that Rosie had been overwhelmed with delight. Later, when it had faded, she pressed it between the pages of a book.

There were other customers who showed her moments of kindness but they were the minority: for the most part they were either indifferent or complaining or simply downright mean. They seemed to have no understanding of the hours, the endless hours, that Aunt May worked, standing pink-faced over the steaming copper or at the kitchen table, iron in hand, with a mountain of clothes in front of her, or of the desperate importance of every penny she earned.

And, in the end, as Rosie well knew, it was the work that killed her aunt. Worn out with no strength to resist her last illness, she gave up the struggle while lying asleep in the big, brass bed in the backroom which for twenty years she had shared with her husband Bob.

She was only 43 when she died, but she looked every day of sixty.

2

Rosie had little time to mourn. After the walking funeral – one hearse and the mourners following on foot – she set to, as her aunt had done, in the scullery and the kitchen, to transform the untidy piles of dirty clothes into neatly-ironed bundles, each labelled with the name of the owner.

Uncle Bob watched her and said nothing. His three sons, Rosie's cousins, Harry, Albert and Ron, watched her and said nothing. Relatives and neighbours, popping in to offer sympathy, watched her and said nothing. But Rosie knew from her uncle's manner that he was thinking, and she guessed that he was thinking about her.

Uncle Bob, a small man with the look of a pugnacious terrier, was going through one of his regular bouts of unemployment and these always made him morose. He was a carpenter, quite a good one, and he was only truly happy when working with his beloved tools. Unfortunately, he was also something of a perfectionist and his total commitment to craftmanship, his steadfast refusal to cut corners did not sit well with most of the local employers, who were more interested in output than quality. His obstinacy, as Aunt May used to put it, had 'cost him more jobs than I've had hot dinners.'

But it was not just the lack of work that stopped Uncle Bob's tongue that morning. He was mourning the loss of a good wife, as was proper, remembering the time when May was young, voluptuous and eager, when nights, and an occasional Sunday afternoon, in the heaving brass bed had been sheer delight.

There had been little enough of that in the past few years: Bob had watched the bright-eyed girl he married decline into a scraggy, sharp-elbowed, greying woman, her face cured to a

10

permanent pink by the steam, with no energy, patience or inclination for the delights that could be found between the sheets. That he had changed also, and was no longer the quick, laughing young man of twenty years ago, was something that simply did not occur to him.

Still, he granted that May had been a good hard-working wife and mother and knew that he would miss her. But death was not an infrequent visitor to Victoria Road and its inhabitants, including Bob, had learned from long experience to pay it a little, brief respect and then dismiss it. Dying, after all, was relatively easy; it was living that threw up the real problems.

This was the thought that chiefly occupied Bob Daines and which was responsible for his silence. And Rosie's instinct had been right. He was pondering the problem of what to do about her.

A plan, a vague plan concerning his own future and that of his three sons, was taking shape in his mind and Rosie played no part in it.

He had never really been in favour of taking the girl into his home: that had been May's doing. She had fought his objections to a standstill, argued with him so fiercely that he had given in out of sheer exhaustion.

3

Rosie was the bastard daughter of May's sister, Ethel. The father was unknown except to Ethel, who had borne that secret away forever when the consumption finally killed her. So Rosie, at the age of nine – perky, cheeky little Rosie with her big impudent brown eyes – had been brought to live with the Daines family. A strange little cuckoo in the nest.

Bob considered himself to be a fair man, and he readily admitted that Rosie had earned her keep. As time went on and she grew bigger, Rosie more or less ran the little terraced house, leaving her aunt free to cope with the laundry. It was Rosie who hearth-stoned the front step, black-leaded the kitchen grate, scrubbed the floors, made the beds, mended the worn clothes and did most of the shopping and some of the cooking, in addition to the twice-weekly laundry round.

Morever, she did all this cheerfully, without complaint, accepting that it was a girl's job to help in the house. It never occurred to her to comment on the fact that Uncle Bob and the three boys (with the occasional exception of Albert, the middle one) never lowered themselves so far as to lift a cup from the table to drink from it, or to touch the old pail that did duty as a coal-scuttle except to hand it to her when it was empty.

Of course, these manifold chores meant that Rosie had no time for school. Indeed, as far as the local School Board was concerned Rose Adelaide Carr did not exist, for Bob Daines had never troubled to register her presence in the house. She had been stopped and questioned in the street on two or three occasions by the School Board Inspector and she had simply lied to him, insisting with a sweet innocence that she actually lived in Basingstoke and was only staying with her aunt for a few days.

She conjured up the inoffensive town of Basingstoke because she had once stayed there, briefly, with her mother. Ethel Carr had been a restless soul, moving from place to place, sometimes in search of employment but more often to follow in the footsteps of her latest lover and so with her, also, there had been no opportunity to send Rosie to school for any worthwhile period.

The longest time Rosie sustained as a scholar was for six weeks at a school in the town called Wolverhampton, which Rosie vaguely recalled as being somewhere up north. The experience was such as to put her off schooling and school teachers for life, for it had been her misfortune to be placed in the charge of a certain Miss Bundle, a tall thin lady with iron-grey hair and coldly-glinting blue eyes.

Miss Bundle also had a long thin scraggy neck and when she became angry the veins on the neck stood out like columns and turned faintly blue. She was angry very often, especially with Rosie, towards whom she developed a positive, if irrational, dislike. It may have been because Rosie was incapable, not from wilfulness but from her very nature, of falling into the silent, frightened submission that characterised the other children, or because Miss Bundle saw in this child a flickering spark of independent spirit and was determined to extinguish such a dangerous manifestation.

At any rate, Miss Bundle focused her steely sights on Rosie and with formidable determination went forth to break her. She abused and threatened the child; she made her the target for bitter mockery; as a hunter sets traps for his prey, she imposed impossible tasks on her, knowing that the uneducated girl could only fail. When the abuse and sarcasm failed she beat Rosie with the cane, beat her time and time again, beat her until her arm ached, beat her until the cane snapped.

And all the time, the teacher searched Rosie's eyes for a hint of fear, a tiny hint only, just enough to give Miss Bundle the satisfaction of knowing that she had won, that the stubborn spirit was broken and the punishment could end. For the truth of it was that Miss Bundle had become weary – and perhaps a little guilty too – of the long contest and wanting nothing more than to bring it to a reasonable conclusion. But pride and a vigorous sense of Christian duty would not allow her to turn back from her self-imposed task until this wayward child had been brought to a state of grace.

Infuriatingly, Rosie showed no sign of submission. At first, her eyes filmed with tears and she looked up at Miss Bundle in bewilderment, as though she could not comprehend what was being demanded of her.

Later, however, she came to recognise, dimly perhaps, that this was some kind of contest, that Miss Bundle wanted something that she could not give, and the stubborn side of her nature took over. So when the exhausted Miss Bundle, the thick veins in her neck quivering with frustration, looked into the brown eyes, seeking desperately for some trace of fear or defeat, she saw only defiance, or a suggestion of mockery or – what was infinitely worse – even a look of pity.

Rosie took her weals and her bruises home with her and said nothing. Her mother bathed the injuries and soothed her daughter, asked one or two questions, but did nothing until the day when she decided that it was time to move on, back to

13

London. Then she went to Buck's the oil shop on the corner, and bought a twopenny cane, a thin pliable cane with a handle.

That afternoon Ethel Carr and Rosie waited outside the school gates until Miss Bundle appeared. Rosie had no notion of what was afoot, although a certain tenseness in her mother's manner indicated that it might be exciting.

When Rosie had identified the teacher, Ethel told her to stand back, then planted herself in the path of the unsuspecting woman.

'Miss Bundle?' she asked, with a deceptive smile.

'Yes,' answered the teacher warily.

'I'm Rosie's mother.'

'Rosie?'

'Rosie Carr.'

'Rosie Carr. Ah, yes.' Miss Bundle looked at Rosie and then back to Ethel. 'She wasn't in school today.'

'No,' said Ethel. 'She won't be coming any more. We're moving away.'

'Oh,' said Miss Bundle, 'I'm sorry to hear that.'

'I bet you are,' said Ethel calmly. 'You'll have to find some other poor kid to pick on now, won't you?'

'I don't know what you mean.' There was fear in the pale blue eyes now, and she attempted to move on. 'If you'll excuse me – '

'Just a minute,' said Ethel in the same calm tone. 'I haven't finished with you yet. I've come to tell you that you are a wicked, spiteful old cow. And to give you a taste of your own bloody medicine!'

And with these words she drew the cane from under her thin coat and slashed at Miss Bundle's sallow face. Taken by surprise, the teacher failed to raise her guard and the cane cut a diagonal mark across her cheek. She screamed and began to run as the cane sang through the air to fall again and again on her arms, her shoulders, her backside.

Ethel was not a fit woman and after a few yards she gave up the chase, threw the cane away, and went breathlessly back to Rosie. By this time a crowd of children had gathered, staring in amazed silence at the extraordinary scene. Some of them

14

smiled secretly but such was the power of Miss Bundle's authority that not one of them found the courage to cheer her undignified rout. There was a certain logic in their attitude: they realised that though Rosie might be leaving they were staying, and no-one wished to take her place as the target for Miss Bundle's excesses.

'Don't stand there with your mouth open like a letter-box!' said Ethel to the astonished Rosie and, gathering up her daughter, she swept away, leaving fifty wide-eyed children in her wake.

That, to all intents and purposes, was the end of Rosie's schooling, a circumstance that worried her not in the least. She was happy to be free of the Miss Bundles of this world and she was kept far too busy to worry about her lack of learning. Aunt May had expressed her concern from time to time, but young Rosie proved so useful about the house that the tired woman soon came to accept the situation.

It was a boon to Bob Daines, for it meant that there was one less problem to solve. Rosie was virtually a free agent, unfettered by any need to attend school; she was also a willing and experienced skivvy. There were few girls of her age who could do what she did around the house.

So, while Rosie got on with the washing, Bob thought it all through. By the next morning he had reached a decision. First, he wrote a letter and waited for six weeks until a reply came in the shape of a bulky registered envelope. He found the contents satisfactory. So far, so good.

His next step was to pay a visit to The Winged Horse, a public house in the High Road.

4

Rosie had just returned with the week's washing and was unloading it at the back door when her uncle came out to her. Even his insensitive eye noticed that the child looked pale and worn-out, and the tiny twinge of guilt that nipped his mind for a moment increased his awkwardness.

'Rosie,' he began.

'Yes?'

She glanced up at him and then continued with her work. There was a lot to do and she had no time for gossip.

'I'm talking to you!' he said irritably. 'Leave that and listen, can't you?'

She stopped what she was doing and stood watching him.

'That bloody pram needs oiling,' he said. 'You can hear it squeaking halfway up the street.'

'I'll put a bit of grease on the wheels,' she replied.

'It wants a proper job doing,' he said. 'I'll get one of the boys to give it a going-over for you.'

With this he went inside again, muttering to himself. He would have been surprised to know that Rosie watched his departure with a relief that had nothing to do with the squeaky perambulator.

She knew, without being told, that her uncle had little time for her. He had never raised a hand to her or shouted at her, that was true, but, by the same token, he had never, by word or action, done anything to show that he included the girl in his family circle. He would chat and laugh and sometimes play with the boys, he would curse them and chastise them, but he kept Rosie at a distance, refusing to be drawn towards her. Aunt May, sensing this, had done her best to make it up to Rosie, but the pressure of maintaining the family meant that she had little time for mothering.

With the death of her aunt, the one point of warmth, of human contact went from Rosie's life. She had suffered such a loss before, when her mother died, but in a way, her aunt's passing was worse. There was no-one else now to whom she could turn, nowhere else to go unless it be an orphanage, and that was a prospect that filled her with a chilling fear. Jessie Hamilton, who lived with an elder sister at Number 39, had spent four years in an orphanage near Glasgow, and her description of the place had made it sound like some hellish prison, where the captives were presided over by an army of Miss Bundles.

It was this fear of the future that had driven Rosie to work even harder in the house, to add the laundry to her already heavy load of chores. Instinctively she knew that her uncle would never accept her for herself: what she hoped to do was to prove to him that she was indispensable. To keep the laundry money coming in was an essential part of this operation, for more often than not it was the only income to reach the family purse.

Last Saturday, Rosie had collected almost fourteen shillings from her customers, and when she handed the money over to her uncle – every penny, including the ha'penny that Major Pauley had given her as a personal extra – he had accepted it with what sounded like a grunt of approval.

The grunt had given her hope. If she stuck to her labours he might come to understand that the family could not manage without her.

So, when her uncle spoke to her about the squeaking pram, she saw this as another small step forward. He had never shown any interest in such things while her aunt was alive: the fact that he wanted the old pram put in order now could only mean that he was expecting her to carry on, that she was consolidating her position.

On such small manifestations did Rosie build her hopes. Her uncle's grudging grunt of approval, his reference to the perambulator, the fact that weeks had gone by since her aunt's death and she was still in the house. Like someone walking alone and afraid through a long black tunnel, she seized eagerly on any indication that there was daylight ahead.

Still, at the back of her mind, huddled like a bright-eyed mouse in a corner, there lingered a thought, a remnant of fear. She could not fasten upon it with any precision but she knew vaguely that it had something to do with the look in her uncle's eye, with his strange awkwardness. She had the feeling – no, nothing so strong as a feeling, more a suspicion – that he had been going to say more, but that he had somehow lost his nerve.

But because she was by nature an optimist and because it was only a tiny suspicion, she refused to dwell upon it.

So, as she lit the copper and prepared the washing, Rosie hummed a little song to herself, and she laughed as she held the Misses Brown's drawers, with their pink bows and lace frills, against herself, wondering how she would look in such absurd garments.

5

That evening, Uncle Bob gave Rosie tuppence and sent her to The Winged Horse for a pint of ale. The Star of India pub was nearer – on the corner of the next street – but her uncle always insisted that she should make the longer journey, on the grounds that the beer at The Winged Horse was superior.

'Don't go to The Star,' he told her for the hundredth time: 'The beer there is like gnat's piss.'

Rosie knew better than to argue but she had difficulty in suppressing a little smile. Many times in the past, when it was raining or she felt really tired, she had saved herself a journey of a half-mile by going to The Star of India and not once had her uncle commented about the quality of the ale. But on this occasion she decided to take no risks and, holding the jug, which was patterned with garish red roses and had a broken lip, she set off.

The weather had undergone a sudden change: the freshening breeze had dropped and the clear blue of the Spring sky had taken on a more sullen hue. It hung over the city like a grey bowl, holding in the sultry air, pressing the gritty heat down on to the streets and, like thousands of other Londoners, the inhabitants of Victoria Road had taken evading action.

The elderly residents sat at open front room windows, fanning their faces with newspapers and drinking hot tea – for the received, if contradictory wisdom, handed down from generation to generation, was that hot tea cooled the blood. Their sons and daughters, the middle-aged and the young-married, had spilled out on to the pavement before their front doors, where they sat on kitchen chairs, exchanging gossip with neighbours.

The older teenagers had long since departed to try their luck on 'Monkey's Parade' in the High Street, the no-man's land that was the recognised jousting arena for unattached boys and girls. In pairs, or larger groups, they strolled up and down, one sex slyly inspecting the other, until a selection was made and they went off to the nearest park together.

The children, unconcerned about the heat, had taken over the road as a playground, their shouts and screams quivering on the air. The boys, among them Rosie's two younger cousins, Albert and Ron, were playing 'Tip it and Run', a street game that had something in common with both cricket and baseball and which probably preceded them both.

At the bottom end of the road a bunch of girls was playing a skipping game. While two of their number swung the rope, the others took turns to rush in and compete to see who could carry on skipping the longest. The rope swung easily at first, to the chant of:

> Old Mother Mason,
> Broke her basin,
> How much did it cost?
> Penny, tuppence, threepence, fourpence . . .

As the amount increased, so did the pace of the rope, and it was only the most expert among the girls who could reach beyond the shilling mark.

A gaudily-painted ice-cream cart, pushed by a dark-haired Italian youth, made its way down the street followed by a crowd of younger children, yelling in chorus:

> Okey-pokey, penny a lump,
> The more you eat the more you jump.

They were hoping that the smiling Italian would hand out free 'tasters' – small portions of crushed and sweetened ice – but he knew that in this oppressive heat he was in a seller's market and that there was no need for such inducements.

Rosie passed through all this activity, exchanging a neighbourly greeting here and there. She was well-liked and among the women there was a good deal of sympathy for her. It was summed up by Mrs Bushnell of Number 22: she watched the

19

girl moving down the street and, shaking her head, said to a neighbour:

'Poor little bitch. She has no life, no life at all. She's nothing but an unpaid skivvy.'

6

In theory, The Winged Horse was managed by Mr Henry Quorn, and it was his name that appeared on the board above the door to the public bar as licensee; but everyone knew that the real boss was his wife, Lucy. Known universally as The Missus, Mrs Quorn was a sort of female Captain Bligh, and she ran the pub with the same ruthless, driving efficiency that Bligh had displayed in the running of his ships.

To be fair, she had little alternative. She had been married to Mr Quorn (who was always referred to, somewhat euphemistically, as The Guv'nor) for some twelve years and the whole thing had turned out to be a grievous disappointment. The handsome, dashing, athletic young man who had swept her off her maidenly feet all those years before, had disappeared with astonishing rapidity, to be replaced by a fat, idle, purple-faced boor with a strong leaning towards lechery and an even stronger taste for alcohol in almost all its forms. The only consolation, she often thought, was that the one tended to cancel out the other: drink increased his lust but diminished the possibility of translating it into performance.

The Missus had grasped the nettle early on in their married life. Realising that Mr Quorn was, if that were possible, an even worse business man than a husband, and that unless she acted he would either drink or gamble away the profits, she had taken the running of the pub firmly into her own hands. Mr Quorn had demurred at first, but his protest had been short-lived: cunning goes with idleness, and he had the wit to understand that if he continued to run the pub his way, there would very soon be no pub to run, whereas with his wife in charge a future of blissful indolence was virtually assured.

She was clever enough to appease his vanity by leaving him

the trappings of authority. In his fancy waistcoat, with the gold watchchain straining against his stomach, his pomaded hair parted in the middle and plastered down flat on either side, his waxed moustache, his gleaming patent-leather boots, he strutted from bar to bar, the living cliché of a successful landlord.

It was this formidable figure that glared down at Rosie as she approached the bar of the snug and put down the jug. She knew Mr Quorn and was a little afraid of him, but he was usually too lofty to acknowledge her existence. Tonight, however, he seemed to look at her with some interest and even rolled out her name in his deep pompous voice.

'Ah, Rosie. Little Rosie Daines.'

'If you please, sir, I'm Carr.'

'What's that?'

'Not Daines, sir. My name is Rosie Carr.'

'I know your name!' he snorted. 'I know who you are!'

'Yes, sir,' she said. 'Could I have a pint of old-and-mild?' And remembering her manners added a polite 'please'.

He frowned a little at this and drew in his stomach, trying to convey the idea that he was the landlord not a potman. Then, turning away, he moved along the bar to the partition that separated the public bar from the saloon. Pausing there, he called:

'Lucy, Lucy, my dear. Have you got such a thing as a minute to spare?'

Rosie heard The Missus call back an answer: 'What is it, Henry?'

The tone of this exchange was polite, even mildly affectionate for, as far as possible, the Quorns tried to sustain a certain public dignity, to hide their hatred of each other behind a fiction of mellow harmony. Towards the end of the day, however, the polish tended to go out of the performance for Mrs Quorn's irritation rose in direct proportion to her husband's intake of alcohol. On this particular evening, since it was early, they were still well into their respective roles.

'The girl is here, my flower,' said Mr Quorn.

'The girl?'

21

The voice sounded sharper, and a moment later The Missus appeared on Rosie's side of the bar.

'What girl?' she demanded and then, her eyes falling on Rosie's puzzled face she added: 'Oh, that girl.'

Not for the first time, Rosie stared in awe at the big, handsome, swelling woman. The Missus's plump body seemed to swell outwards above and below the waist, where it was constrained by a whalebone corset. The full rounded bottom curved against the long skirt and her firm ample breasts strained upwards and outwards, their snowy peaks just showing at the neck of her blouse.

Her mass of rich honey-coloured hair, coiled, twisted, plaited and frizzed, was piled on her head like a crown and held in place by dozens of hairpins and two ornamental combs. Mr Quorn was not a short man, but his wife's hair and her high-heeled button-up boots promoted her above him by a good six inches.

She had a good skin, as creamy and smooth as the asses milk in which she washed each day. She had heard or read somewhere that Gertie Millar, the popular musical-comedy actress, bathed in asses milk and swore by it as an aid to the complexion. Ever since then The Missus had despatched one of the pot-boys to the Donkey Dairy at Turnpike Lane three times a week to collect a gallon of milk.

In addition to all this, she spent an hour or so each day on the care of her skin, applying a selection of the latest oils, lotions and creams in liberal quantities, followed by a careful application of make-up. The effect was unusual, not say, striking. She favoured what might be described as the 'peaches and cream' look and, though this may have suited her in younger days, the girlish doll-like face now contrasted in an extraordinary way with the maturity of the remainder.

This face looked down at Rosie and wrinkled its nose in displeasure. A drift of heavy perfume encircled the girl, assaulting her senses so violently that she stepped back a pace.

'I wasn't expecting you till next week,' said The Missus.

'No, ma'am,' stammered Rosie, baffled by this statement.

'The arrangement was next week,' said The Missus. 'It was quite clear.'

'I rather think the child has come to get this filled, my pet,' said Mr Quorn. He indicated the jug with a little nod.

The Missus looked at the jug and then back to Rosie and emitted a little grunt.

'You're not as big as I thought,' she said. 'And you don't look strong.'

'She don't look strong at all,' echoed Mr Quorn. 'Hardly a pennorth of meat on her. Boil her down for dripping and you wouldn't get enough to fill an egg-cup.'

The Missus silenced him with a look and walked all round Rosie, surveying her from top to toe.

'Are you strong, girl?' she demanded.

'Yes, ma'am,' answered the bewildered girl.

'Well, we'll have to see about that,' said The Missus. 'That is something we'll have to see about. For the moment, we will reserve judgment, as they say. But bear this in mind, girl, bear this firmly in mind. We have no room for weaklings here. No room at all. Weaklings and idlers are not welcome in this establishment. You understand me?'

'Yes, ma'am,' Rosie replied, now utterly confused.

'We have one word for weaklings and idlers,' said Mr Quorn. 'One word. Out O-U-T out. We show them the door.'

'Exactly!' said The Missus. 'O-U-T.'

She looked at Rosie once more, sniffed, and marched away into the other bar. As the connecting door closed behind her, Mr Quorn leaned across the bar and said confidentially:

'That woman is a jewel. A pearl. Only one fault.' He tapped his chest. 'Heart. Heart as big as Chelsea Barracks. Rules her head, you know. You can count yourself lucky that she's taken to you, Rosie. You've found a second mother there, a second mother.'

Rosie had no ready reply to this and she was relieved when Mr Quorn, unbending a little, filled her jug, took the tuppence and dismissed her.

Rosie's real mother had always maintained that unexpected events, good or bad, always came in threes. If you met one Hottentot, you were sure to meet two more; if you found a sixpence, you could expect to enjoy two further bits of luck; and one piece of bad news would have two others treading on its heels.

Rosie had never given this dubious theory much thought, but by the end of the evening she was beginning to believe that there might be something to it.

There was, first of all, the extraordinary manner of her reception at The Winged Horse. The more she turned it over in her mind, the more mysterious it became. The Missus had spoken of some 'arrangement', something about not expecting Rosie till next week.

On her way back to Victoria Road, Rosie gnawed at the problem without resolving it entirely. Had her uncle arranged for her to work for The Missus? To do her washing perhaps? Or some skivvying? The thought of more washing on top of everything else, or of some additional job, frightened her. She could hardly cope with what she had to do now, there were simply not enough hours in the day.

The second event in the sequence was the thunderstorm or, rather, not the thunderstorm itself so much but what happened as a result of it. As Rosie left the pub, the distant cannonade of thunder was already rumbling on the still air and, within minutes, the sky seemed to tear itself apart. Soon the spatter of rain became a deluge, bouncing off the pavements and turning the gutters into swirling streams that raced each other to the gurgling drains. Rain spewed in bubbling sheets from roofs and shop blinds and gathered in great pond-like puddles that spanned the width of the streets. Rain poured down on Rosie with such ferocity that she was soaked through to the skin in seconds and to seek shelter would have been a meaningless exercise.

And, worst of all, rain splashed into her jug, watering the beer more effectively than any pot-man at The Winged Horse.

It was this that concerned Rosie most of all. She had no

coat, nothing with which she could cover the jug, so she tried to protect the contents by holding her free hand over the top. But as she edged forward awkwardly, all her concentration on the precious ale, she missed her footing on a curb, made a desperate effort to recover, and dropped the jug.

It fell with a crash which, in her ears, seemed to outdo the thunder, broke into a dozen pieces, and the old-and-mild was borne away to the nearest drain.

Appalled, she stared down at the wreckage. What should she do? To go back to The Winged Horse for more was out of the question: she had no money and no jug. The only thing she could do was to go home and face the wrath of her uncle. She felt a heavy dull pressure in her stomach as she stood there contemplating this prospect, but it seemed to pass as quickly as it had come, and she turned her head towards Victoria Road.

'You took your time!' he said gruffly as she entered the kitchen and stood before him, water dripping from her clothes and forming puddles at her feet. Then, looking at her empty hands, he added sharply: 'Where's the ale? What happened?'

She stuttered an explanation and offered to return to the pub for more.

'Do you think I'm made of money?' he demanded. 'Do you think I've got money for you to throw away like confetti at a wedding?'

Suddenly, because she was wet and exhausted and frightened, and because the ache in her stomach had returned, and because she felt that she could take no more, Rosie began to weep. Her eyes big with tears, she turned from him and stumbled into the scullery.

He followed her a moment or so later and found her sitting at the mangle-board, sobbing her heart out. He felt the prick of conscience for the second time that day and, touching the damp and bedraggled girl on the shoulder he muttered awkwardly:

'Don't take on. It's all right, it's all right. It doesn't matter. Accidents will happen.'

The touch, the tiny little bit of human contact, set her off again. She swung round and pressed herself against her uncle, clinging to him and sobbing. He waited in embarrassment until this new storm had subsided. Then he said:

'You're wet through. You'd better get dried off and get to your bed.'

She released him and stood up slowly, dabbing at her eyes with the back of a hand.

'I saw The Missus at The Winged Horse,' she said, her voice crackling on the words. 'She was funny. I don't mean funny – I mean – what she said.'

'What did she say?' He stepped back a pace, his face reddening slightly.

'She said – she said something about not expecting me until – until next week.'

'Ah, yes,' he said. 'Well. Yes. I was going to tell you about that.'

'About what?'

'I'm leaving, Rosie. Leaving here. I wrote to my brother in Canada. He's done well out there. He's sent the money so that I can join him. He's got a job lined up, you see. So I'm leaving. Soon. With the boys.'

'Canada!'

She stared at him, trying to take in what he had said.

'I was going to tell you, of course.'

'You – and the boys?'

'That's the ticket.'

'And what about me?'

The fear showed in her eyes and he said quickly: 'Oh, you'll be all right, Rosie. I've fixed you up. That's what The Missus meant, don't you see? You start there next week. I mean, you don't think I'd leave you to fend for yourself, do you? No, it's all fixed. You live in at the pub, general work and all that. All found and a shilling for yourself each week.'

There was a little silence and then she sighed and nodded, saying nothing. She picked up a towel and put it over her wet hair.

'You're a lucky girl, Rosie. A job, a roof over your head, all your meals. You could learn pub work. It's an opportunity a lot of girls would give their right arms for.'

'Yes.' She moved to the door. 'Goodnight, Uncle.'

'It's for the best,' he said. There was a touch of desperation in his tone as he tried – as much for his own sake as for hers – to convince her of the rightness of his decision.

She turned back to him. Her voice was small and thin. 'Couldn't I come? You want someone to look after you. I'd work. I'd – ' The words tailed away. His eyes had already given her the answer.

'I'm not a pair of bloody braces,' he said, his guilt forcing him into anger. 'I can't hold you up as well as everyone else. I've got enough with the three boys. I can't take on no more.'

She nodded again and opened the door. As she went into the kitchen he shouted after her:

'You ought to be grateful! I've fixed you a good job. A good job! You ought to consider yourself lucky! You're an ungrateful little cow!'

8

As Rosie undressed for bed, peeling off her wet clothes, she saw that her drawers were stained dark red, that blood was trickling from between her legs.

That was the third thing. The job at The Winged Horse, the broken jug, and now this. Her first period.

Her aunt had warned her in a vague, uncomfortable way about such a development. And from Jessie Hamilton, who was fourteen, she had gathered more precise information, so the event was not entirely unexpected. All the same, on top of everything else, it was frightening, and as Rosie tried to staunch the flow and bound herself with some strips from an old sheet, she felt the absence of her aunt – of another woman – more than ever, and the tears came again.

The storm had passed and she lay awake for a long time, watching the high-riding moon through the window. She closed her eyes and imagined that she was out there, flying over the rooftops, flying away, as free as the moon.

But where? Where would she go? Where could she fly?

CHAPTER TWO

1

Few people would have believed it, but once she had settled in and the initial feeling of shock and disorientation had passed, Rosie actually liked being at The Winged Horse. It would be wrong to suggest that she enjoyed the work (although there were some parts even of that which did give her pleasure, like polishing the brass rail around the bar, or, as she grew older, taking a turn at serving the customers) but it never occurred to her to complain, or to question a punishing schedule that kept her on her feet from six in the morning until ten or eleven at night. Her one respite – and that came only as a result of some outside pressure – consisted of a Sunday off every fortnight, and one evening free each week. The evening off was a moveable feast, depending on the whim of The Missus.

The truth was that Rosie had never known anything other than a life of hard work and so she took it all for granted. And, in the streets around the pub she saw enough grinding poverty to make her thank her lucky stars that she had, at least, a roof over her head, a bed to sleep in, and food in her belly.

There were other compensations too. Her bright, outgoing nature, her cheerful optimism and – as she developed in confidence – her ready humour, made her many friends and it was in these rough-and-ready and often incongruous friendships that she found her greatest pleasure.

There was Mr Softley, for example, the pub's pianist and entertainer who, in a sense, became her greatest friend, a sort of cross between mentor and benevolent uncle. He came in

28

five evenings each week, from Tuesday until Saturday, to play the old piano in the Saloon Bar and generally entertain the customers. For this service he was paid ten shillings per week, plus dinners and tips. The tips usually came in the form of drinks from the customers but, since Mr Softley was not a heavy drinker, he worked out an arrangement with The Missus by which she re-sold most of his free drinks and split the proceeds fifty-fifty. In a good week, he could earn as much as a pound in wages and tips.

Mr Softley, who knew which side his bread was buttered, had developed a special relationship with The Missus. The relationship stopped well short of anything high-seasoned or improper (indeed, there were those who suggested that Mr Softley's tastes did not lie in that direction) but he flirted with and flattered her, teased her and made her laugh, in a way that was as effective as it was extravagant. He appealed to her innate snobbery and had become a sort of licensed jester, the only person, in Rosie's experience, who could transform the normally proud and lofty Missus into a fair imitation of a giggling schoolgirl.

It was widely rumoured that Mr Softley had once been a concert artiste of some prominence, and there were a dozen differing theories to explain why he had been reduced to his present circumstances. But Rosie knew nothing of this. She only knew that in the whole of her life she had never seen anyone so magnificent as Mr Softley.

A tall man of late middle-age, he gave an impression of slightly faded artistic gentility. An abundance of white hair combed back over a high domed forehead fell in a majestic mane on to the collar of a worn velvet jacket; a silk tie flowed from the neck of a ruffled white shirt; black pin-striped trousers brushed worn but polished shoes. He had immaculate if somewhat grandiose manners and, when he chose, a sly and cynical tongue. He was a tenor – quite a good one – and his speaking voice bore the unmistakeable stamp of a public school background.

Mr Softley was looked upon as a character by the regular customers of the pub and his virtuosity at the piano, together with his encyclopedic knowledge of their favourite ballads, was much admired. All the same, he did not make friends easily. The casual bonhomie was something he put on with his job, and he made it difficult for anyone to penetrate beyond this screen and reach the private man.

It was almost a year before Mr Softley seemed to notice Rosie. When she smiled at him in her usual cheerful manner he simply looked back at her without expression, as if to suggest that skivvies were not worthy of his attention. Rosie thought it very odd that a man who could play the piano so well and encourage the customers into song should be so miserable. She noted a certain sadness in the mild blue eyes and wondered what could possibly trouble such a splendid man. But she held him in too much awe to approach him further.

Then, early one evening, a stranger came into the bar. He was a man of about thirty-five, thin and weedy, and he brought with him a small home-made wooden cage in which there was a collection of doleful-looking birds. A notice nailed to the top of the cage announced the man's trade.

ALF COPPINS–BIRD TRADER
GENUINE WILD SINGING-BIRDS FOR SALE
Chaffinches and Linnets – 6 pence
Blackbirds – 9 pence

Rosie happened to be in the bar, wiping down the tables as Mr Coppins chatted to Mrs Oates, one of the regulars, and tried to persuade her to make a purchase.

'They're all genuine, lady,' he said, 'you can bet your best boots on that. Guaranteed wild singing-birds.'

'How do I know that?' said Mrs Oates, looking doubtfully at the birds huddled in the cage.

'Because I caught them meself, didn't I?' said Mr Coppins. 'I was out in the country this morning, wasn't I? Snared the little beggars meself.'

'They look half-dead to me,' said Mrs Oates.

'Ah, they'll soon perk up, missus.' He poked a finger at one of the linnets. The bird fluttered uneasily and looked up with a glazed eye. 'There, see?' continued Mr Coppins. 'Full of life. Give him a drink of water and a peck of groundsel and he'll sing out like a bleeding champion. Listen, you can have any one of the linnets for fourpence. Special reduction.' He produced a brown paper bag from his pocket. 'I'll shove him in this so that you can carry him home. How about that?'

'How do you catch them?' asked Rosie, looking at the captive birds with a mixture of curiosity and sympathy.

'Well, lovey,' said Mr Coppins, turning to her with a well-oiled smile, 'I'll tell you. 'There's no pain in it, if that's what's worrying you. All you do is spread a bit of bird-lime on the branches and – whoosh. They're caught. No hardship. Matter of fact, I reckon the little beggars look upon me as a benefactor. I mean, they don't have to forage for themselves no more, do they? I mean, they're looked after now – good homes, plenty of seed – what more could they ask for?'

At that moment one of the linnets came to life and dashed itself against one side of the cage and then the other, trying in vain to spread its wings in the confined space. Eventually it gave up and resumed its former crouched position. It seemed to Rosie that the sharp little eyes were looking at her in reproach.

'I'll buy that one!' she said impulsively. 'I'll buy that one for fourpence.'

'Ah,' he said, 'ah. Not that one, lovey. That's a rare beauty. That'll cost you sixpence. One tanner.'

'Fourpence,' said Mr Softley.

Mr Coppins turned and saw Mr Softley standing at his elbow. 'Did you speak, or did the wind blow?' he asked aggressively.

'That is a linnet, is it not?' asked Mr Softley.

'Well, it's not a bleeding nightingale.'

'In that case, the price is fourpence. That is what you told this good lady.'

'He's right.' Mrs Oates confirmed the statement with a nod. 'He ain't wrong, he's right.'

'Not that one,' said Mr Coppins stubbornly. 'That one is a tanner.'

'What a horrible little man you are,' said Mr Softly. He turned to the other customers. 'Ladies and gentlemen. Did any of you happen, perchance, to hear what price this pathetic creature asked for his linnets?'

'Fourpence,' said a woman emphatically.

'Fourpence,' said an elderly man.

'Fourpence,' said Mr Holloway, a coal-heaver, and as he spoke he turned and glowered massively down at the bird-trader.

'All right, all right,' said Mr Coppins, beating a retreat. 'Fourpence it is. You got the best of the box there, lovey. I'm robbing myself. Fourpence.'

Rosie reached in the pocket of her apron and brought out a piece of white rag tied in a knot. She caught Mr Softley's eye as she began to unravel the rag. He was looking at her with a puzzled, slightly disappointed expression. Blushing, she counted out four pennies, leaving herself three, and put the rag back in her pocket.

Mr Coppins opened a little gate in the cage and drew out the frightened bird.

'Do you want it in a bag?' he asked.

'No,' said Rosie.

Once again, she was aware of Mr Softley watching her. She took the little creature from Mr Coppins. It strained against her grip and then settled. She could feel its quivering fear on her palms.

'Where will you keep it?' asked Mr Softley.

'I'm not going to keep it,' said Rosie. 'I'm going to let it go. Birds like this aren't meant to be caged up.' And, surprised by her own boldness, she turned to the bird-trader and said: 'If I had the money, I'd buy the whole lot and let them all go free!'

She marched to the door of the pub and went into the street. A smoky sun stood poised on the edge of the world and the light was just beginning to fade.

'There, my little beauty,' she whispered. 'Off you go, off you go.'

She opened her hands. The bird did not move for a moment, but then, spurred by fright, it pecked ungratefully at her finger, bringing a little bubble of blood. The linnet fluttered, its wings brushing her hand, lifted off and beat its way upwards. She watched with a smile as it perched on the rim of a roof on the opposite side of the road, as if pausing for breath, and then took off once more, fluttering away towards the setting sun. Rosie sucked her finger ruefully and wondered if such a tiny creature would be able to find its way home.

She felt a hand, a light touch, on her shoulder and looked up to see Mr Softley standing there. He smiled down at her, and gave her a quiet, rather solemn nod of approval. He touched her wounded finger and looked gravely at the faint smear of blood.

'One of life's lessons, little Rosie. Never expect gratitude.'

2

After this incident, Mr Softley took a definite interest in Rosie and tried, in a subtle and indirect way, to make life a little easier for her. Among other things, he had a quiet and confidential word with Mr Parker, a respected local business-man and magistrate, about the fact that Rosie worked seven days a week with no time off. Mr Parker, who was an occasional customer, had a word in turn with The Missus. Since he also happened to be a member of the local Licensing Committee, Mr Parker carried some weight and, shortly afterwards, The Missus took Rosie aside and announced that, out of the unfailing goodness of her heart, the girl would be allowed one evening off each week and every other Sunday.

At nights, after the pub closed and while she was cleaning up, Mr Softley began to stay behind and talk with Rosie. In a sense, and without realising it, he started the education she had so far missed. He had travelled a great deal as a young man and he told her magical and exciting stories about countries of which she had only vaguely heard, of France and Germany and Italy, of America and Australia. It pleased him to see her eyes widen in disbelief as he spoke of the great trains with their sleeping-cars, of buildings in which people travelled to the upper floors in moveable rooms called elevators, of the magnificent houses with armies of servants where he had performed at private parties, of animals called kangaroos which carried their young in pouches, of rivers full of crocodiles and of far-away places which were almost entirely inhabited by black or brown or yellow people.

Rosie had a bright enquiring mind and, after thinking over what he had told her, she would go back to him with question after question, pressing him until he was forced to disengage out of sheer mental exhaustion.

It was elementary stuff, perhaps, but it was exactly what Rosie needed, opening her up, as it did, to the fact that there was another world beyond the boundary of the High Street. For the first time, she began – in a vague, unformed way – to regret her lack of schooling.

One memorable Sunday, encouraged by Mr Softley, she gathered her courage and took a tram-ride into that other world. It was the first of many such trips and, in time, she found her way to Hyde Park, the Tower of London, Buckingham Palace, the Houses of Parliament and many other places to which Mr Softley directed her.

But what she liked most of all was to take the tram in the opposite direction, away from the city, travelling to the end of the line and then walking to such places as Hadley Wood or to the countryside beyond Edmonton. The open country gave her a great sense of release, a refreshening of the spirit which she would have found difficult to explain even to Mr Softley. She carried a taste of the country back with her whenever possible in the shape of clusters of bluebells, buttercups, primroses or – best of all – bunches of sticky-buds which she would watch day by day, in silent delight, as they slowly opened into bright green leaves.

It was a time of constant discovery for Rosie. Mr Softley's old upright piano had always held a fascination for her, and one afternoon when the pub was closed and both The Missus and The Guv'nor were out, she opened it up and began to play with the keys. She found, to her astonishment, that she had a natural ear for music and within a half-hour she was able to pick out the tune of 'The Last Rose of Summer', one of Mr Softley's most popular renderings.

She could hardly wait to convey her delight at this accomplishment to her friend. To her surprise, his reaction was muted. She could not understand that she had aroused the professional in him, that in his eyes the piano was a serious instrument, not made for tinkling fingers.

'That is not the way, Rosie,' he said with unaccustomed severity. 'The piano is a majestic instrument and it must be approached with respect. I am a poor practitioner myself but I know sufficient about it to – '

He checked, seeing the disappointment in her eyes, and shook his head. 'Oh, dear. Oh, dear, oh, dear. Forgive me, little Rosie. That must have sounded unbearably pompous. Forgive me. I must be getting old. Of course, you have done well. Remarkably well. Clearly you have an ear, as they say. I'll help you all I can.'

'I know I could never play like you,' she said. 'I only want to play for fun.'

'Nothing wrong with fun,' he said, 'nothing wrong with fun at all.'

After this, he encouraged her to practise whenever the opportunity occurred. He soon abandoned any attempt to teach her written music, from which she shied away like a frightened colt, and apart from a little advice here and there, left her to develop in her own way. She had a remarkable ability to hold a melody in her head and translate it on to the piano and, within weeks, she was able to strum a dozen or more simple tunes with fair competence.

It gave her an extraordinary sense of delight to hear the music rising from her fingers, and with this delight there went a little ripple of pride. At last she had achieved something for herself and the accomplishment, small as it was, helped to build her confidence.

3

Rosie's self-confidence, however, was still fragile and, one evening some weeks later, might have suffered a fatal setback had it not been for the friendship – and cunning – of Mr Softley.

It happened after one session in which she had played 'The Lost Chord' all the way through with hardly an error.

As she finished and turned to look at Mr Softley to see if he approved or no, she saw the formidable figure of The Missus bearing down upon them. Rosie jumped up quickly, her heart pounding, tensed for the coming storm.

'What is going on here?' demanded The Missus.

'Ah, my dear lady,' said Mr Softley, wheeling round and putting on the special smile and voice that he reserved for The Missus. 'I might have known it, I might have known it.'

'Known what, may I ask, Mr Softley? Known what?'

'I am afraid our secret is out, Rosie,' sighed Mr Softley. 'Our little secret, our little surprise has been discovered.' He gave Rosie's arm a little surreptitious squeeze, signalling her to silence.

'Secret? Surprise?' The Missus looked from the man to the girl and back again, demanding an answer.

'You guessed, didn't you?' said Mr Softley. 'You knew all the time. Oh, what a shrewd woman you are, to be sure. I should have realised that it is impossible to hide anything from you.'

'Mr Softley, you are keeping this girl from her work!' said The Missus. But the tone was easier now, less strident. Mr Softley was clearly winning, as he usually did.

'Oh, it really is too bad of you, dear lady,' he continued, in the same sorrowful tone. 'It was going to be a surprise. You have ruined this child's magic moment. Ruined it.'

'Mr Softley, will you please tell me what you are talking about?'

'We have no choice, I fear, Rosie. Perhaps you had better explain to Mrs Quorn,' said Mr Softley.

Rosie had not the slightest notion of what to say but mercifully, before she could speak, Mr Softley hastened on: 'No, no. It is better, perhaps, that I should speak. Dear lady, if I may?'

He drew The Missus aside, as if the subject was too grave to be discussed in front of a young girl and lowered his voice:

'You look radiant tonight, dear lady. I dare hardly look in your eyes for fear of their brightness.'

'Now, Mr Softley,' she said, 'none of your monkey-shine!'

He allowed his fingers to brush her hand. 'Oh that I were a glove upon that hand that I might touch that cheek!'

'That's enough, Mr Softley,' she said girlishly. 'Fine words butter no parsnips. You can't get round me, you know.'

'Is that a challenge, dear lady?'

'Mr Softley!'

'I'm sorry. I go too far, I go too far. Forgive me. But the fault is yours. I look at you and my tongue is driven to excess.'

'What is this secret you were talking about, Mr Softley?'

'Oh, that. It is of little consequence now. The truth is that the girl wanted to show her gratitude to you in some way. I know, I know, you are not accustomed to gratitude, you do not expect it. You are too generous, you know that, don't you? You give too much of yourself. But you'll never change, it isn't in your nature to change. At any rate, to cut a long story short, the girl worships you. And with reason, with reason. You are her benefactor, you took her in, you gave her a home. How, she asked herself, how can I demonstrate my gratitude? Out of her slender resources, she could buy nothing of worth. I found her pondering the question one day, near to tears. I took pity on her, suggested a solution. I would, I said, teach her to play your favourite ballad on the pianoforte. When sufficiently accomplished, she intended to play it to you as a surprise. On your birthday, perhaps. A child's gift, dear lady, a child's gratitude expressed in melody.' He sighed. 'There – it is out, you have forced it out of me.'

There was a long pause as The Missus digested this. She looked at the quivering girl.

'Rosie!'

'Yes, ma'am!'

'I appreciate the thought, don't think I don't.'

'Yes, ma'am,' repeated the puzzled Rosie.

'But you're a skivvy here. Just a skivvy. Don't go getting big ideas in your head. You are paid to work, not to muck about on the piano. Is that clear?'

'Yes, ma'am.'

'As long as that's understood. Now, you'd better finish the clearing up. All these lights burning cost money, you know.'

'Yes, ma'am. Thank you, ma'am.'

The Missus moved to the door. Mr Softley moved with her and opened it for her.

'You are an angel,' he whispered.

'Don't spoil the girl,' she replied, 'don't go spoiling her.' She smiled, tapped his face as though in mock rebuke, and sailed out.

Mr Softley closed the door and leaned against it, drawing in a deep breath and shaking his head.

'A well, Rosie, a bottomless pit!' he said, with wonder in his voice. 'That woman is a bottomless pit. The more fanny-nanny you pour into her, the more she takes. It's outrageous, incredible. I keep thinking that I've gone too far, over-reached myself. But no. She is a woman who cannot be over-flattered. Oh, dear. Oh, dear. I feel quite ashamed of myself.' Then seeing that the girl was standing silent and crestfallen, he went to her. 'Cheer up, Rosie. All's well that ends well.'

'I don't think I ought to play any more,' Rosie said in a small voice.

'And why not, pray?'

She shrugged her shoulders and he saw that the tears were not far away. He put a finger under her chin and tilted her face upwards. Searching her eyes he said gently:

'Is it because of what she said? Is that it?' Her silence answered him and he went on: 'Listen to me, little Rosie. You may be a skivvy, but you are also a human being. A person. You won't always be a skivvy, that will pass, but you'll always be a person. Remember that, little Rosie. You're growing up – every day I've seen you growing in confidence. You have intelligence and wit and a big, big heart. And beauty too – soon you will be a beautiful woman. With that sort of equipment, you can make yourself a good life, a fine life. Have faith in yourself, little Rosie, believe in yourself. I tell you now, you are worth a dozen Mrs Quorns. Are you listening?'

She nodded, tears gleaming through the beginning of a smile.

'That's better,' he said, 'that's much better. Now, do you know what you are going to do? You are going to sit down at that piano, Miss Carr, and you are going to play "The Lost Chord" all the way through. Do you hear me? Come along – sit down and play!'

Miss Carr! It was the first time anyone had called her *that*!

She wiped her eyes with the back of her hand as the smile took command and sat down at the piano.

4

The Winged Horse stood on the corner of the High Street and Fortune Street, and it was in the Fortune Street market that Rosie met and made most of her other friends.

Starting outside the pub with Big Bessie's jellied eel stand, the stalls stretched down Fortune Street on either side, crowding into the roadway and leaving only a narrow avenue between for access.

Rosie loved to slip away for a half-hour if she could, especially on Saturday night, and wander through the market. She liked Saturday night best because then the stalls were lit up with hissing naphtha lamps, the market was crowded with eager, bustling customers and the stall-holders vied good-humouredly with each other to attract attention. It was a magic place, roaring with noise, teeming with life and rich with the earthy smell of vegetables, the tangy scent of oranges and apples.

Big Bess, who was built like a shire horse and had a voice to match, took a fancy to Rosie from the beginning. There was an element of pity in her attitude, for she had a shrewd idea of the amount of work Rosie was expected to do at the pub and of the long hours the girl had to put in. Big Bess had no love for The Missus who had tried several times, without success, to have her moved from her pitch outside The Winged Horse, on the grounds that she constituted a nuisance.

There was a certain justice in the complaint for, when Big Bess was in full cry, her voice could be heard in every bar and room of the pub. Rosie loved to hear the big woman's spiel:

'Fresh today! All fresh and luverly! Jellied eels, cockles, whelks – all fresh in today. Luverly grub! Come on – try these whelks, missus. One dish of them and you'll be chasing your old man round the kitchen table! All luverly! Here we are, mister – a plate of cockles fresh from the sea – guaranteed to put hair on your chest! Luverly – all fresh and luverly!'

To Rosie, the way Big Bess cajoled and teased the passing parade was as good as a comedy turn, she felt that she could listen to her forever. In between the spiels, Big Bess would refresh herself with great gulps of stout from a large jug – 'oiling the old tonsils', she called it. And she would push a dish of jellied eels in Rosie's direction, saying with a broad wink:

'Get that lot inside you, Rosie. Eels is good for a growing girl. They'll make your hair curl.'

Rosie liked the jellied eels and ate them at every opportunity, but her chestnut-coloured hair never seemed to respond to the encouragement. When she let it down at night, unpinning the scrawny bun in which it was confined, the thick, rich hair remained as straight as ever.

5

There was another market character called Tommo the Toff who was to become Rosie's friend although in her first two years at the pub he seemed scarcely aware of her existence. Rosie did not find this surprising for Tommo was a handsome dashing young man at least six years her senior and he seemed to have the pick of the attractive girls in the neighbourhood.

Unlike the others, Tommo did not have a regular line: he seemed able to turn his hand and voice to the sale of anything. His speciality was to buy up goods that had been damaged by fire or flood, the stocks of bankrupt shops or what the factories called 'seconds' and sell them off at his stall.

The first time she saw and heard him, Rosie stood as

though transfixed, staring in admiration. Perched on a wooden box, he towered above the crowd, a slim, sprightly, impudent figure in a flamboyant waistcoat with what seemed to be a gold watch-chain stretched from pocket to pocket, drain-pipe trousers of a deep purple hue with knife-edge creases, and a shining top-hat on his head.

On that first occasion, he had acquired a stock of vases, ornamented with a Chinese design, from one of his mysterious sources, and was exercising all his skill to unload them on to a crowd of potential, if somewhat wary, customers.

'Now, come along, ladies and gentlemen. I'll tell you what I'll do. I will first take up this magnificent vase. Look at that workmanship, ladies and gentlemen! Look at the artistry of that design! These vases, ladies and gentlemen, were made in Shanghai, China, at the world-famous Tong pottery. Do I tell you a lie? I do not! Perish the thought. Every one of these magnificent vases, ladies and gentlemen, is stamped on the bottom – if you will pardon the word – with the Tong pottery sign.'

Tommo held the vase out so that all could see a curious dagger-shaped T on the base of the vase. Then he flicked it with his finger, bringing forth a low bell-like tone.

'Here that? Hear it ring? Sound as a bell. Now, ladies and gentlemen, I'll tell you what I am going to do. I have here one gross of genuine Tong vases originally ordered by a famous West End emporium which shall be nameless. I could tell you a long story about how they came to be offered to your friend, Tommo the Toff, but I can see that you're all getting fidgety to buy. And I don't blame you. I do not blame you. With one of these genuine Tong vases on your mantelpiece you will have a precious heirloom. Now, this is what I am going to do. I am going to surprise you. No, I am going to shock you. Do you know what these genuine Tong vases are being sold for in London, Paris, Rome, Timbuctoo and other famous capitals? No? I'll tell you. They are going for five pounds, nineteen shillings and sixpence! Five pounds, nineteen shillings and a tanner! But am I asking that, ladies and gentlemen? I am not. Am I asking five pounds? I am not.

41

Do I ask four pounds, three pounds, two pounds or even thirty bob! I do not! Not even one pound, not even ten shillings, not even five, not even a half-crown! I am giving them away, ladies and gentlemen, giving them away at the ridiculous price of ninepence each. Nine pennies only. Nine pennies for a genuine Tong vase! And that's not all, ladies and gentlemen, that is not all!'

He passed the vase down to his young assistant and produced four sovereigns from his pocket. One by one he sent the glittering coins spinning into the air, counting them off as he did so and catching them in his top hat.

'I have here four golden sovereigns, fresh from the Royal Mint! Four sovs, ladies and gents – one, two, three, four! What am I going to do with these beautiful sovs? Watch carefully – remember the quickness of the hand deceives the eye!'

In full view, he took the coins from the hat, flicked each one up once more and clinked them in his hand. Then jamming his hat back on his head he jumped down from the box and passed his hand quickly back and forth over the array of vases. The audience strained forward, listening. There were four distinct and audible chinks.

When he resumed his perch, he held out his hand to show that it was empty.

'Gone, ladies and gentlemen! Gone! Where? You saw for yourself. Four of you are going to turn up trumps, four of you are going to be lucky! Four of these genuine Tong vases contain a brand new golden sov! Now, who's going to be first? Don't all rush now, let the dog see the rabbit! Ninepence for one of these magnificent, genuine Tong vases!'

But there was a rush and Tommo and the boys were kept busy handing out the vases and taking in the money. Rosie watched in wonder as some thirty vases were seized by eager hands and rattled and searched for the sovereigns. As far as she could see, no-one was lucky enough to find the money and after a while the people drifted away, shaking their heads and muttering, though for the most part the disappointment was fairly good-natured.

When she asked another friend, Dave Culley about this, he laughed.

'Sure, that's one of Tommo's tricks. The sovs don't go in, do they? He flicks the vases with his finger to make it sound as if they do, then palms them. It's a fair wonder how them people fall for his spiel time and time again. It's greed, Rosie, human greed!'

After this, Rosie had mixed feelings about Tommo. She didn't think it was right for him to cheat the people like that, yet on the other hand, she could not help but admire his cleverness.

6

Dave Culley was an Irishman who scraped a living from the sale of song sheets. Dave's tiny pitch was wedged in between Sam Hoddle's greengrocery stall and the china stall run by Bert Galvin. He displayed some of his wares on a small stand and flourished others under the noses of passers-by:

'Don't forget your song-sheets! Don't forget your song-sheets! All the latest, as sung by the uncrowned monarchs of the music-hall! Don't forget your song-sheets! Tuppence a sheet only – two pennies a piece. "Are We to Part Like This, Bill": "Nellie Dean": "Any Old Iron": "Roaming in the Gloaming". Don't forget your song-sheets! All the latest as sung by Marie Lloyd, Harry Champion, Vesta Tilley. Don't forget your song-sheets!'

Dave was a regular at The Winged Horse, a quiet, mild man when sober but a roaring, fighting Irishman when he had a few pints inside him. On such occasions, the mere mention of Ireland was enough to set him off into a furious tirade about the duplicity of the British.

Once, when he had been worsted in a fight, and was staggering drunk, Rosie had steered Dave to his home in Walpole Road, two streets away and seen him safely inside. She had then returned to the pub, where he had left his precious stock, and hidden the song-sheets safely away in her attic-room until the next day. Dave was quite sure that he had lost his stock and his relief when he saw it again was as glowing as his gratitude.

'Oh, you're a darlin' girl, Rosie, a darlin' girl! From now on in, you can count me as a true friend, count on Dave Culley through thick and through thin. I never thought I'd lay me eyes on them sheets again and that would have been the busting of me. Yes, you're a darling, a darling girl! I'll never forget you for this, you can take a solemn oath on that!'

The following Saturday, Dave gave Rosie a little necklace, the first piece of ornamentation she had ever owned. The necklace was made up of tiny shells threaded together and, next to the flowers and trees which were her first love, she thought the perfectly-shaped little shells were the most beautiful things she had ever seen. She wrapped the necklace in a piece of clean cloth and put it away in the cardboard box in which she stored her few precious possessions – the book, with Major Pauley's rose and other flowers and leaves pressed in it, an embroidered handkerchief, a big, worn, leather purse which had once belonged to her mother, and a little bag containing six multi-coloured glass marbles – called alleys – that her cousin Albert had shyly pressed upon her on the day she had left Uncle Bob's house to begin her service at The Winged Horse. And in a creased envelope, she stored two birth certificates, her own and her mother's.

Yet another friend was Mr Crooks, the cats-meat man. During the day he drove around the streets in a pony and trap selling portions of horse-flesh on wooden skewers at a ha'penny a time, but at night he opened up a stall in the market. It was a smart stall, always clean and freshly-painted, with the legend 'Pussy's Butcher' painted above it, but Mr Crooks, in his straw hat and striped apron, more than matched it in splendour.

Over the years, Mr Crooks had developed something of a reputation as an animal doctor: besides cats-meat, he also sold a range of his own medicines and ointments for use in the treatment of sick cats and dogs. On his daily rounds and at the market-stall, he was often called upon to advise on a sick or wounded animal and there seemed to be few conditions which did not respond to his care.

He also offered another useful and necessary service. For the sum of sixpence (or, in some instances, for a reduced fee of threepence or even for nothing) he would put down an old or hopelessly sick dog or cat and dispose of the body. Everybody knew that these sad operations were carried out in a shed adjoining the stable in the big yard at the side of Mr Crook's corner house in Mafeking Street, but *how* he carried them out no-one knew or had even dared to ask. It was enough to see his skill and tenderness with a sick animal to know that he was incapable of inflicting pain on any creature.

Mr Crooks was a Methodist, which is to say that he was never seen in The Winged Horse or any other public house, went regularly to Chapel and bible class, and saw to it that his children attended Sunday School regularly. But he was not fiercely sectarian or narrow-minded in his attitudes. It was his view that some of his Chapel colleagues did the cause a great deal of harm by portraying God as a joyless disciplinarian. He believed that there was enough misery in the world without Christians adding to it and that God enjoyed a good laugh and a bit of fun as much as he did.

Rosie met him quite by chance when The Missus found the pub cat, Ginger, scratching its ear, and told Rosie to take it along for Mr Crooks to look at. She gave the girl sixpence, with the injunction:

'I want to see some change out of that, Rosie! I'm not made of money. I haven't got a fortune to spend on cats.'

Mr Crooks placed the struggling Ginger on a table at the back of the stall that he kept for such examination, quietened him with a scrap of meat, and looked at the offending ear. Nodding, he told Rosie to hold Ginger down while he wrapped a piece of clean cloth around the end of a pencil, dipped it in an antiseptic solution and cleaned the ear, after which he smeared it inside with a sharp-smelling vivid green ointment.

As he worked, Mr Crooks questioned Rosie. 'You're the girl who works for Mrs Quorn, aren't you?'

'Yes.'

'What's your name?'

'Rosie. Rosie Carr.'

'You seem to be a respectable young lady. I'm surprised that your parents allow you to work in that place. It's little better than a gin-palace.'

Rosie had seen a real gin-palace from the outside only once in her life, in Upper Street, Islington, near Collins Music Hall. Huge and garish, it made The Winged Horse look colourless by comparison. She wondered how The Missus, who prided herself on running a superior establishment, would have responded to Mr Crooks' description. Aloud, she said:

'I haven't got any parents.'

'I see. I see.' Mr Crooks looked at her and smiled, a kindly smile. 'Well, that makes a difference. A significant difference, I should say. However, you do have a father in heaven, you know. A father who cares. Do you go to Sunday School, Rosie?'

'No, sir.'

'You should, you know, you should. How old are you?'

At this time, Rosie was fifteen and she said so.

'Hmph!' grunted Mr Crooks. 'You don't look fifteen. Still, that means you are old enough for Chapel. Do you know the Methodist chapel in West Green Road?'

'I've passed it, I think.'

'Next Sunday, don't pass it, come in. We're a friendly crowd. You'll like it. Come in and say hello to your heavenly father, and to Jesus. Remember that Jesus died on the cross to save us all.' He handed Ginger back to Rosie. 'There. He has a sore in the ear. Put some of this green ointment on it twice a day and it will clear up in no time. That will be four-pence.'

'Thank you, sir.' Rosie took the little cardboard box of ointment, handed over the sixpence and received her tuppence change.

Mr Crooks looked at her, pursing his lips and brushing a finger over his neat clipped moustache. 'You won't forget about Chapel?'

'I have to work every other Sunday,' she said nervously.

46

'Wicked,' he said, 'wicked! Oh, not you, Rosie, not you. I can see that you're not wicked. No, I mean it is wicked that you should have to work on the Lord's Day. When is your next Sunday off?'

'This weekend coming, sir.'

'I tell you what, Rosie. Come to tea at my house. Number 11, Mafeking Street. It's on the corner, you can't miss it. Come at four o'clock – how's that? Mrs Crooks will be delighted to meet you, and so will the family. I have a daughter Tess, who is just your age. Will you come?'

Rosie drew back a little, overcome by shyness. And suddenly she felt conscious of her appearance and knew that she could never go. Apart from the worn skirt and blouse she was wearing under her apron, she had one dress, bought at Ma Bishop's second-hand clothes stall in the market and that, too, was hardly suitable for visiting Mr Crooks' home.

He seemed to read her thoughts, for he said with a smile: 'Come as you are. We're plain, ordinary folk. No need for dressing up.' He tapped his chest. 'It's what's in here that counts, Rosie. That's what God sees. You'll come then? I can tell my wife to expect you?'

Rosie nodded, mumbled her thanks, and hurried away. On the short journey back to the pub, she felt a kind of panic rising within. What had she done? Despite what Mr Crooks had said, she knew that she could not go in her present clothes, nor in the dress that was hanging in her room, her so-called Sunday dress. That was all right for her solitary excursions, but it would never do in company. But she had said she would go. What excuse could she now make to back out of it?

Later that night, finding her looking unusually grave and pensive, Mr Softley asked her what was wrong and eventually, after a little gentle questioning, eased the story out of her.

He said nothing, but the following evening, with a solemn little bow, he presented her with a brown paper parcel and said:

'A small birthday gift, little Rosie.'

'But it isn't my birthday,' she said, wide-eyed.

'Not your ordinary birthday, perhaps. We'll call it your official birthday. After all, if the King of England can have two birthdays, why shouldn't one of his loyal subjects?'

'What is in it?'

'Ah,' he said, tapping his nose. 'Ah. That would be telling.'

Later, in the privacy of her room, she unwrapped the parcel with quivering fingers to discover that it contained a blue dress with white trimmings and a pair of short button-up boots. They were almost new and far outshone anything else she possessed: what was more, the boots were a perfect fit and the dress almost so – all it needed was a tuck here and there. How on earth had Mr Softley guessed her size so accurately, she wondered?

So, on the Sunday, Rosie set forth, her heart thumping, to fulfil her first social engagement. When she arrived at Number 11, Mafeking Street, she lost her nerve and walked past the house. She turned back after a little while but shyness overwhelmed her once more and she would have passed the house again but for the fact that Mr Crooks happened to see her from the parlour window. He hurried down and ushered her in.

It was the first of many visits. Mrs Crooks, a stout motherly soul, took to the girl at once and little by little Rosie was drawn into the family circle. In the daughter, Tess, she found a friend of her own age, someone with whom she could talk and gossip on equal terms, the first such real friend she had ever had.

Again, it was exactly what Rosie needed at this time. With her mother she had been constantly on the move from one furnished room to another and, at Victoria Road, her Uncle Bob had always kept her at a distance, accepting her presence there with surly reluctance.

Now she felt almost part of a family. There was always a smiling welcome for her, she was accepted for herself alone and for no other reason. It was another small boost to her blossoming self-confidence.

It was not all sweetness and light and friendship, however: there was a darker side to life at the pub and in the streets around it that Rosie came to know in all its squalor and viciousness.

Early each morning, for instance, a line of ragged, barefoot children would form outside the back door of The Winged Horse, waiting for Rosie to dish out the scraps of stale food, the leavings from customers' plates, that had accumulated in the waste bucket. It was a smelly mixture of bones, bits of meat and bread, vegetables, strips of fat and fishbones, all gooed together with greasy gravy, but the kids waited eagerly, holding out tin plates or basins or grubby bare hands for their share of the dismal feast. Rosie had seen and known poverty and hunger, but the sight of these pale faces and glowing eyes never failed to move her.

The Missus made much of this morning exercise, proudly confiding to her friends and customers that it was her way of 'doing a little bit to help the less fortunate'. She took care to see that no food that could be used again found its way into the bucket, but Rosie often managed to slip the odd sandwich or ham-bone past the vigilant eye of The Missus and pass it on to the children.

Then there was the time when Lil, one of the neighbour-hood prostitutes, came staggering into the public bar with blood pouring from savage wounds in her head and body. She collapsed just inside the door and Rosie rushed to help her. As she knelt over the woman, she saw that her skull had been split open; blood was bubbling up through the grey roots of the dyed hair and trickling thickly down the rouged cheeks. Her right arm hung at a strange angle as though broken at the elbow and her hands were slashed as if by a knife. Lil stared glassily at Rosie and it took the girl a full half-minute to realise that she was dead.

The Missus, partly out of hysteria and partly for fear of the reputation of her house, collapsed in a faint and had to be helped upstairs. It was left to Rosie to cope with the situation until police and ambulance arrived to take charge. It turned out that one of Lil's customers had gone berserk and attacked her with a meat-axe.

Later, in her room, Rosie's self-control broke and she lay on her creaking bed, weeping and shivering so violently that her teeth chattered. She had nightmare visions of Lil, of that ugly V-shaped wound in her head; the warm, sickly smell of blood clung to her nostrils.

It was Rosie's first experience of violent death. Not long after this, she was to have her first taste of another sort of violence.

She had spent part of her evening off with Tess Crooks and, after a good-night cup of cocoa in the kitchen, was making her way happily back to The Winged Horse. To do so, she had to cut through a narrow passage called Brown's Alley which connected Wilmore Road with Fortune Street.

As she entered the shadowy alley she saw three men standing together some thirty yards ahead and heard them laughing together. She hesitated for a moment, wondering whether to turn back and go the longer way round via the High Street, but she was tight for time and decided to press on.

The men fell into silence as she approached. Quickening her step and lowering her head she made to hurry past, but one of the group stepped in front of her.

'Hello, dearie,' he said, with a leer.

He thrust his face close to hers and she caught the sickly reek of stale beer. She stepped back, only to find that the other two were now blocking her retreat. The first man, heavily-gutted, pressed his bulk against her, forcing her back into the others. He wore a ragged donkey-jacket and moleskin trousers fastened with straps below the knee; his face had not seen a razor for days and the leering mouth was toothless save for a few blackened stumps.

'How about a kiss, dearie?' he said drunkenly. 'A little goodnight kiss?'

She pushed him away and tried to move on, but he grabbed her arm and pulled her back. She struck out with her free hand, her nails clawing the coarse skin.

'You bloody cow!' he shouted and releasing her arm he struck the back of his hand across her face with such force that she staggered back and would have fallen but that the others caught her.

'Right!' said the first man. 'Let's have her! Hold her down! Hold the bitch down!'

They forced her to the ground. She struggled violently, clawing and kicking, but they were too much for her and pinned her back, one holding her arms and the other forcing her legs apart. The first man pulled up her skirt, ripping it as he did so, and she felt his heavy hands fumbling with her drawers.

One of the other men dropped a hand on her left breast, squeezing it painfully, and his heavy quickening breathing stirred her to fresh struggles.

'Hold her still!' shouted the first man. 'Hold the cow still! You can have her after me.'

A long scream of terror burst from her lungs and he struck her again. She lay back, turning her head from one side to the other in anguish: her nose was bleeding and she felt the salty taste of blood on her tongue.

'No, no, no. Please, please,' she moaned.

The first man thrust his hand between her legs.

'Now – here's a very nice bush,' he said. 'A lovely little bush. And a sweet little hole! Well, we'll soon fill that, dearie.'

He knelt above her and she saw him fumble with his belt and trousers. Then, as he began to press down on her, she heard a shout.

'Hey, there! What's going on?'

There followed a clatter of running footsteps, coming nearer. The man above her disappeared, the others released her and fled. A moment later she looked up into the concerned face of Tommo the Toff and saw, as in a mist, three other faces looking down at her.

They helped her up, straightened her clothes, applied a handkerchief to her bloody nose. But nothing, it seemed, could stop the sobs of fear and shame that shuddered out of her.

'It's all right now,' crooned Tommo, holding her to him. 'All tickety-boo. It's all right now.'

Rosie could not stomach the thought of facing The Missus that night and eventually she persuaded Tommo to lead her back to the Crooks' home, where she fell sobbing into the big comforting arms of Mrs Crooks.

It was two days before she went back to work. Mr Crooks went to see The Missus and although he did not disclose what he had said, she sent word that Rosie should not return until she was quite better.

That was easier said than done. It took much longer than two days for Rosie to recover from the shock. She felt a deep sense of shame, a feeling of *uncleanness*, which lingered with her for months. And many years later, the thought of that encounter in Brown's Alley could still bring her out in a sweat of fear and fill her stomach with nausea.

CHAPTER THREE

1

'How are you, my little lolly-dolly?' asked Tommo the Toff placing his battered top-hat on the bar and smiling across at Rosie.

'I'm as fit as a flea at a picnic,' said Rosie. 'And I am not your lolly-dolly.' She drew a pint of draught ale from the pump and placed it before him. 'Fourpence, if you please.'

He put down the money and dropped his hand on hers as she went to pick it up. 'Rosie,' he said, 'I've been thinking.'

'Did it hurt?' she asked, pulling her hand away.

'Not so you'd notice,' he said. 'No, straight up. Why don't I take you up the Empire on your next night off?'

'Give over!' she said. 'I got my reputation to think of. If I'm seen out with you, it won't be worth a light!' But the quick, half-surprised smile she gave him contradicted the dismissive tone in her voice, and as she moved along the bar to serve Dave Culley she was conscious of a little inner flutter of excitement.

Ever since that incident in Brown's Alley, Tommo had demonstrated an increasing interest in Rosie. He had called at the Crooks' house the following morning to enquire how she was and to hand in a bunch of violets. Thereafter, when she returned to work, he had taken to visiting the pub more frequently and had sought her out whenever possible.

Their exchanges were never very deep, usually taking the form of a kind of flirtatious badinage in which he mocked and teased her good-humouredly with Rosie responding in much the same fashion. It had taken Rosie a little time to adjust herself to the game but as the weeks passed she was giving

Tommo as good – and better – than she got, much to the delight of those who happened to be listening.

The interest was not only on his side, however. Rosie found herself thinking more and more of Tommo as the weeks went by. She looked for him in the bar and was disappointed when he did not show up and within the limits of her resources she began to pay more attention to her appearance. For most of her work she wore a coarse, sackcloth apron and, in the past, had never bothered to remove it when running errands outside the pub; it had simply never occurred to her to do so. But now, whenever she went out, Rosie removed the apron and replaced it with a clean, crisp white one, the emblem of working-class respectability.

She acquired from Dave Culley a picture postcard of Zena Dare, the musical comedy star, and tried as best she could – and with a little help from her friend Tess Crooks – to copy Miss Dare's hairstyle. To her chagrin, it proved not only unmanageable but impractical in terms of work, since the hair took an hour or more to put in place and then kept escaping from the pins which were supposed to hold it there; moreover, the change came in for some ribald remarks from customers and acid comments from The Missus.

Such opposition only served to make Rosie the more obstinate. She sought the advice of Lily Hoddle, whose father ran a greengrocery stall in Fortune Street Market. Lily was two or three years older than Rosie, a bright pretty young woman whose attractive appearance was much admired by both sexes. In no time at all, Lily came up with a compromise solution.

'It's too long, Rosie, too long by half. Look, it's nigh on down to your waist. You'll never be able to keep that blooming lot in order. You'll have to cut it, lovey, you'll have to cut it.'

'Cut it?' said Rosie in dismay.

'Not much,' said Lily, 'not too much. Trim it a bit like. There'll be plenty left but you'll be able to keep it tidier.'

Rosie gave a deep sigh.

'It'll be all right,' said Lily reassuringly. 'When I've finished you'll look like a Sunday afternoon treat.'

And so the deed was done and to Rosie's delight the treatment worked. Even The Missus seemed to approve, for she said, with a sniff:

'That's better, Rosie, that's much better.'

And when Tommo first saw the new hair-style; he threw up his hands in mock surprise and said:

'Who's this then? The face is familiar, but I don't seem to cotton the Barnet Fair. May I enquire your name, princess?'

'Leave over, Tommo,' said Rosie blushing. 'Get on your bike!'

'Rosie,' he said in an astonished voice. 'It's Rosie! I'd know that voice anywhere. But the appearance – Rosie, Rosie – blow me tight – you look better than a basket of oranges!'

It was shortly after this exchange that Tommo invited Rosie to go to the music-hall with him and, after the usual ritual bout of verbal sparring, she accepted. And it was about this time that one of Rosie's most cherished dreams became a sort of reality.

She began to fly.

2

To be exact, Rosie only imagined that she could fly. Common sense told her that it was only a dream but the experience was so sharp, so vivid, that it had, for her, all the quality of truth and she found it hard to believe that her soaring flights above the rooftops were only a fantasy, a sort of trick played by her subconscious mind.

The genesis of the dream lay in the signboard of the pub, the garish painting of the winged horse, which hung only a few feet from Rosie's attic window. At first Rosie had hardly noticed the sign: it was one of those familiar things which were part and parcel of the everyday scene and so passed without attention. Then, one wet and gusty day, she went to close her window against the rain and heard the board creaking and heaving in the wind. She saw it almost for the first time and it seemed to her that the winged horse was straining to escape, struggling to leap into the sky. She watched fascinated as it swung this way and that, its nostrils flared, its wild eyes staring at her as if in appeal.

That evening she asked Mr Softley about the sign and he told her the legend of Pegasus, the winged horse, of how, with his help, an ancient Greek warrior named Bellerophon had been able to defeat many enemies, and of their attempt to fly to heaven.

Rosie did not fully understand all that Mr Softley told her and she thought that some of it was a little far-fetched, but the story quickened her imagination and she thought how wonderful it would be if she, too, could have wings and fly the heavens or, better still, if she could ride Pegasus and go with him to all those wonderful places that Mr Softley had told her of in the past. How marvellous to be free, to ride the wind, to soar through the clouds, to look down on the earth, on Tommo and The Missus and the market, and see them without being seen!

And one night it happened. At one moment she was lying in bed, half-awake and half-asleep and the next, as if by some miracle, she was astride the winged horse, clinging to its mane, her flannel nightdress flapping around her ankles. Up and up into the starry sky they rose, the great wings beating the air, until the moonlit streets below looked like a maze of silvery canals with dolls-houses lining each bank. Now Pegasus spread his wings and began to glide, wheeling and turning with such smooth grace that Rosie felt as if she would explode with the sheer delight of it all. She laughed aloud and the winged horse appeared to understand for he half-turned his head and neighed in happy unison.

It was the freshness, the *cleanness* of everything that Rosie found so amazing. The air lay cool and sweet on her skin: the sleeping suburb below seemed to be purged of its ugliness and squalor and looked like some enchanted city, hung with chains of golden fairylights.

Rosie had no recollection of going back to the pub, but she woke in her bed in the pale light of morning filled with a sense of utter contentment and happiness. She went to the window and looked out at the winged horse, her friend. In her imagination he smiled at her and pricked up his ears as if to acknowledge their secret.

After this, they went on several dream-journeys together, never travelling far, simply circling over the landscape she knew so well and, occasionally, moving out to the country-side she had visited on her Sunday excursions or, at other times, picked up the flowing line of the Thames and following it until they looked down on its wide bridges and glided over the top-most turrets of the Tower of London or the Houses of Parliament.

Rosie grew in confidence with every flight, no longer clinging on desperately, but riding freely; and she learned to manoeuvre the winged horse so that by a touch of a foot or hand he would turn this way or that, or simply hover like a swallow on spread wings. He came to know her voice also and to respond to a gentle word of command.

Of course, there were nights when the dream just would not come, when Rosie was so tired that she fell into a deep dream-free sleep, or when, despite an intense effort of concentration, her mind and body would not respond and she remained earthbound. After a while she realised that the dream of flight was capricious, that it visited her of its own accord and could not be wished or ordered into her mind. Most often, it fell upon her unexpectedly and, in time, she understood that this was the way of dreams, especially the good ones.

She told no-one of her friendship with the winged horse and of her flights on his broad back, not even Mr Softley or Tess Crooks. Some instinct told her that to speak of it would be to destroy it and that possibility was too dreadful to contemplate. So she kept her peace and, whenever she looked up at Pegasus, she would smile at the thought of the secret they shared and fancy that he was smiling too.

3

It wasn't long before Rosie began to have doubts about the wisdom of her decision to go to the music-hall with Tommo.

She had never been out with a young man before: her only knowledge of such matters had been gained at second-hand from friends like Tess Crooks and Lily Hoddle, or from what she had observed from behind the bar of the pub, and this had left her with a general impression that all young men were predators.

'They are only after one thing, lovey,' said Lily darkly. 'Their minds run on tram-lines and always in the same direction.'

'But you go out with a lot of boys,' Rosie protested.

'That don't signify,' said Lily. 'I'm not saying I'm against fellers. I like some of them. And I don't mind a bit of a kiss and a cuddle, nothing wrong with that. But most of them don't want to stop there. Hands like bloody gypsies, wandering all over the place, know what I mean? And if you give them an inch, they'll take a foot, and before you know where you are, you've got one up the spout, know what I mean?'

'Up the spout?'

'You're in the pudding club, lovey. Lumbered. And when you start looking for the feller, you find he's scarpered. No, it's not worth it, Rosie. My advice to you is – have a good time but if the bloke starts coming the old acid, put your knee in where it hurts – know what I mean?'

From Tess Crooks, as might be expected, Rosie received advice of a more demure character although the general drift was much the same. Tess had recently broken off a relationship with a young man named William Wales whom she had first met at Chapel, where he was a Sunday School teacher They had been out together on a half-dozen occasions and it had looked, for a time, as if the affair would develop into something of a more permanent nature, but, quite suddenly, Tess banished him from her life and he no longer appeared at Chapel.

Privately, Rosie thought that Tess was well rid of William, who in her eyes was a pompous young chap with an exaggerated opinion of himself. At first her friend was reluctant to speak of the matter but eventually, when she learned that Rosie was to go out with Tommo, she described the shameful incident in graphic detail, as though to convey a warning.

It seemed that one evening, after Bible Class, Tess and William had been entrusted with the task of locking up the Chapel hall and returning the keys to the caretaker. There was no-one else within hearing distance when she told Rosie what happened then, but she spoke in a whisper nevertheless, as if she hoped to keep it from the ears of God.

'It was only the second time I'd let him kiss me,' she said. 'The first time was just a quick goodnight peck. I mean, on the cheek, not on the lips. But this time he pulled me round as we were putting the prayer-books away and kissed me right on the lips. Well, I didn't really mind that so much and I let him do it again. He was holding me real tight and the second time he kissed me so hard that I could feel his teeth through his lips. And then – and then – do you know what happened?'

'No,' said Rosie, eager for Tess to get to the point.

'I felt his tongue in my mouth!' said Tess.

'Ugh!' said Rosie in disgust.

'His tongue!' said Tess. 'Licking the inside of my mouth! It was horrible.'

'Horrible!' Rosie agreed, trying to imagine what it would be like to have someone else's tongue inside her mouth and, more than that, why anyone would ever wish to do such a strange thing.

Then, moving like a toad in the back of her mind, there came the recollection of what had happened to her in Brown's Alley not so long before, of the terror that had overwhelmed her, of those rough mauling hands. She shuddered involuntarily and, with an effort, shut out the memory, concentrating her attention on what her friend was saying.

'And then,' said Tess, lowering her voice still further, so that Rosie had to crane forward to pick up the words, 'and then – guess what he did.'

'What?' Rosie's voice was a whisper also.

'He squeezed my front,' said Tess.

'What?'

'He squeezed my front.' Tess looked down at her breasts and laid a hand between them in a gesture that explained all.

'No!' said Rosie in disbelief.

59

'He did!' Tess took her hand away and looked at it briefly, as though it were unclean.

'What did you do?' asked Rosie.

'I smacked his face! Really hard. Well, honestly, I was so shocked. I was trembling all over. Then he started saying he was sorry and all that, but I told him I never wanted to see him again. I mean – to do a thing like that! Tess shuddered at the recollection and hissed the next words. 'The beast!'

These conversations left Rosie in a state of some mental confusion. She knew that Tommo had a reputation with the girls, that he was widely talked of as being 'a bit of a lad'. On the other hand, he was well-liked in the market and Big Bess had once said that he would make a good catch for any girl who could pin him down. And Rosie could not deny that she liked him, liked his cheeky good humour, his generosity and – yes – she liked his looks. Tall and handsome, with laughing impudent blue eyes, he was a man almost any girl would be proud to call her beau.

But was he, as Lily Hoddle had said, only after one thing? Was he like Tess Crooks' William – the sort of man who kissed with his tongue and fondled a girl's breasts?

Rosie tried not to dwell on such unthinkable things, but her mind kept coming back to them. She found herself imagining what it would be like to be kissed and touched in that way and was half-ashamed to feel a ripple of response in her body, a strange tingling sense of excitement that almost immediately produced a reaction of guilt. It wasn't right to feel that way, it wasn't decent. Could it mean that, at heart, she was a bad girl?

She thought of her mother and of the various men who had flickered through her life. Rosie had known them as uncles, Uncle Fred, Uncle Albert, Uncle Harold and – oh – two or three others. She knew now, of course, that they were not uncles at all but lovers, men who had briefly taken up with her mother and then passed on. Rosie had often slept in the same room and heard them gasping and grappling in the double bed, wishing they would stop whatever they were doing so that she could get to sleep.

Had she inherited a certain sinfulness from her mother? Was there bad blood in her?

The strange thing was that she could not really bring herself to think of her mother as a sinful woman. She remembered only the times when they had snuggled up in bed together and the comforting warmth of her mother's arms around her: she remembered the bright impetuous laugh, the gay teasing, the games they played. And her prettiness, she remembered how pretty her mother was, as pretty sometimes as a picture.

Her mother had loved her, that she knew. If there had ever been a doubt of that it had been resolved when Rosie was eight and one of the uncles – she thought it was Uncle Fred but she couldn't be sure – had begun to abuse and beat her for some small offence. Her mother, hearing Rosie's screams, came running in and, without a moment's hesitation, picked up the bread-knife.

'Leave her!' she had said, 'leave her! If you lay another finger on her, I'll do for you!'

Rosie, looking at her mother, could see that she meant every word. At any moment she expected the bread-knife to descend. But the man had stopped, surprised, and turned his temper on her mother – though Rosie noticed that he kept well away from the quivering blade.

'I've had enough of your bloody brat, sitting around, picking her bloody nose, giving me lip! It's her or me – make up your mind!'

'That's easy!' Her mother's voice had been sharp with contempt. 'You can get! Skedaddle! Take your things and get! And good riddance!'

The man had left in dark bitterness, muttering half to himself, and only when he had descended the stairs did her mother set down the knife. Then she said:

'Did you give him lip?'

'No, Mum,' said Rosie.

'You sure?'

Rosie thought for a moment. 'Well,' she said at last. 'I said he stunk of beer and sweat.'

'You said that!'

61

'I didn't mean anything. And it's true.'

Her mother smacked her across the face with such force that Rosie cried out.

'That's for lipping your elders!' said her mother.

And then she embraced Rosie, holding her close, and said, with a laugh in her voice:

'Don't worry, Rosie, love. He wasn't worth a spit. And you're right – he did stink! You and me, we'll manage fine on our own.'

After which she had given Rosie tuppence, sent her out to buy fish and chips, and they'd had supper together, eating the fish and chips out of the greasy paper, licking their fingers and laughing together.

Of course, they did not manage alone together for long. Another uncle appeared, an uncle who was informed from the beginning that Rosie came first in her mother's affections. But Rosie never forgot the incident with the bread-knife or the fish-and-chip supper that followed; it was one of the best evenings in her life, perhaps *the* best.

But remembering all this did nothing to help her resolve the problem of her relationship with Tommo. Was he taking her out because he truly liked her or was he hoping to lure her into the sort of shameful and dangerous situation that Lily Hoddle had spoken of?

In the end, it was Rosie's strong streak of commonsense that decided the matter. There was no point in speculating. The only way to find out Tommo's intentions was to go out with him. If he behaved badly, then that would be the end of it. She would show him in no uncertain terms that she was not the sort of girl with whom men could take liberties.

The decision pleased her because it chimed with her own inner wishes. She really wanted to keep the date with Tommo and began to look forward to it with increasing excitement.

4

For his part, Tommo had no doubts about the matter. Up to the time of the incident in Brown's Alley he had scarcely been aware of Rosie: to him she had simply been the young kid at the pub. But coming upon her attackers so suddenly had enabled him to see her for what she had become – an attractive and shapely young woman. He had caught a brief but fascinating glimpse of creamy thighs and swelling breasts and the sight had surprised and excited him.

The story of the attack had gone around the neighbourhood and in the telling of it Tommo had emerged as something of a hero. In truth, he had done very little except fortuitously to appear with his friends at the right moment, but he accepted the adulation (and the free drinks that went with it) in exactly the right tone of engaging modesty.

It was natural, therefore, and only right that he should show a benevolent interest in the girl he had so pluckily rescued. The little gift of violets had been a genuine measure of concern as had his later solicitous enquiries about her welfare.

But later, when Rosie returned to the pub and her spirit revived, Tommo's interest took a deeper turn. He found that she had a tongue and wit as sharp, if not sharper than his own. He was used, on the whole, to having matters his own way when it came to verbal duels, but in Rosie he had met an opponent who was more than worthy of him. This both amused and disconcerted him: he sensed, though he could never bring himself to admit it, that Rosie was above him in intelligence and, moreover, that she had an independence of spirit that would not be easy to overcome. These uneasy thoughts bruised his vanity and made him the more determined to meet this challenge.

So, the more he thought of Rosie, the more involved he became, and he saw but one end to it all. His physical desire for her grew in intensity with each day: he could scarcely see her, even at a distance, without feeling the fierce heat rising in his loins. He sensed that he would have to tread carefully with this one, that she would not be so easy or so willing as some of the other girls he had known; but have her, he would, he was determined on that. And when that objective had been achieved it would bring a double victory, a double satisfaction, for he would have subdued and overcome not only her flesh but something of her spirit also.

Tommo kept a record of his conquests on the barrow that he used to carry goods to market. Down one of the wooden shafts he had carved a series of notches, each one commemorating the successful seduction of one young lady or another. The record was already a formidable one: there was no more room on the left-hand shaft and it had now become Tommo's driving ambition to start on the other side and to mark the occasion with a notch for Rosie.

Guided by a combination of native cunning and experience, he decided that their first outing – the projected visit to the music-hall – should be regarded as a sort of overture and no more. His main objective on this occasion would be to build Rosie's confidence, to make her feel that he was someone to be trusted. If he made his move too soon or too clumsily, she could be frightened off. The softening-up process might well take more than one evening, and turn out to be expensive, but the remembrance of those creamy thighs had been burned on his mind like a brand so that each time he thought of Rosie, Tommo knew that she would be well worth the effort and the money.

5

As they sat side by side on the top deck of a Royal Blue horse-bus which took them along the High Road, and Seven Sisters Road and down past the park to the Finsbury Park Empire, Tommo had to admit that Rosie had done him proud. She was wearing a costume of sandy brown which might have been made for her and had a little matching hat pinned to her neatly piled-up hair. The colour of the costume seemed to pick up and highlight the rich auburn of the hair and the total effect was one of charming simplicity. There's no denying, thought Tommo, that our Rosie has a touch of class: no-one would think to see her that she works in a public-house or has spent her life skivvying.

What Tommo didn't know was that Rosie had build up her wardrobe for the evening mainly by judicious borrowing.

The costume belonged to Tess Crooks and had to be returned, unmarked, on the morrow. The hat and the hand-bag came from Lily Hoddle; the white gloves had been purchased for threepence from a second-hand stall. The perfume had come, amazingly enough, from The Missus who, meeting Rosie on the stairs on her way out, had said with unusual magnanimity:

'Well, well! Quite the little madam, aren't we!' Then she'd sniffed and added: 'You've got no scent! Must have a bit of scent on you, girl. Might as well do the job properly. Here, go into my bedroom and help yourself.'

Reluctant to offend the Missus, Rosie had taken up the offer. But unlike The Missus, who soaked herself in perfume each evening, she had the good sense to use the bottle sparingly. The result pleased her and intrigued Tommo, adding a subtle touch to her personality.

Tommo had taken some care with his appearance also. Clad in his Sunday-best pearl grey suit, with a smart curly-brimmed bowler in place of his workaday topper, he might well have been taken for a respectable bank clerk rather than a spieler in the market. The only concession to flamboyance was the plum-coloured waistcoat that showed beneath the high-collared jacket and the thick gold watchchain that stretched from pocket to pocket across his stomach. Rosie thought he looked very smart and was quietly proud to be seen with him.

Oddly enough, a certain shyness overcame them at first and they travelled in virtual silence, their tongues unusually still. It was as though, now that the moment had come, neither knew what to say to the other. All their previous meetings, apart from the occasional brief exchange, had taken place with other people around: this was the first time they had been alone together and a kind of awkwardness arose between them, an awkwardness that was hard to break down. The problem was further compounded by the fact that this was also Rosie's first outing with a beau, and she was not sure how to behave.

Thus she made an initial mistake when the conductor came round to collect the fares and she began to fumble in her

65

purse for the necessary coppers. Tommo pushed her hand down and said gruffly:

'I'll get them, I'll get them!'

Rosie saw a touch of pink in his cheeks and realised at once that she had commited a social gaffe and embarrassed her escort. She had 'shown him up' which, according to Lily Hoddle, was one of the worst things you could do to a young man.

As the bus crossed Green Lanes by the Manor House pub, Rosie tried to break the stiff silence.

'Lovely evening,' she said. 'It's a lovely evening.'

'Yes.'

'Really lovely.'

'Yes,' he said again.

'Mind you,' she said, after a lengthy pause, 'it's only to be expected. I mean, it's the end of May. The weather should be on the turn.'

'Yes,' said Tommo, and added reflectively, 'We had a rotten April.'

'Oh, didn't we?' explained Rosie. 'Really rotten.'

'Rotten,' said Tommo, nodding.

Really, thought Rosie, this is worse than the previous silence and she wondered whether the rest of the evening would go in the same way. She was quite relieved when they arrived at the stop near the Empire.

Tommo seemed to brighten up once they arrived in the foyer of the theatre. He waved to and greeted several people, mainly young men of his own age, and appeared to be quite at home in the bustling, brightly-lit atmosphere. Pulling out his watch and clicking it open, he said:

'Ah, we're in good time. We'll have a little drop of wet, eh?'

Without waiting for a reply, he steered her briskly towards the bar, where the barman greeted him by name.

'Evening, Tommo.'

'Evening, Dick,' said Tommo. 'A pint for me and a port-and-lemon for the lady.'

'No!' said Rosie, more quickly and sharply than she intended.

'What?' said Tommo in surprise.

'Not port-and-lemon,' said Rosie.

'Oh,' said Tommo. 'Then what will it be?'

'I don't think I want anything.' But as soon as she had spoken she saw by the look on his face that she had committed another gaffe and she added quickly: 'Well, perhaps I'll have a Vitapop.'

They kept a small stock of Vitapop at The Winged Horse and Rosie knew that it was guaranteed to be non-alcoholic.

'Vitapop!' said Tommo, in a voice tinged with disgust.

'Don't keep it,' said Dick, and managed in those three words to imply that no self-respecting barman would be seen dead with the stuff.

'All right then,' said Rosie quickly, in a small, almost inaudible voice. 'I'll have a lemonade.'

'A lemonade, Dick,' said Tommo, and Rosie saw a quick look pass between the two men.

Another long silence as they stood sipping their drinks, a silence in which they exchanged little awkward smiles. Rosie began to think that there might be something wrong with her appearance: she was certainly more quietly dressed than the majority of other young women in the bar and wondered whether Tommo was disappointed on that score. Privately, she considered that some of the women present looked down-right common and told herself that Tommo or anyone else was welcome to them.

A young man came up behind Tommo and banged him on the back so hard that the beer slopped over the rim of Tommo's glass on to his shoes.

'Wotcher, me old Tommo!' said the newcomer.

'You clumsy bugger!' said Tommo.

'Sorry, me old china.' The young man stared approvingly at Rosie. 'You got company, I see. What's this then? Another notch for the old barrow?'

'Shove off, Mick,' said Tommo angrily. 'Why don't you shove yourself off!'

The young man shielded his mouth with an open hand and lowered his voice. 'What's Liz going to say about her, then, eh? She'll have your guts for garters, Tommo!'

'Shove off!' said Tommo with more emphasis, 'shove off!'

'You want to watch him, girl,' said the young man as he moved away, a smile on his face. 'He has two like you for breakfast every morning.'

'Flannel mouth!' said Tommo, and as he glanced awkwardly at Rosie, she saw that the pink spots had returned to his cheeks and that he was sweating slightly.

'What did he mean about the barrow? A notch on the barrow?' asked Rosie.

'Take no notice,' said Tommo. 'He's barpoo. All gammon and cabbage. Come on, let's go in.' He was beginning to realise that he'd made an error by bringing Rosie to one of his regular haunts and that they would be better off in the safety of their seats.

He had splashed out on two of the more glamorous stall seats, known as fauteuils, in the hope of impressing Rosie but she had heard someone mention the price of the seats and was mildly shocked by his extravagance. One shilling and sixpence for a seat in a music-hall, three shillings for the two of them, seemed to be a dreadful waste of money.

'You didn't ought to have done it, Tommo,' she whispered. 'I'd have been just as happy in the Gods.'

'Nothing but the best for you, Rosie,' he said with the air of a man of unlimited resources.

'You didn't ought to have done it,' she said again, but with less emphasis and he knew that he had at last scored a point, for she squeezed his arm as if to say thank-you, and as she sunk into the seat he could feel her quivering excitement.

'You been here before, of course,' he said.

'Never!' breathed Rosie, 'never! I've never been to a music-hall ever.'

'Ah,' said Tommo. 'Well, it's a good bill. Ought to be good.'

She stared around, drinking it all in – the balcony and gallery rising tier upon tier to the high ceiling in which, so she'd heard, there was a dome which was sometimes opened to the night sky on hot summer nights. Flanking the stage on either side were the boxes in which three or four young swells, in full evening dress, were already settling with their gorgeously attired young ladies. Rosie didn't think too much of the boxes: she felt that to sit in one would be like something on view in a shop window.

Next she turned her attention to the stage. The area above and around the vast curtain that screened the opening was painted with a rather gawdy representation of flowers, plump gilded cherubs and even plumper ladies who, but for a discreet scrap of veil here and there, would have been utterly naked. The curtain itself was entirely given up to advertisements: VINOLIA SOAP, HOLLOWAY'S PILLS, BORWICK'S BAKING POWDER, PINK'S JAM, LLOYD'S WEEKLY NEWS, BOVRIL, WATNEY'S ALES, and R. WHITE'S GINGER BEER. Rosie had seen similar advertisements for these familiar products hundreds of times and was able to recognise most of them: still, she thought it odd that they were allowed to appear in such a beautiful place.

Presently this curtain was whisked away to reveal lush dark-red drapes. The conductor of the orchestra, his head just visible above the pit, came on to applause and his unseen orchestra began to play. Then the house-lights dimmed, the footlights glowed, the drapes opened with a swish, and the show began.

From that moment on, Rosie was utterly lost in the wonder of it all. Tommo had to rouse her at the end of the first half and she drifted through the intermission in a dream, longing to get back to her seat.

It was, as Tommo had said, a good bill. There was no chairman as in the old type of music-hall for this was more of a variety show, featuring ten acts in all. Among them were some of the top names in variety – Paul Cinquevalli, the famous juggler, C.H. Chirgwin who called himself The White-Eyed Kaffir, a famous chorus line called The Palace Girls and, at one point, a spectacular effect – introduced as a representation of Niagara Falls – when an opening appeared at the back of the stage and thousands of gallons of water – real water! – began to tumble down in a roaring, glistening sheet. Rosie was sure that the water would flood into the theatre and she rose to her feet to look until angry shouts from behind forced Tommo to pull her down.

The top act was a singer called Vesta Victoria. The whole audience seemed to know her and her songs and could scarcely wait to join the choruses of such popular numbers as 'Daddy Wouldn't Buy Me a Bow-wow' and 'Waiting at the Church'. Rosie had heard these songs many times back at the pub and she lifted her voice with the others, enjoying every moment.

And then, as if all this wasn't enough, a portly gentleman appeared on stage to make an announcement.

'Ladies and gentlemen, for your final entertainment this evening, the management is proud to bring you, without extra charge, the very latest in moving pictures! Filmed by the Bioscope Company! Ladies and gentlemen, we proudly present "Ellen's Escape!" '

Then the great theatre went quite dark, a white screen descended from above, a pianist began to play, and a flickering tongue of light appeared from behind. It was incredible! Rosie had seen photographs before but the ones she saw now were actually moving! It did not matter that the movements were jerky and awkward, she scarcely noticed that. The wonder of it was that the people on the screen seemed to be alive!

The story was short but rather frightening and Rosie was soon caught up in it. At the climax, when Ellen had been tied to the railways tracks by the villain, and the hero was riding to her rescue, she found herself urging him on aloud. It did not matter since most of the other members of the audience were shouting too. As the hero struggled to untie Ellen's bonds and the train drew nearer and nearer, Rosie sunk into her seat and shielded her eyes, afraid to watch. But she heard a cheer from the audience and opening her eyes again she saw that the train had swept past and that Ellen was safe in the hero's arms.

After all this, it was hard for Rosie to come back to reality. It wasn't until they were in the street, outside the theatre, and the girl in the blue coat came swaggering up to Tommo that she came down from the heights, back to earth.

'Hello,' said the girl, 'hello, hello, hello. And what have we here?'

'Hello, Liz,' said Tommo, glancing quickly and awkwardly at Rosie.

'What's the matter, Tommo?' said the girl. 'You look as sick as a nine-pound note. Didn't you expect to see me? Is that it? Didn't you expect to see me?'

'Now look, Liz – ' Tommo began, but she cut across him.

'I'm looking. Oh yes, I'm looking all right! You didn't think I'd be here, did you? You thought I was in Southend for the week. Well, I was, only I got fed-up, d'you see, and I thought I'd come home early and look up my feller. You remember him, don't you? Name of Tommo. And here's a bit of jam! I find him, don't I, I find him first crack. With a bit of fluff hanging on to his arm!'

A small crowd had gathered in anticipation of some further entertainment, and Rosie plucked at Tommo's sleeve.

'Come on, Tommo,' she murmured.

'Oh, no you bloody well don't!' said Liz.

Hands on hips, she now turned her full attention to Rosie, blocking the way forward. Rosie recognised her now: she had appeared at The Winged Horse with Tommo on two or three occasions in the past, but that had been some months ago and there had not appeared to be anything significant in the relationship. Before he had set his sights on Rosie, Tommo was always turning up with one girl or another.

'Now,' said Liz, pushing back a strand of carrotty-coloured hair that had escaped from its pins, 'now, my girl.' Rosie caught the sharp odour of beer as Liz thrust her red face to within an inch or two of her own. 'I got nothing against you, nothing. But he's my feller, see? Mine! If you didn't know that before, you know it now. So what do you do? I'll tell you what you do. You hop it. Double quick. Scarper. Vamoose. Otherwise I'm liable to spoil your looks, such as they are!'

Rosie, uncertain of how to respond to this attack, glanced quickly at Tommo. He tried to interpose himself between the two, but Liz pushed him back and grabbed the front of Rosie's costume jacket. 'Well? You heard me, you ain't got cloth ears. Move! Move!'

'Let me be!' protested Rosie.

'I warned you!' screamed Liz. She pulled Rosie forward: Rosie resisted, and one of the lapels of the jacket came away in Liz's hand. Rosie looked down in horror as the crowd cheered.

'You bitch! You bloody bitch!' she cried.

A surge of anger overwhelmed her and she hurled herself at Liz. The other girl staggered backward under the onslaught, tripped over a by-stander's foot and fell sharply and painfully on her bottom. As she yelled, the crowd cheered even louder.

Rosie stood over the fallen Liz and held a warning finger into her face.

'You touch me again, you lay a finger on me, and I'll cripple you. I mean it.' She made a derisory gesture in the direction of Tommo. 'As for his lordship, you can have him. With rings on. Good riddance!'

Liz, making no attempt to rise, burst into tears.

Rosie picked up the piece of torn cloth, drew herself up, and walked off with all the dignity she could muster. Tommo made a move to follow her.

'Rosie. I'm not her feller. She had it all wrong.'

'I'm not interested,' she replied coldly.

He touched her arm but she shook herself free and the look in her eyes stopped him in his tracks. He could only stand and watch as she stalked towards the bus stop.

The young man who had spoken to Tommo earlier in the evening now appeared. 'You can't say I didn't warn you,' he said.

'Let's go and get a drink,' said Tommo. 'Women! I laid out over four shillings tonight on tickets, fares, drinks. Four bob! Wasted.'

As they moved away, Liz ran after them and grabbed Tommo's arm. 'I'm sorry, Tommo,' she wailed, 'I didn't mean it. It was just seeing you with her – '

'Get away!' said Tommo roughly, pulling free. 'We're

finished. I've had enough of your bloody antics. Now, get away. Leave me alone.'

'Don't, Tommo,' she cried pathetically, 'don't. I'll kill myself.'

He threw a coin at her feet. 'Good idea,' he said cruelly. 'Make a good job of it. There's a tanner – buy yourself some flowers to put on the coffin.'

At this moment, Rosie came back. She had simmered down somewhat, but her tone was still terse.

'Listen,' she said, 'listen. Are you her feller?'

'No, Rosie, no. I swear to God,' said Tommo fervently.

'Why did she say you were, then?'

'She's stewed, can't you see? Pissed as a newt. We been out together a few times, that's all. She just thought she could frighten you off.'

'Then she's got another thought coming, hasn't she?' said Rosie.

'I've just told her to clear off,' said Tommo. 'I told her, we're finished. God's truth, Rosie.'

'All right, all right,' she said briskly. 'Don't stand there like a cup of cold tea. Take me home.'

Tommo looked at his friend, shrugged, and meekly followed Rosie.

7

On the ride back, Rosie sat in silence while Tommo tried to clear the issue of Liz.

'Because we went out together a few times she took it for granted that we were – well – that I was her regular. I never said nothing like that to her. She's all right when she's sober, I'll give her that due. But when she gets a few drinks on board she's a pain. I'm glad to see the back of her.'

When Rosie made no response, he went on: 'Sorry about your costume. I'll get it mended. I'll get it invisibly mended, so you won't notice.'

'You'd better had,' said Rosie grimly. 'It don't belong to me. It belongs to Tess Crooks.'

Another long silence, broken eventually by Tommo, who said with the air of a penitent schoolboy:

'I suppose this means – well – I got a line on this pony and trap, see. I was going to borrow it on your next Sunday off – run you out into the country. Don't suppose that's on now.'

To his surprise, Rosie began to giggle.

'What's up now?' he said in an aggrieved tone.

'Your face!' she said. 'You look like a dying duck in a thunderstorm!'

He smiled, she laughed, and all the tension between them dissolved. She took his arm in a gesture of forgiveness and they sat happily together in the dimly-lit interior to the end of the ride. At the side door of the pub he made no attempt to kiss her goodnight. Instead, he shook her hand and said:

'Thanks for coming, Rosie.'

'That's all right,' she replied formally. 'I quite enjoyed it. Thank you for taking me.' She was surprised at the handshake and half-hoped that he would kiss her.

'What about that outing then, on your next free Sunday?'

'I'll see,' she replied. 'Ask me when the time comes.'

Tommo left her with mixed feelings. He wasn't sure how to measure the evening. It had come good in the end, but he saw now that his original estimate of Rosie had only been half right. She was tough, no bones about that: the way she had stood up to Liz and bundled her over had been a real eye-opener. But he sensed that it went beyond that.

He found it difficult to shape the thought. It was simply that with all the other girls he'd known he had been cock of the walk, the undisputed superior. They had fallen for his spiel, his impudence, his swagger. Apart from the odd one here and there, they had deferred to him. Some had even thrown themselves at him, without shame. Yes, he'd had the occasional awkward one, like Liz, but never anyone quite like Rosie. No girl had ever spoken to him as Rosie had done, after the scene with Liz. And he had never so meekly responded to an order, never!

Now he had the uneasy feeling that the traditional roles had been reversed, that if their relationship continued he would be playing second fiddle to Rosie.

Then he chided himself for bothering with the problem. She was one girl out of many, he could manage without her. After all, wasn't he Tommo the Toff? No kid of seventeen was going to put him down! Squaring his shoulders, pursing his lips into a whistle, he made his way towards the Paradise Cafe where the door to the back room was always open and where he knew he could find some convivial friends, a game of pontoon, and a few jugs of beer. Even so, despite the company and the soothing effect of the ale, Rosie kept pushing her way into his thoughts and would not be denied.

Had he been able to read Rosie's mind, Tommo would have been disappointed to find that he figured there only as a kind of small-part player. As she undressed for bed, Rosie was remembering the stage show, reliving the glamour and magic of it all. The incident with Liz was already half-forgotten, she could think only of the music, the songs, the comedy, the laughter.

Despite everything, it had been a wonderful evening, like catching a glimpse of another world! And she found herself singing one of the songs she had heard that evening:

> Oh, she was as
> Beautiful as a butterfly
> And as proud as a Queen
> Was Pretty Little Polly Perkins
> Of Paddington Green!

CHAPTER FOUR

1

Rosie was on duty in the public bar on the night the police came. She'd had little to do with policemen and did not immediately place the two solemn-looking men in heavy tweed suits who advanced towards her.

'Evening, gents. What'll you have?' she asked.

'Get your mistress, girl!' said the older of the two men. He had a big bushy moustache, which spread out across his square, florid face to link up with long gingery sidewhiskers. Above this the brown eyes were as hard as bullets, brooking no argument.

'Who shall I say, sir?'

'Tell her Inspector Clemence of Tottenham CID wants a word.'

Rosie found The Missus in the kitchen, checking the supplies.

'Rozzers!' said The Missus, feeding a bit of boiled ham into her mouth. 'Pestilence! They're a pestilence! Clements, did you say? Haven't seen him around for ages.'

She wiped her hands on a cloth, checked her appearance in the piece of cracked mirror that hung above the sink, assumed an appropriate smile and went through to the bar, with a curious Rosie in tow.

'Ah, Mr Clemence,' said The Missus. 'Nice to see you. You've been neglecting us, you know. I was beginning to wonder.'

'Evening, Mrs Quorn,' said Clemence.

'I have a very nice drop of Scotch whisky. I know you like whisky – '

'This is not a social call, Mrs Quorn,' said Clemence reproachfully.

'Oh,' said The Missus. She seemed to be a little flustered by this. 'Nothing wrong, I hope?'

'I hope so too, Mrs Quorn. I sincerely hope so.' He turned to his colleague. 'This is Detective Constable Roberts.'

'Evening, ma'am,' said the young officer politely. The Missus inclined her head in response. Roberts looked past her and fixed his eyes on Rosie, who was hovering just behind The Missus. He had an open, handsome face and, when Rosie gave him a little smile, he responded in kind. Then, as if remembering his position, he cut the smile quickly and replaced it with a look of stern concentration. Rosie suddenly heard Mr Softley's name and turned her attention to Inspector Clemence.

'Do you happen to have in your employ a certain Wilfred Blake Softley?' asked Clemence, lowering his voice a little but still managing to insert a certain pomposity into his tone.

'Mr Softley? Oh, yes. He plays the piano in the saloon. Tuesday to Saturday.'

'Ah. So he would be here now?'

'Upstairs. Changing into his togs,' said Rosie quickly.

'I trust – ' began The Missus.

'I would like a word with your Mr Softley,' said Clemence. He glanced around. 'Is there somewhere private, perhaps?'

'There's my parlour. You could use that.'

'Capital! If you could ask Mr Softley to step into your parlour for a little talk, I'd be obliged. You need not mention us. Say that you wish to see him.'

'Rosie – you heard,' said The Missus. 'Fetch him! And look sharp!' She turned to the Inspector and added, in a milder tone: 'This way, if you please.'

Rosie sped upstairs to the small dressing-room and knocked on the door.

'Mr Softley?'

'Yes? Who is it?'

'Rosie.'

'A moment.'

Rosie waited impatiently. She sensed that a drama was

77

developing, a drama which involved the police and Mr Softley and in which she was playing a small, peripheral part. The door opened suddenly and Mr Softley stood before her, buttoning his waistcoat. He spoke with an unaccustomed sharpness.

'Well, what is it? What is it?'

'Compliments of The Missus. She would like to see you in the parlour as soon as possible.'

His eyes searched her face. He looked drawn and anxious. 'Did she say what it was about?'

'No.'

'Is she alone?' Rosie hesitated and he continued in a kinder tone: 'Rosie, little Rosie. We're friends, are we not? Allies. Is The Missus alone?'

'She's got two men with her.'

'Two men?' She saw him stiffen. 'Do you know them?'

'No.' She shook her head. And then, because, for the first time, an impossible thought occurred to her, the thought that Mr Softley might be in trouble with the police, and because they were friends, she added: 'But I know they are police-men. Detectives from the CID.'

She felt him stiffen as she spoke, saw the wild terror race across his eyes. Some of this fear communicated itself to Rosie, and she trembled uncontrollably. In a whisper she said:

'Are you all right?'

There was no reply for a long time. He was leaning against the doorpost, with one hand gripping the edge of the door and she saw that the knuckles of this hand were white. Eventually he drew breath and nodded:

'Tell – tell them I'll be down directly. Thank you, little Rosie.'

2

The parlour was a small, square room just off the saloon bar. Equipped with a sofa, a couple of armchairs, a small table and a roll-top desk, this was The Missus's sanctum, the place from which she conducted the business affairs of the pub or to which she occasionally retired for privacy. The Missus led the way in and indicated one of the armchairs.

'There we are, Mr Clemence,' she said. 'Make yourselves comfortable. Are you sure I can't tempt you to some of that prime Scotch whisky?'

'Well, perhaps. Since we are in the privacy of your parlour, Mrs Quorn. That would be very kind.'

'Most kind,' said Roberts.

'My young colleague will take a draught ale,' said Clemence sternly.

'Most kind,' repeated Roberts with slightly less enthusiasm and gave The Missus a pale smile.

She went out into the saloon to order the drinks and came back immediately.

'I hope you won't keep Mr Softley too long,' she said. 'His public will be waiting.'

'That depends, Mrs Quorn,' said Clemence smugly, 'that all depends.'

'On what?'

'On the judge and jury, I should say, wouldn't you, Roberts?' Clemence chuckled. 'Oh, yes, it will depend on the judge and the jury.'

'Exactly right, sir,' said Roberts dutifully.

'I don't understand,' said The Missus with an anxious frown. 'I mean – you said you wanted to speak with him. Surely it doesn't go beyond that?'

Clemence hesitated, as if debating the question in his mind. Then he replied with a question of his own:

'Mrs Quorn, how long have you known Mr Softley?'

'Five years. Almost six.'

'You would, from your observation, say that he was a man of good character?'

'Oh, excellent,' she replied. 'He is an educated gentleman, you know, his family background is very – well, I mean – I understand he comes from a very fair background.'

'Odd that he should work here, isn't it?' said Clemence. 'I mean, if he is well-connected.'

'This is a very respectable house,' said The Missus with a touch of hauteur.

'Oh, indeed. I know, I know. All the same, it makes you wonder, doesn't it?'

They were interrupted by the arrival of the drinks and these, in turn, were followed by Rosie.

'Mr Softley says that he will be down directly,' she said.

'You did not – ' The Inspector eyed her keenly.

'I said The Missus wanted to see him,' said Rosie, blushing slightly under his scrutiny. She felt certain now that Mr Softley was in danger of some sort and her only thought was to help him.

'Get back to your work, Rosie,' said The Missus. And, as the door closed behind the girl, she turned to Clemence. During the short interlude since his last question her quick mind had been picking away at the problem and the consequence of this mental debate was that she had decided to backtrack a little. It was obvious that Mr Softley was in trouble with the law and if that were so, she did not intend to get herself tarred with his brush.

'We were talking about Mr Softley, Inspector,' she said. 'Well, as I said, he is a man of good character. However, that being said, I must add that he is a man of good character *as far as I know*. As far as I know, if you get my drift. I have no complaints about his work here, none at all. But that is all I know of him, Inspector. What he does, what he gets up to when he leaves here, I wouldn't know from Adam, if you follow me.'

The Inspector nodded gravely and sipped his whisky. 'About his work here, Mrs Quorn. Has he – has he ever brought a companion with him? A friend?'

'Companion? Friend? You mean, a lady friend, is that what you mean?'

The two police officers exchanged a quick look, and it crossed The Missus's mind that they were amused by her reply. But Inspector Clemence showed no sign of this as he said gravely:

'No, ma'am. I do not mean a lady friend.' He leaned towards her. 'Look, Mrs Quorn, you are a woman of the world. May I speak frankly?'

'By all means.' She felt a little tremor of excitement, an

excitement that was almost sexual, stir in her flesh.

'Your Mr Softley – ' he began.

'Not my Mr Softley!' she said sharply, now more than ever determined to put a distance between herself and whatever misdeed had been committed.

'Mr Softley then,' went on the Inspector. 'I tell you this for your own good, Mrs Quorn. Strictly speaking, I suppose I should keep quiet. On the other hand, common decency tells me that I should not stand by and see your trust abused, if you follow me.'

'Yes,' mumbled The Missus who, in truth, was becoming more confused by the moment.

'Did you know that the man who calls himself Mr Softley to you, is in fact somebody else?'

'He changed his name to Softley quite legally, by deed poll,' said Detective Constable Roberts.

'Quite so, quite so,' said Clemence quickly. 'But that is irrelevant. The question is – what did he change his name from? And the answer, Mrs Quorn, is that his former name, the name he was born with, was Oates. Wilfred Blake Oates. Does that name ring a bell with you?'

'I – I – can't say,' said The Missus, looking from one man to the other. 'No, I don't think so.'

'Are you familiar with the crime of buggery, ma'am?' asked Clemence abruptly.

'No,' said The Missus faintly.

Roberts suddenly coughed and seemed for a moment to be choking in his beer. When he had recovered he said apologetically: 'Sorry, sir. Went down the wrong hole.' For some reason this remark seemed to set him off again and it was another minute before they could continue.

'As I was about to say, ma'am,' said Clemence, 'as I was about to say. Your Mr Softley – our Mr Softley if you prefer – when he was still Mr Oates, was sent to prison for two years for the crime of buggery.'

'Oh, my goodness,' said The Missus and collapsed heavily on to the sofa.

'Yes,' said Clemence softly. He seemed to be enjoying himself, to enjoy spelling out the details. 'He was found guilty of fornication with – of having had carnal knowledge of – another person of the same sex. A young man. In short, buggery.'

'I can hardly believe it,' murmured The Missus. Clemence leaned towards her, his eyes glittering, his lips moist. 'He is a pervert, ma'am. A pervert. In the common jargon, a poof. And if there is one thing I cannot stand, Mrs Quorn, it is a poof. I can understand murder, larceny, fraud, I can even understand rape, if you will pardon the term. But one think I cannot understand and never will understand, one thing that revolts me is a poof. Some people say they should be pitied. Pitied! I'd horsewhip every one of them! I'd flog some decency into them! Ugh! The thought of two men – together –'

He caught a look from Roberts and stopped suddenly. When he continued, it was in a quieter more controlled tone:

'Well, there it is, ma'am. And we are here this evening because we have reason to believe that Mr Wilfred Blake Softley née Oates, is up to his old tricks again.'

'Oh, no,' said The Missus.

'Oh, yes, ma'am. A complaint has been laid.'

'A complaint?'

'I cannot say more at this stage except that the complaint appears to be well-founded. But even if nothing comes of it, at least you know what sort of chap he is. At least you can be on your guard.'

'He'll never set foot inside here again!' said The Missus grimly.

The Inspector looked at his watch. 'Where is the fellow? He's taking his time!'

'Shall I go and rouse him out, sir?' asked Roberts.

'No,' said The Missus quickly. 'I'll find him for you. I – I wouldn't want any – you know – any fuss or disturbance over this.'

'Of course,' said Clemence, twirling his empty glass.

'Help yourself while I'm gone,' said The Missus. 'Plenty more where that came from.'

She had recovered from the initial shock and her dominant feeling now was one of anger. She did not share the Inspector's moral indignation, she had been around too long and seen too much for that, but she was angry. Angry with herself, when she remembered all the flirtatious incidents, the amorous dallying, that had passed between Mr Softley and herself. True, it had all come to nothing and now, she thought bitterly, now I understand why! And her anger enveloped Mr Softley: she felt that he had betrayed her, taken advantage of her good nature and made her look a fool.

She went up to look for him herself, because this also gave her an excuse to go to the bedroom and tidy her hair and make-up. When this had been done to her satisfaction, she moved along the corridor to the dressing-room and knocked on the door.

'Mr Softley!' she called sharply.

There was no reply. She turned the handle and the door yielded. The room was empty, but Mr Softley had obviously changed into his performing clothes for his other things were hanging in the closet. She went to the top of the stairs and listened. No sound of piano music or singing rose from the saloon. Where had the man got to?

A thorough if discreet search of the pub got them nowhere and it could only be assumed that Mr Softley, anticipating trouble or having been tipped off, had made good his escape. The two police officers went round to his lodgings to make further enquiries while The Missus, harassed by customers, drafted Rosie in as a temporary pianist.

In a sense, Mr Softley had made good his escape. No-one had thought of looking in the cellar and it was there that The Guv'nor found him. He was swinging from a rope attached to a hook in a ceiling beam which the cellarman used as a kind of hoist for lifting the beer barrels, and he had been dead for at least an hour.

3

There were times when Rosie found it very hard to work out what God was up to. She wondered, not in any sense of self-pity but with genuine bewilderment, what she had done to offend him. Why did the people she loved most always die? Her mother, her aunt and now Mr Softley – why them? They were good, kind, fine people too, which made it worse. If people had to die, there were plenty of villains around. Surely God ought to turn his attention to them and leave the good ones alone!

Of course, there were some who said that Mr Softley was not a good man, who hinted at unspeakable crimes and suggested that his departure was a kind of blessing. Rosie spoke up with spirit whenever she heard this view, defending her friend stubbornly and shaming most of his detractors to silence. But the rumours continued, quietly and discreetly fuelled, if Rosie had only known it, by The Missus herself, who was busily working off her wounded pride at the expense of her late pianist.

Rosie guessed that Mr Softley had committed a crime of a special sort, that he had broken some kind of social taboo; the whispers that accompanied the mention of his name, the shaking of heads, the scandalised looks, all indicated that he had touched some nerve in the community. But again, Rosie could not help but notice that those who were quickest and most savage in their condemnation were always the ones who had the least to boast about in terms of their own characters.

No-one spoke directly to Rosie on the subject, some because they thought her too young to have knowledge of such matters, others because they knew of her fierce loyalty to Mr Softley. However, from a word here, a bit of overheard gossip there, Rosie built up a fair picture of Mr Softley's supposed crime and after the inquest, which brought in a verdict of 'suicide while the balance of his mind was disturbed', she was able to talk to young Detective Constable Roberts about the matter. She went up to him outside the courtroom and said bluntly:

'I'm Rosie Carr. I work at The Winged Horse.'

'Ah, yes, miss. I remember you.' Roberts touched his cap politely, a gesture that pleased Rosie. She noticed that his bright eyes were very dark, almost black.

'Have you got a minute?' she asked.

'For you? Any time,' he replied.

'I want to ask you about Mr Softley,' she said.

'Ah,' he said guardedly. 'In what connection?'

'Now, don't go all official on me,' she said, with a touch of annoyance. 'That verdict – balance of his mind disturbed. That means they think he was barmy at the time he did it, right?'

'More or less.'

'That's tripe,' she said. 'I saw him that evening, remember? He wasn't barmy, but he was desperate.' She thought of the look of terror in Mr Softley's eyes.

'Look,' he said gently. 'Why not forget it? All over now – water under the bridge.'

'Not for me, it isn't. He was good to me, he was a good friend. Look, I haven't just come out of the egg, I've been around. Why did you want to see him that night? And why was the poor devil scared out of his wits?'

After an initial hesitation, he told her about Mr Softley's previous conviction and the circumstances which had led to his suicide. He had, Roberts told her, become involved with a young man of nineteen, the son of well-to-do parents.

'Involved?' asked Rosie.

'You asked for it,' said Roberts with a sigh. 'They lived together, like man and wife. Slept together in the same bed. Understand?'

'I'm not daft!' said Rosie, blushing slightly. 'Go on.'

Roberts then told her that the young man's parents had found out about the association: they had tried to force their son to return home and, when he refused, they had filed a complaint to the police, naming Mr Softley.

'That's about the size of it,' said Roberts. 'Anything else you'd like to know?'

'That's enough for one day, thank you,' Rosie said politely. 'Poor Mr Softley. No wonder he was frightened.'

'It was his bad luck that the complaint came to Inspector Clemence. He's got a chip on his shoulder when it comes to – well, people like your friend.'

'Poor Mr Softley,' she said again.

'When's your night off?' he asked, after a pause.

'Who wants to know?'

'I do.'

85

'What for?'

'Stone me!' he said. 'What do you think? I thought you might let me take you out.'

'Come off it!' she said teasingly. 'What do you think people are going to say if they see me walking out with a *rozzer*?'

Before he could respond, she moved on; but, a few yards on, she took the sting out of her words by turning to give him an impudent wink. He smiled and touched his cap again, in acknowledgement.

That night, after the pub had closed, Rosie sat in her room and thought about Mr Softley. What she had learned about her friend had not in any way affected her feeling for him. She did not understand how two men could love each other in that way but she felt no sense of shock or disgust, reasoning that God had made people the way they were and that it was not up to her to sit in judgment on his handiwork.

She regretted now that she had not made the effort to get closer to Mr Softley. From the beginning their relationship had been one-sided, she had been content to let him do all the giving. Now she saw how selfish she had been. What an effort it must have been for him to put on his smiling evening face for the customers! What torment he must have gone through! And how alone he must have felt, how utterly friendless and alone!

Tears misted her eyes as she remembered what he had once told her, his rich, rather theatrical voice echoing in her mind:

Listen to me, little Rosie. You may be a skivvy, but you are also a human being. A person. You won't always be a skivvy, that will pass, but you'll always be a person. Remember that, little Rosie.

That had been a sort of turning-point in her life, the moment when she had first learned to have respect for herself. She would always owe Mr Softley that. And who, out of all her friends, could replace him? There was no-one to whom she could go and talk so frankly, no-one who would understand as he had understood. For the first time in months she felt a loneliness, a vulnerability, that quickened her tears.

4

The unexpected death of her old friend had certain immediate and some long-term consequences for Rosie. Mr Softley could not possibly have known what these would be, but it seemed to Rosie, when she thought about it later, that even in death he was still exercising some benevolent influence on her life.

The first thing to happen was that The Missus, seeing an opportunity to save a few shillings, informed Rosie that she could take over as pub pianist on a permanent basis. She spoke as if she were doing Rosie a great favour.

'I am putting my trust in you, Rosie. I can only hope that you won't let me down.'

'Thank you, ma'am,' said Rosie. She waited for the other woman to continue, but all she heard was a brusque dismissal.

'Well, don't stand there gawping, girl. Off you go.'

But Rosie had come a long way from the child of thirteen who had once trembled in the presence of The Missus. She stood her ground and said:

'What about wages?'

'Wages?'

'Do I get something for the extra work?'

'Extra work? I thought you enjoyed playing the piano.'

'I do, ma'am, I do. I'm not saying I don't. But it is extra. And you'll be saving what you paid Mr Softley.'

'What the late Mr Softley received by way of remuneration is not your affair!' said The Missus sharply. 'In any case, he was a professional. You don't expect to get the same, do you?'

'I need something,' Rosie said, sensing a victory. 'I mean, I shall need a couple of decent frocks and that. Can't play to the customers in my old clothes, can I?'

'How much are we paying you now?' The Missus knew the answer to this question very well, but she was playing for time.

'Four shillings a week,' replied Rosie.

'Plus room and full board,' emphasised The Missus.

'Plus room and board,' said Rosie.

'Hmph. I should have thought that was enough. More than enough in this day and age.' The Missus gave one of her martyr-like sighs. 'But that's always the way. Young people – no gratitude. No gratitude. All they think of is Number One. Self first, self second, self last. I should have known. I should have known. But I judge other people by my own standards, that's the trouble. That is where I go wrong.'

Rosie waited while The Missus continued in this vein. She knew that the woman found it painful to give way on a matter of money and that behind this mournful tirade The Missus was working out how little she could get away with and, at the same time, making the mental adjustment necessary to even a minimal concession. She stopped at last and said:

'I'll give you an extra shilling a week.'

'Half-a-crown,' said Rosie. 'That's what I had in mind. Another two shillings and sixpence.'

'A half-crown! I am not made of money, girl!'

'A shilling won't get me far,' said Rosie. 'Can't buy much with a shilling. Like I said, I'll need some frocks and a bit of paint and powder. And I'll have to keep my hair special. I mean you don't want me looking like I just came out of the workhouse, do you, ma'am?'

'I'll give you two shillings,' said The Missus. 'Not a penny more.'

'And the same arrangement about the tips?'

'What arrangement?' said The Missus stiffly.

'Like you had with Mr Softley,' said Rosie. 'I keep the cash tips. And when somebody buys me a drink, you re-sell it and I get half the doings.'

'Very well,' said The Missus and added icily, 'Is there anything else?'

'Well,' said Rosie, emboldened by her success so far. 'If I'm playing the joanna I won't be able to serve behind the bar, will I? So you'll need someone to fill in. And while you're at it, we could do with a bit of help with the odd jobs during the day.'

'Perhaps,' said The Missus, the chill still singing in her voice, 'perhaps you would like to take over the running of the pub? I mean, don't let me stand in your way, will you?'

'No, no,' said Rosie, 'not in a million years. I didn't mean to stick my beak in your business, ma'am. Only making a suggestion.'

'Which I will bear in mind,' condescended The Missus. 'Which I will bear in mind.'

5

The following Sunday, after morning Chapel, Rosie met Tommo and drove with him in a borrowed trap out to Cockfosters and Hadley Wood. Rosie was reluctant to go at first but Mr Crooks persuaded her that after the strains of the past week the change would do her good.

It was a fine, sweet spring day and Tommo kept the sturdy little grey pony moving along at a cheerful pace, but Rosie, who normally enjoyed such moments of freedom and showed her pleasure openly, was unusually quiet during the first part of the journey. Tommo tried to draw her out without success and in the end he gave up the effort and did not try again until he stopped at The Cherry Tree inn to get water for the pony and some liquid refreshment of a stronger sort for himself.

Quite a lot of other people seemed to have been struck with a similar idea. All the seats and tables, both inside and out were occupied and, in the end, they joined three or four other couples on the forecourt. Tommo left Rosie sitting on the grass in the warm sunshine and went inside. He sank a pint of ale in one, without pausing for breath, and promptly ordered another pint, a lemonade for Rosie, and two tuppeny roast beef sandwiches, one thick and one thin. He borrowed a tray, piled a side plate with some of the free pickles and niblets of cheese that stood on the counter, and picked his way carefully through the crowd back to Rosie.

He set the tray down between them and offered her one of the sandwiches. 'I brought a thin one for you, Rosie, made with thin bread. I like a thick one myself, bread cut like doorsteps.'

She nodded and nibbled abstractedly at the sandwich. He had never known her so quiet for so long and wondered what he could do to break through to her. His original timetable in regard to Rosie had gone sadly astray: four or five weeks had passed since their evening at the Empire and this was the second Sunday they had spent together, but he had to admit that his original objective remained as elusive as ever.

He could not explain why. It was simply that, when faced with a suitable opportunity to advance his cause, his heart seemed to go to his boots, his nerve to desert him. Why she, alone of all the girls he knew, should have this effect upon him defied understanding or explanation.

Nor could he understand why he bothered to pursue Rosie when there were easier pickings that were his for the taking. In a vague sort of way he realised that she represented a challenge, and that pride and vanity made it necessary for him to continue the pursuit: to give up without achieving his goal would be a savage blow to his self-esteem and to his hard-won position as the local Casanova. Yet even this did not entirely explain away his attitude. Was there another, even more serious reason behind his increasing interest in this girl?

It was that word *serious* which frightened him. Had he fallen into a trap of his own making, was he becoming serious about Rosie, with all that implied in terms of commitment and marriage?

Marriage!

There were certain words, certain things, for which Tommo had always reserved a special scorn. Love and marriage were the chief among these, the principal targets for his cynicism. But of late, to his shame, he had been forced to ask himself if his strange and almost total preoccupation with Rosie was a manifesto of love. Worse, in a mad moment, he had even pondered the idea of marriage. If there were no other way to win her, would be – as a last resort – agree to wed her?

Of course, he had dismissed both suggestions out of hand. But the frightening thing was that they kept coming back, wriggling through his defences, challenging him again and again. There was no-one with whom he could discuss this predicament for he would have been ashamed to reveal so much of himself to his friends. So the argument raged on inside. Did he love Rosie, in the full sense of that embarrassing and terrible word? He could not imagine himself ever telling Rosie, or any other girl for that matter, that he loved her. There was something unmanly in the idea, a suggestion of weakness.

These were some of the thoughts that buzzed like bees in his mind as he watched the silent Rosie. She sat with her back to a tree, looking as though she were in a daydream, the drink and the sandwich neglected at her side. He felt a sort of airiness inside, a surge of pleasure and excitement, as he looked at her: there was no doubt that she was a real beauty, an absolute stunner. Once again the word *class* surfaced in his head. It was a word he much admired, just as he admired those people who possessed it. Rosie had class, no argument there; it sat on her as naturally as a crown on a Queen.

'A penny for them,' he said.

She looked surprised at the interruption, then gave him a wan little smile.

'I'm sorry,' she said. 'I'm not much company, am I?'

'What's up?' he asked.

'Nothing. Everything,' she said listlessly. 'Don't let's talk about it.'

Afraid that they would lapse into silence again, Tommo said quickly: 'I was born near here.'

'I didn't know you'd been born,' said Rosie. 'I thought they cut you out of a quarry.'

She spoke automatically, as if she were simply going through the motions of maintaining their usual badinage. He seemed to sense that her heart wasn't in the remark for he went on:

'No. Straight up. I was born about a mile from this pub.'

It occurred to Rosie that she knew little or nothing of Tommo's background and she said: 'Your people still live here?'

'My mother – yeah. The old man kicked the bucket ten – twelve years ago.'

'Do you ever see your mother?'

'Not if I can help it.'

'Tommo, that's terrible! Your own mother!' Rosie was genuinely shocked.

'She's a wicked old cow,' said Tommo. 'Always was, always will be. I got nothing to thank her for. She lives with a jug of ale in her hand. I don't remember a time when she wasn't pissed. Drove my old man to an early grave, poor old sod. We'd have starved but for him. She didn't care, she didn't give a light for us or for anyone else come to that. If you were on fire, she wouldn't give you a bucket of water to put the flames out. The day after the old man died I hopped the twig. I got out.'

'Did you have any other family – brothers, sisters?'

'Three sisters. They'd all gone by the time Dad packed it in. She drove 'em out, the old woman. I was a lot younger than them – a sort of afterthought. Or more like an accident, you might say.'

'What are your sisters doing?'

'Two of them got spliced. One lives in Manchester, the other is in Australia somewhere. The third one – Amy – she works up Piccadilly way, on the game. Leastways that's what she was doing last time I heard of her.'

'Don't you care?' asked Rosie.

'Not particularly,' said Tommo. 'It's her life.'

Indeed, he had spoken throughout without emotion, as though he were recounting some fictional story in which he had little interest. 'Wouldn't mind seeing Nellie again,' he continued. 'That's the middle sister, the one living down-under. She took me in when I ran away from home, looked after me for a couple of years. Nellie's not a bad sort. For the rest, I don't give a stuff.'

Rosie looked at Tommo as though she were seeing him for the first time. She had always thought of him as a sharp-witted, appealing, and very attractive rogue, a young buck without a care in the world, and in a sense that was true. But now she saw that this wasn't the whole story. He was like her in that he had never had a real home, except for brief periods, and he had been forced to make his own way, to learn the bitter lessons of survival in the hardest school of all – the streets. She felt a glow of sympathy for him and, if there hadn't been so many other people around, would have taken his hand. Instead, she smiled.

'That's more like it,' he said. 'Feeling better?'

'A bit.'

And then Tommo, instead of building on this small advantage, destroyed her mood again in a few words. He said:

'You still got that iron-hoof on your mind?'

'Who?'

'The pianist bloke. Mister-bleeding-Softley.' He should have been warned by the glint in her eyes but he blundered on regardless: 'You want to forget him, girl. Good riddance to bad rubbish. A bloody poof, an iron-hoof! We're all well rid of him!'

She stood up suddenly, and he scrambled up beside her. She was quivering between anger and grief, tears glistened in her eyes.

'I'm going!' she said.

'What have I done now?' he asked in genuine bewilderment. 'What have I said?'

'If you don't know, that makes it worse!' she said sadly, and stalked away. He rushed after her and pulled her to a halt, oblivious of the heads that were turned in their direction.

'Rosie!' he urged. 'Pack it in, pack it in!'

'Will you let me go?'

'Every time we go out you end up by creating a scene!' he said angrily. It was almost the truth.

'Then you'll be well-rid of me, won't you?' she replied. Pulling away, she moved on.

'Where you going?' he demanded, blocking her path.

'Home.'

'How?'

'I'll get a bus. Or I'll walk. Now – will you get out of my way?'

'Rosie,' he said grimly, 'so help me, Rosie, if you don't come down off your high horse, I'll belt you one!'

'Once! You've only got to hit me once, Tommo, and that's us finished. Once!' She spoke quietly but with such force that he backed down.

'For God's sake, Rosie, I don't know what to make of you.

Straight up. Will you tell me what I've done? What I said to bring this on? If I upset you, I'm sorry. There! I don't say that too often, I can tell you. But I'm saying it to you now. I'm sorry. Satisfied?' She hesitated and his exasperation surfaced again.

'Right!' he said, 'right! I can't do no more. You want to walk? Right, Miss Rosie-bloody-Carr. Walk! You can walk to hell and back for all I care!' He turned on his heel and began to make his way to the pony-and-trap.

Rosie stood watching him, thinking that in many respects he was like a schoolboy. What was the use of being angry with him? He hadn't even realised that his words had hurt her. He didn't know any better, that was the truth of it, and it did no good to quarrel with him. At least, he had apologised and, as he had said, that was no easy gesture.

After ten paces or so, his resolution weakened and he turned to see if she were following. They stood looking at each other for a long moment and then, smiling, she went to him. Taking his hand she said:

'Come on back, I haven't finished my sandwich.'

She reached up and kissed him on the cheek, a move that brought murmurs of mocking approval and some applause from the audience of customers. Tommo grinned and acknowledged the reception with a stylish bow while Rosie, following his example, dropped a neat curtsey to either side.

6

In a secluded clearing in Hadley Wood later that afternoon, as the pony grazed and Rosie picked bluebells, Tommo, who had a certain bull-like obstinacy and never knew when to leave well alone, blundered in again.

'Back at The Cherry Tree, Rosie. What did I say to put your back up?'

Fortunately, Rosie was now in a more cheerful frame of mind. She said: 'Let's forget it, Tommo, shall we?'

'No, honest,' he persisted. 'I'd like to know.'

'Don't you remember what you said about Mr Softley?
Don't you even remember that?'

'What did I say? I said he was an iron-hoof. What's wrong
with that? I mean, it's the truth.' Tommo's forehead was
creased in honest perplexity as he tried to work out why
Rosie should have taken umbrage at his words.

'Tommo,' she said quietly, 'if that's all you can find to say
about him, then it's best you should say nothing at all.'

'Look,' he said earnestly, 'no offence. Don't take offence,
Rosie. But that's what he was. Everyone knows that.'

Rosie could see that he had not understood and that there
was no point in pursuing the question.

'Let's leave it, Tommo, eh? You'll never understand how I
feel, not if you live to be a hundred. Only one thing I got to
say. You run Mr Softley down all you want to, call him what
you like. But don't do it while I'm around, that's all. Now,
let's drop the subject.'

'But Rosie – ' he began.

'Drop it, Tommo!' she said sharply. 'Unless you want to
start me off again – drop it! Once and for all.'

'All right, all right!'

She smiled at his tone. 'Bet you think I'm a right old
nagger, don't you?'

'No,' he said gloomily, 'but I don't understand you half the
time, that's for certain.'

'I'm sorry. I didn't realise I was all that complicated.' She
laughed in his face and, on impulse, kissed him on the cheek.

It was all the encouragement he needed. He pulled her
round and took her in his arms. She held her head back,
avoiding his lips and said mockingly:

'What do you think you're doing?'

'I know what I'm going to do!' he said.

'Well, take it easy,' she said. 'Don't crush my bluebells.'

She wriggled free and laid the flowers in the shade. As she
straightened up he seized her again and kissed her. It wasn't
pleasant at first: he was too impatient and urged his mouth
against her with such force that it hurt. With an effort she
pulled back and whispered:

'Take it easy, I said. Gently does it, gently.'

Instinct rather than experience guided her as she returned the kiss, pressing her full lips against his, lightly at first and then with greater insistence. It was sweet and exciting now: she could feel the pleasure quivering in her flesh, feel his trembling response. He eased her backwards and slowly lowered her to the ground. For a moment, it seemed as if she were going to protest, but he sealed her lips with his own and she lay back, her eyes closed.

She shuddered as he began to caress her breasts, moulding his hand to their roundness. Even though she was guarded by a dress, a petticoat and a chemise, it seemed as though he were touching her directly. A warm rainbow-like mist coloured her mind and, as she felt her nipples harden, she writhed in pleasure, clinging to him with greater passion, willing him to go on.

His hand moved lower, gliding over her dress, gliding up and down her thighs and again she felt her flesh respond. A pause, which seemed like an eternity, and then she was aware of a hand under her skirt, a hand sliding up her leg, fingers fumbling under the leg of her drawers.

She began, instinctively, to struggle, moving her body and doing her best to stop the moving hand, but Tommo was past stopping now and the more she struggled the more insistent he became. Rosie felt the taste of salt in her mouth and suddenly the memory of that night in Brown's Alley came flooding back, filling her with terror. Gathering all her strength, she pushed him away and rolled free.

'No, Tommo, no!' she moaned.

He bore her down again, 'Aw, come on, Rosie. Just a bit of a cuddle. No messing, I promise. I won't put it in unless you say so.'

'No!' She screamed so desperately that he pulled away, terrified that someone might have heard. Rosie stood up and straightened her clothes with trembling hands. Tommo watched her grimly.

'You know what you are?' His tone was heavy with disgust. 'You know what they call tarts like you?'

'I'm sorry, Tommo,' she said in a small voice. 'I'm sorry.'

'You're a CT, that's what you are. A bloody cock-teaser!'

'I'm sorry,' she said again.

'You wanted it as much as I did!' he said savagely. 'You were panting like a bitch on heat!'

It was true, she thought. She had wanted him. Did it mean that she was a bad girl? Had she inherited her mother's nature, would her life develop in the same way? Yet, on the other hand, fear had overcome desire. Fear of what? Fear of pregnancy, of what Lily Hoddle had described as being in 'the pudding-club'? Or was it a deeper fear? The terror had started from the moment Tommo had actually touched the bare flesh under her drawers. Even now, the recollection made her shudder for she had not felt his hand but that of an unknown man with a leering, toothless mouth; and at his touch all the sickening revulsion had returned. Would she ever be able to allow a man – any man – to touch her, to make love to her, without invoking the devil faces of that nightmare in Brown's Alley?

She began to gather up the bluebells. He sat with his arms around his knees, more sulky now than angry.

'Bitch!' he murmured.

'That'll do, Tommo,' she said wearily. 'I said I'm sorry. If I gave you the wrong impression, I'm sorry. I wasn't trying to lead you on.'

'I believe you, thousands wouldn't,' he said.

'And you needn't talk so high and mighty!' she said, with more edge to her voice. 'You had no right to take such liberties? Do you really think I am that sort? Easy – good for a quick roll on the grass? If that's your opinion of me, you'd better think again.'

And then, remembering what the young man had said to Tommo in the bar at the Empire, Rosie made an inspired guess. 'I'm not going to be another notch on your barrow, Tommo. Don't run away with that idea!'

'A notch? On my barrow? Don't know what you're talking about!' he said.

But his face had reddened and Rosie could tell from the bluster in his tone that she had scored a direct hit.

'Well,' she said, 'are you going to take me home or shall I walk?'

'Come on,' he said.

They drove home in virtual silence arriving about a half-hour before the pub was due to open for the evening session. Rosie was not surprised when Tommo left her with a brusque, rather surly farewell and without suggesting another date. She went quickly inside determined not to allow her disappointment to show.

The bluebells were drooping badly and she realised that she had been wrong to pick them. They looked weak and somehow colourless, pale reflections of the bold purple flowers that had caught her eye. It hasn't been a good day for any of us, she thought ruefully.

She went into the kitchen to get a bowl and water for the bluebells and found The Missus there, preparing a snack for herself and The Guv'nor.

'Ah, Rosie,' she said, 'you're back early. I'm glad. I've been on the go all day. Can I leave you to open up the bars while Mr Quorn and me has a little snack?'

Strictly speaking, Rosie was entitled to the full day off, including the evening and it was on the tip of her tongue to tell The Missus as much, but she held her peace. Better to keep busy, she thought, than to sit in her room and brood over the misfortunes of the day.

'All right, ma'am,' she said.

'In the morning,' said The Missus, 'I want you to move your things down to the spare bedroom on the first floor. The one Mr Softley used as a dressing-room. You'll be more comfortable there.'

Compared to the attic, the spare room was indeed a splendid place: but Rosie had been in the attic for four years and grown attached to it.

'I don't mind the attic,' she said.

'Nonsense!' said The Missus. 'You'll be much better off downstairs. Besides, I need the attic for the new potman.'

'New potman?'

'Starts tomorrow. Recommended by Mr Parker. One of his unfortunates. A young man from his down-and-outs hostel.' The Missus sighed. 'I should have said no. There are plenty of good potmen available, men with experience. But that's me all over, soft-hearted. That's my trouble. Always willing to help the unfortunate of this world – not that I get any gratitude for that. We'll have to train the new man, Rosie, and hope against hope that he turns out all right. Ten minutes, dear – open up in ten minutes.'

As the door swung behind The Missus, Rosie sighed. In one week, she had lost Mr Softley and forfeited Tommo's friendship; now she had to move out of the room which had been her little private refuge for so long. It was strange, she thought, strange how nothing remained the same, nothing ever stood still. You got used to one lot of circumstances, adjusted yourself to them and then – whoosh ! – everything changed and you had to start all over again. It was the same with people. They came into your life, you learned to like them – even to love the best of them – and then, when you needed them most, they went away or kicked the bucket on you.

And where was God while all this was going on? What was he doing? Why did he allow so many bad things to happen? Why was he so indifferent to what was happening on the earth he had created?

And then, stealing in without notice, surprising and shocking her, came another extraordinary, frightening question.

Was there a God? Did He exist?

It was a shattering thought, so shattering that Rosie sat down at the kitchen table to grapple with it. She felt a sense of guilt, as if she had put out a hand and touched the devil. She wished – oh, how she wished! – that Mr Softley had been there to help her find an answer. She closed her eyes to shut out the question but it persisted and in desperation she began silently to pray:

'Oh, God, dear God, dear Jesus, I believe in you, I do honestly. But give me a sign, please, give me a sign to show that you are there, to show that you exist.' She opened her eyes and caught sight of the breadknife lying on the table and said, aloud this time, but in a frightened whisper: 'Lift that breadknife! Just a few inches. Please! Please God, give me a little sign – please, then I'll never doubt you again!'

She watched the knife for a full minute, concentrating with all her being, but there was no response.

CHAPTER FIVE

1

Rosie slept well that night. The fresh air, the emotional ups-and-downs of the day and an unexpectedly busy night in the pub had all combined to make her so tired that she fell asleep almost as her head touched the pillow. When she woke in the morning at her usual time of 5.30 the night had worked its magic and she felt all her natural optimism come bubbling back. The problems of yesterday were still very real to her but they did not seem as menacing or important now.

Looking out of her window at the golden beginning of what promised to be another fine day, she apologised silently to God for what now seemed to be the foolish doubts of the previous evening. And to the winged horse she said aloud:

'Got to move, got to move downstairs. But don't go fretting yourself. I've got a room at the front so we can keep each other well in view. You'll have the new bloke up here. Don't know what he's going to be like, mind you. One of Mr Parker's down-and-outs The Missus said. Poor devil will be glad of a nice room like this, eh? Look after yourself, Pegasus. I'll be seeing you.'

She washed and dressed and went cheerfully down to the kitchen. The fire in the big range had been banked up so that it would stay alight during the night and her first task was to rake it thoroughly and open the draught control so that the embers glowed with new life. Then she topped it up with fresh coals, filled the kettle and set it to boil, and opened the door to the urchins who were waiting for the morning handout.

'Well, well,' said Rosie, surveying the ragged group, 'who have we got on the ear'ole this fine morning then?'

'Morning, Rosie,' they chanted, pushing forward, 'morning! Any leavings, Rosie – and left-overs. Please, Rosie.' Skinny hands held out tin basins and chipped plates, unnaturally bright eyes stared up at her from thin pallid faces.

'All right, all right, get into line then and we'll see what we've got,' she said.

She distributed what had been collected in the waste-buckets and – in the absence of The Missus – thrust a slice of new bread and a piece of cheese into the hands of those whom she knew to be the most needy, maintaining a running commentary as she did so:

'Here we are then, young Elsie. A bit of bread and a chunk of cheese. Never mind the tea-leaves on the cheese – they'll wipe off. Potato mash and gravy for you, Charlie. Blime ole pole, Ginger, you want to tell your ma to get busy with the Sassafrus Oil – your hair is running alive! Don't come near me – I don't want your fleas! Here, Lucy, a bit of beef and a couple of mutton bones – make a nice drop of stew, they will. Danny – now what have we got left? Ah, half an apple and a bit of fruit cake. Now that's the lot. Off you go. Scoot! Skedaddle!'

As she was finishing, Rosie became aware that a young man was hovering shyly in the background. She glanced at him but said nothing at first, putting him down mentally as yet another backdoor beggar. Although Rosie discouraged adult beggars it was not unusual to find one tagging onto the queue of children. She judged this young man to be about twenty: he was very thin, so thin that his shabby coat hung from his shoulders as though from a clothes-hanger, and his skin had that slight saffron tinge which she knew from experience to be a sign of poverty and hunger.

Only when she had sent the last child on his way did she make a move towards him. On an impulse, because it was a fine day and she felt in a cheerful mood, she cut a hunk of bread, topped it with a slice of boiled bacon, and thrust it into his hands.

'Here!' she said. 'Put that where the trams won't run over it. And clear off sharpish, before The Missus comes.' He looked at the bread and ham and back to her in slow surprise and she added sharply: 'Go on! Eat somewhere else. If you're caught here, you'll get a flea in the ear'ole, and I'll very likely get the sack! So hop it, will you, hop it!'

'Mr Parker sent me,' he said, and spoke so quietly that she had to ask him to speak up. 'I've been sent by Mr Parker.'

'You're the new potman!'

'Yes. Sort of.'

'Well, why didn't you say so! I'm sorry. I didn't realise. Don't stand there then, come in, come in. Wasn't expecting you until later. Your room's not ready yet. Sit down at the table. Daresay you could do with a cup of tea. I could. I've got to make one for The Missus and The Guv'nor. What's your name?'

He was sitting at the table by now, perched rather nervously on the edge of the chair, clutching the bread and ham in one hand and a small straw case in the other.

'Frank Lambert,' he said, in the same low voice.

'What? You'll have to speak up, y'know.'

'Frank Lambert.'

'Frank. Good. Frank by name and frank by nature, eh?' She rubbed a hand against her apron and held it out: 'My name's Rosie, Rosie Carr. Nice to meet you, Frank.'

It took him a few seconds to disengage from the bread and shake the proffered hand. A tiny smile broadened his face and lit up his eyes and she saw that he was quite handsome. She made to pick up the bread but he beat her to it in a swift, almost frightened movement. And then, as though ashamed, he put the food down again and said:

'Sorry.'

'I was only going to make you a proper sandwich,' she said.

'Thank you. This will be fine, thank you.'

Now she noted something else about him. He had what the locals would have called a 'posh' voice: the accent was not unlike that of the late Mr Softley, the accent of an educated man.

'You're hungry, eh?' she asked.

102

'A bit,' he admitted.

'They don't exactly feed you up at Mr Parker's hostel, do they?' she said. 'I've seen it. Bread and workhouse scrape.'

'Workhouse scrape?'

'Haven't you heard of that?' she said. 'Bread and margarine. And they put the marge on with one spread of the knife and take it off with the other.'

Rosie took the steaming kettle from the range, made a pot of tea and set a tray for The Missus and The Guv'nor. Each morning it was her job to take tea and hot buttered toast to them in their bedroom. The toast was all that Mrs Quorn ate for breakfast but for her husband it was simply an appetiser. When he felt ready to face the day he would descend to the kitchen and put away what he liked to call a proper English breakfast of chop, bacon, eggs and fried bread. Rosie cut some bread, put a slice on the end of a toasting fork and handed it to the young man.

'Here, might as well make yourself useful. You make the toast while I fry you some bacon and eggs. You look as if you want feeding up.'

As he held the bread towards the glowing fire-bars he said:

'Does that happen every day?'

'What?'

'Those kids lining up for scraps.'

'Every day.'

'It's hard to believe,' he said, shaking his head.

'Why?' she asked. 'You've seen hungry kids before, haven't you?'

'I didn't mean that,' he said. 'I meant . . . ' He checked himself and muttered: 'It doesn't matter.'

'No,' she said. 'Go on. What were you going to say?'

He turned wide, grey enquiring eyes to her face in a look that was faintly disconcerting: she had the feeling that he was measuring her. And she found herself measuring him in return, thinking that her first impression had been wrong. This young man was not in the usual run of down-and-outs and he was certainly no ordinary potman: there was a quiet assurance in his manner, a suggestion of subtle strength and intelligence that marked him out as different. She felt as

103

though those grey eyes were boring into her and with an effort she broke the spell:

'What are you bossing at me like that for?'

'I'm sorry,' he said politely. 'I didn't mean to stare.'

'Come on,' she said. 'You were going to say something about those kids.'

'Nothing really,' he replied. 'Except, that to see them, without shoes, lining up for scraps, you would be hard put to believe that Britain is the richest country in the world, wouldn't you?'

'I wouldn't know anything about it,' Rosie said.

'It's true. The richest country in the world. And yet we cannot feed our children or put shoes on their feet!'

'We can't make toast either!' said Rosie sharply and pointed to the toasting-fork. The slice of bread was a blackened, smoking crisp.

'Sorry,' he said with a grimace.

'You've made a good start,' she said. 'Let me give you a tip – what was your name again?'

'Frank. Frank Lambert.'

'Let me give you a tip, Frank. In this place, you'd better concentrate on your work and forget about the blooming Empire! The Missus is a bit of a slave-driver and if she catches you day-dreaming or laying down on the job, she'll have you out of here so fast your feet won't touch the ground.'

'Thanks, Rosie. I'll remember that. I'm not afraid to work.'

'Good,' she said briskly. 'Glad to hear it. Here, get this lot inside you. And don't tell The Missus I gave you a cooked breakfast. She'd have a fit with her leg up.'

She set a plate of bacon and eggs before him, together with two thick slices of bread and butter and an enamel mug filled with hot, sweet tea. She noticed that he did not fall upon the food as Tommo might have done in his place, but ate with a kind of polite, disciplined control, as though he were holding himself on a careful rein.

And she noticed also, as she was preparing fresh toast for The Missus, that he was staring at her once more.

'You're doing it again!' she said.

'I beg your pardon?' He seemed surprised. 'What am I doing?'

'Staring. Staring at me.'

'You must be used to that,' he said.

'No, I'm not. Why should I be?'

'Well,' he said, 'you are very beautiful. Exceptionally beautiful. Don't you know that?' He delivered this extraordinary statement in a straightforward, serious voice, as if he were referring to a picture or to a certain view, and as if he was simply announcing an obvious fact.

As for Rosie, she was so taken aback that, unusually for her, no ready retort came to her lips. It was not until she had served The Missus and The Guv'nor with their tea and toast and was on her way back downstairs that she had gathered herself and felt ready to hit back. There would be no more of that sort of nonsense from Mr Lambert, she told herself. He had been in the pub five minutes and he was already taking liberties! Well, she would put him in his place, once and for all.

In the event, Rosie had to defer her rebuke. Frank Lambert had been existing for some months on scraps of food and the odd bowl of soup. His stomach had got out of the habit of digesting a full square meal and the unexpected bounty of breakfast had proved to be too much for it.

Rosie found him in a corner of the yard, his face yellow, his body heaving, as he spewed up all that he had just eaten.

2

By eight o'clock Rosie had cleared her things from the attic, made the bed and generally tidied up. She took Frank up to show him the lay-out and was rather perturbed to see how breathless he was after climbing the three flights of stairs.

'Are you all right?' she asked.

He nodded and after a few moments managed to speak: 'Yes – I'm – fine.'

'Well, you don't look it!' she said bluntly. 'Sit down and rest a minute.'

The bed squeaked as he sat down and a strange little sound, half-croak and half-whistle came from his throat as he struggled to draw breath. She watched him anxiously, but after a while his breathing came more easily and he gave her a little apologetic smile.

'Sorry,' he said.

'You're in a bit of a state, you know that,' she said.

'I'll be all right.'

'You done this sort of work before? I mean – have you ever worked in a pub?'

'No,' he replied, and added hastily: 'But I'm not afraid of work.'

'Just as well,' she said wryly. 'It's all go. I can tell you.'

'How long have you worked here?' he asked.

'Donkey's years. Since 1906. Nigh on four years.'

'You like it?'

'There's worse jobs. And beggars can't be choosers.'

'Where do you come from? Have you any family?'

'Questions!' Rosie smiled. 'If questions were feathers, you'd have enough to stuff a mattress.'

'Sorry. I didn't mean to pry.'

'Oh, I don't mind,' she said. 'My life's an open-air meeting. I haven't really got a family. My mother's dead and I never knew who my father was. I suppose I'm what you call a bastard. I lived with Aunt May until I was thirteen, then she put in for a harp – '

'Put in for a harp?'

'Kicked the bucket. Put down her knife and fork. Died. She was lovely, my Aunt May. She was good to me. Anyway, as soon as the funeral was over, my uncle told me to hop it.'

'He turned you out?'

'Sort of. He made it clear that I wasn't exactly his idea of Christmas. He fixed me up with this job and then he scarpered. Emigrated actually. To Canada.'

'You've had a hard life, Rosie.'

'Could have been a lot worse.'

'Did you never ask yourself why?'

'Why what?'

'Why. Why life has to be like that. Why kids should be starving, lining up for you to dole out scraps?'

'That's the way things are.'

'But it isn't right, Rosie.'

'Right! Wrong! Who cares what's right or wrong? Nobody that I can see. It's always been the same and neither you nor anybody else will change it.'

'I'm not sure about that, Rosie.'

'Well,' she said, 'I know one thing. I can't stand here gassing to you or The Missus will have my guts for garters. I'm going down. And you'd better come and present yourself to her ladyship. She'll be up and around in about ten minutes.'

As she went downstairs Rosie shook her head in wonder and disbelief. She had not met Frank Lambert before today – he had been in the house scarcely more than two hours – yet she was already talking to him as if she had known him for years, telling him the story of her life, answering his constant stream of questions!

There was something strange and intriguing about him, she could not deny that, a touch of the same sort of mystery that had distinguished Mr Softley. How was it that people of their background and obvious intelligence had ended up working in a pub? She thought she now knew at least part of the answer in Mr Softley's case, but what about this new young man? Rosie resolved that next time they talked she would be the one who asked the questions!

3

When Tommo came into the bar at midday, there was no trace of the sullenness of the day before: like Rosie, a night's sleep had restored his spirits and, to her relief, he behaved as if there had been no argument or difference between them. As was his custom, he drank the first pink down without pause, ordered another, and then slapped a paper bag down in front of her.

'There you are, Rosie, girl. A present!' he said.

'For me, Tommo?'

'Well, it's not for Marie Lloyd, is it? Of course it's for you. Wouldn't do for anyone else anyway. Well, don't you want to see what it is?'

Several of the regulars pressed Rosie to open the bag and crowded round as she did so. Blushing a little, she produced a pair of white drawers; closer inspection by the admiring company revealed that each leg had been embroidered in gold with the letter R and decorated with much lace and ribbon. There was a chorus of approval from the appreciative audience.

'Tommo!' said Rosie. 'What am I supposed to do with these?'

'Wear 'em, of course, what do you think. Mind you, I reckon you should let me help you try them on – just to see if they fit like.'

'Chance would be a fine thing!' she said. 'Where did you get them – or mustn't I ask?'

'Had 'em made special, didn't I?' said Tommo. 'Special for you. Paid extra to have R for Rosie embroidered on.'

'You don't expect me to believe that, do you?' she said. 'Come on, tell the truth and shame the devil. Where did you pinch them?'

'Pinch 'em?' said Tommo in a pained voice. 'I don't go around half-inching ladies' drawers. No, I bought 'em, didn't I? Paid good money for 'em.'

'Where?'

'The big house up at Winchmore Hill. People died and the agents were selling off the contents. So I go up there, don't I, to pick up a few bargains. One of the job lots was the ladies underwear. Normally, I wouldn't be interested in ladies underwear – '

'Not much!' interjected a burly drayman.

'But I see the R on the leg of these drawers,' Tommo continued, 'and I thought – they'll do Rosie a treat. So I chucked the handle in after the hammer and bought the bundle.'

'Are they really for me, Tommo?' asked Rosie.

'I told you, didn't I?'

'Thanks. Thanks ever so. They're lovely.'

Rosie wrapped up the drawers, put the parcel away at the back of the bar and went to keep an eye on a discussion that was taking place at one of the tables between two regular customers – One-Eyed Joe, an unemployed navvy, and Ivan, a Russian refugee who had come to Britain after the failure of the 1905 revolution. One-Eyed Joe had taken a drop too much and Rosie knew that it would not be long before the debate erupted into a row. Indeed, the turning-point seemed to have been reached as she arrived at the table.

'If you don't like this country, mate,' Joe was saying in a threatening tone, 'why don't you bloody well go back where you came from?'

'But I am liking this country. I am liking him very much,' answered the little bearded Russian, who looked for all the world like a college professor.

'Now, wait!' said One-Eyed Joe, striking an attitude. 'Now just you hang on a minute. Did you or did you not – did you or did you not say – ' He paused, having lost the thread of his accusation and Rosie took his arm.

'Come on, Joe, my old beauty,' she said. 'Time you went home and dropped anchor.'

'Wait!' said One-Eyed Joe, pulling free. 'I am not going to stand by while some foreign git runs down this country!'

'I am sure Mr Pootilo didn't mean any harm,' said Rosie.

'The name is Putilov,' said Ivan. 'Putilov.'

'There you are!' said Joe triumphantly. 'A bloody Russki! We take 'em in, and the next thing, they're running us down!'

'Come on, Joe,' said Rosie.

'I am saying the truth. I am saying that the working peoples of this country do not have economic or political freedoms. This is what I am saying!' said the Russian, shaking his head seriously.

'I agree! You're absolutely right, my friend.'

Rosie turned to see Frank Lambert at her elbow. He had been carrying a tray of empties across the bar and had set this down in order to join the discussion.

'Now, don't you start!' said an exasperated Rosie. 'I've got enough with these two!'

'But this gentlemen is absolutely right,' said Frank earnestly. He addressed himself to One-Eyed Joe. 'Do you really believe that this is your country?'

'Are you calling me a bleeding foreigner?' asked Joe.

'I'm asking you a straight question,' said Frank. 'Is it or is it not your country?'

'Of course it bloody well is!'

'Do you own any of it?'

'What do you mean?'

'You say it's your country. All right. How much of it belongs to you?'

'You've got a button missing, mate, you're up the stick,' said Joe.

'That's what I thought,' said Frank. 'It's your country but you don't own a square inch of it. Why? Because it all belongs to the landlords, the landowners.'

Rosie left One-Eyed Joe and turned her attention to Frank. 'Have you blown your top?' she asked in an urgent whisper. 'If The Missus comes in and finds you arguing with a customer, that'll be your lot, you bloody fool! Now, take that tray out of here and get on with your work!'

'But – '

'No buts!' she said firmly. He was breathing heavily and a thin film of sweat lay on his pallid skin. 'Are you all right?' she added in a quieter, anxious tone.

'Yes. I'm fine.'

'You don't look it to me. Here, get rid of that tray and then go down the cellar. You can have a rest there. I'll cover for you. Go on.'

'I can manage,' he said.

'My Gawd,' said Rosie, 'I never met anyone like you for an argument. Will you hop it?'

He nodded and moved off with the tray. By this time One-Eyed Joe's wife had located her husband and was in process of dragging him away. She was a small woman, half the weight and height of Joe, but she appeared to be in complete command and he went like a lamb.

Rosie went back to the bar in time to see that The Missus had intercepted Frank and instructed him to carry a large wooden crate into the next bar. The crate was filled with bottles of stout and Rosie watched anxiously as Frank struggled to lift it from the floor. He managed to raise it to the level of the bar and rest it there while he struggled for breath.

'Here, let me help you,' said Rosie, going to him.

'No.' He shook his head. 'I can manage.' Gritting his teeth, he lifted the crate and staggered towards the door leading to the other bar. He had almost reached it when he stopped suddenly: he half-turned, looking at Rosie in mute appeal and then the crate slid from his arms and crashed to the floor. Fortunately none of the bottles broke, although they rolled around in all directions. Frank stood looking around in a sort of daze and swaying slightly; then he too went down, striking his head against the fallen crate. By the time Rosie reached him, he was unconscious and blood was bubbling up through a cut on his forehead.

'What is it? What happened?' The Missus came hurrying through and checked as she saw Frank. 'What's wrong with him?'

'He fell. He's hurt himself bad. He's out cold,' said Rosie, kneeling by Frank.

'Fell? How did he come to do that?' asked The Missus belligerently.

'Because the poor devil is half-starved, that's why!' said Rosie. 'Got no nourishment in him.' She looked up at Tommo, and at Dave Culley, who were watching from the bar. 'Tommo! Dave! Don't stand there like two empty glasses. Help me get him upstairs.'

'I thought he was in a bad way when I first clapped me eyes on him,' said Dave. 'Didn't look as if he had the strength to kneel and kiss the foot of the Pope!'

'Hold on a minute,' said The Missus. 'If he's that ill, he'd be better off in a hospital – or back in the hostel.'

'He doesn't want a hospital,' said Rosie. 'He just wants some food in his belly and a bit of a rest. He'll be all right in a bit, ma'am, you'll see.'

'I don't know – ' said The Missus.

'Mr Parker wouldn't like it if he heard you'd sent him away, ma'am. He wouldn't, would he?'

'Hmph!' said The Missus and turned to her husband. On those rare occasions when she could not make up her mind she invariably asked his view, working on the principle of heads I win, tails you lose. If his advice turned out to be good she would always take the credit and if it proved faulty he was allocated the blame. 'Mr Quorn, you are the landlord here. What do you wish us to do?'

Stone the crows, thought Rosie as she staunched the flow of blood with her apron, the poor devil will bleed to death if they don't make up their minds soon!

'What to do, my pet?' said The Guv'nor. 'That is a problem. That is in the nature of a problem.' He scratched his stomach and frowned, wrinkling his forehead with the effort of thought.

'The best thing,' said Rosie, 'the best thing would be to see how he is in the morning.'

'Exactly,' said The Guv'nor, grasping this rescue line with both hands. 'We'll take the matter under advisement in the morning.'

'We ought to get a doctor in to see him,' said Rosie.

'A doctor!' said The Missus. 'And who will pay the bill, may I ask? Who will bear the cost?'

'Here,' said Big Bess. She banged a sixpenny piece down on to the bar counter. 'We'll have a whip-round. There's a tanner to kick it off.'

Within a couple of minutes Big Bess's sixpence had been joined by a collection of other coins, amounting to a total of three shillings and eightpence. Tommo put in sixpence on his own account and shamed The Guv'nor into matching this contribution.

Seeing the way the wind was blowing, The Missus put in fourpence to bring the amount to four shillings and then promptly took charge of the medical fund.

'I'll settle with the doctor,' she said, and turned to Dave Culley. 'Dave, would you go and ask Dr Rhys to call in as soon as possible?'

'I think Dr Wallace would be a better bet,' said Big Bess.

'Oh,' said The Missus coldly. 'I always have Dr Rhys. He's very good.'

'He's Welsh,' said Big Bess dismissively. 'Never liked the Welsh. Now, Dr Wallace – '

'Oh, for Gawd's sake!' cried Rosie. 'He'll die while you lot stand there arguing! Just get a doctor, will you?'

'He's not going to croak,' said Tommo. 'Leastways not yet. He's coming round.'

'Don't stand there, then!' she said. 'Help me get him upstairs.'

As they helped the half-conscious Frank to his feet and moved him towards the stairs, Rosie heard Big Bess make a chilling comment:

'He's hungry, all right. All skin and bone, wants feeding up. But it's not just that. I've seen it before. You can tell by the eyes. I'll lay all Lombard Streeet to a china orange that he's got the consumption.'

4

The doctor, when he called an hour later, neither confirmed nor denied this opinion. They had settled for Dr Rhys in the end and to Rosie's unpractised eye he seemed to be extraordinarily perfunctory, not to say offhand, in manner. Pronouncing the wounds to be superficial, Dr Rhys bound up Frank's head and then, oblivious of Rosie's presence, pulled back the bedclothes and began to examine him. Rosie politely turned her head away for the half-minute or so it took the doctor to assess the problem and decide what needed to be done. He took Rosie outside on the landing to discuss the matter.

'How long has he been working here, girl?' he asked in a tired voice.

'He only started today, sir,' said Rosie.

'Where did he come from?'

'Mr Parker sent him, sir. He was in Mr Parker's hostel. Where he was before that, I don't know, sir.'

'I see. Well, you look a sensible girl. I daresay you know what's wrong with this young man as well as I do.'

'He needs feeding-up, sir?' said Rosie tentatively.

'That's right. He's got the most common complaint in London, girl. I see it a dozen or more times a day. Malnutrition is the official word. A better description would be hunger, starvation.' He sighed, then continued more briskly: 'Now, as I say, you look to be an intelligent lass. So I will not offend that intelligence by prescribing tonic pills or bottles of pink water disguised as medicine. You understand me?'

'No, sir. I mean, yes, I think so.'

'He needs rest, nourishing food and some considerate attention. They are the only medicines that will help him, you see.'

'You mean he has to stay in bed, sir?'

'Of course. A week at least. And he'll need beef tea, milk puddings, eggs, fruit, that sort of thing.'

'Oh, lor,' said Rosie.

'I know,' said Dr Rhys in a tone of resignation. 'I might as well prescribe a month in Switzerland. But it is nourishment he needs. Has he anywhere else to go?'

'I don't know sir. I suppose he might go back to the hostel.'

'To Mr Parker's hostel for destitute young men? What rest, nourishment and attention do you think he'll get in that cold monument to Mr Parker's piety? Oh, don't get me wrong, Mr Parker means well and does many good works. But he doesn't really understand the problems. He thinks a man can exist on stale bread and scrape, a bowl of watery soup and a prayer. Send the patient back to the hostel if you want to kill him off – do that by all means. But if you want him to recover, then he will need food, rest and care.'

'Yes, sir.'

'What's your name, girl?'

'Rosie. Rosie Carr, sir.'

'Well, Rosie, will you undertake to look after him?'

'As best I can, sir.'

'No-one could ask more than that.'

'There's only one thing, sir,' stammered Rosie.

114

'Well?'

'I am not sure how The Missus – I mean, Mrs Quorn – I am not sure how she'll take it. She won't like the idea of him lying up here.'

'I'll talk to Mrs Quorn,' said Dr Rhys. 'Leave that to me.' He smiled for the first time and Rosie, revising her earlier impression, decided that he was a nice man and a good doctor. 'I won't call again unless you send for me, Rosie. No point in running you into needless expense.'

He unfastened his black bag and took out a small round white cardboard box. 'Change the dressing in the morning and put some of this ointment on the wound. In a couple of days he won't even need a bandage.'

Rosie never knew what Dr Rhys said to The Missus but he appeared to have something of the late Mr Softley's flair in that area. The Missus complained as usual and told Rosie that the work would have to be done with or without Frank, but she made no mention of him leaving.

Rosie thought it better not to push her luck, so she waited until The Guv'nor and The Missus took their afternoon nap and then made her patient some beef tea and an egg custard. He stirred as she brought in the food and opened his eyes.

'Here,' she said, 'get this inside you.'

'I ought to get up and get back to work,' he said.

'There's no work for you today,' she replied, 'nor for a few days yet. Doctor says you've got to rest.'

'Mrs Quorn won't like that.'

'Mrs Quorn will have to lump it then, won't she? Now come on – sit up and eat this while it's hot.'

He tried to struggle up in the bed but the effort proved to be too much for him and he dropped his hands listlessly.

'I don't think I can eat, Rosie,' he said.

'You're going to eat if I have to hold your nose and force it down,' she said firmly. She propped him up in the bed, wrapped a cloth around his neck to serve as a napkin, and spoon-fed him, ignoring his occasional protest. And she thought how odd it was that she should have met this young man only a few hours before and now she was sitting on his bed, nursing him like a baby!

Only when he had consumed all the beef tea and at least half the custard did she relent. 'There,' she said, wiping his mouth, 'that'll do for now. Keep on like that and you'll soon be as fit as a flea at a picnic.'

He took one of her hands in limp, cold fingers. 'You have beautiful hands, Rosie.'

'My hands? Beautiful? You want your eyes tested,' she said briskly.

But a moment or so later, on the landing, she paused and held her hands up for examination. They were quite shapely, she had to admit, but the nails were cracked and the skin rough and reddened as a result of the constant washing of dishes and glasses in water strenghtened with soda. They didn't look in any way special to her and certainly not beautiful.

That was twice in one day that he had used the word beautiful to describe her. It was stupid, of course, but all the same she couldn't help feeling pleased.

It had been an eventful day in many ways, and it hadn't spent itself yet. Later, when she slipped out for a breath of air, Big Bess hailed her:

'Hey, Rosie-girl, heard the news?'

'What news?'

'The old king's fallen off the perch.'

'You're having me on!' said Rosie.

'No. Straight up. King Edward's snuffed it. We got a new king now. King George the Fifth.'

'Strewth!' said Rosie. She had vague memories of the time when the old Queen died, of people wearing black armbands, of black-edged pictures of Victoria in windows, of street parties and bunting and holidays when King Edward was crowned. But after all the excitement things had settled down again and life had gone on much as before.

'Well,' she said, 'I'm sorry to see him go. But either way, it won't make much difference to the likes of us, will it?'

CHAPTER SIX

1

By early evening, news of the death of the old King, the 'uncle of Europe', had spread through the district. Shop-keepers put up their shutters, stallholders closed up well before the usual time and, as if urged by a common instinct, they all descended upon The Winged Horse to raise a glass in respectful memory of the late monarch.

Of course, it did not stop there. One glass led to another: toasts to the old King had naturally to be followed by a more cheerful salute to George V, his successor and, in no time at all, what had started as a wake developed into a rip-roaring, full-throated party.

Rosie was kept so busy, at the piano or behind the bar when the pressure was really on, that she had little time even to think of the patient upstairs, let alone time to break off and go to see him. Halfway through the evening, enticed by the party atmosphere and egged on by Tommo, she broke her own self-imposed ordinance and agreed to take a port-and-lemon. She had eaten very little that day and the effect of the drink was electrifying. Within minutes she was playing the piano and leading the singing with a new sprightliness while the assembled customers linked arms and hurled themselves into a hectic dance:

> Knees-up, Mother Brown,
> Knees-up, Mother Brown,
> Under the table you must go,
> Ee-eye, ee-eye, ee-eye-oh.
> If I catch you bending

I'll saw your legs right off
Knees-up, knees-up,
Don't get the breeze-up,
Knees-up, Mother Brown!

She followed this with another old favourite, 'Comrades'.

Comrades, comrades, ever since we were boys,
Sharing each other's troubles,
Sharing each other's joys.
Comrades when manhood was dawning
Faithful whate'er might betide
When danger threatened, my darling old comrade
Was there, by my side.

It was during the communal singing of this ballad that
Rosie became aware of a young man standing to one side of
the piano. When he caught her eye, his face broadened into a
smile and he lifted his glass a little as though to greet her. His
face was vaguely familiar but she was not able to put a name
to it until she was called from the piano yet again to help
relieve the pressure at the bar.

'Hello, Rosie.'

She looked up and saw that the smiling young man had
followed her. 'You'll have to take your turn!' she said. 'I've
only got one pair of hands.' And then, looking briefly into his
eyes, she remembered the handsome detective-constable and
said: 'Oh, sorry. It's you, Mr Roberts.'

'Stan Roberts,' he said. 'I'm not on duty.'

'Whether you are or not, you'll still have to wait your turn!'
She smiled, taking the sting from the words.

Later, during a lull, he said, 'Can I buy you a drink?'

'Lor, no!' she said, with a little giggling laugh. 'I've had
one and that's enough. Made me feel quite squiffy.'

'It is an occasion,' he said.

'Yes,' she said. 'To look at them, you wouldn't think the
King had died, would you? Wonder what he would say if he
could see them?'

'He wouldn't mind, I'm sure,' said Stan Roberts. 'Anyway,
I'm celebrating something else.'

'On your own?'

'Oh, I had a couple of mates with me to begin with, but they slid off back home. Well, they're married, d'you see. Hooked. I'm on my own, I don't have to report to anyone.'

'That's nothing to boast about,' she said tartly.

'I wasn't boasting. Just stating a fact.'

'And what have you got to celebrate?'

'Promotion. I've been made up to sergeant. Detective-Sergeant.'

'Oh,' she said mockingly. 'Sergeant! It will cost a shilling to talk to you soon!'

'What about celebrating with me, Rosie?'

'When?'

'Tomorrow night.'

'Screw your head on, sergeant! Some of us have to work.'

'Your next night off then.'

'That's not till Thursday.'

'All right. It's a date.'

She was about to protest that he was taking too much for granted when she was swept away by another wave of customers demanding drinks and her services at the piano. When, at last, there was another lull, she found a red-faced and rather drunken Tommo at her elbow.

'Hello, my little lolly-dolly,' he said. 'And where have you been all my life?' He pulled her close and tried to kiss her, but she pushed him away.

'Give over, Tommo.'

'How about a little walk after you close up?'

'Walk? I doubt I'll have the strength to walk upstairs. Anyway, I thought you were done with me after what happened on Sunday.'

'Oh, that,' said Tommo airily. 'Well, you did carry on a bit. Gave me a right old jacketing. But I've forgotten that – no hard feelings on my side.'

'Thank you!' said Rosie acidly. 'Thank you very much. I'm much obliged, I'm sure. Very good of you.' And on a wicked impulse, remembering what Frank Lambert had told her, she said: 'Tommo. What do you think of my hands?'

'Hands?' He looked down at them, puzzled.

'Hands!'

'How do you mean?'

'See anything special about them?'

'Oh, come off it, Rosie. Hands is hands. What do you expect me to say?'

'Nothing,' she said with a touch of bitterness. 'It doesn't matter.'

Detective-Sergeant Roberts chose this moment to come up to Rosie. 'Thursday, then,' he said. 'I'll pick you up here at six.'

It was on the tip of Rosie's tongue to tell him that she was otherwise engaged or to make some other excuse but, before she could speak, Tommo intervened:

'What's that! What are you talking about?' And, in a more belligerent tone: 'You keep away from her, do you hear me? Keep your hooks off!' He poked a finger into Stan's chest as if to underline the words.

'Don't do that,' said Stan mildly.

'I'll bloody well do what I like!' said Tommo. He belched noisily and then attempted to repeat the gesture, but Stan grasped his wrist and held it. Tommo seemed surprised by the strength of the other man's grip.

Stan turned his dark eyes on Rosie. 'Is he your feller?'

'No,' said Rosie, 'no, he is not. Not in a million years.'

'Rosie!' Tommo protested.

'I wouldn't have him if his backside was hanging in diamonds!' she said firmly.

'Then that's that,' said Stan. 'I have to go now. Is it all right for Thursday – six o'clock, here?'

'That will be lovely,' said Rosie, giving Tommo a defiant look.

Stan released Tommo's wrist. 'Sorry, old sport.' And as Tommo took a half-threatening step towards him, he said with a smile: 'Now, we don't want any trouble, do we?'

Something in the quiet tone made Tommo check. Stan nodded and made his way out, pausing briefly at the door to send Rosie a smile.

'Now,' said Tommo, 'what the hell was all that about?'

'You heard,' said Rosie.

'You're not going out with that buckaroo!'

'Who's going to stop me?'

'I will! Don't think I won't!'

'Tommo,' said Rosie patiently, 'it's got nothing to do with you. Who I choose to go out with is my affair. I'm not your girl, you don't own me or my time. So long as we get that clear, we can be mates, friends. Got that?'

'I'll lay for that bloke,' said Tommo darkly. 'I'll do him an injury.'

'I shouldn't try it, Tommo,' she said drily.

'Why not?'

'Two reasons. In the first place he's a copper – a sergeant. So he's liable to run you in for disturbing the peace. And in the second place, I reckon you might get more than you bargained for.'

'A bogey! You're going out with a bloody bogey!' Tommo stood blinking at Rosie and he looked so put out and perplexed that she forgot her irritation and felt sorry for him.

He isn't half as tough as he likes to make out, she thought, he's mostly bluster. When Stan Roberts had stood his ground, calling the other man's bluff, Tommo had backed down quickly. The impudence, the spiel and the bravado were real enough but they were like something put on to cover a weakness, to disguise the inner man. Oddly enough, the thought drew her closer to Tommo. The fact that he was uncertain and vulnerable made him somehow more human. She smiled to herself, thinking how strange it was that men should be regarded as the stronger sex when they were so obviously weaker than women. Tommo, for instance, Tommo was like a child; what he needed was not so much a girl but a mother. He needed someone to look after him.

2

As the evening dwindled to its close Tommo became drunker and noisier than ever as if he was determined to demonstrate his defiance and independence to Rosie and to everyone else. When The Missus called 'Last Orders' and began pointedly to prepare for closing, he was one of a group of stall-holders from the market who lingered behind, singing.

PC Johnson, a burly, bearded constable, came into the bar as if on cue and stood looking sternly at the noisy little crowd.

'Come along, ladies and gents!' called The Guv'nor, trying to show PC Johnson that he was doing his best to maintain order. 'Time, please. On your way, if you please.' He nodded to Rosie who began to put out the lights.

Dave Culley, the mild and gentle one, suddenly erupted. Lifting his glass he roared: 'Here's to a free and unfettered Ireland and to hell with the murdering British!'

'That's enough!' said the policeman. 'You heard the landlord. Move on. Move on.'

Dave lurched forward and thrust his face to within an inch of Johnson's beard. 'I say – long live a free and unfett – '

He got no further because Big Bess, concerned for her friend, pulled him away abruptly.

'He don't mean no harm, Mr Johnson,' she said apologetically. 'He's never been to Ireland in his life.'

'It's a lie!' screamed Dave, 'it's a lie! My father was Irish, my mother was half-Irish – '

His voice grew less audible as, helpless in the massive hands of Big Bess, he was dragged out to the street.

'Now let's be having the rest of you,' said Johnson.

Tommo sauntered over to the policeman, waved a languid hand in the direction of The Guv'nor and The Missus and said in a whisper that could be heard in the four corners of the room:

'Ah, officer. Constable. I'm glad you came. I have a complaint.'

'Yes,' said Rosie. 'A moving tongue – that's his complaint.'

'They've been at it again,' said Tommo, loftily ignoring the interruption. 'The minute your back's turned, constable, they are at it.'

'What's he on about? What's he saying?' said The Guv'nor.

'He's drunk,' said The Missus scornfully. 'He's as full as a boot.'

'Hop it, Tommo,' said Johnson, 'hop it.'

'All right,' said Tommo. 'Say no more. Just remember, I warned you, officer. They have been at it – I give you my solemn oath on this – they have been at it the whole, entire evening.'

'Been at what?' asked The Guv'nor. 'What have we supposed to have been at?'

'Ignore him, George,' said The Missus. 'I told you, he's stewed, drunk to the eyeballs.'

'I accuse this man and woman, constable,' said Tommo. 'I accuse them – '

'Give over, Tommo,' said Rosie. 'The joke's gone far enough. Drop it, eh, drop it?'

He pulled away from her touch. 'I have a public duty. Officer, take those two into custody!'

'On what charge?' asked Johnson good-humouredly.

'Ah,' said Tommo, laying a finger along the side of his nose. 'Ah. What charge? You may well ask.' He swayed slightly and creased his forehead in concentration. Then he smiled broadly. 'Watering the beer! That's the charge!'

'Get out of here before I chuck you out!' yelled The Guv'nor.

'You?' said Tommo. 'Chuck me out? What will you use for an army?' He planted the top-hat on his head and banged it down. 'Do not concern yourselves. I have done my duty and now I will take my leave of you.'

He swayed to the door and turned for a moment: 'One other thing, constable. The woman is the real brains behind it.'

'What?' said Johnson

Tommo pointed a finger at The Missus. 'That one. The female woman. The one with the hair and the – oh, never mind – run them both in – your sergeant will tell you which is which. Chin-chin!'

As the doors swung behind him, The Missus carried a large tot of whisky across to the policeman.

'That Tommo will get himself hung one day – that tongue will get him hung,' she said. 'Here, have this to warm your cockles, Mr Johnson.'

'Thank you, Mrs Quorn,' said Johnson. He sipped the whisky appreciatively. 'Ah, no water in that, I'll be bound.'

'That's the best stuff.' The Missus lowered her voice. 'I'll leave a drop more of the same and a couple of beef sandwiches in the usual place at the back – just to warm you up during the night, eh?'

'That'll go down very well, Missus. I'm much obliged.' Johnson turned to Rosie. 'Yes, that feller of yours is a bit of a character, young Rosie.'

'What feller?' asked Rosie.

'He's all right as long as he don't take things too far. I can talk to you, Rosie. You've got a good sensible head on your shoulders. Tell your Tommo to watch the company he keeps – tell him to keep his nose clean.'

'He's not my feller!' said Rosie. 'Once and for all, he's not my feller!'

'I'm sorry,' said Johnson mildly, 'I thought – '

'You know what thought done, don't you?' said Rosie. 'Thought thought he'd shit himself and when he put his hand down his trousers he found he had!'

'Rosie! There is no need for coarseness!' said The Missus, shocked at the reception of this obscure cockneyism.

'Well,' snapped Rosie, 'it makes me wild! Everyone jumping to conclusions. Tommo is not my feller. Nobody's my feller!' And with this she stomped off into the other bar.

'Young people,' sighed The Missus. 'Young people today. I don't know what the world's coming to.'

'They're given too much,' said Johnson. 'They have it too easy.'

'Yes,' said The Missus, nodding agreement. 'Exactly. They have it too easy.'

'And they don't know when they're well off.'

'No, they don't,' said The Missus. 'But we're to blame. Oh yes, I blame our generation. We've allowed the young too much latitude.'

'You have taken the words out of my mouth, Mrs Quorn,' said Johnson solemnly. 'That is it exactly. We've given them too much latitude.'

'And now we're paying the penalty,' said The Missus.

'And now we're paying the penalty,' said Johnson.

They shook their heads from left to right and back again in exact unison and time, as if they had been rehearsing together for weeks.

3

It wasn't until she began to climb the stairs that Rosie realised how exhausted she was. It was an effort to put one foot in front of another and she longed to get to her bed. But she had to feed her patient and see that he was settled for the night and her own comfort would have to come later.

He was sitting up in bed reading a book when she entered the room and to her unpractised eye he seemed to look better already, as if even a few hours rest had done him good.

'You shouldn't be reading, you should be resting!' she scolded him mildly.

'Oh, but I am resting!' he said and gave a deep sigh of pleasure. 'This is heaven. To lie here and read. Marvellous!'

'Well, put it down now. I've brought you some warm bread and milk with brown sugar, a glass of milk in case you want a drink in the night, and a bit of fruit I managed to get in the market. An apple – that's a Grannie Smith that is – and a couple of oranges.'

She set down the tray holding all these things and removed the book from his hands.

'Do you read much, Rosie?' he asked.

'When do I get time?' she replied. 'Now, eat that. Mind now, it's hot.'

He plunged the spoon into the steaming bread and milk and lifted a spoonful to his lips. In a second he was spluttering with pain and the spoon dropped back into the bowl. Some incoherent words bubbled from his open mouth. Rosie shook her head.

'I told you it was hot.'

'Ooh,' he said, gasping for air. 'Ooh. I burned my tongue.'

'Serves you right,' she said, showing no sympathy.

When he had recovered, he tackled the dish with more care, taking a little at a time and testing it carefully.

'You can borrow that book if you like,' he said.

'I told you, I don't have time to sit around reading,' she said. 'And in any case, I don't really understand about books.'

'You'd understand this one. The truth lies between the covers, Rosie, the real truth about our lives.'

'I don't need a book to tell me that!'

'But it tells about the future too. It's called *Merrie England* and it's by Robert Blatchford.'

'Never heard of him.'

'He's a marvellous man. What he writes is so simple, so obvious. He shows how we can abolish poverty and build a wonderful future for everyone.'

'The future?' said Rosie. 'I don't think of the future. I take each day as it comes – and that's hard enough.'

'I know, I know it's hard,' said Frank earnestly. 'But that's exactly what I mean. It should be better. It could be better. I mean – there must be something more you want from life. Isn't that true?'

'I could do with a little more sleep,' she said with a small wry smile.

'I'm serious, Rosie.'

'So am I. I'm on my feet from six in the morning to eleven or twelve at night. Do you wonder I get tired? I'm tired now. You know what I'd like more than anything else? To lie in one morning! Just to lie there and sleep. Oh, I'd give a year's pay for that!'

'And that's all?'

'That's all.'

'No,' he said, 'I don't believe it.'

'Whether you do or not, it's the truth.'

'All right. Perhaps it is true, perhaps that's all you want for yourself. But take those kids this morning. Do you think it right that children should have to beg for scraps? That children should live like that?'

'It's always been the same, and it always will be,' said Rosie.

'No!' said Frank. 'It can be changed, it will be changed, Rosie. When we have a truly people's government at Westminster. When that day comes, Rosie, there will be no kids without shoes or food, no unemployed, no poverty. Life will flow like music! People won't live like animals any longer, they'll live in clean beautiful cities without hatred or fear. They'll be real, dignified human beings.'

His eyes shone as he spoke, as if he were actually seeing a vision of the future. And for some reason she was reminded of a time when, at the age of five or six, her mother had taken her to a big store at Christmas time. Rosie could not be sure but she thought the store was Whiteleys, a huge, crowded, overwhelming palace of a place that made her feel very small and frightened. However, she did remember clearly that she had not been over-impressed with Father Christmas himself, whose breath smelt of beer and tobacco but afterwards, when her mother took her to the Fairy Bower, she had been almost speechless with wonder and delight. For months, years, afterwards she remained convinced that she had actually been to fairyland and kept a vision of the magic bower glowing in her mind.

Frank reminded her of the child she had once been. He, too, was seeing visions. The difference was that she had grown up and knew that her Fairy Bower had been a deception, made out of coloured lights, pasteboard, tinsel and paint.

Aloud she said: 'Sounds all right. But I'll believe it when I see it.'

'It won't come without effort, Rosie,' he said earnestly. 'Nobody is going to deliver a new life to your door. We have to work for it. You and me – all of us.'

'Me?' she said tolerantly. 'What do you expect me to do?'

'For a start, take this book. Read it. Learn about our ideas. Take it, Rosie, please!'

He held her with his clear grey eyes and thrust the book into her hands. Once again, she felt a strength emanating from this strange young man. It seemed as if he were looking deep into her heart and a sudden unexpected wave of shame swept over her, shame at her own inadequacies. She was hard put to keep back the tears. Taking the book she turned away and said, with as much briskness as she could command:

'All right. I'll take it. Anything to keep you quiet. Now – is there anything else you want before I go to my bed?'

'No, Rosie, thank you. I'd like to go on talking but I mustn't. You need your rest. Thank you for everything.'

'What have I done?' she said lightly. 'Now eat your supper and get as much rest as you can, do you hear me?'

'I hear you,' he said smiling.

As she smoothed the bed clothes he took one of her hands. 'Now, that's enough of that,' she said with a smile. And, on an impulse, she bent over and kissed him gently on the lips.

'Goodnight, lovey,' she said.

4

When she arrived at her own room, Rosie knelt down and pulled the old cardboard box from beneath the bed. She liked to go through the box at least once each week and tonight, despite her tiredness, she felt the need to look at and to touch its contents once more. The marbles given her by Cousin Albert, the two birth-certificates, the rose from Major Pauley, the purse, the embroidered handkerchief, the necklace of shells, the programme from that night at the Empire – these and other things were hers and hers alone, they belonged to no-one else either in whole or part. And, in a strange but satisfying way they gave Rosie a feeling of belonging, a sense of identity: it was as if this battered box contained the proof that she did, in truth, exist as a person.

She opened the purse and from an inner compartment drew out her mother's wedding ring, a thin worn circle of gold, and slipped it on. It was too big – though not by much – and turned easily on her finger. She closed her eyes, picturing her mother, wondering about her unknown father.

Frank Lambert had spoken of the future. What did the future hold for her? When she had told Frank that she lived from day to day, that she had never given thought to the future, she had been speaking the truth. But now, for the first time, she felt a vague, unformed dissatisfaction with her life. It made her feel uneasy, unsettled, even irritable with herself. But what could she do?

It was unthinkable that she should remain a barmaid forever but, on the other hand, pub work was the only job she knew. Marriage? Of course, that had its attractions, but she had seen too many girls rush into marriage, seen their spirits and health crushed by poverty, seen them lose their bloom and wither like leaves in autumn as they bore child after child. And her turn of mind was too practical to dream, as some girls did, that one day a rich and handsome young man would fall hopelessly in love with her, marry her, and carry her off to a life of unbelievable luxury.

Once, she recalled, she had thought about becoming a nurse. Her mother had taken her to visit a friend in a hospital near London Bridge. Rosie remembered nothing of the patient or the other circumstances but her imagination had been fired by the sight of the nurses. One in particular had spoken to Rosie as she waited outside the ward, looking down on her with a warm smile. She had looked so beautiful in her cool, fresh uniform, she had conveyed such an impression of gentleness and kindness that Rosie had never forgotten her. Even now, if she closed her eyes and concentrated hard, she could pick up the clean sweet scent of that unknown nurse.

But later her mother, not meaning it unkindly, had responded to Rosie's tentative question on the subject with a finality that utterly crushed any idea of nursing as a job.

'It's no good, Rosie. You need education for that. More education than you'll ever have, lovey.'

The book Frank had given her lay on the bed and Rosie put out a hand to touch it. Education? That was the barrier? Without education she could not hope to better herself. But she was seventeen, moving towards eighteen, and she had forfeited her chance of schooling years ago.

She shook her head, annoyed that she should allow herself to indulge in such self-pity. Her life was not so bad. At least, she had a roof over her head, a bed to sleep in and food in her belly. There were thousands in worse condition and instead of bemoaning her lot she should count her blessings. She had managed without books and education so far, and managed very well. There were other things in life after all.

And, as if in response to this thought, she heard a shrill whistle from the street outside. She knew at once that it was Tommo and, as the whistle was repeated, she got up and went to the window. Pulling back the curtain, she saw Tommo standing in the back of the trap in which he had taken her out to Hadley Wood. The same sturdy pony stood patiently between the shafts and one of Tommo's market friends, Flash-Harry Green, sat holding the reins. Tommo put two fingers from each hand into the sides of his mouth and repeated the whistle yet again as Rosie opened the window.

'Give over, Tommo!' she called in an urgent whisper. 'You'll wake the whole neighbourhood.'

But Tommo, who had clearly taken more drink since leaving the pub, would not be silenced.

'Rosie, my old darling, my beauty, my lovely piece of crockery! Tommo is here, Tommo is waiting.'

'Give over, Tommo!' she hissed. 'You'll get me the sack! Give over!'

Tommo now adopted what he imagined to be a musical stance and began to strum an invisible guitar as he raised his voice in song:

> Are we to part like this, dear
> Are we to part this way?
> Who's it to be?
> That copper or me?
> Don't be afraid to say.
> Though everything's over between us
> Don't ever pass me by
> For you and me still friends can be
> For the sake of the days gone by.

The window just along from Rosie opened during this musical interlude and an astonished Guv'nor stuck his head out. He was soon joined by The Missus, her abundant hair enclosed in a white nightcap.

'Hook it, Tommo!' shouted The Guv'nor. 'Hook it!'

'I'll get the police on you!' yelled his wife.

Tommo crossed his hands across his heart and looked yearningly up at The Missus.

'Ah, there she is! The light of my life! And who is that with her? No, it can't be! Do my eyes deceive me? It's a baboon, a red-arsed baboon! Flash-Harry, look – take a butchers! If that ain't Beauty and the Beast may I never touch another drop of liquor!'

'Rosie! Are you responsible for this?' called The Missus.

'No, ma'am!' said Rosie hastily and appealed to Tommo once more. 'Tommo, you've had your joke. Go home and let folks get their rest.'

'We're going for a moonlight drive, Rosie!' called Tommo. 'How about coming? No charge. A lovely drive in the moonlight.'

'If you go with him, you needn't bother to come back!' said The Missus.

About a dozen people, most of them as far gone as Tommo, had gathered around the trap and he now began to lead them in song, serenading Rosie and conducting vigorously as he did so:

> You are my honey, honey-suckle
> I am the bee,
> I'd like to kiss the honey sweet
> From those red lips, you see.
> I love you dearly, dearly
> And I want you to love me.
> You are my honey, honey-suckle,
> I am the bee!

The singing, which began on a robust note, diminished in strength as it progressed. Rosie could not understand the reason for this at first, but then she saw PC Johnson standing on the corner, arms akimbo, grimly observing the scene. Others had noticed him too, and by the end of the chorus the supporting crowd had melted away, leaving Tommo and Flash-Harry as the only surviving voices.

131

Unperturbed by this defection, Tommo extended his arms once more and began to sing:

> Speak to me, Rosie!
> Say what I long to hear . . .

PC Johnson stepped forward suddenly and Tommo's voice trembled away into silence. He met the constable's grim look with a grin, banged his topper on his head and said brightly:

'Lovely evening, officer. Touch of rain in the air though, I think.'

'Tommo,' said Johnson. 'I'll give you five minutes to get home. If I catch you out again tonight, I'll have you for disturbing the peace, drunk and disorderly conduct, obstruction, being in charge of a conveyance while under the influence of alcohol, and anything else I can put tongue to.'

'Mr Johnson – ' Tommo began.

'Five minutes,' said Johnson.

Tommo shrugged, raised his hat in salute to Rosie and to The Guv'nor and The Missus and said:

'Goodnight, my beauty. Goodnight all. Sleep tight and don't do anything to frighten the horses.' He took the reins from Flash-Harry and stirred the pony to action.

'Come on, Ada, girl. Step lively. Up a shade, Ada, up a shade.'

He was soon lost to view. Johnson looked up at the window. 'You'll be all right now, ma'am.'

'He really is getting beyond a joke!' said The Missus.

'Oh, he's harmless enough, ma'am,' said Johnson. Rosie could not be sure, but she thought he sent a wink in her direction as he spoke.

As Rosie closed the window and pulled the curtains, something dropped at her feet and rolled across the floor. With a shock she realised that she had forgotten to take off her mother's ring. She retrieved it safely and replaced it in the purse.

But the incident sent her mind back to the theme of marriage. Perhaps it need not be so bad, she thought. If she married a good decent man, there was no reason why it shouldn't work out. But who?

There was Tommo, but with him she would never be sure. She liked him, even loved him in a maternal sort of way, but, underneath that extrovert personality, her instinct told her that there was a kind of weakness. She could not define it, except that it was a weakness of character, but it made her wary.

Then there was the Detective Sergeant, Stan Roberts. She hardly knew him, but he seemed to be a decent straightforward chap. There was a quiet strength to him that she liked and, if his promotion was anything to go by, he was bright enough to get ahead. But she really didn't know him.

And then there was the strange earnest young man upstairs in her old room. She hardly knew him either, but, in an odd way, she felt that she did. There was strength in this man too, a different strength perhaps from that of Stan Roberts, but she sensed that he was not someone to be easily deflected from a set course.

There was something else too. She wasn't sure about Stan, but with the other two there was an element of impractibility in their make-up, a touch of helplessness which intrigued and moved her. She felt the urge to comfort and help them.

What rubbish, she told herself abruptly. Two of the men were virtual strangers and the third was an irresponsible madcap womaniser! She must be out of her mind even to think of marrying any one of them. She wasn't yet eighteen, there was time enough, more than enough, to worry about that sort of thing!

Even so, as she lay in the dark, she wondered what it would be like to have a man lying next to her. An excitement prickled her flesh and she stirred restlessly, uneasily, half-ashamed of such feelings. Then she remembered that she had forgotten to say her prayers and she prayed hurriedly to God to forgive her for bad thoughts and to keep her good.

CHAPTER SEVEN

1

'Well,' said The Missus, with grim humour, 'and how is his lordship today?'

She must have crept up the stairs, the cunning old cow, thought Rosie, for until the door burst open she had not heard a thing. And this meant that she had not had time to hide the dish of lamb stew and the tapioca pudding which she had sneaked up for Frank Lambert's midday meal.

The Missus advanced to the bed and surveyed the dishes on the tin tray. She sniffed the air aggressively, glared at Rosie and said, with sweet sarcasm: 'You're being well looked after, I see, Mr Lambert. Nice bit of neck of lamb that, smells very nice.'

'It's scrag-end,' said Rosie. 'Two pennorth of scrag-end.'

'And what is that, then?' said The Missus, pointing at the pudding. 'Tapioca, if I'm not mistaken. And made with some of my fresh cream milk I'll be bound.'

'The doctor said –' Rosie began.

'I am well aware what the doctor said!' cut in The Missus. 'It is easy for doctors to talk. They're my provisions on that tray, not the doctor's. I'm the one who is paying not Dr Rhys.'

It was on the tip of Rosie's tongue to point out that, after paying Dr Rhys the two shilling fee for his visit, there was a balance of two shillings in the pot – in The Missus's purse in fact – but she decided that it would be more tactful to hold her peace.

'I am very grateful, Mrs Quorn,' said Frank.

'I'm sure, I'm sure. What I want to know is when I may

expect you downstairs. We were run off our feet last night. We can't go on doing your work as well as our own, you know.'

'He's in no fit state!' said Rosie.

'Oh, I'm much better,' Frank said. 'I'll come down and start work this afternoon.'

'Good,' said The Missus. 'That's all I wanted to hear.' She marched back to the door, the bare floorboards creaking beneath her tread. 'Rosie!' she beckoned. 'A word, if you please!'

Rosie glanced warily at Frank, then followed The Missus out to the landing, closing the door behind her.

'Now,' said The Missus in a low tense voice, 'just what do you think you are playing at?'

'I don't know what you mean, ma'am,' replied Rosie. The statement was not entirely true: she did have a fair notion of what was on the other woman's mind.

'It's bad enough that you steal my food!' said The Mussus. 'That's bad enough, in all conscience. But to steal my time as well, that is going too far, too far. I'm paying you – remember that! Not him in there, not the doctor! Your place is downstairs, my girl, downstairs working, not sitting around up here playing nursemaid to that muttonhead!'

'I'll pay you for the food, ma'am,' said Rosie.

'I fully intend that someone should pay! I don't intend to be out of pocket over the likes of him. He's been nothing but a nuisance since the moment he arrived. I was a fool to take him in. It's always the way. I let my heart rule my head and people take advantage of me.'

Guided by long experience, Rosie waited quietly while The Missus ran on in this vein and interposed only as she showed signs of petering out.

'Beg pardon, ma'am. But the doctor said that Mr Lambert ought to rest for three or four days – a week.'

'A week!' The Missus snorted like a restless horse. 'Oh, yes. He told me as much! Very good of him to make so free with my staff! I ask you – the man comes here, works for an hour or so, and then falls down! He's done nothing – nothing – to earn his keep. And I am supposed to keep him in idleness for a week! Why don't you make it a fortnight – a month – a year! Why don't you go out on the street and bring in a dozen idlers like him and put them to bed and feed them my best food!' The Missus paused for breath and lifted a warning finger. 'He starts work this afternoon or he's finished. Out. I'm not running a hostel or a hospital. I've told you before and I'll tell you again – '

A furious, rasping bout of coughing from the attic interrupted this new diatribe and The Missus paused to listen. Rosie watched her anxiously.

'How long has he had that cough?' asked The Missus.

'It's not really a cough,' said Rosie. 'More an itch in the throat.'

'Fiddle-faddle!' said The Missus. 'That's a cough, if ever I heard one. And that cough is telling us something, Rosie. Now, you tell me, tell me the truth. Has he been bringing up blood?'

Remembering the bright red splashes she had seen on the rags Frank used as hankerchiefs, Rosie said: 'A few spots. I mean, not much.'

The Missus shook her head, and there was a new note of sympathy in her voice. 'It won't do, Rosie. It just will not do. That young man is sick, too sick for the sort of work I need him for. I should have seen that from the beginning. As usual I allowed my heart to rule my head. He'll have to go, for his own sake.'

'Where? What will he do?'

'I don't know. That's not my affair. But I can't have him here, coughing all over the customers, I really can't. There is a limit.' And then, perhaps because she saw the distress in Rosie's eyes, The Missus said defensively: 'It'll be better for him, Rosie. He needs to be out in the open, not stuck in a smoky bar. Well, you heard that cough. Terrible! He needs fresh air in his lungs. And the work – it will over-tax his strength. No. A couple of weeks of that – less – and he'll collapse again. If he stays here, he'll get worse, not better. Blind Freddie could see that!'

Rosie, remembering what Big Bess had said, listened to this with growing apprehension. 'Is it – do you think he has the – ' She checked, unable to pronounce the dreaded word.

The Missus had no such reluctance. 'Consumption, Rosie. If he's not eaten up with the consumption then I'm a one-legged Hottentot. That cough, that tells the whole story.'

'Perhaps we ought to send for Dr Rhys,' said Rosie.

'What good will that do? He'll only confirm what I've told you. What's the point of throwing good money after bad?' The Missus sighed. 'Why is it that these things always happen to me? Always to me. I try and do someone a good turn and this is how I get paid. I tell you something! I'm going to have it out with Mr Blooming Parker when I see him! I know why he sent that boy to me. He wanted to get shot of him, he didn't want a consumptive on his hands, the old hypocrite!'

She paused to draw breath, then went on. 'Now, Rosie, listen. He can stay here one more night. One more. Tomorrow he must go. I'm sorry, but that is now it must be. I look to you to tell him.' She moved to the stairs. 'Now, I must go and see about getting another potman.'

'If you please, ma'am – ' Rosie began.

'No!' said The Missus. 'My mind is made up. Don't attempt to change it. That young man must go – it's not right to have him here, it's not healthy.'

She stomped off down the stairs. Rosie turned back to the attic, but when she opened the door she saw that Frank had his eyes closed and was drifting off to sleep.

What, she wondered, what will become of him?

2

Later that afternoon, on her way to the Donkey Dairy to collect a gallon of asses milk for The Missus, she saw Dr Rhys park his familiar tricycle outside a house, unstrap his black Gladstone bag and go inside to make a call on a patient. She waited, growing more nervous by the minute, until he came out again and then approached him.

'Begging you pardon, sir.'

'What is it?' he said wearily. 'What is it now?' He recognised her then and gave a wan smile. 'Ah, it's you, cariad. From The Winged Horse. What's your name again?'

'Rosie, sir.'

'Ah, that's it. Well, what's the problem?'

She hesitated, feeling a sudden sense of guilt. Leaning on the saddle of the tricycle he looked worn and tired, as if he had been up all night. Perhaps that is it, she thought: her aunt had told her once that doctors and undertakers were never short of customers.

'Is it about the young man?'

'Yes, doctor.'

'Taken a turn for the worse, has he?'

'No, not really, sir. But The Missus – Mrs Quorn, that is – I mean – well, she says he has to go tomorrow, you see. He's lost his job like.'

'Why is that?'

'The Missus doesn't think he's up to the work.'

'She could be right there.'

'What I wanted to ask, sir, if you don't mind, what I wanted to ask was – well – is it the consumption, doctor? Is that what he's got?'

'What makes you ask that?' he snapped, and glared at her fiercely, as if rebuking her for treading on forbidden territory.

'I just thought – ' Her voice petered out in face of his stare.

'Leave the thinking to me, will you?' he said. And then he added with more kindness. 'Tuberculosis? Without proper tests and further examination I cannot say with complete certainty. On the other hand, all the indications are there. Yes – if you want a blunt answer – I believe the young man has what you call the consumption. I could have told you as much yesterday, but there was really no point.'

'He ought to go to a hospital.'

'He ought to go to a lot of places. Switzerland, for example. So did the hundreds of others around here – people who are in the same condition as your young man – or even worse.'

'He isn't my young man,' said Rosie.

'Then you can count yourself lucky.'

'I've heard that there are special places you can go to if

you've got the consumption. Special hospitals in the country and that.'

'Oh, there are,' said the doctor, 'there are indeed. The only trouble, cariad, the only trouble is that such places cost money. A great deal of money. To be a patient in a TB clinic costs more for a week than you can earn in a year.'

'Don't they have any free ones, I mean like for poor people?'

'There are some, not many. Run by various charities. And they have waiting lists as long as the Old Kent Road.'

'Then what's to become of him? She's kicking him out – he's got to go tomorrow.'

He cocked his head to one side and gave her a little quizzical look. 'If he isn't your young man, why are you so concerned about him?'

'Well, someone has to worry, don't they? Someone has to care,' she answered defiantly.

'Yes,' he said, nodding. 'But not many do. Not many do.'

'There's nothing can be done for him, then?' she asked.

'I'll make enquiries at one or two of the charities I mentioned. But I don't hold out much hope.'

'So that's it!' said Rosie, with a touch of anger. 'He can't pay for one of those posh clinics, there's no place in the others, so what's left? A six-foot plot in the bone-orchard!'

'Something like that, Rosie,' he said calmly. 'It isn't right, it isn't just, but that's the way it is. I could name you a hundred people in the same situation – two hundred – more.'

She nodded, aware once again of the weariness – almost a kind of hopelessness – in his eyes, as if the daily battle against disease was becoming too much for him.

'I'm sorry to have bothered you, sir,' she said.

'That's all right,' he said gently and smiled. 'You feel free to bother me any time you like. Look upon me as a friend, Rosie.'

The smile seemed to lift the tiredness from his eyes and to make him look quite young. Rosie had mentally registered him as elderly – fifty at least – but now she realised that her calculation had been ten years out, if not more. He was only middle-aged really and quite good-looking in a craggy sort of way. She returned his smile and repeated her thanks.

'Wait,' he said, as she turned to go. 'Have you asked the young man – what is his name again?'

'Frank Lambert, sir.'

'Have you asked him if he has any friends or relatives he can go to? He's a well-spoken lad, sounds as if he might come from a good home.'

'If he had a good home, he'd naturally go back to it, wouldn't he?'

'Not necessarily. He may have reasons. It's worth pursuing, Rosie. Talk to him.' He looked down at the milk-can in her hand. 'What is that for?'

'I'm on my way to the Donkey Dairy to get milk for The Missus.'

'Asses milk?'

'Yes, sir.'

'What does she do with it?'

'She washes herself in it.'

'Good Lord? Why on earth does she do that?'

'Reckons it's good for the skin. If she had her way, if she could afford it, she'd have a bath in donkey milk every day.'

'Good Lord!' he said again, his eyes glinting with amusement. 'A regular Cleopatra!'

'Sir?'

'Never mind. I must push on.' He swung himself on to the saddle of the tricycle. 'Goodbye, Rosie. Don't be afraid to come to me if you need help at any time.' He smiled. 'You're a good person, Rosie. But remember – you can't carry the troubles of the world on your back. You can't be responsible for every lame duck that comes your way. Think of other people to be sure, but don't forget to spare a thought for yourself sometimes. Bye, cariad.'

He gave a wave of his hand and began to pedal away. She watched him, wondering about the strange name he had called her. Cariad? And she smiled, thinking again that he was quite handsome for his age and certainly very nice.

Dr Rhys, for his part, was thinking how strange it was that someone like Rosie should blossom in this bleak, poverty-stricken landscape. In his experience it was not true, as some woolly-minded romantics claimed, that poverty ennobled. He knew only too well that, for the most part, it turned people into beasts, particularly the men; the elementary struggle for day-to-day survival made them selfish, cunning, ignorant and cruel.

But there were exceptions. Every now and then, in the course of his duties, he would come across someone who stood out from the brutish crowd, someone whose character had been steeled and refined by the struggle.

There was a woman he knew, a patient who lived in Campbell Road, Finsbury Park, a slum road that had the reputation of being the worst street in North London. She was poor and burdened with children like most of her slum neighbours, but somehow she had found the strength and the will to resist all the sneers, to overcome the incredible difficulties, and to teach herself to read and write. Then she had gone on to educate herself beyond this, creating for herself a small private world of learning amid the turmoil of the family and the street and, in the process, winning the respect of her neighbours who came to her in increasing numbers for advice and help.

There were others like her. Another patient, a man of vivid natural intelligence and indomitable spirit, had organised the workers at the local boot-polish factory and led them in a successful struggle against intolerable conditions. He could think of about a dozen such people, men and women whose qualities had risen triumphant above their circumstances. And there were some, a few, who had escaped the slums and managed to make something of themselves.

But for the great mass there could be no escape and this was why the doctor wondered about Rosie. She had intelligence, no doubt of that, she was as bright as a button: and there was beauty there too, a glowing beauty that reflected her lively and generous spirit. Would she fade, as so many had faded? Would she be trapped into a slum-marriage, and sacrifice all that native intelligence, that potential, to a husband and family? How often he had seen that happen! He could not see a wedding, with its noisy happy cockney crowd,

141

without wondering what the bride and groom would look like in four or five years, what mark poverty would lay upon them.

He had armoured himself against such feelings with a show of professional objectivity and a certain cynicism. Without such protection his job would have been more painful, less bearable. So, now, as he pushed the tricycle up a hill, he rebuked himself for his sentimental lapse. He had been a fool to allow himself to be drawn towards Rosie's innocence and warmth. There was nothing he could do either for her or for the young man in the attic. If he allowed himself to become involved in a personal sense with the problems of every patient he would have no rest, no peace.

All the same, in contradiction of these thoughts, he resolved that on the morrow he would call in on Frank Lambert and take another look at him. And to confirm this decision he stopped and made a note to this effect in his rounds-book.

As he remounted he made another note, a mental note this time. The tricycle was getting too much for him: It was heavy and slow and gave no protection against the vagaries of the weather. Before the next winter, he would go into the question of buying one of the new motor-cars that seemed to be catching on so fast.

3

For The Missus and The Guv'nor it was a fairly typical afternoon. He lay on the bed in his undervest, long under-pants and socks, fast asleep and snoring while she sat before the mirror of the wash-stand engaged in the never-ending struggle to preserve her youth and improve her beauty. She was so engrossed in this labour of love that she was surprised when her husband spoke:

'Don't tell me you're still at it!'

'Lor!' she said. 'It's awake! Rip Van Winkle has opened his eyes!'

'The hours you spend at that bleeding mirror,' he said. 'The hours!'

He rose from the bed, stretched his arms and scratched his belly. Then, bracing himself deliberately and cocking his backside, he released a long triple blast of farts.

'George!' said The Missus.

'Better out than in,' he said.

'You're disgusting. You're a pig, that's what you are, a pig. And I'll tell you something – you snore like a pig. I hardly got a wink last night with your snoring.'

'You know what you can do if you don't like it,' he said. 'Sleep somewhere else.'

'Don't tempt me,' she said. 'It would be a pleasure.'

'Ah,' he said. 'You say that now. But think what you'd be missing.'

And moving over he circled her with his arms and muzzled her neck. She jumped up and tried to move away, but he held her wrist.

'Give over, George!' she said. 'I'm not having any of that.'

'Ah, come on, pet,' he said, pulling her to him. His free hand went to her breast, and she slapped it down.

'No, George! You're not deaf. I said no!'

'Why not? Come on, you used to like it in the afternoon.'

He pulled her in again and forced his mouth against hers. She resisted strongly at first but, as his hands grew more insistent, her resolve seemed to weaken.

She knew that her husband required three things of life – drink, food and sex, not necessarily in that order. If his appetites were appeased, he was governable, but if he were deprived of any of the three he could be troublesome in the extreme. She seldom enjoyed sex with him since it was largely a one-sided, smash-and-grab affair but she had learned to resign herself to the act in the interests of peace. Still, she tried one more feeble protest.

'George, stop it! I'm all dressed!'

'That's soon remedied!'

He threw her back on the bed and pulled her skirt and petticoats up to her neck.

'No, George, not like this!' she protested.

'Shut up!' he said excitedly, his trembling fingers fumbling with the elastic of her new rayon knickers. As he did so, a

143

knock at the door distracted him momentarily and, seizing her opportunity, The Missus rolled from under him, stood up and shook down her skirts.

'Who is it?' she called sweetly.

'Rosie, ma'am,' came the reply. 'I brought your donkey-milk.'

'Tell her to hook it!' hissed The Guv'nor.

But The Missus was already on her way to the door, patting her hair as she went. She frowned at the waiting Rosie.

'Took you long enough!'

'Sorry, ma'am.'

'And how many times must I tell you? It is asses milk, not donkey milk.'

'Sorry, ma'am.'

'All right, all right! Put it down by the wash-basin. I'm going to my parlour.'

As The Missus made to move past Rosie, The Guv'nor said sulkily:

'Aren't you coming back, my pet?'

'This pub doesn't run itself!' she said. 'I've books to make up, there's ordering to be done.' And with that she made for the stairs, thankful for this escape, no matter how temporary.

Rosie put the can of milk down as ordered, glad to be relieved of its weight, and turned to follow The Missus.

'Rosie!' said The Guv'nor and she stopped. His small bright eyes flickered over her body.

'Yes, guv'nor?'

'It's my back.' He put a hand over his right shoulder and winced. 'The screws, the old rheumatics, playing me up again. Can you see any oils on the table there?'

Rosie searched the table-top and came up with a bottle of macassar oil. 'This what you mean?'

'That's the stuff. The Missus was going to give me a rub. You do it, will you?'

Rosie hesitated. In the last few months she had grown a little uneasy about The Guv'nor's attitude: there had been a certain amount of mauling in the bar, and at odd moments, when her attention had been elsewhere, she had felt his hands slide briefly across her bottom or brush lightly against her breasts. So far there had been nothing serious, nothing she could not cope with, nothing that was beyond the small change of a barmaid's life. It had happened at odd times with various customers and she had learned to ignore the wandering hands or, at most, lightly to rebuke the offenders. If you worked in a pub, you had to learn to live with that sort of thing and not make too much of it. Of course, if a customer took too many liberties that would be a different matter, but so far that sort of problem had not arisen.

The Guv'nor was also a different matter. In a way, she was dependent upon him for her food and shelter, she could not treat him as she would a customer. The Missus ruled the roost, but if Rosie offended or upset The Guv'nor, he had the power to make her life unbearable, to force her out of a job. So she had approached the matter warily, keeping out of his way when possible, giving him little or no opportunity to grope her.

'Come on,' he said. 'The shoulder. It's been giving me gyp all day.'

'All right,' she said briskly. 'Turn over.'

'Turn over?'

'I can't get at your back unless you lie on your front, can I?'

She propelled him round on the bed until he was lying face downwards, rolled his undervest up to his neck and poured some of the linament into a cupped palm.

'That the place?' she asked, as she set to work, running her hands distastefully over the ripples of blubber. His flesh made her think of mottled dough, although it was sweatily warm to the touch.

'A bit lower,' he breathed. 'That's it. Ah, lovely, that's lovely.'

'Bacon-fat's the best thing for this,' she said. 'Or pork dripping. Finest thing out.'

'Never in your life,' he said. 'That's Rowland's Macassar Oil, that is. Royalty uses that, my girl.'

'I'm surprised,' she said. 'I didn't think royalty suffered from the screws.'

'They're human, same as we are,' he said.

'There,' she said, rubbing her hands, 'that should do you.'

145

'Wait,' he said and rolled over. 'Give us a rub here.' He indicated his left shoulder. 'I got a twinge there.'

'I thought it was the other shoulder.'

'Both shoulders! I should know!' he said.

As she leaned over him, he reached up suddenly and pulled her down.

'Rosie,' he breathed. 'Rosie!'

He clasped her to him, pressing his lips against her face. She could smell the oily wax on his moustache, the stale odour of his breath and all the terror of that night in Brown's Alley came rushing back to her. And, in the same moment, he forced one of her hands downwards to his crotch.

Some instinct told her not to scream and, forcing her hand free, she struggled silently, beating at him with a small clenched fist so fiercely that he had to let her go.

She stood for a full half-minute listening to his agonised panting, sucking in her own breath.

'Rosie,' he whined, 'be kind to me. I didn't mean to hurt you. I haven't had any real love for years. That old cow, that's not love. Please.' He forced himself up on one elbow. 'Look. I won't touch you. But you touch me. That's all I want.' He put a hand to his crotch. 'Here. Hold me here. There's a gold sovereign in my waistcoat pocket, Rosie. It's yours, if you hold me here. There's no harm in it. Toss me off, Rosie, and you can have the sovereign.'

She was to remember afterwards how pathetic he looked, how revolting and yet pathetic. But at this moment it was revulsion that overwhelmed her and, hard on its heels, came a wild and violent hurricane of anger, as all the bitterness and frustration of the past few weeks, the past few years, exploded in her head like a charge of dynamite. She was angry not only for herself and her own humiliation, but for her mother and her aunt, for Mr Softley and for Frank Lambert, for the urchins who queued for scraps each morning, for the weariness of Dr Rhys and for the hundreds of sick people he had told her of, people who were worse off even than Frank. Her rage encompassed the whole rotten world, everything that made such things possible.

Rosie was surprised that she did not scream or shout, astonished that with such a storm raging inside her she should still maintain some measure of control. In a low dangerous voice, she said:

'Guv'nor, listen to me! I swear to God that if you come near me again, if you lay a finger on me, I'll finish you! That's a promise. I mean every word I say. Touch me once more and I'll pass the word down the market. I'll tell Tommo and Dave and Big Bess, I'll tell them all and leave them to deal with you. They'll take a knife to that – that *thing* of yours, they'll cut out your lights and your liver. And if they don't I will or my name's not Rosie Carr. You won't be able to walk round here again, you won't be able to crawl! Listen to what I say. Remember, for it's the solemn truth. God's truth.'

She had the satisfaction of seeing the gleam of fear in the watery eyes before she swept from the room.

The anger subsided as quickly as it had come and in the solitude of her own room she wept as she had not wept in a long, long time.

4

Frank Lambert slept all the afternoon and for half the evening and when he awoke at last he was conscience-stricken at his failure to report downstairs for work as he had promised. He decided to dress and go down but, as he tried to move to the chair over which his clothes were hanging, the floor began to behave in a most extraordinary fashion, tilting steeply one way and then the other in the manner of a see-saw. Moreover, a strange white mist had somehow entered the room: it swirled above the chair and seemed to swallow it up so that his clothes were lost to view. The mist tickled his throat and, as he began to cough, the floor gave a last convulsive jerk that sent him crashing to the floor.

It was there that Rosie found him when she went to the attic after closing-time with some pigeon pie and the rest of the tapioca pudding. She managed with a struggle to get him into the bed and then ran downstairs to the bar for a brandy. The Missus was busy in the parlour, The Guv'nor had gone to bed, and there was no-one to question her action: in any case, Rosie was in a militant mood and she was determined to take the brandy with or without permission.

Frank opened his eyes and gave her a wan smile as she came back.

'Hello, Rosie.'

'Never mind the hellos.' She was rather breathless after running up the stairs and sat down on the edge of the bed. 'Here, drink this.'

'What is it?'

'Never mind what it is – drink it! It will do you good.'

He looked at her doubtfully, but she pressed the glass to his lips and he took a tentative sip.

'Whisky!' he said, making a face.

'Wrong. Brandy.'

'But I don't drink.'

'This isn't drink, it's medicine. Now, come on, down the hatch! You need something. You look like death warmed up.'

He got most of the brandy down and they sat in silence for a few moments. Gradually a touch of colour came back to his cheeks.

'That settles it once and for all,' said Rosie at last. 'You couldn't go back to work even if The Missus wanted you, which she doesn't. And you can't stay here. We'll have to find somewhere for you to go, somewhere you'll be looked after.'

'Mrs Quorn said she doesn't want me?'

'What did you expect? You're sick, you're not up to the work. Mr Parker should never have sent you here in the first place.'

'I'd have done anything to get out of his rotten hostel. I couldn't stand the regular daily doses of piety. Or the way he favoured me over and above the other poor devils because he thought I was a better class of person.'

Rosie remembered that Mr Softley had been able to wring favours from Mr Parker, most notably when he had been persuaded to intervene with The Missus to get Rosie some time off. Had that happened because Mr Softley was an educated man, 'a better class of person'? Rosie's attitude towards Mr Parker had always been near to reverence but now she was beginning to have doubts. Had The Missus been right when she'd said that Frank had been sent to her because Parker did not want a sick man on his hands? Aloud, she said:

'I wouldn't be too quick to knock Mr Parker or his hostel. You might have to go back there.'

'God forbid!' said Frank fervently.

'Have you got any better ideas?'

'About what?'

'Where you could go. I've racked my brains and I can't come up with any answers.'

'I'll find somewhere,' he said.

'The state you're in? Easier said than done.'

He retched suddenly and broke into a violent fit of coughing. It seemed to convulse his entire body and when he had finished she saw the ominous signs of blood on the clean white rag he had been holding to his mouth. She soaked another piece of rag in water and wiped the film of sweat from his forehead.

'See what I mean?' she said gently. 'You're as weak as a day-old kitten. Listen – have you got any family you could go to? Mother and father – brothers and sisters – someone who could take you in?'

'No,' he said quickly, 'no-one.'

'Ah, come on,' Rosie said. 'Don't give me that old acid. You must have some family.'

He smiled thinly. 'I haven't seen them for over two years, Rosie, haven't seen or heard of them.'

'Why not?'

'It's a long sad story.'

'Never mind that! Would they take you in?'

'Even if they would, I wouldn't go.'

'You're making as much sense as a three-legged horse!' she said half-angrily.

He sighed. 'How can I explain it?'

'Try putting one word after another.'

'I fell out with them, Rosie. Not so much with my mother but with my father. You see, when I left college, he wanted me to go up to university and read law.'

'Read? I don't get it.'

'Study law. With a view to becoming a barrister. But I had other ideas. I met a friend at college who was a bit of a rebel, you see, and he talked to me about the Labour Party, lent me books and pamphlets. Occasionally we sneaked off to meetings. Anyway, the upshot was that I became a Labour supporter myself. A socialist, if you like. You know what that means, don't you, Rosie?'

'No,' she said blithely. 'Something bad, I expect. And I suppose the idea of you being a what-do-you-call-it – a socialist – got up your father's nose?'

Frank smiled. 'He didn't like it. But he liked it even less when I told him that I didn't want to go to university.' He looked at her earnestly, his eyes searching her face, as if he were afraid that she might be secretly mocking him. 'I want you to understand, Rosie. You see, I'd always lived a sheltered, privileged life. What did I know about working-people – the people I wished to serve? So I'd decided to leave home and go to live among them, to share their lives. I mean, the only thing I knew about the poor was what I'd read in books. That's not enough! How can you talk about empty bellies if you've never known what it is to have one?'

'So your father kicked you out?'

'It was a bit of both. I would have left anyway. I'd grown disgusted with the way we lived. My parents are not wicked people – in a way, I love them, but their life-style, their snobbery disgusted me.'

'I think you must have a screw loose in your head! You gave up a good home to join the ranks of the poor!' She shook her head and added tartly: 'You thought you'd be doing us a favour, did you?'

'No! It wasn't like that, Rosie. I just believe that in order to change the misery of the people you have to understand that misery, to share it.'

She shook her head again, utterly bewildered. 'And what did you find out?'

'I've learned more in two years than I ever learned at school or college.'

'And bloody nigh killed yourself doing it. I hope you think it was worth it!' She took his thin hand in hers and lowered her voice to a whisper. 'Frank. Listen to me. You are very sick. Do you know that?'

He nodded. 'Yes.'

'Do you know how sick?'

'I think so.'

She took a breath and her voice trembled as she said: 'Do you know that you will surely die if you go on like this? I mean it. Do you want to die?'

'No. But I'm not the only one with this sickness. There are thousands in the same boat. And I will not save myself while they go under. I am not going to buy my life with my father's money.'

He's like a child, she thought, bright-eyed, innocent and obstinate. And irritating! But instinct told her to move cautiously and quietly and so, after a pause, she said:

'What's your father's job? Or doesn't he have to work?'

'Oh, he works all right. Busy as a beaver. He's a barrister, quite a famous one, a KC no less.'

'KC?'

'Kings Counsel. And he's in Parliament. He's an MP.' He checked suddenly and frowned. 'That is between us, Rosie. You won't tell anybody?'

'Who is there to tell?'

'Promise?'

'I promise. Now, you'd better get some sleep.'

He clutched her fingers. 'Don't go.'

'I'm tired. I've work to do tomorrow.'

'Have you read the book I gave you?'

She drew back. 'When do I get time to read?'

'You should find time, Rosie. A little time each day. The truth is in that book – the sharp, plain truth. You will read it, won't you?'

She was conscious of the blood burning in her cheeks, of salt tears pricking at her eyes, and she cried out as if in pain:

'Leave me alone! Why can't you leave me alone!'

151

'Rosie – what is it? I'm sorry if – '

She swept his words aside. 'You come down here, slumming it, talking about living like the poor – what do you know? Why don't you go back to your posh home and leave us be? If you want the truth, I can't bloody well read or write, nothing except my own name. There! I was ashamed to tell you, though God knows why! Why should I be concerned about what the likes of you think? You can keep your book and your fancy ideas, I'm not interested!'

In the short time he had known Rosie, he had seen only the cheerful, optimistic, practical side of her nature and the evident distress that lay behind this outburst surprised and moved him. With an effort he pulled himself up in the bed and said:

'It doesn't matter, Rosie, it doesn't matter!'

'It matters to me!' she responded angrily. And then, flinging out an arm she repeated: '*It matters to me!*'

The arm connected with the dish of tapioca and sent it crashing to the floor. This small insignificant accident which the everyday Rosie would have dismissed with a laugh, now seemed to her to be the last straw, a kind of climax to another exhausting, frustrating day.

Rounding on the hapless Frank, she cried: 'Oh! Bugger! Bugger it! Now look what you made me do!'

She picked up the broken bits of pottery, scraped the pudding from the floor and wiped the floorboards clean – all this in utter silence. Then she marched grimly to the door and went out.

A moment or so later he heard her voice and when he looked up she was standing in the doorway with the old familiar, indestructible, impish smile on her face.

'Sorry about the pudding,' she said. 'You'll have to be satisfied with the pie. Eat it up now – I'll see you in the morning.'

'What about tomorrow?' he asked. 'If I've got to get out – '

'Don't worry about that,' she said cheerfully. 'We'll think of something. 'Night.'

'Goodnight, Rosie,' he said.

CHAPTER EIGHT

1

That night, Rosie went to bed in a state of some confusion, not to say bewilderment. It seemed to her that life was moving too fast, each event treading on the heels of the next at such speed that, before she had time to cope with one problem a new one appeared above the horizon.

Uppermost in her mind was the question of Frank Lambert. She had told him she would think of something – but what? He did not seem to be prepared to help himself, so what could she do for him? What an extraordinary young man he was! At times, so innocent, almost childlike; at others, obstinate to the point of stupidity. And yet, with all this, he was bright and intelligent and brave. She did not really understand his ideas: on the surface, they sounded rather far-fetched and not very practical. But at least he believed in something. He wanted to help people, to raise them up out of the gutter and, God knows, there was plenty of room for that. And unlike so many others he was prepared, in one of Tommo's phrases, to throw the handle in after the hammer, to put his whole being behind his opinions.

Opinions apart, there was also something in his personality which intrigued and held Rosie. He had spoken to her as no other young man before, telling her that she was beautiful, that she had beautiful hands. When he spoke thus and fixed her with his keen grey eyes she felt a strange and fanciful excitement tug at her heart.

Behind Frank there lurked this new problem of The Guv'nor. What had happened that afternoon was frightening in its implications for the future. She had successfully

153

warded him off but, in doing so, she knew that she had made an enemy. It was unlikely that he would touch her again but he was a cunning, mean, vindictive man and he would surely seek ways to revenge himself for her contemptuous rejection of his advances. He was The Guv'nor after all, and he was quite capable of putting such pressure on The Missus that Rosie would be sacrificed in the interests of marital peace.

And, by this route, she came back to herself once more. What on earth had possessed her to tell Frank Lambert that she could not read or write? Held back by shame she had never told anyone before, not even her friend, the late, lamented Mr Softley. There had been times in the past when she suspected that Mr Softley knew of her letterless state but, if that were so, he had been too courteous and sensitive to mention it. And there had been other times when only her quick wit had prevented others from learning her shameful secret.

In a sense Frank was different. He was not of her background or class and, in any case, he was passing through. Tomorrow he would be gone, he did not matter. But to reveal her illiteracy to those around her, to expose herself to their pity or mockery, was something her pride would not allow her to contemplate.

For, to Rosie, it was a matter of shame, of burning shame. She felt somehow handicapped, incomplete, as if her illiteracy was a kind of dread disease, distancing her from others. True, there were many people around her with the same handicap but she felt no community with them; instead, she looked upon those who could read and write, especially the children, with a mixture of envy and shame. Increasingly in recent months she had found herself staring at the incomprehensible pages of a newspaper or a book in a state of bitter frustration. She knew that those mysterious letters and words held the key to a world from which she was barred by her ignorance. And the most stupid thing of all was that pride, stubborn pride, prevented her from doing anything to break down that ignorance!

Rosie fell asleep with these thoughts chasing each other around her head. She was young and healthy and exhausted and so she slept well: when she woke on the stroke of six, the jumble in her head had cleared and, where Frank Lambert was concerned, her subconscious mind had come up with what seemed to be a possible way forward. As soon as she had completed her early morning chores, Rosie put a shawl over her head and shoulders and went round to see Mr Crooks.

2

The weather had taken a sudden yet typical turn overnight and the fine spring sunshine of the past few days had yielded to a bleakness that had more than a touch of winter in its make-up. The lowering sky was a heavy battleship grey and, although it was not actually raining, the atmosphere oozed a sort of dampness, so that by the time Rosie reached Mafeking Street, her shawl was covered with gleaming tear-like drops of water, as if the wool were weeping.

'Good gracious Rosie!' said Mrs Crooks when she opened the door.

She had a dust-cap on her head, a well-used overall covering her comfortable body, and her face and hands were smudged with streaks of black. 'You've properly caught me on the hop. I'm in the middle of black-leading the kitchen stove.'

She pushed a stray lock of hair back under the dustcap, depositing another smudge of black on her forehead as she did so. 'Come in, love, come in! What a change, eh! Like a November day.' And as she closed the door, she added, as if the thought had suddenly struck her: 'Nothing wrong is there?'

'No, no,' said Rosie. 'I wondered if Mr Crooks was around.'

'He's in the shed, cutting up the catsmeat. Tell me, love, have you had your breakfast?'

'Yes, thank you.'

'Wouldn't you like a cup of tea?'

'I can only stay a few minutes. I must get back.'

'Well, all right then.' Mrs Crooks put one reasonably clean

finger under Rosie's chin and tilted it upwards. Usually she carried with her a fresh scent, rather like full-cream milk, but today she smelt strongly of soot and ash. Smiling she said: 'Are you sure nothing is wrong, love?'

'No, everything is fine. Truly. I just want to have a word with Mr Crooks – ask his advice.'

'Well, if he can help, he will, you know that, Rosie. Come on through.'

She led the way down the passage into the kitchen, which had been carefully prepared for the assault on the stove. The chairs were stacked on the table and covered by a sheet and another sheet hung over the dresser. The clock and the ornaments and the collection of horse-brasses which were Mrs Crooks's chief pride had all been taken down and stacked away, lest they be corrupted by soot and dust.

'You must excuse the state of the place, Rosie. I've been giving the stove a thorough old do, cleaning out the flue and everything. I thought it was going to be fine, didn't think we'd need a fire. But as soon as I've got this polished, I'll have to light one, I'm afraid. And that will start the soot and the dust going all over again! No end to it, no end to it at all! Go through, dear, you know the way. You'll find Mr Crooks in the shed.'

Rosie went through the scullery and out at the back door. The house stood on a corner and the yard was much bigger than most of its neighbours, large enough to take a stable for Mr Crooks's pony, a lean-to shelter for the trap, and a roomy hut which served as store-room, work-shop and occasional surgery for sick animals. A pair of sturdy gates provided direct access to the street.

The smell of soot gave way to the strong tangy scent of horse-flesh as Rosie entered the shed. Mr Crooks in a striped blue-and-white apron was cutting a haunch of meat into thin slices and so engrossed was he with this task that he did not notice his visitor. As for Rosie, she watched in fascination as the long thin blade sliced through the meat with a flashing almost breath-taking precision. It occurred to her that either the knife must be very sharp or the horse meat a good deal more tender than the mutton they served up in the pies at

The Winged Horse. She waited until Mr Crooks laid down the knife and then moved forward.

'Why, Rosie!' he said. 'What brings you here?'

He picked up a swab and began to wipe his hands, smiling down at her. Rosie smiled back, responding to his warmth. From the beginning, she had instinctively trusted this big man, with his strong yet sensitive hands, his broad honest face.

'I came to see you, Mr Crooks,' she said.

'Well, well!' he replied. 'I'm flattered. I'm complimented. A visit from a beautiful young lady – that doesn't happen every day of the week!' Leaning towards her, he lowered his voice to a mock confidential whisper: 'Did you see the Old Cheddar?'

Rosie knew this household by now and she understood at once that Mr Crooks was referring, more or less affectionately, to his wife. However, in the early days she had been mystified by the term 'cheddar' and it was only later she found out that it was descended from the cockney rhyming slang for Missus – 'cheese and kisses'.

'Mrs Crooks is cleaning the stove,' Rosie replied.

'Then we had better talk here and keep out of her way,' said Mr Crooks. He waved Rosie towards an old cane armchair and pulled up a box for himself. When they were seated, he said:

'When the Old Cheddar attacks that stove it isn't safe to go anywhere near. She turns that kitchen into a battlefield. And that blacklead brush of hers is like a deadly weapon. That's why I keep that armchair out here. This hut is my refuge, you see, a very present help in trouble.'

'She keeps the place very nice,' said Rosie, remembering the many times she had seen her own face dimly reflected in the beautifully black-leaded stove.

'No denying that,' said Mr Crooks, 'no denying that at all. If people attacked the devil and his works in the same fashion as the Old Cheddar attacks dirt and grime, there'd soon be no sin left in the world. Mark you,' he added, his eyes twinkling, 'I wouldn't much like that. A world without a little bit of sin would be rather tame, eh? Nothing to put a good fighting Christian on his mettle.'

He chuckled to himself as he dug under his apron into a waistcoat pocket, produced a worn silver snuff-box, and sniffed in a pinch of snuff. 'Right, Rosie,' he said, 'what can I do for you?'

'I've come about one of the men at the pub,' she said hesitantly.

'Oh, yes?' He eyed her keenly.

She told him about Frank Lambert, gathering confidence as she went on. When she had finished, he smoothed his greying moustache with a thumb and finger and said:

'This young man is very ill, you say?'

'He has a cough fit to frighten the dead. And he's as weak as a twig. The doctor reckons it's the consumption.'

'And Mrs Quorn intends to put him out today?'

'Yes.'

'Couldn't he go back to Mr Parker's hostel?'

'It would be the death of him.' She paused. 'He will die anyway if he doesn't get proper care and treatment and that. I wondered – I mean – by all accounts his father is a toff, a real toff. He could afford to look after Frank. I was thinking – I was thinking – perhaps I ought to go and see him.'

'I take it that this young man of yours is not on the best of terms with his parents?'

'Not as far as I can make out,' said Rosie. 'His Dad is the main trouble, I think. He got the dead needle when Frank said he wanted to live with the workers and went and jacked in the home and everything.'

Mr Crooks smiled, picturing the scene. 'I'm not surprised. It was a funny thing to do.'

'Daft!' said Rosie. 'Just plain daft.'

'On the other hand,' said Mr Crooks, 'there is something to be said for someone who is determined to practise what he preaches. Your young man was following a good example. Our Lord Jesus Christ did the same thing.' He took another pinch of snuff. 'You think it would help to see the father, do you?'

'I don't know. He might tell me to shove off. But I can't think of anything else.'

'It's certainly worth a try. Do you know where to find Mr Lambert senior?'

'I'm not sure. That's one of the reasons I came to you. Frank says he's a big nob in the law and he's also a what-do-you-call-it – something in Parliament.'

'A member? A member of Parliament?'

'I think that's what he said.'

'Then you are home and dry, Rosie. You can go to the House of Commons and ask to see him.'

There was a small silence, then Rosie muttered: 'I don't think I'd have the nerve. Not to go there.'

'Why, Rosie,' said Mr Crooks, 'you are one of the bravest persons I know.'

'I'm not sure about that. The thought of walking in that place, without so much as a by-your-leave. No, I'd be scared out of my wits.'

'You could write to him first. Write a letter and ask for an appointment.'

'No!' said Rosie, rather too quickly, and she felt her cheeks redden. 'A letter takes time, something's got to be done today.'

'Ah, I'm beginning to understand,' said Mr Crooks, coming to the root of the matter at last. 'You'd like me to come with you to see the young man's father, is that it? Is that why you came?'

'I couldn't think of anyone else I could turn to,' said Rosie meekly.

'Rosie Carr!' he said with an assumed severity. 'You are as quick as a whippet and as cunning as a fox!' He shook his head and stood up. 'You do realise that he may not be in Parliament today? He might be engaged in a law suit or he might be away. Anything.'

'I just thought it might be worth a chance,' she said.

'Well, maybe so.' He sighed. 'All right Rosie. We'll go this afternoon. It'll make a nice outing.'

'I'm ever so grateful,' said Rosie.

'I'm sure,' said Mr Crooks drily. 'Now, if I'm to take the afternoon off, I'd better get started on my rounds. Don't want all the cats in the neighbourhood to complain, do we? I'll meet you on the corner of Fortune Street and the High Road at – say – three o'clock this afternoon?'

'I'll try and make it,' said Rosie. 'I've got to ask The Missus for time off first.'

'You'd better make it, my girl,' said Mr Crooks. 'For one thing is certain. I am not going on my own!'

The thought suddenly occurred to Rosie that Mr Crooks was almost as nervous about the enterprise as she was herself.

3

To Rosie's surprise, The Missus conceded the afternoon with a minimum of fuss. Rosie did not go into detail about the nature of the expedition, confining herself to the statement that Mr Crooks was taking her to see someone who might help Frank Lambert. She got the impression that The Missus had a conscience about turning the young man out and would be relieved if he were found somewhere to go.

Fortunately, the weather had put on a more cheerful face by the afternoon although just to be on the safe side, Rosie took along an umbrella she had borrowed from Lily Hoddle. She wore her best – indeed, her one and only costume – a neat burgundy-coloured outfit, with a white blouse edged with Nottingham lace. Both the blouse and the costume had been bought with her first earnings as a pub pianist. Mr Crooks, who arrived ten minutes late and apologised profusely, said that she looked as smart as a freshly-scraped carrot. Rosie did not understand this but it sounded complimentary, so she let it pass.

She made no reference to Mr Crooks's appearance, thinking that it would not be in keeping for her to do so, but he was dressed in his best dark-grey Chapel suit and looked the essence of respectability.

They travelled most of the way by electric tram, making three changes, and at a quarter past four they were facing a stern, bearded policeman at the entrance to the House of Commons.

'Yes?' said the policeman.

'We've – I mean – we've come to see Mr Lambert, MP,' stammered Mr Crooks. It struck Rosie once again that her

160

companion was, if anything, more nervous that she was herself.

'I take it you mean *Sir Roger* Lambert?' said the policeman, emphasising the title.

'Sir?' said Mr Crooks. 'Yes. Oh, yes, that would be right.'

'Have you got an appointment?' said the policeman.

'Well, no, not exactly,' said Mr Crooks.

'Are you constituents of Sir Roger?'

'Well, no, not exactly,' said Mr Crooks again.

Rosie thought it was time she took a hand. She put on her sweetest smile and said: 'We've come to see Mr – I mean Sir Roger – on a sort of family matter, you see. Very personal.'

'That is it exactly,' said Mr Crooks, gathering his courage.

The policeman smiled at Rosie appreciatively and directed them to repeat their request to his colleagues who were on duty in the main lobby. They walked up a long solemn corridor, spoke to another policeman, and were allowed through on to the marble floor of the central lobby. There were a lot of people about, some simply waiting, others talking in low serious voices. A faint, musty, bookish smell hung in the air. To Rosie, the people, the surroundings, had an air of awesome importance: it was almost an impertinence that she, Rosie Carr, should be there at all. This, after all, was the highest place in the land, the place where all the laws were made. She grew steadily more nervous as they waited while the card bearing their names and the nature of their business was borne away in search of Sir Roger Lambert by a lofty attendant in white tie and tails who carried himself like a guardsman.

They waited and waited. A half-hour slipped by. Some of the seats that ringed the lobby were vacant but Rosie and Mr Crooks remained standing, unsure as to whether these places were reserved for visitors of special importance. If I'd been on my own, Rosie thought to herself, I would have bolted for home a long time ago.

Mr Crooks whispered: 'Do you see who that is?' He nodded towards a tall handsome man with a mane of wavy hair who was moving across the lobby.

'Is it him?'

161

'No, no!' he hissed. 'That is Ramsay MacDonald.'

'Oh,' she said, being none the wiser for this information.

'He is the leader of the Labour Party!' said Mr Crooks.

Rosie looked at the tall man with more interest, remembering that Frank Lambert had spoken of something called the Labour Party. She watched as MacDonald put an arm lightly around the shoulders of an elderly woman and, with a smile on his face, led her away. He seems respectable enough, she thought; on the other hand, I don't suppose he would be allowed in this place if he were otherwise. Another thought occurred to her.

'Have they got any women in Parliament?' she asked. 'I mean, what you call members.'

'Women?' Mr Crooks smiled. 'Politics are not for women, Rosie.'

'Why not?' she asked.

'Not equipped for it. Politics is a man's game.'

Rosie considered this. 'But what about being Queen, like Victoria?'

'Being Queen is not the same.'

Mr Crooks spoke in such a tone of authority that Rosie did not pursue the subject, despite the question that surfaced in her mind. If a woman was good enough to be Queen of England and all that, why wouldn't she be good enough to be a member of Parliament?

Mr Crooks nudged Rosie. 'Sh. I think this might be him.'

She followed his look and saw a tall, imposing-looking man standing beside an attendant who was nodding in their direction. Her first impression was one of blackness. The frock-coat and trousers were a dull black and, above the stern angular face with its spiky black eyebrows, the hair, one lock of which fell with a sort of deliberate casualness across his forehead, was as dark and shiny as the stove in Mrs Crooks's kitchen. The only touch of lightness was provided by the stiff white butterfly-winged collar from which his square chin jutted aggressively. Rosie felt the nervousness come tingling back as he strode towards them.

'Mr Crooks?' The voice was deep and resonant, a perfect match for the formidable body.

'Yes, sir.' Mr Crooks brought his feet together and straightened up, as if he were coming to attention before a superior officer.

'And you are Miss Carr?' He looked at her fully for the first time and she was quick to see a faint almost imperceptible relaxation in his manner, a hint of surprise or admiration in the dark brown eyes. In an odd way, it gave her a little confidence.

'Yes, Sir Roger, sir,' she replied. She wasn't sure whether it was the custom to curtsey to MPs, and compromised with a little respectful bob.

'I am in committee. I have to get back in a few minutes. What is the nature of your business?' asked Lambert. There was no encouragement in his tone.

'It's a personal matter, sir,' said Mr Crooks.

'Yes, yes.' There was a note of irritation in Lambert's voice.

'We – that is – we should like to talk to you about your son.'

'My son?' He looked startled, as if taken off balance, but he quickly recovered his composure and glanced quickly at Rosie.

'My son?'

'Yes, sir,' she replied. It occurred to her that he might have more than one son, so she added: 'Frank. Frank Lambert.'

A young man came up at this moment and touched Lambert on the arm. At the same time he smiled at Rosie and said politely:

'Excuse me.' Turning to Lambert, he said: 'This meeting about salaries for MPs. It's at five o'clock tomorrow, Committee Room 12. You will be there, Roger?'

'What? Oh, yes.'

'Good.' The young man smiled at Rosie once more, and there was a certain bold impudence about his look that brought from Rosie the hint of a smile in return. He was dressed in a neat pearl-grey suit with blue cravat, but the clothes seemed wrong for him somehow. With his light almost flaxen-coloured hair and blue eyes he reminded her of a picture of a sea captain which she had seen once in a copy of *Chums Annual*.

'Sorry to butt in,' he said.

As he walked away, Lambert said: 'You'd better come with me.' He led the way through an archway into a short corridor which was lined on each side by long green-covered benches. Lambert indicated a suitable place and the three of them sat down side by side. A little further along, and on the opposite side, two or three couples were engaged in low-voiced conversation and there was a constant traffic of people passing to and fro. It seemed to Rosie to be an odd place to choose for a private conversation.

'Now, what is this about?' said Lambert. His voice was laced with hostility and as Mr Crooks opened his mouth to respond, he held up a forbidding hand and added: 'No, wait. First, let me establish your credentials. Are you related? This young lady, is she a relative, a niece, perhaps?'

'No, sir,' replied Mr Crooks. 'Rosie is a family friend. A good family friend. She asked me to come with her today.'

'To lend her what one might loosely call moral support?'

'You might say that, sir.'

'And may I ask what you do? Your job – profession?'

'I am a trader in catsmeat,' said Mr Crooks, blushing slightly.

Lambert nodded, sniffing the air in disdain as if he had caught the whiff of catsmeat.

'And do you know my son, Mr Crooks?'

'No, sir. Not exactly. Rosie's the one who knows him.'

'Ah!' said Lambert, nodding grimly. 'I see. It is Miss Carr I have to be concerned with. Well, before you say anything, Miss Carr, let me tell you one thing. It might save time for both of us. If it is your intention to ask me for money, the answer is in the negative. N – O. If, as a result of – of a relationship with my son, you have problems – if you are in any sort of trouble – that is something that you must resolve with him. Do I make myself clear?'

Rosie did not take all this in at first, though as the general drift of it sunk in, she felt her face reddening and her indignation rising. What kind of man was this? The pompous insult was bad enough, but the most extraordinary thing was that he had not even bothered to enquire after his son, to

164

show any concern for him whatsoever. She was too full to speak but fortunately Mr Crooks found both the confidence and the courage to respond.

'That is a very offensive statement, sir. I am surprised that a gentleman of your standing should make accusations without benefit of facts.'

'I made no accusation!' replied Lambert irritably.

'I beg your pardon, sir, but you did. By implication. By implication. If you had a daughter and someone spoke to her in the same way, you would have the right to be offended as I am now on Rosie's behalf. Is it because she is poor and uneducated that you automatically think the worst of her? I tell you this, Sir Roger, you would have to march for a month of Sundays to find a kinder, better, more respectable girl than Rosie.'

And with this, Mr Crooks stood up and took Rosie's arm. 'Come along, Rosie. We shall do no good here. Let us go.'

Rosie shook her head. 'No. We can't just leave it. Something has to be done.' She turned to Lambert, her fear of him swallowed by a quiet anger. 'You can think what you like about me, mister. That's your privilege. It's water off a duck's back as far as I'm concerned. But your son. What about your son? Do you care anything for him? Does it matter to you that he's dying – that he will surely die if he doesn't get help?'

'What?' Lambert looked up at Crooks. 'Is this the truth?'

'It's God's truth, sir.'

It all came out then and, when Rosie had finished, Lambert sat in silence for a full minute. Rosie's anger at the man had died long since and now, seeing his stricken face, she felt only pity. He seemed to have shrunk inside his coat, his face had taken on softer lines. She remembered something Mr Softley had once said. She hadn't understood it then but she did now. He had told her:

'Rich and poor are equal in two things, Rosie. Death and grief.'

Lambert looked at his watch. 'It's almost five-thirty. Rather late to organise anything tonight. Do you think your landlady, Mrs Corn – '

'Quorn,' Rosie interrupted with a smile.

'Do you think Mrs Quorn would let Frank stay for one more night? Tell her that I will pay her, I will pay her well. I'll be over to collect him first thing in the morning.'

'Oh, that's wonderful, wonderful!' said Rosie, her eyes shining.

Lambert reached into a pocket and produced two sovereigns. Handing them to Mr Crooks, he said: 'Give these to Mrs Quorn. They should satisfy her of my intentions and pay for the extra night.'

'More than pay, sir,' said Mr Crooks. 'Very generous. Thank you.'

'Thank me!' Lambert shook his head. 'No. But I thank you, I thank you both. And, Miss Carr, I owe you an apology. What I said – '

'It's all forgot,' said Rosie. 'Least said, soonest mended.'

'At least, let me offer you some tea?'

'No, sir. We best be going. I've got to get back to the pub, you see.'

'If you are out of pocket in any way – '

Rosie checked him. It was surprising, but she felt quite at ease with him now, almost as if their original roles had been reversed.

'No, love. Don't spoil it, eh? Keep your money. We got here and we'll get back. See you tomorrow. Don't be late.'

As they were about to move off, the young man with the flaxen hair and blue eyes came up once more. He stood deliberately in front of Rosie, blocking her progress and looking at her with smiling admiration.

'No,' he said. 'I cannot let you go yet. Not until Sir Roger has introduced us.' He turned to Lambert. 'Come along, my dear chap. You've had the young lady to yourself for the past hour. Introduce me, dammit!'

Lambert seemed none too pleased with this approach and he did the honours brusquely. 'Miss Carr – Mr Crooks – may I present Mr Russell Whitby, Member of Parliament.'

'I am delighted to meet you, Miss Carr,' said Whitby. To Rosie's astonishment he bowed, took her hand and kissed it lightly, so lightly that his lips only just brushed her fingers:

166

she was much more aware of his beard tickling her skin and suppressed a sudden inclination to laugh.

Whitby turned now to Mr Crooks, inclining his head gravely and said: 'Mr Crooks, sir. My pleasure.'

Neither Rosie nor Mr Crooks were quite sure how to respond to all this and it was Lambert who came to their rescue. 'Excuse us, Whitby,' he said, 'Miss Carr and Mr Crooks are just leaving. They are in something of a hurry.'

And with this, he took Rosie's arm and began to lead her to the entrance. As she turned there to say goodbye to him and to confirm the arrangements for the morrow, she saw the tall, broad-shouldered figure of Whitby standing in the centre of the lobby. He was looking straight at her and, as she caught his eye, he smiled yet again and dipped his head in salute.

When they reached the street, Rosie took a deep breath. 'Phew,' she said, 'I'm glad that's over. I feel as if I've just taken off a pair of tight boots.'

'You carried it off very well,' said Mr Crooks.

'I couldn't have managed without you. You were marvellous. The way you spoke out, I mean. I'm ever so grateful.'

And later, on the tram, she asked: 'What did you think of that feller?'

'Oh, not so bad once you get under the crust. He tried not to show it, but he's obviously very fond of his son.'

But Mr Crooks had mistaken the object of Rosie's question. She had been referring not to Sir Roger Lambert but to the young man with the flaxen hair. She decided not to correct Mr Crooks or to press the point, lest he thought she was too taken up with the brief encounter.

Mr Crooks said: 'Mind you, the hardest bit is yet to come.'

'What's that?'

'What is the young man – Frank Lambert – going to say when you tell him? From all accounts, he is an independent character. Suppose he refuses to go home?'

It was quite remarkable to see the transformation in The Missus once Rosie had recounted the events of the afternoon. She had begun by scolding Rosie for being away so long but as the story emerged she became amiable in the extreme. The two sovereigns clearly pleased her, but even more potent in bringing about a change in attitude was the revelation that the father of the sick young man upstairs was an MP, a famous lawyer and, most impressive of all, a Knight of the realm, Sir Roger Lambert, KC, MP, no less. And his son was in her house!

'You should have told me, Rosie,' she said, 'you should have told me before you went. I would have gone with you myself. I'm sure I don't know what Sir Roger must have thought. I mean Mr Crooks is a very respectable man – '

'Mr Crooks was wonderful!' Rosie interjected. 'I couldn't have done it without him.'

'No doubt, dear. But he is a catsmeat man,' said The Missus, putting Mr Crooks firmly in his place. 'I mean, there are limits. Still, what's done is done. Sir Roger is coming here tomorrow, you say?'

'First thing in the morning, ma'am.'

'Hmph.' The Missus eyed Rosie keenly. 'I hope you did not give him a false impression. I may have said things, but you know me, I hope. I had no intention of turning young Mr Lambert out, not in his conditon. That would be contrary to my nature. I'm sure you know that.'

'Yes, ma'am,' said Rosie. In fact, she had not painted too harsh a picture of The Missus to Sir Roger, so that she was able to add with perfect truth: 'All I said was that Frank was very ill and ought to be moved away from here as soon as possible.'

'Good,' said The Missus. 'Capital. Dr Rhys came again this afternoon, while you were out. He was very pleased at the way the young man is being looked after. Now, come along, we mustn't neglect our patient. Let us go and see that he is comfortable.'

Crikey, thought Rosie, smiling to herself as they climbed

the stairs, he's *our* blooming patient now! And then her amusement vanished as she remembered what Mr Crooks had said on the way home. Frank had not yet been told of her interview with his father and of the plan to take him home. How would he react? She would have preferred to tell him herself, privately, but all that was out of her hands now. The Missus had taken possession of the field and was in full cry.

'Well,' said The Missus, bustling into the attic with her best smile well in place, 'and how are we – ' The words faded and the smile turned to disapproval as she saw that Frank was sitting on the edge of the bed, struggling to get dressed.

'What are you doing!' she demanded.

'You said – '

'You will get back into that bed at once!' she interrupted. 'You are in no fit state to go anywhere tonight! Goodness gracious me, I've never heard the like! What kind of woman would I be if I let you go in your condition! Rosie, help me get Mr Lambert back into bed!'

'But you told the doctor,' Frank protested. 'You told him that it was not convenient for – '

'I told him that until you could be taken to a place where you would have proper care and attention, I would see that you were looked after. That is what I told Dr Rhys, and that is what I meant. Convenient? No, I cannot admit that it is convenient. I have a business to run. But I have a heart, I hope. A good many people would vouch for that, I dare swear. Now, back into that bed, if you please.'

She advanced on the hapless young man and began to pull off his trousers, brushing aside his feeble resistance. 'Oh, this is no time for modesty. I'm a married woman and yours won't be the first pair of legs I've seen. And if Rosie hasn't seen a man's legs before, she soon will, so it makes no odds!'

Rosie did not quite see the point of this for, beneath his trousers and shirt, Frank was wearing a long fawn-coloured wollen undergarment that stretched from his neck to his ankles and which did duty both as under-vest and underpants. She had seen him in this outfit on two or three occasions while making his bed and been unimpressed. In her book it was just the sort of outfit to put a girl off men for life.

Frank was too feeble to struggle and seemed relieved when he was back in the bed. He looked helplessly at Rosie, as if hoping that she would provide some explanation for this abrupt turn-about in his circumstances, but Rosie could only make a face at him and wait for The Missus to subside. There seemed to be no likelihood of that for some time.

'Rosie!' she said reprovingly. 'Just look at the state of these sheets! And the pillow-case! What have you been thinking of? I shall want these changed before you go to bed tonight, my girl! I'll give you a pair of fresh sheets and a pillow-slip from my personal cupboard.' She smiled at Frank. 'I keep them in lavender, you know. And I must see if Mr Quorn has a night-shirt he can loan you. We can't have you sleeping in your underwear. Are you listening to me, Rosie?'

'Yes, ma'am.'

'Now, food. Let me see. I have a chicken in the larder. Yes. Some nice tender breast of chicken with plenty of broth. That's the stuff to build you up. And a nice egg custard. I'm sure we can tempt you with that, eh, Mr Lambert?'

'It's very good of you, ma'am,' said Frank, in a tone that revealed his continuing bewilderment, 'but I am not really hungry.'

'Now, we mustn't have that!' said The Missus, lifting his head and thumping the pillow. 'We don't want Sir Roger to think we've been neglecting you, do we?' She dropped his head back on to the pillow, but he lifted it immediately:

'What did you say?'

'Oh, nothing,' said The Missus. For the first time, she showed a trace of embarrassment and glanced quickly at Rosie, as if for help.

'What did you say about – about Sir Roger?' asked Frank. He looked from one to the other for an explanation.

'Well,' said The Missus, gathering herself, 'I suppose you will have to be told sometime. Rosie, you'd better explain.'

'Me?' said Rosie, aware of Frank's stare and of the hostility behind it.

170

'Who better, since you went to see him,' said The Missus, making a pretence of smoothing the top sheet.

'You've seen my father?' asked Frank accusingly.

'This afternoon,' whispered Rosie. 'You see – '

'And a lucky thing for you that she did!' said The Missus, back on course and in full sail. 'Rosie asked me for the time off and naturally, I gave it to her with a good heart. She went to see your father – Sir Roger – with my full blessing. And the upshot of it all is that he is coming here tomorrow morning – in person, mind you, in person – to take you home.'

'Rosie,' said Frank, 'is this true?'

'Yes.' She nodded.

'You promised!' His voice was bitter, his eyes sharp with reproach.

'I had to do something!' she replied, with a touch of anger. 'You won't help yourself, so someone has to, promises or no promises. You need care and all that. Who else could I turn to?'

'And if I say I won't go with him?'

'You'll go all right,' she answered grimly. 'You'll go if I have to carry you down myself. And don't think I wouldn't!'

'That's the ticket!' said The Missus.

He turned his face away from them then and would say no more. Rosie waited a moment or so and then said:

'All right. If he wants to sulk, let him. But he can sulk on his own as far as I'm concerned.'

5

Later that night she went up to change the sheets as bidden. The Missus had already taken Frank some chicken broth and an egg-custard but these dishes stood on the table by the bed almost untouched. Food apart, The Missus had clearly been active in other directions: a bright counterpane now covered the greyness of the blankets, a couple of rugs broke up the bareness of the floorboards, a clean white cloth covered the table on which, besides the broth and the custard, there was a bowl of fruit.

'Crikey!' said Rosie, 'she's really been pushing the boat out, hasn't she!'

He remained silent, looking at her with listless eyes.

'Oh. We've still got the hump, have we?' she said crisply. 'Well, that suits me. Now, let's have you out of that bed for five minutes while I change the sheets.'

As she advanced to the bed, he suddenly took her hand, holding it with surprising strength. 'Rosie. Why? Why did you do it?'

She sat down on the edge of the bed, shaking her head. 'I told you, lovey. I had to. No other choice. Oh, The Missus is blowing all hot now but that's only because she's suddenly found out that your old man is a toff. If he doesn't turn up tomorrow, if he changes his mind and doesn't come at all, she'll soon blow cold again. And then it will be marching orders for you, old china. The street.'

'Rosie, I don't want to leave.'

'I told you, one way or another, you've got no choice.'

'I don't mean that. Don't you understand?'

'I'm trying to. Look, I know it means swallowing your pride. I know you don't want to be beholden to your father, but needs must when the devil drives. What good will you be to that – what-do-you-call-it – that cause of yours if you make a dead martyr of yourself?'

'Rosie, I love you!' Frank almost shouted the words.

It took a moment for the words to sink in. She looked at him in bewilderment, unable to respond in words.

'I mean it, Rosie. I truly love you. You are the best and most beautiful girl I've ever met.'

'Now,' she replied, gathering her wits, 'don't let's have any of that rubbish!' She tried to remove her hand but he held it tight.

'I love you, Rosie. I think I fell in love with you that first morning. I can't describe what it is like. I think of you night and day, you are never out of my mind. I listen for your footsteps on the stairs, I count the minutes waiting for you to come. I love you.'

172

There was quite a long silence, and then she said gently:
'Listen. You think you love me – '

'I know I do.'

'You've only known me a couple of days.'

'Two days, two years. What does it matter? You can't measure feelings by the clock. I love you.'

'All right. I believe you, thousands wouldn't. Now, I tell you what you have to do. You have to go home tomorrow and you have to get well. When you're better, completely better, that'll be the time to talk about love.'

'If I do that, will you promise – '

'No, I'm making no promises. I've broke one I made to you already. No. Get better, then we'll both be in a position to talk. Right?'

'As long as there's some hope – '

'While there's life, there's hope,' she said cheerfully. 'Now, let's have you out while I change the sheets.'

To him, and even to herself, she seemed surprisingly calm and matter-of-fact, but she could feel her heart pumping as though in desperation and her head felt as though it were filled with flying birds.

CHAPTER NINE

1

An eager early morning sun woke Rosie, throwing its bright beams on to her face. She tossed back the sheet and relaxed for a while in the caressing warmth; the problems of the day ahead surfaced only slowly and, as usual, they did not seem so bad in the light of this new morning. Indeed, she felt oddly happy and light-hearted, as if this day had a special quality that set it apart from others.

She could only trace the source of this happiness back to the previous evening, to what Frank had said to her. Of course, it was foolish, impossible, nothing would or could come of it. In a few hours, he would be gone and she would probably never see him again. But whatever happened, the fact was that he had said he loved her, and this was the first such declaration of her life.

Was he in love with her? She had no doubt that he thought he was. She had known him only a short while but she had seen enough to realise that he was incapable of insincerity. On the other hand, he had shown himself to be a naive, impractical, dreamer of dreams. She loved his talk of a new world, she admired his willingness to sacrifice himself for his ideals, but her commonsense stopped short of accepting what she saw as impossible visions. And then again, she thought ruefully, it may be that I haven't the intelligence to understand his ideas.

Did she love him? It was an intriguing thought. There was something compelling about him, something that made him seem different from the other men she knew. And there was a gentleness there too, a quality she had seen little of in her life.

From the beginning Frank had treated her as an equal, as a person in her own right and, Mr Softley and one or two others apart, that too had not come her way very often. Yes, she was drawn to him, no doubt of that. But was that enough? If it came to the point could she marry him, live with him, and be happy?

She pulled herself sharply away from this line of thought. Rosie, she scolded, who is being fanciful now, who is dreaming dreams? Frank hadn't mentioned marriage or any such thing. In any case, the idea was an impossible one. Not only was he a very sick young man, he was also from a different class. It was impossible to imagine that his father, Sir Roger Lambert, KC MP, would accept Rosie Carr, an uneducated barmaid as a member of his family! Stick to your own kind, she warned herself, above all, keep your feet on the ground.

She got out of bed and pulled off her nightgown. The sun's rays bathed her flesh, giving it a light golden texture and, for a few moments, she stood there turning her body this way and that in an effort to see it reflected in the small and inadequate mirror on the wash-stand. Was she beautiful, as Frank had said? The legs were long and slim, the hips narrow, the stomach gently rounded, the breasts firm and high. And the face, the face wasn't too bad either. The eyes were clear and wide, the nose straight, the lips full and generous but not too much so. She was lucky with her teeth too. The looks of so many girls were spoiled by poor, discoloured teeth, but hers were white and regular.

Yes, she supposed she was what might be called beautiful. Frank had said as much and yesterday the handsome MP with the corn-coloured hair had stared at her with open, insolent admiration. Other men had done the same. She wondered what it would be like to lie in bed with a man, to be as naked as she was now and to feel his hands sliding across her skin.

She began to dress hurriedly, conscious of a tingling moistness between her thighs and of an exciting glow in her flesh which had nothing to do with the sun and everything to do with this sudden invasion of wicked thoughts. The sooner she covered her body the better.

She went downstairs, dealt with the inevitable queue of waifs, made a pot of tea and prepared a light breakfast for Frank. He was awake when she took it in to him and seemed to be refreshed and rested.

'I've brought you a boiled egg and some nice thin bread-and-butter,' she said. 'And I don't want you leaving anything. You can't travel on an empty stomach.'

'Rosie,' he said, 'I've been thinking.'

'Not again!' she said with a little smile. 'All that thinking will be the death of you!'

'I've been thinking about what you said. You're right, of course. I've got to shake off this illness, get myself fit, otherwise I'll be no good to you or to anyone else.'

'Now you are beginning to make sense,' she said.

'For one thing, I don't have the right to talk to you – I mean, talk about the future – until I am fit and well. But when I am, when I am back on my feet, we will talk about it. You promised me that.'

'I don't remember making a promise,' she said. 'Still you get yourself better, like you said, then we'll see.'

'I meant what I said, Rosie. I love you.'

'Now,' she said, 'don't start that again.'

'I only want you to remember,' he said. 'When I'm away, I want you to remember. That's all.' And, after a pause, he added: 'Will you come and see me?'

'I don't know about that,' she said warily.

'Please,' he said. 'If I send you the address, will you come?'

'We'll see,' she said again, 'we'll just have to see. Now, I must get a wiggle on. Work to do. When you've had your breakfast, you'd better get washed and dressed. Your father said he would be here early. Can you manage on your own?'

'Yes, I'll be all right.' As she moved to the door, he checked her. 'Rosie.'

'What is it now?'

'Would you do something for me?'

'Like what?'

'Something for yourself too.'

'Well?'

'You won't be offended by what I'm going to say?'

176

'How do I know until you've said it?'

'I want you to learn to read and write.'

She flushed angrily. 'That's my business! I was a fool to tell you. There's no call for you to stick your nose into – '

'Rosie,' he interrupted, 'Rosie! Don't be annoyed. I only want to help. You see, there is a thing called the Workers' Educational Association. The WEA. It's run by ordinary people, really, nothing to get alarmed about. They run classes in all sorts of subjects – evening classes for working-people. They even have a course for people like you – you know, people who through no fault of their own have never learned to read or write.'

'When would I get time to go to such a thing?'

'You could try. I met the local secretary once – a woman called Margot Jones. She lives not far away – in 27 Lands-downe Road. You could go and see her. At least you could do that. Will you?'

'I can't just go and knock on the woman's door – '

'You can! She wouldn't mind at all.'

'How much does it cost?'

'Whatever you can afford. In your case, they probably wouldn't charge anything.'

'I'm not out for charity,' she said proudly. 'I can pay my way.'

'Of course. Anyway, Margot Jones will explain it all to you. Margot Jones, 27 Landsdowne Road. Will you remember?'

'I expect so,' said Rosie.

'Think how marvellous it would be to be able to read books and newspapers, to write letters! You are clever, Rosie, naturally clever. You'll pick it up in no time. I mean it.'

For the third time, Rosie said: 'Well, we'll see. We'll just have to see.'

2

Clearly, Sir Roger Lambert's notion of what was early morning differed in a marked degree from that of Rosie and of the general mass of people in the area around The Winged Horse. He arrived at last, shortly after ten o'clock, when Rosie had almost given him up.

She was made aware of his presence by one of her regular urchins whom she had posted to keep watch. This youngster came rushing into the bar where Rosie was polishing the brass rails in a state of some excitement, shouting:

'He's coming, Rosie, he's coming!'

'All right, Danny,' she said, 'no need to shout.'

She gave a final rub to the length of rail, put the polish and dusters out of sight, and washed her hands, doing everything quite deliberately for she was quite determined not to be rushed, to stay calm. He had taken his time, she told herself, so I will take mine. She touched up her hair, removed the coarse apron and went to the door.

A motor-car had just come to a halt in the street outside, a long, gleaming, magnificent monster of a motor-car. Admittedly Rosie had no great experience of such vehicles, but she had never seen one quite so splendid as this. The passengers were protected from the weather by a roof and windows, the seats looked to be upholstered and the metal work shone like mirrors. A burly man in a blue uniform, cap and shining black leather leggings leaped from his seat behind the steering-wheel and opened one of the doors. At the same time he barked haughtily at the crowd that gathered to watch and admire!

'Stand back there! Stand back, if you please!'

It took Rosie a moment or two to recognise Sir Roger, for he had discarded his black legal and parliamentary outfit and was wearing a brown tweed Norfolk jacket with knee-breeches to match. In these clothes and in these familiar surroundings, she thought he looked smaller and certainly less formidable.

Rosie moved forward but before she could greet him she was pushed aside and The Missus swept past her. She had on a brand-new dress in the latest fashionable colour of purple, and her hair was piled and pinned up in Queen Alexandra style. The scent of her perfume could be picked up at ten paces. 'Dressed up like a sore finger,' was how Rosie described her later to Tess Crooks, 'dressed up like a sore finger, speaking as if she'd got a pickled onion in her mouth, and smelling like a blooming flower-shop.'

It was a reasonable description in the circumstances. The Missus advanced on Sir Roger, extended a plump beringed hand and said, in a carefully-rounded tone:

'Do I have the honour of addressing Sir Roger Lambert?'

'I am Sir Roger Lambert, yes,' he said brusquely, lifting his hat in acknowledgment but ignoring the hand.

'Ah,' the Missus realised that the out-stretched hand was superfluous to requirements and withdrew it with no trace of embarrassment. 'May I be permitted perhaps to introduce myself in person? I am Mrs Quorn, landlady of this establishment.'

'The landlady? Ah, yes. Capital.' Sir Roger pulled out a watch and studied it briefly. 'I have little time, Mrs Quorn. Is my son ready to leave?'

'Perhaps, may I be permitted to suggest that we move inside?' said Mrs Quorn in the same affected voice. She glanced at the crowd, as if to indicate that it would be better for him not to be seen in such company.

'As you wish,' said Sir Roger. As he moved to the door his eye fell on Rosie and he stopped before her. His long stern face relaxed in a smile, and raising his hat, he said:

'Miss Carr. A great pleasure to see you again.'

'Good morning, Sir Roger, sir.' She dropped him a little bob.

'How is my son?'

'Much the same, sir. He had a good night, I think, and is well-rested.'

'Is he able to walk?'

'Oh, yes, sir. He isn't strong, but he can walk. But he is very ill, like I said. He's going to need a lot of doctoring.'

'And he shall have it, rest assured of that. I have a specialist standing by at home.'

He smiled again and nodded, then went inside where he was greeted immediately by The Guv'nor. It was Mr Quorn's usual custom to slump around the house before the midday opening in old trousers and a worn cardigan but this morning, like his wife, he had dressed up to the occasion. Indeed, it seemed as if he had decided to outshine The Missus, for he was wearing his newest waistcoat, a garment of such striking redness that, in Rosie's eyes, it made him stand out like a Royal Mail post-box.

No, she thought, as he bobbed towards Sir Roger, not so much a post-box as a bird. With his plump red belly and little beady eyes he reminded her of a robin she had once seen hopping around in Hadley Wood.

'Welcome, sir, welcome!' said The Guv'nor in his deep throaty voice. 'Mr Quorn at your service.'

Sir Roger nodded politely. 'My pleasure.'

'A glass of something?' said The Guv'nor, waving a hand towards the bar. 'I have a good Madeira, if that's to your taste. Or French brandy, the best, no rubbish. Scotch whisky, if you'd prefer it.'

'I won't just now, if you don't mind,' replied Sir Roger. 'It's a little early in the day for me.'

'What I do have,' said The Guv'nor, 'is a very special cream sherry if – '

'No, my dear,' said The Missus. 'We mustn't press the gentleman. You heard what he said.'

'Very well, my pet,' said The Guv'nor, sending just the hint of a scowl in her direction. 'That is a fine motor-car you have, sir. I caught a view of it from upstairs. A remarkable machine, if I may say so.'

'A Daimler,' said Sir Roger.

'Ah,' said The Guv'nor, as if he had expected nothing less. 'You can't beat a Daimler, they say. Have to go a long way to beat a Daimler.'

'These motor-cars,' said The Missus. 'They're becoming quite the thing. Fair taking over. Won't be long before you'll be hard put to find a single horse on the streets of London.'

'I doubt that, my pet,' said The Guv'nor, 'I very much doubt that.'

'Mark my words,' she said.

The conversation faded and there followed a long, awkward silence. At least, it seemed long to Rosie although it lasted only a few moments. She was relieved when a little, impatient cough from Sir Roger filled the void.

'I assume we are waiting for my son?'

'Shall I go and help him down, ma'am?' said Rosie quickly.

'Of course, girl, of course. Don't stand there. Can't you see that Sir Roger is in a hurry!'

As Rosie moved towards the stairs she heard The Guv'nor start to speak and she paused beyond the door to listen: 'A fine young man, sir. It has been an honour and a privilege to have him under our roof. Been like one of the family, he has. We shall miss him. And if I may say so, sir, if I may be so bold as to make the point, Mrs Quorn there has been like a mother to him. No, no, my pet – no use your denying it. She's too modest, sir, that is her trouble. Her principal fault, you might say. Modest and generous. No half-measures with this lady. She's been like a mother to that lad, and that's the Bible truth.'

Smiling at this comedy, Rosie moved on up the stairs, out of listening range. As she followed the curve of the stairs towards the attic, she heard a furious burst of coughing and, hurrying on, found Frank sitting half-way up. His small bundle of possessions lay on the stair beside him.

'What do you think you're doing?' she demanded.

It took him a full minute to bring the cough under control and answer her. 'I heard the commotion outside. Saw the car. Thought I'd come down.'

'You should have waited for me,' she said reproachfully. She moved the bundle aside and sat down beside him. 'Feel bad, do you?'

'I'll be all right in a minute.'

'It'll take more than a minute before you're all right, my lad. That chest of yours is going to be a long job.'

'How is my father?'

'Oh, he'll pass, with a good push.' She paused. 'You're always asking me to make promises. Will you make me one?'

'If you're going to ask me to forget you, not to see you again – '

'No, nothing like that.'

'Then I promise.'

'When you get better again, promise that there will be no more of this living like the workers – all that rubbish. There's no rhyme nor reason to it. There are enough sick and hungry people in the world without you adding to their number.'

'I can't give up what I believe in.'

'I didn't say that. Did I say that? Believe what you want, but don't kill yourself doing it.'

He nodded. 'I promise.'

'Cross your heart and hope to die?'

'Cross my heart.' She felt him take her hand and a little tremor of feeling, of affection, quivered within her.

'I shall miss you, Rosie.'

'I'll miss you too.' And that's the truth, she thought, the gospel truth.

'Truly?'

'Truly.'

'You are really beautiful, Rosie. A beautiful person.'

'Now,' she said gently. 'None of that. You'll give me big ideas.'

'I love you.'

'Yes. So you said before.' She pulled her hand away. 'We must get you downstairs. Your father will be champing at the bit.'

'Wait,' he said. 'I don't want to say goodbye to you downstairs, in front of everybody.' He took her hand again. 'Not goodbye. Au revoir. Au revoir, my darling Rosie, and bless you for everything.'

She felt the tears prick at her eyes and, on impulse, leaned forward and kissed his cheek. He drew her to him then and kissed her lightly and very tenderly on the lips. She cupped a hand against his cheek and felt tears there. They stayed together for quite a long time, exerting no pressure, their lips just touching, then she broke away suddenly and jumped up, brushing her eyes with the back of her hands.

'That's enough of that!' she said briskly. 'Come on, my old soldier, let's get you downstairs.'

Not for the first time, Rosie wondered why so many people, men especially, were afraid to show their true emotions. Apart from her mother, Frank was the only person who had ever called her 'darling' or given voice to his feelings.

Yet here was that same Frank, the young man who a few minutes ago had wept at the thought of leaving her, standing before his father as stiff as a plank and speaking to him as to a stranger. And Sir Roger was no better. She had played the scene over in her mind a half-dozen times, trying to visualise how they would react to each other, but none of her mental pictures had been like this!

'Hello, father.' Very calm, very cool.

'Frank.' Very stiff and formal.

A pause, then: 'Sorry to have put you to all this trouble, father.'

'No trouble. Least I could do.'

'Is mother all right?'

'Oh, yes. She keeps as well as can be expected. She'll be all the better for seeing you.' Another pause, longer than before, and then Sir Roger continued: 'Well, I think we should take our leave of these good people and be on our way.'

Rosie found it all very disappointing. She had hoped to see an emotional reunion, her romantic instincts cried out for it, but both Frank and his father seemed determined to remain stiff and aloof, masking their feelings. Perhaps, thought Rosie, perhaps that's the way toffs behave to each other. It was all very strange.

Stranger still was the surprise Sir Roger had in store for her. He stood for a moment, plucking at his lips with a finger and thumb as if trying to make up his mind about something and then, turning to The Missus, he said:

'Mrs Quorn, I wonder if it would be possible for me to borrow Miss Carr for a few hours?'

'Miss Carr?' The Missus did not immediately connect this title with Rosie and it took her a second or two to gather herself. 'Miss Carr? Oh, you mean Rosie.'

'She seems to be an excellent nurse and I thought she might be of some use on the journey. If she wouldn't mind, that is. And there is my wife. Lady Lambert is not well enough to travel and she has expressed a wish to meet Miss Carr so that she might thank her for all she has done.'

Crikey, thought Rosie, The Missus is not going to like that. Nor did she. Her eyes rested on Rosie, glinting like steel, and her voice was edged with ice, as she replied:

'Well, Rosie, you are a free agent. You heard what the gentleman said. You must decide. It is up to you. Don't let considerations of work influence you. We shall manage for a few hours without you, I have no doubt of that. Well?'

Rosie looked at the grim face of The Missus, and knew that she was silently ordering her not to accept. She was about to say no, the word was almost on her tongue, when Sir Roger, who had read the situation well, cut in crisply:

'Then it's settled. Thank you, Mrs Quorn, it is very good of you. I will see that Miss Carr is delivered back safe and sound by mid-afternoon at the latest.'

'Very good of you, I'm sure,' said The Missus coldly.

'We do recognise – my wife and I – that we are in your debt also, Mr Quorn. And Mrs Quorn of course. We should like to recompense you in some measure for what you've done.'

'Why, thank you – ' Mr Quorn began.

'That will not be necessary,' interjected The Missus. 'It is good of you, Sir Roger, but we did what we did for the young man because – well – we know of no other way. We turn no-one away from these doors, sir. I fancy you might find a good many people to vouch for that. As for the cost of the accommodation, of the beef-tea and the milk-puddings and the chicken and all the rest of the special invalid food, I am content to bear that burden. What is money compared to the care and comfort of one in need? No, I am sure I speak for my husband on this. We did not go into this for payment, sir, and we ask no payment now. I am right, I hope, Mr Quorn?'

'As always, my angel,' said Mr Quorn, though not with any excess of enthusiasm.

'I apologise if I unwittingly offended,' said Sir Roger gravely. 'Your sensitivity on this matter does you much credit. Perhaps I might make an alternative suggestion. Suppose I were to leave, say, five pounds in your keeping. As a donation. Yes, let us call it that. A donation towards the charitable work to which you are both so deeply and sincerely committed.'

'Well,' said The Missus, 'that puts the matter in a different light entirely. That does put a new complexion on things. Five pounds is a very generous sum. A person could do a great deal of good with five pounds at her disposal. But I must leave the decision to my husband. He has a head for such matters.'

She beamed in the direction of The Guv'nor knowing that on this subject at least she could trust his judgment, although he seemed a little surprised to be thus consulted. He pulled at his ear and murmured to himself as though debating the pros and cons of the problem, and then delivered his verdict:

'As you say, my pet, five pounds will go a long way. I think, in the circumstances, we might accept the offer. Thank you, sir.'

'Capital!' Sir Roger counted out five sovereigns and made as though to hand them to The Guv'nor. The Missus was too quick for him, however, and interposing herself between them she accepted the money with a smile.

'Thank you. There will be a good many people who will bless you for this.' She turned sharply on Rosie. 'Don't stand there, girl! Sir Roger hasn't got all day. Go and tidy yourself up, make yourself presentable!'

'There is no need – ' Sir Roger began.

'No-one goes from this house looking like a tramp! We are humble people, but we have our pride, I hope. Hurry, Rosie!'

Unable to believe her good fortune, her heart thudding with excitement, Rosie fled to her room.

4

Ten minutes later, Rosie emerged from The Winged Horse. She had put on her burgundy-coloured costume and her best hat, a simple boater-shaped creation encircled by a broad red ribbon that matched the costume. The waiting crowd greeted her like a visiting princess, applauding and cheering. Blushing slightly, she dropped them a cheeky, half-curtsey in response.

There were more cheers when the stiff-necked chauffeur held the door open for Rosie. She almost spoiled the effect by a slight stumble on the running-board, but she recovered quickly and took a seat next to Sir Roger and opposite Frank.

A familiar face appeared at the window and she saw Tommo looking at the interior of the motor-car in grinning astonishment. He glared at Rosie and pulled the door open. Oh no, Rosie thought in panic, don't show me up, Tommo, please don't start creating a scene! Don't show me up!

'Strike me pink!' said Tommo. 'We are putting on the dog!'

She felt the heat burning in her cheeks. 'I'm going visiting.'

'With these toffs?' He grinned cheekily at the Lamberts.

'Yes. Please, Tommo, shut the door. You're holding us up.'

The motor-car shuddered as the chauffeur cranked the engine into life and Tommo jumped back.

'Watch your step, Rosie!' he shouted. 'Remember what the old woman said. When a girl goes out with a gent she should keep one hand on her purse and the other on her ha'penny.'

'Stand clear, if you please, stand well clear!' ordered the chauffeur. He closed the door and climbed in behind the wheel. A couple of small explosions drove the crowd back and then the car jerked forward.

Tommo raised his battered top-hat in an ironical gesture of farewell, the crowd cheered again, a few urchins formed themselves into a running escort for a hundred yards or so, and then they were free and clear and heading down the High Street at a steady fifteen miles an hour.

It took Rosie a good five minutes to recover from her embarrassment. Inwardly, she was seething with anger. I'll clean that Tommo when I see him, she told herself fiercely, I'll put a new face on his bloody head. I'll put the lid on his bloody antics. Showing me up like that! I'll kill the bugger, I'll murder him!

Sir Roger was evidently thinking of Tommo also, for he interrupted Rosie's silent threat of vengeance with the comment:

'The young man in the top-hat seemed to be a most amusing character.'

'He likes to think so,' said Rosie, 'he likes to think he's a funny party. Not in my book. In my book he's about as funny as a corpse at a funeral.'

'Oh,' said Sir Roger, slightly taken aback, 'I thought he might be a friend of yours.'

'A friend? Of mine?' She sniffed indignantly. 'Never in a million years. I wouldn't have him as a friend if – ' She was about to say 'if his backside was dripping with diamonds' but remembering herself in time she finished with: 'if he was the last man on God's earth.'

Frank smiled at her and she smiled back, relaxing a little and telling herself not to be silly, not to allow her disgust with Tommo to spoil this outing. After all, here she was, little Rosie Carr, skivvy and barmaid and part-time pub-entertainer, riding in a motor-car for the very first time in her life! She would enjoy herself and let Tommo go hang!

In a surprisingly short time they had left the streets of terraced houses behind and were out in the country beyond Edmonton, moving along the Hertford Road towards Enfield Lock and Waltham Cross. On either side the land rolled gently to the horizon, neat fields of green and brown broken only by the occasional grand house or small clusters of farm buildings and cottages. The trees were bright in their fresh spring green and in the small orchards the cherries and apples were draped in shawls of pink and white blossom.

At one point, a score or more of birds, disturbed by the unfamiliar noise of the motor-car, rose in protesting flight from the edge of a wood. Rosie caught the flash of glossy, colourful plumage: green necks rising to heads that were splashed with red, black crescent markings on the plump brown bellies. Frank saw her wondering look and said:

'Pheasants.'

'They're beautiful!' said Rosie.

'They're a good eating bird too,' said Sir Roger drily.

'People eat them?' said Rosie, aghast.

'Don't you approve?' asked Sir Roger.

'It's wicked,' said Rosie. 'To kill and eat something so beautiful.'

'You eat chicken, I suppose?'

'When I can get it, yes.'

'And beef and mutton?'

'Yes,' said Rosie, sensing that she was being led into a trap.

'I see,' said Sir Roger. 'You don't mind if the plain ordinary creatures of the field are killed and served at table. It is only the colourful ones that you are concerned with. An interesting viewpoint.'

'You're sending me up,' mumbled Rosie, feeling the flush in her cheeks yet again.

'It's a mistake to argue with my father,' said Frank. 'He can never forget that he is a lawyer and a politician. He loves to score debating points.'

'I'm sorry,' said Sir Roger, 'I didn't mean – ' He leaned forward and patted Rosie's hand. 'I'm sorry.'

'That's all right,' said Rosie cheerfully. 'My fault. I was born with my brains in my boots.'

'At any rate, you are enjoying the drive?'

'Oh, it's lovely! Really lovely!' replied Rosie, her eyes sparkling. 'It was ever so good of you to bring me.'

'A pleasure to have you,' said Sir Roger courteously. He glanced out of the window. 'Ah, almost there. Are you familiar with this part of the world?'

'No,' said Rosie. 'Furthest I've been is Edmonton. Or Hadley Wood. Except when – ' She was about to mention the early travels with her mother but, deciding that this might lead to awkward questions and embarrassing answers, she checked and added: 'I don't even know where we are.'

'Cheshunt,' said Sir Roger. 'Just beyond Waltham Cross. We have a family house here. It's where Frank was born.'

To her left, through the fringe of trees that lined the road, Rosie saw that the farms had now given way to parkland. She caught a glimpse of ordered lawns, the glint of water and, rising above terraced gardens, a large rambling house. And soon she had a clearer view of the house as they drove in through a pair of huge white ornamental gates. It stood at the end of a long wide drive, its mellow red brick and mullioned windows glowing in the sun. Stone the crows, thought Rosie, it must have a hundred rooms!

'Walton Manor,' said Sir Roger with a little smile. He was clearly enjoying Rosie's bemusement.

'This is where you live?' she whispered, her eyes wide.

'Oh, yes. This is our home. And Frank's.'

'Crikey!' said Rosie. But what she was thinking might have surprised him.

All those rooms, all those windows, all those stairs to scrub and wash and polish and keep clean and tidy! I'm glad it's not my blooming house!

5

The journey had tired Frank and he was taken upstairs immediately on arrival, to be attended and examined there by two doctors. One doctor, thought Rosie, would have been enough. They probably charged twice as much for a visit as Dr Rhys, which meant that their combined fees could be as much as eight shillings or more!

But then extravagance seemed to be the order of the day in this incredible house. For one thing, there appeared to be servants everywhere, men servants, women servants, grooms, gardeners, stable-boys. While she was waiting for Lady Lambert to see her, Rosie was taken to the kitchen by the housekeeper, Miss Pritchard, and she counted at least four people, women and girls, at work there, quite apart from others who came and went. As for the kitchen itself, Rosie had never seen such a place, never seen so large a stove, so long a table, so big a dresser, so many shelves stocked with so many dishes and provisions. She calculated that the kitchen at The Winged Horse would fit into this one at least four or five times.

Miss Pritchard was a short sturdy lady of middle-age,

dressed in a severe dress of black bombasine. Her dark hair, streaked with grey, was brushed up in the prevailing style and bound into a large bun. A cluster of keys rattled on the chain-belt at her waist. Rosie found it hard not to stare at the small black growth on her left cheek from which three or four hairs stuck out like small quills or at the fringe of hair on her upper lip, which was the nearest thing to a moustache she had ever seen on a woman. To match this, the housekeeper had a voice that was almost masculine in its depth and resonance.

Miss Pritchard was a bustler. She bustled about from place to place, from person to person, moving at a speed not far short of running, scarcely pausing to sit down or draw breath. Her orders, reprimands and cajoleries were issued in the same brisk way and came out in short sharp bursts, rather in the manner of smoke signals, leaving no-one in any doubt as to who was in command.

Rosie was fascinated by her and Miss Pritchard, in turn, was clearly intrigued by the sudden appearance of this young lady. The one thing already clear was that Miss Rosie Carr was not on a level with the people upstairs. To someone of Miss Pritchard's experience, the clothes and the style (or lack of it) underlined this truth, while the fact that Sir Roger had despatched her to the kitchen placed Rosie firmly in her proper social station.

Still, there were other unexplained aspects of the matter, so Miss Pritchard, in between her domestic forays, set out to satisfy her curiosity.

'Have you come far, Miss Carr?'

'Oh, miles. Miles,' said Rosie, gulping down a mouthful of ham sandwich.

'From where, may I ask?'

'Tottenham, ma'am.'

'Your home is there?'

'Lor, no. Well, yes, I suppose in a way. I work in a pub, you see. Do you know The Winged Horse, corner of Fortune Street and the High Road?'

'I am not acquainted with public houses either in Tottenham or anywhere else!' said Miss Pritchard, with more than a hint of rebuke in her voice.

'Ah,' said Rosie, unabashed. 'It's a good pub. If ever you find yourself down Tottenham way, you want to pop in. The saloon, mind, not the public. Public wouldn't suit you at all.' And, remembering herself, she added: 'If you'll pardon me for saying so, ma'am.'

'You live in this public house, do you?'

'Oh, yes. Got a nice room. Used to have the attic, but now I've got a lovely room on the first floor.'

'And what do you do there?'

'Oh, all sorts. Lots of skivvying work. Help behind the bar most nights, and I play the joanna – I mean the piano – in the saloon. To entertain the customers. I like that, I really enjoy that.' She wasn't sure whether the look in Miss Pritchard's eyes reflected shock or wonder, so she added: 'I'm not a real piano player, not a proper one. But I can knock out most tunes.'

What on earth is Sir Roger doing with a girl of this sort, thought Miss Pritchard. Then she remembered Frank's arrival. Was that the association? She was prevented from pursuing this question by the arrival of Mr Pooley, the butler. Tall, broad-faced, with sleek silvery hair, he carried himself like a guardsman. His calm aloofness was a perfect contrast to the flurry that Miss Pritchard seemed to generate.

'Sir Roger and her ladyship wish to speak with you, Miss Pritchard.'

'With me, Mr Pooley?' She seemed surprised. 'Are you sure you don't mean Miss Carr here?'

'I am quite sure, Miss Pritchard,' said Mr Pooley coolly. 'Your presence is required in the drawing-room.'

No love lost between those two, thought Rosie. And she smiled inwardly as, before following Miss Pritchard to the stairs, the butler gave Rosie the sort of appraising look with which she was now becoming familiar. More surprisingly, the hauteur cracked for a split-second as he half-closed one eye in a conspiratorial wink. He's a cheeky one, Rosie decided. I bet the maids have to keep an eye out for him!

Fifteen minutes later, it was Rosie's turn. She was ushered into the drawing-room where Sir Roger and his wife were waiting. Miss Pritchard stood respectfully to one side, with a long-suffering look on her face. To Rosie, the room seemed enormous and its furnishings impossibly rich and fine: she felt dwarfed and a little frightened by it all. Morever, she had an uncomfortable feeling that she was on show, that she was about to be put to some kind of test.

'So you are Miss Carr!' said Lady Lambert, nodding. 'Come nearer, girl, and let me take a good look at you.'

Rosie reddened, stepped forward and dropped a small curtsey to the large, glittering woman who sat upright on the sofa, facing her. The glitter came from a motif of small shining stones which decorated the top of her dress, from the jewellery at her throat, the rings on her plump fingers. Polite company might have described the lady as buxom but Rosie knew no such word and in her straightforward mind she registered Lady Lambert as fat.

The broad face remained quite handsome, but below this a massive body, squeezed out from the waist by corsets, strained like rabbits in a bag against her dress. When she moved the rolls of flesh quivered uneasily before settling into position. There was a hint of kindliness in the eyes and the fold of the face, but the general impression was one of aristocratic certainty and stiffness.

'Hmph,' said Lady Lambert. 'Your name is Rosie, I believe?'

'Yes, ma'am.'

'Hmph. We shall have to change that. I understand that you are at present employed in a public house. Is that correct?'

She made it sound as if The Winged Horse was only one small step removed from a brothel. Rosie could not make head nor tail of these questions or where they were leading and she felt the slightest tremor of resentment. For one wilful moment she felt like telling this fat woman to mind her own business, but she controlled the impulse and replied simply:

'Yes, ma'am. I work in a pub.'

'Hmph.' A pause, then: 'Yes, Miss Pritchard, I agree. Something might be made of her.'

'My dear – ' Sir Roger began.

'Please, Roger,' said his wife, cutting across him. 'This is my province.'

Sir Roger gave Rosie a little apologetic smile and she wondered why. But not for long.

'Rosie,' said Lady Lambert and stopped immediately, clucking her gums. 'We really must do something about that name, Miss Pritchard. It sounds so – so common.'

'Of course, your Ladyship,' said Miss Pritchard humbly.

'Alice would be very suitable,' said Lady Lambert. She turned to Rosie. 'Do you like Alice?'

'I don't know her, ma'am,' answered Rosie, growing more bewildered by the minute.

'I didn't mean – ' said Lady Lambert, then shook her head: 'Oh, never mind. The point, girl, the point is this. My husband and I have decided to do something for you. You were helpful to our son and we wish to help you in return. You appear to be a bright, presentable girl. Miss Pritchard tells me that she has talked with you, and she is of the opinion that you could fit in here – in time and with the proper training. So we have made a place for you on the kitchen staff. The important thing is that you will be in no moral danger here. You will now be able to leave that dreadful public house and begin a new clean life.' She smiled benignly and put the tips of her fingers together. 'Now, Carson will drive you home, so that you can collect your things, then you will come straight back here. The sooner you begin the better.'

'I don't understand,' said Rosie.

'We are taking you under our roof, under our protection. Do you understand that?' said Lady Lambert in a tone of infinite patience.

'My dear, perhaps the girl – ' said Sir Roger, only to be interrupted yet again by his wife.

'I am sure that the girl – Alice – is capable of answering for herself, Roger.'

'My name is Rosie,' said Rosie, beginning to gather herself.

'Not in this house, not while you are in our employ.'

'I'm not in what-do-you-call-it – your employ!' said Rosie,

slipping the leash on her temper: 'I didn't come here for a job. I don't want a job. I've got a job. I've got a good job!' She turned on Sir Roger. 'You've got no right to bring me here and try and talk like this. What do you take me for? What do you think I am? I'm not a bit of china you can move from one shelf to another without so much as a by-your-leave! I know I'm only a common girl, a barmaid, but I'm a – a – ' She hesitated, feeling for the words, until something that Mr Softley had told her surfaced in her mind and she went on: 'I'm a human being! A person! I know I'm not in your class, but I'm a person, a human person!'

'Well, I never!' said the astonished Lady Lambert.

'Disgraceful!' said Miss Pritchard.

'I'm sorry if I shouted,' said Rosie, more quietly. 'If you'll pardon me, ma'am, I must be getting back.'

'Don't be foolish, girl!' said Miss Pritchard.

'Don't call me girl,' snapped Rosie. 'I've got a name. It's Rosie Carr, and I'm not game to change it for you or anyone else.'

She wasn't quite sure how she got out of the room and she was still quivering with anger when the motor-car appeared in the drive to take her back. She heard Sir Roger say:

'I'm sorry, Miss Carr. Believe me, it wasn't meant in quite the way my wife put it. We really did want to help, to show our gratitude.'

'I'm not looking for help or gratitude,' said Rosie. 'Anyway, it's over now. Say goodbye to Frank for me.'

'Of course.'

She climbed into the motor-car, desperate to get away from this place, but then she remembered that no-one had told her the doctors' verdict.

'What did they say about Frank?' she asked.

'He is very, very ill, as you said. He is going to rest here for a week or two, and then he is to go to a sanatorium in Switzerland.'

'Ah,' she said. 'That's all right then.'

He held the door open for a moment longer. 'Miss Carr, I truly am sorry. It was misguided and foolish. My fault. Will you remember, please, that if you do need help at any time, I am your friend. Don't be afraid to call on me. I mean that.'

'Yes,' she said. 'Thank you.'

It wasn't until the car had left the house well behind that the reaction set in and she began to weep. She felt ravaged inside, alone and vulnerable, and the threatening future seemed to offer no clear road ahead.

CHAPTER TEN

1

For the next two or three weeks a welcome calm closed around Rosie's life. She settled back into the regular, comforting routine of her work in the pub, glad to be free for awhile of outside pressures and emotional uncertainties.

She found some comfort in her new friend, Stan Roberts, the policeman, who was reserved to the point of being taciturn and as composed as Tommo was flamboyant. On their first evening out together she found his silence a little hard to take, until she realised that stillness was part of his nature. He appeared to be content to let others do the talking, to sit back and observe the world. There was nothing dour in his attitudes for, from the look in his eyes, he seemed on the whole to be amused by what he saw.

She grew to like his quiet confidence, and his wry sense of humour; above all, he exuded a feeling of strength and reliability which relaxed her to an extraordinary degree. Unlike Frank and Tommo, he made no demands on her. With these two she had felt herself to be the stronger and, with Frank in particular, she had given of her strength freely and willingly. With Stan Roberts there seemed to be no such need; he had strength enough of his own, strength enough for the two of them perhaps.

She knew now that she was not in love with Frank Lambert. It had nothing to do with her friendship with Stan Roberts, nor with that disastrous visit to the Lambert home in Cheshunt, although that had confirmed in her mind the impossibility of any long-term relationship between them. No, it was simply that, as the days passed, Frank's image faded and she found herself thinking of him only occasionally and not with any particular excitement.

Of course, she would never entirely forget him. How could she ever forget the first man to tell her that she was beautiful, to declare that he loved her? But for all that, her natural commonsense told her that their brief time together had been but an interlude in her life, and she suspected that, for all Frank's protestations of love, it would not be long before she became a remote memory to him also, as blurred and faded in his mind as an old photograph. Rosie felt no bitterness or cynicism about this, accepting it calmly as a simple fact of existence.

With Tommo, it was different. He featured in Rosie's life much as usual except that now it looked as if he had grown tired of chasing her, and had reverted to his old ways. He came into the bar with a succession of cheeky, laughing girls and made much play of showing them off, as if he were challenging Rosie to react; but she guessed his game and maintained an outward indifference to his antics, giving him as good and better than she received when it came to a battle of words. Her inner feelings veered between a kind of bitter amusement and downright anger although pride would not allow her to admit that there was any element of jealousy in her attitude.

Oddly enough, this falling-out with Tommo prompted Rosie to pursue the idea of learning to read and write. It was an act of defiance on her part, as if she were determined to prove to herself that her mind was centred on other, more important, things than Tommo the Toff and his lady-friends. In truth, Tommo's behaviour played only a small part in her decision. A whole confusion of developments, building up over the months, had led her to this point. As, for example, the interview with Frank's mother at Cheshunt which had affected her more deeply than she realised. Lady Lambert had behaved towards Rosie as if she were a natural inferior, as if her natural place was in the kitchen, as if she had a natural right to order the girl's life and, indeed, was performing an act of extraordinary kindness in doing so.

It was the condescension that had stirred Rosie's anger and

roused her pride. She was not ashamed to be a skivvy and a barmaid and she had no great driving ambition to be anything else, at least at the moment. She did not mind taking orders from The Missus or being scolded by her, for The Missus paid her wages and such was her right. But this did not apply to outsiders like Lady Lambert: they had no right to treat her like a *nothing*, to talk to her as from on high, to order her about.

There was no reason to suppose that learning to read or write would change this situation but instinct told Rosie that it was the first step. In any case, she had put off the decision far too long.

And so, one afternoon she gathered her courage and went to see the lady of whom Frank Lambert had spoken, the lady from the Workers' Educational Association. Margot Jones of 27, Landsdowne Road.

2

'Yes?' said the little woman briskly and without any note of welcome in her voice.

'Mrs Jones?' asked Rosie nervously. She had been surprised to find that Number 27 was a small shop with windows which were curtained on the inside and plastered with posters and notices on the outside. Rosie had passed the door three or four times, before summoning the will to ring the bell and this cold reception had done little to strengthen her resolve. Moreover, she realised almost as she spoke that she had fallen into error, for her quick eyes saw that there was no wedding ring on the woman's hand.

'*Miss* Jones.' The reply was sharp and reproving. 'What do you want?'

'Mr Lambert said I should come,' said Rosie. The words came out in a quick tremulous burst. She wished fervently that she hadn't come, that she could turn and fly.

'Lambert?' Behind the steel-rimmed spectacles the grey eyes, shining like polished pebbles, surveyed Rosie in sharp disbelief. 'Never heard of him.'

'Oh.' This was all that Rosie could manage. She began to turn away.

'Wait!' The tone was peremptory. 'Do you mean Frank Lambert?'

'Yes. That's him.'

'Well, why didn't you say so? I haven't seen him for weeks. Where has he got to?'

'He's – he's gone away. He's ill.'

'Hmph.' Miss Jones seemed to consider this statement for a moment and then discard it. 'Why did he send you?'

'He said – he told me – that – '

Miss Jones interrupted her impatiently. 'If you've come about the classes, the enrolment is in the evenings. Monday, Wednesday, Friday.' She flung out a hand to indicate a large printed notice in the side window. 'If you'd taken the trouble to read that, you would have saved yourself the trouble of knocking, to say nothing of my time.'

'Yes,' mumbled Rosie. 'Sorry to have troubled you.' Once again she turned away, thankful now that it was all over. Miss Jones, however, had other ideas.

'Well, you're here now. What was it you wanted to know?'

'It doesn't matter,' said Rosie.

'Tch. Tch.' Miss Jones made a little clicking sound of disapproval. 'It must matter, or you wouldn't have come. What classes are you interested in?'

'Classes?' Rosie tried to gather her thoughts. 'Oh. Well, you see, Frank – Mr Lambert – said that you – I mean – ' But she found it impossible to tell this strange, fierce-looking little woman of her ignorance and she mumbled: 'It really doesn't matter.'

Miss Jones studied Rosie for a long moment and clicked her gums in disapproval once more.

'Tosh! Don't keep saying that it doesn't matter! It is quite obvious to me that it matters very much. Come in.'

'Pardon?'

'I said – come in. Come along. I do not intend to conduct a conversation in the doorway. Close the door behind you.'

Miss Jones led the way through the main area of the shop which had been converted into a lecture room where plain wooden forms and a variety of old chairs faced a lectern and a blackboard. The floor was bare and the boards creaked underfoot. All around the room there were books, nestling together on improvised bookshelves made of pine planks resting on loose red bricks. Dozens of books, perhaps hundreds – certainly more books than Rosie had ever seen before. The room was bleak, there were ominous patches of damp on the ceiling but, somehow, the books invested the place with dignity, colour, a feeling of authority. She looked at them with awe.

Miss Jones entered a tiny room at the rear of the shop, removed a pile of leaflets from a chair and told Rosie to be seated: then she dumped the leaflets on the floor and, squeezing her way past heaps of pamphlets and yet more leaflets, settled herself behind a small, untidy desk. Rosie's nervousness had now turned to bewilderment. All that paper, all those words! She had the uncanny feeling that she and Miss Jones were on an island, cut off from the world outside by these towering cliffs of books and documents.

While Miss Jones searched the crowded desk for some papers, Rosie studied her. She was small, no more than five feet in height, and her position behind the desk made her look smaller. Rosie found it difficult to guess her age: she plumped for forty but would not have been surprised if someone told her that this estimate was out by ten years, one way or the other. The small body was sturdy enough but rather shapeless, with an almost flat, mannish chest. She wore a white blouse with a cameo brooch at the throat and Rosie noted with approval that, unlike the surroundings, the blouse was fresh and clean. The nicest feature about her, Rosie decided, was her eyes. She had removed her spectacles and the wide grey eyes looked far less formidable and altogether more kindly than they had on the doorstep.

'Ah,' said Miss Jones, triumphantly flourishing a printed form, 'here it is.' She picked up a pen, plucked a hair from the nib with thumb and forefinger, and dipped it into an inkwell. 'Now. Name.'

'What?' said Rosie.

'Name. Name. You have a name, I presume?'

'Yes. Carr. It's Carr.'

'First names?'

'Rosie.'

'Rosie?' Miss Jones frowned. 'Is it Rose, Rosa or what?'

'Rose. Rose Adelaide Carr.' Rosie moved as if to get up. 'Look, I'll come back, I – '

'Sit down, sit down,' ordered Miss Jones. Rosie sat back but she was beginning to get the measure of this woman now, beginning to resent her domineering tone.

'Address?'

'The Winged Horse, High Street,' said Rosie.

'You live there?' asked Miss Jones, without too much surprise.

'I live there and work there,' said Rosie. 'Nothing wrong with that is there?' she added defiantly.

'Nothing at all, nothing at all,' said Miss Jones mildly. 'Righteo. Which classes are you interested in? See here's the list – run your eye over that.'

She passed a leaflet across the desk. Rosie took it and made a pretence of studying the print. The paper fluttered as her hands trembled.

'I'll have to think about it – I'll come back and let you know,' she said, getting to her feet.

'Oh, God!' said Miss Jones suddenly. 'Oh, my God! I see it now.' She thumped her forehead with the palm of her hand. 'Maggie – you are an idiot, a fool, a short-sighted chump!'

'My name isn't Maggie – ' Rosie began, more perplexed than ever by this sudden outburst.

'Not you, not you!' interrupted Miss Jones. 'Me. Me! I'm talking of myself. Oh, what a chump I am! Sorry, sorry, sorry, sorry! Forgive me. Sit down, sit down, sit down! Truth is I am single-handed here and sometimes there's so much to do I can't see the wood for the trees. But I make no excuse. I should have known better. My job to know better. I do apologise if I embarrassed you.' She thumped her forehead yet again.

'That's all right,' Rosie mumbled as she sank back into her chair. What an extraordinary turn-about, she thought. In a few seconds the woman's attitude had completely changed and she still could not fathom out what had happened to

201

cause such a transformation. She wondered whether this banging of the forehead had somehow shaken up Miss Jones's brain and rearranged her thoughts into a more congenial pattern.

'Hmph,' murmured Miss Jones, giving herself another whack. 'We nearly lost you there, didn't we? It's my attitude. I know, I know. I'm very conscious of it. When the pressure is on, all my worst faults come to the fore – impatience most of all. Sorry, sorry, sorry, sorry.'

'No need for that,' said Rosie, who was beginning to be embarrassed by this fulsome confessional.

'No,' said Miss Jones. 'Quite correct. I mustn't go on about it. Time's precious. To business. Now, let me make sure I get it right this time – don't want to put my big foot in it again. You came – now you must not be offended at my asking this – ' she paused and smiled apologetically. 'You see, that leaflet – you were looking at it upside down. You've come about the literacy class. Am I right? You mustn't be afraid or ashamed to tell me.'

'Literacy?' said Rosie, uncomfortably.

'Reading, writing and so forth.'

'Yes, I want to learn like.' Rosie spoke breathlessly, expelling in a rush the words that had been suppressed for so long.

'Capital. Well, that wasn't too difficult, was it?' Miss Jones consulted the partially-filled form. 'Rose. You won't mind if I call you Rose?'

'No. Only most people – I mean – I'm always called Rosie.'

'Rosie. Yes. Better. More friendly, Rosie. And you shall call me Maggie.'

Rosie's sense of relief at having at last taking the first step towards her goal was so great that she showed no surprise at this sudden switch to first names. Indeed, she was beginning to like this strange woman whose moods seemed to be as changeable as a Spring day.

'Frank – Frank Lambert said your name was Margot,' Rosie ventured, anxious to get it right.

Miss Jones snorted. 'It is, it is. But I can't stand it. Too unbearably bourgeois. So it's Maggie. Maggie Jones.' She smiled. 'You can't get anything more working-class than that, can you?'

Rosie smiled tentatively, not knowing what to say. She didn't know the word *bourgeois* but she had understood the general drift of the statement and was quietly puzzled by it. How strange these educated people were! She suspected that Miss Jones, like Frank Lambert, came from a secure, well-to-do background: yet both had this funny notion about becoming part of the working-class.

Rosie had never been given any choice in the matter, she had been born to poverty and the lower classes and looked likely to remain in that position; she saw no particular virtue in it nor indeed in working-class life itself. Why anyone should want to change a perfectly good name like Margot for something as common as Maggie, or risk his health as Frank had done, simply because they imagined that this would identify them with the workers was beyond her. In a sense she admired the dedication, but for the most part such conduct struck her as plain daft. She pulled away from these thoughts as Miss Jones began to speak again.

'How would Wednesday evening suit you? Wednesdays at half-past seven?'

'Oh, I can't do the evenings,' Rosie said. 'I can never do a regular evening. I'm working, see. In the bar. I get one night a week off. It's usually Thursday but it often changes. And I get every other Sunday.'

'I see. What hours do you work, Rosie?'

'I get down in the kitchen at half-past six in the morning and I finish around eleven at night.' Seeing the frown on Miss Jones's face she added cheerfully: 'Oh, it's not as bad as it sounds. I get a half-hour each for my meals and most afternoons, after we close, I can usually manage a couple of hours to myself. Like today. The grub's good and I've got a nice room. Oh, don't worry – I'm one of the lucky ones!'

'So it seems,' said Miss Jones, in a tone that carried very little conviction. 'Tell me, Rosie, why did you not learn to read and write? Didn't you go to school?'

Rosie was surprised at the ease with which she answered these questions. As she calmly described the circumstances of her upbringing she realised that the sense of shame about her lack of education had gone. Now that the decision to learn had been taken she felt eager to get on with it. When she had finished, Miss Jones said:

'Yes. I see. Does your employer know that you can't read or write?'

'The Missus? She never asked and I never said. Anyway, writing and that doesn't come into the reckoning much, not in my job.'

'Well, Rosie,' said Miss Jones, pressing the fingers of her hands together, 'we have a problem. The literacy classes are on Wednesday evenings, as I said. And you say you cannot manage Wednesdays. In any case, judging from the hours you work, I doubt if you'd have the time or the energy to study.'

'Study?'

'Of course. It's not just a question of attending a class. You would have to study at home.'

'I'd do it, I really would. I'd find the time somehow,' said Rosie eagerly.

'Not much good if you can't attend the class, is it?'

'You mean – it is only Wednesday nights – '

'Exactly. That is the problem.'

The disappointment hit Rosie like a stab of pain. To be thrown back now, after all the effort, after forcing herself to come thus far, was almost more than she could bear. And on the heels of disappointment came despair, a feeling that the opportunity would never come again, that she would have to live with her ignorance for the rest of her life. She fought to hold back the tears that were already filming her eyes.

Perhaps Miss Jones guessed what was on the girl's mind for she said: 'You really want to learn, do you?' Rosie nodded, and felt the great black shutters that had closed on her dream open wide again as Miss Jones continued: 'Then we must find a way, mustn't we?'

Rosie looked at her, scarcely daring to speak.

'You said you can get away most afternoons for an hour or so. Well, Rosie, how would it be if you came here one or two afternoons a week? And, if the prospect isn't too frightening,

I will try to teach you myself. How would that be?'

They talked for a little while longer, but that is how it was arranged. Rosie walked back to the pub with a sense of elation, of freedom such as she had seldom known. She felt as though she wanted to share her happiness with the whole world; not to tell people what she was going to do, of course, but simply to let herself go, to hug someone, to laugh, to sing.

As if in answer to her mood she heard music and, on the corner of Brereton Road, opposite the football ground belonging to Tottenham Hotspur Football Club, she saw Red Charlie with his piano-organ. The nickname had nothing to do with his politics but derived from the fact that he always wore a faded red army tunic, a relic of his service in the South African War.

He was so astonished when Rosie came running across and clasped him to her in an excited hug that his hand slipped from the handle and the music faded away with a groan.

'What's that in aid of, Rosie?' he asked when she pulled away.

'Nothing, Charlie,' she said. 'I just felt like it!'

'Blimey, girl, you must be in love,' he said.

'Love? Ha! Much better than that, Charlie, much better than that!'

She waved and moved on again. Charlie watched her, smiling and thinking that Rosie was a real card. She'd make some lucky man a good wife but she'd be a real handful all the same.

Rosie had settled down a little by the time she reached the pub, which was just as well, for she was met by Big Bess with some startling news, news that stopped her high spirits in their tracks.

'It's Tommo,' said Bess. 'They've knocked him off. The police. He's been collared.'

3

At the police station, Rosie asked to see Detective Sergeant Stan Roberts. The portly sergeant on duty at the desk wanted to know the reason but she insisted that it was a personal matter and, in the end, he told her to wait. She was directed to a wooden form in the corridor where she waited for a half-hour, sitting in worried silence next to a man in moleskin trousers who smelled of paraffin and a thin woman with a vicious hacking cough.

Rosie had not been inside a police station before and she felt vaguely frightened by the atmosphere, by the constant procession of grim-faced constables moving in and out. One officer brought in a drunken prostitute, holding her in a painful arm-lock as she screamed obscenities at the world. Rosie recognised her as Fanny Bray, a girl who plied her trade in Fortune Street. Seeing Rosie, Fanny yelled:

'Hi, there, Rosie! The stinking rotten gits have pinched you too, have they? Bastards, they're all bollocky bastards!'

'Hello, Fanny,' said Rosie, blushing deeply.

Stan Roberts arrived at last, clearly glad to see her and full of apologies for keeping her waiting.

'I'm sorry, Rosie. I was on a case with the Inspector. Didn't know you were here until a couple of minutes ago. Is it about Tommo? Is that why you've come?'

'Yes. I've got to talk to you, Stan.'

'There's a cafe just round the corner. Come on, I'll buy you a cuppa and we can chat there.'

Betty's cafe was a popular venue for local artisans and for those who worked in public transport. It was an ideal place in which to hold a private conversation for the seats, set at right-angles to the side-walls were rather like church pews with high wooden backs which closed each table off from its neighbours. The atmosphere smelled pleasantly of fried bacon and hot toast.

The tea came hot and strong in large cups and Stan, who said he had missed his midday meal, had two thick slices of toast spread with beef dripping, over which he sprinkled generous measures of salt and pepper.

Rosie came directly to the point. 'Why have you nicked Tommo? What's he supposed to have done?'

'Not supposed, Rosie. He's done it all right. I'm afraid he's in strife this time.'

'What's he done?'

'Sh! Keep your voice down. I'd get it in the neck if they caught me chinning it over with you.' Stan's own voice was little more than a whisper. 'The charge is receiving stolen property.'

'No,' said Rosie. 'Tommo wouldn't do a thing like that!'

'You've got to believe it, Rosie. Three gross of saucepans, two gross of frying pans. Part of a load that went missing from a warehouse in the Midlands two weeks back. And the bloody fool was caught in the act – flogging them off on his stall at bargain prices!'

'He could have bought the stuff, couldn't he? I mean, bought it on the up-and-up. He wasn't to know it had been nicked.'

'That's what he says. Well, I mean, what else could he say? But we reckon he's done it before. We've been keeping a weather eye on him for months. There could be other charges.'

'The fool,' murmured Rosie, 'the stupid bloody fool!'

'You best keep out of it, Rosie,' said Stan. 'Let the law take its course.'

'I can't. I can't. How can I? Someone has to help him.'

'There's nothing you can do,' said Stan. 'No point in getting yourself involved.'

He glanced round quickly, then slid his hand across the table to rest on hers. She gave him a weak smile and shook her head.

'Poor Tommo,' she said. 'Poor stupid bloody Tommo.'

'Stupid is right,' said Stan.

'Did you – was it you who knocked him off?' she whispered.

'I was only doing my job,' he said defensively.

'Yes.' She nodded. 'I'm not blaming you. I mean, you'd run me in if you had to, wouldn't you?'

'Don't talk like that, Rosie,' he pleaded.

'Sorry,' she said, 'I didn't mean anything. Like you said, you have a job to do.' She paused. 'Where is he?'

'In the nick.'

'Could I see him?'

'Rosie, I couldn't – '

'Please. He's got nobody.'

'Why do you want to see him?' asked Stan bitterly. 'He's not worth a drop of your spit!'

'I can't turn my back now, Stan, you must see that. I can't turn my back on him now.'

'Do you – I mean – are you and Tommo – '

She interrupted, squeezing his hand. 'No. No. There's nothing between us. Except maybe friendship. Let me see him – just for a minute. Please.'

He studied her face for a moment, then nodded slowly. 'All right. I'll try and fix it. Can't promise, but I'll do my best. Come on.'

4

Stan had said that the cells below the Station were no fit place for Rosie and so they brought Tommo up to the detention room and Rosie was allowed five minutes alone with him. She had to clench her hands into fists to control her nervous trembling as the heavy door was unlocked and locked again behind her.

Tommo was sitting on the edge of a bunk bed and he looked up with the quick frightened eyes of a boy as Rosie entered. Then he rose, attempting without much success to banter after his old fashion:

'Rosie! Rosie! Well, here's a sight for sore eyes! My own little lolly-dolly! Rosie! Rosie!'

She shook her head, unable to respond. The room itself was dispiriting enough, with its scratched olive-green walls, barred window, and cold cement floor. A chipped chamber-pot peeped out from underneath the bunk and the only other furnishings were a bare wooden table and a chair from which the back had either been removed or broken off. The smell of urine and damp hung in the air, stinging the nostrils. If this is the detention room, thought Rosie, what must the cells be like!

But it was Tommo and the way he looked that shook Rosie

more than anything else. She had always seen him as tall and well-built, a handsome figure of a man, but today he looked smaller and weaker, as if he had somehow shrunk, dwindled within his clothes. And shaking her head, knowing that, at all costs, she must not cry, she went to him.

'Tommo, oh, Tommo.'

His arms locked around her almost in panic and he held her in shuddering silence for a full half-minute, clinging on as if she were his only earthly comfort. She could feel his fear tingle her own flesh. Gradually she eased herself free and, with an effort at lightness said:

'Well, this won't get the washing dried and ironed! Tell me what happened, Tommo.'

'It's all wrong, Rosie. The bogies have got it all wrong. I didn't pinch anything, straight up.'

'They say you – what-do-you-call-it – something about stolen properly. Receiving – that's it – receiving stolen property.'

'I didn't know the stuff had been half-inched, did I? I mean, how was I to know? I bought it from this geezer in Islington. Paid good bees-and-honey for it, paid cash down. All fair and square. On my life, Rosie, that's true, as true as a box has four corners.'

'Did you know this man?'

'No, not really. Called himself Sid.'

'Sid what?'

'I don't know, do I? You don't ask every bloke you meet for his birth-certificate, do you?'

'Would you know him again?'

'Oh, I'd know him if I saw him. Little runt. Short and dirty as a winter's day.'

'Where did he get the stuff?'

'Said he's bought it up in the Midlands from a factory that had gone bust.'

'And you believed him?'

'Oh, give it some air, Rosie. In my line it don't do to ask a lot of questions. If you see a bargain, you grab it – both hands – know what I mean?'

'Yes, I know what you mean,' said Rosie, with a sigh in her

voice. 'You wanted to believe it, so you did. And now you're really in the apple-cart.'

'It'll be all right, you'll see. I mean, I didn't know the stuff was hot. That's the point.'

'Do you know where this bloke hangs out? This Sid feller?'

'No. I met him in the King's Head in Upper Street, Islington. Near the Angel. He had the stuff in a shed round one of the back-alleys. It was all fixed and done in an hour.'

'Is that how you always do your business?'

'I do a lot of it that way,' he said defensively. 'Buy a bundle, sell a bundle. I've got to earn a living.'

'I'm asking,' she said, 'not criticising. Only Stan – Mr Roberts – said there could be other charges.'

Tommo's face went white. 'He said that?'

'Yes. Other charges.'

'The bastard! The bastard!'

'Tommo, he's only doing his job.'

'Oh, yes,' Tommo said bitterly. 'Only doing his bleeding job! He sticks one on me so that he can have a clear run with you. Doing his job.'

'That's not fair, Tommo. Who do you think fixed it for me to see you? Maybe he won't do you any favours but he'll play straight, I'll wager that.'

'I believe you, thousands wouldn't,' said Tommo. 'You sound as if you fancy him.'

'Oh, Tommo, don't talk so daft!' Rosie said impatiently. 'I don't fancy anyone. Now, let's talk sense, shall we?'

'Other charges?' said Tommo, after a pause. 'Did he say what?'

'No.'

'It's a load of swosh. I mean, what other charges? I run a straight business. Clean as a button-stick. Maybe I was a bit of a mug with this last load but they can't hang you for that.'

'Tommo, I've only got a couple of minutes. Is there anything you want?'

'What do you think? I want to get out of this hole.'

'You'd better get some help, Tommo.'

'Like what?'

'One of these law people. What do they call them – a solicitor.'

'I can't afford solicitors! They charge the earth! I'm skint – broke. I've had a bad trot with the horses lately and I put my last few quid into buying that stock. Now the rozzers have taken the lot. Besides, I don't trust lawyers. They'd take the milk out of a blind man's tea and then come back for the sugar.'

The key rattled in the lock and Rosie said quickly: 'I have to go. Is there anything you want in the personal line? Clothes and that?'

'I'll manage,' Tommo said. 'Only one thing. You know where I live?'

'Compton Road?'

'That's it. Could you go there for me?'

'I don't fancy that,' said Rosie.

The area just beyond Compton Road, an untidy haggle of a dozen twisted streets and narrow festering alleys, was known as The Compo. It lay in a hollow and it was as if its inhabitants had trickled down the surrounding hills to settle like sludge at the bottom. For all their hunger and poverty, the people Rosie knew best, the people who lived in and around Fortune Street, were affluent beyond the wildest dreams of the denizens of The Compo.

For here was the very bottom of the social heap: a dark nightmare of a place which contained the greatest concentration of slums, poverty, disease, filth, despair, drunkenness, violence and crime this side of Hoxton and Bethnal Green. During the day the police only ever entered The Compo in force, mounting odd raids with a dozen or more men. At night they left well alone.

Al this went through Rosie's mind and must have been reflected on her face, for Tommo said reassuringly:

'It's all right. Don't fret. I live at the top end, No. 3. You can't even smell The Compo from there, except if the wind's in the wrong direction. I'm in lodgings with a family called Finn. If you could just pop in – tell Mrs Finn I've been called away like, on business and ask her to feed Kitchie.'

'Kitchie?'

'Short for Kitchener. My canary.'

Rosie smiled. 'You've got a canary?'

'Why not?'

'I don't like to see birds in cages.'

'This one has never known any different. Lovely company – sings like a beauty.'

'Cone on now,' said the policeman from the open door.

'The seed's in a biscuit box under the bed,' said Tommo. 'Thanks for coming, Rosie. It'll be all right, you'll see. I'll be out of here faster than you can shake a tick. And on Sunday we'll take a ride out to Hadley Wood again – how about that?'

'That's a date,' said Rosie, with as much conviction as she could muster.

She turned back as the door closed, just in time to catch a brief glimpse of Tommo as he sat on the bunk and covered his face with his hands.

CHAPTER ELEVEN

1

Rosie negotiated the trip to Compton Road without difficulty. She was relieved to find that the house where Tommo lived was indeed at the top end of the road, on the crest of a long hill and a fair distance from the dark Compo valley. Number 3 was a small, neat terraced artisan's house and Mrs Finn a plump clean motherly woman. She was clearly puzzled by Tommo's message and curious to know more, but Rosie pleaded ignorance and managed to keep her questions at bay.

Conscious that she had over-run her time, Rosie hurried back to The Winged Horse with as much speed as she could make. Matters were not helped by the rain that began to bucket from the sky when she still had a half-mile to go, and she arrived both breathless and soaked.

She slipped in through the back door, hoping to get to her room and change out of her sodden dress before confronting anyone. She could still hardly believe what had happened to Tommo: the enormity of the problem frightened her and she wanted a little more time to think on what to do. But in the kitchen she met George Briggs, the new potman, colloquially known as Sailor, who was dragging himself around the kitchen, making up sandwiches and snacks, with a look of martyrdom on his face.

Sailor, a former cook on merchant ships, had given up the sea following an accident which had left him with one leg shorter than the other. A long, boney man with sad watery eyes, he always held his head tilted to one side as though he were expecting fate to deal him a blow in the face and was taking avoiding action. The Missus had selected him from a queue of thirty-two applicants for two reasons: he had worked in pubs before and knew something of the trade and he was cheap.

'The Missus is chasing after you, Rosie,' he said. 'Been asking for you every ten minutes. She's in a right mood.'

'Where is she now?' asked Rosie.

'In the parlour.'

'I'll slip upstairs and get out of these wet things. If you see her, tell her I'm back.'

'What about these snacks? It's not my job to make the snacks. That's your job. But she said I was to get on with it,' he grumbled.

'I know,' said Rosie. 'It's terrible hard work. Cutting bread, lifting those heavy sandwiches. You want to watch out, Sailor, you could rupture yourself!'

Before he could reply she gave him a sweet sarcastic smile and was gone.

'Oh, there you are!' said The Missus acidly, when a drier Rosie at last presented herself. 'It's very good of you to show up. I'm sure we are all grateful. May I presume to ask where you have been?'

Rosie said nothing of her visit to Miss Jones (that was to be kept secret for as long as possible) but she made the most of Tommo's predicament, hoping that curiosity would divert The Missus's anger. Her ploy was successful for The Missus forgot all about Rosie's shortcomings and plunged headlong into this new and sensational development. She plied Rosie with questions, which the girl answered as best she could and when it was clear that she had garnered all the information available, she folded her arms across her bosom in an attitude of righteousness and said:

'Well, Rosie, I am not surprised. I cannot say in all honesty that I am surprised. I am not one to sit in judgment, as you well know. A good many people would vouch for that, I'm sure. I keep an open mind, an open mind. But there's no doubt that Tommo does sail near the wind sometimes. He does sail very near the wind.'

'He wouldn't do anything really bad,' said Rosie.

'You don't know,' said The Missus portentously. 'We none of us know. Oh, I'm not talking about murder or anything like that. But other things – oh, yes, other things. A man's mind is a mystery, Rosie. A mystery. We don't know what goes on in a man's head. But I will tell you one thing. One thing I do know. Men are ruled by two things. Greed and lust. And you mark my words – greed is at the bottom of Tommo's trouble.'

Rosie hardly listened to this, although she made a show of doing so. An idea had been sliding around in her mind and suddenly she took firm hold of it.

'Well,' she said, 'I'd better get a wiggle on.' And, at the door she paused and added with a deliberately casual air: 'Would it be all right, ma'am, if I took my evening off tomorrow instead of Thursday?'

'What?' The voice was sharp and wary. 'I should think you'd had enough time off lately without asking for more!'

'I don't want any more time,' said Rosie, 'only my regular evening. But I'd like to take it tomorrow.'

'I don't know,' said The Missus, adopting her long-suffering tone, 'I don't know. As far as I can see I don't have any say in the matter. I'm only the landlady. I'm nobody. I don't count. You seem to come and go as you please whatever I say.'

'It's all right then?'

'I suppose so.'

'I'm ever so grateful,' said Rosie.

'So you should be,' replied The Missus. 'But watch your step my girl. Don't play on my good nature. I know I'm soft, too soft for my own good sometimes, but there is a limit, you know. A definite limit.'

'I think you're lovely,' said Rosie and, on impulse, she gave The Missus a quick kiss on the cheek. She was gone before the astonished woman had recovered from this extraordinary piece of familiarity.

Later that night, in the privacy of her room, Rosie opened the old cocoa-tin in which she kept her savings. It contained a total of six pounds, four shillings and threepence. She put it in her purse, ready for the expedition she had planned for the morrow.

So, for the second time within a few weeks, Rosie found herself in the central lobby at The House of Commons waiting to see Sir Roger Lambert. The difference was that this time she had come alone and she was already beginning to regret the absence of Mr Crooks. She missed his sturdy support for, as the minutes ticked away, her small stock of confidence began to dwindle at an alarming rate. She felt small and insignificant among the imposing-looking people who stood around the lobby talking in low, grave voices. What was worse, she felt a growing need to use a lavatory but she could see no door marked LADIES and she could not summon up the courage to ask for directions.

At last, as her need grew more acute, she made up her mind to abandon the entire project and head for the street and the nearest public convenience.

'Miss Carr!'

Rosie had almost reached the door when she heard her name and turning she found herself confronting the young flaxen-haired man to whom she had been introduced on her last visit. She tried desperately to remember his name, conscious that she was blushing furiously.

'Russell Whitby,' said the young man as if he had guessed her confusion. He smiled, and across her mind there flashed the thought that she had never seen such clear, vivid blue eyes.

'Ah. Yes. Pleased to see you,' she said, and extended a hand, hoping that this was the proper thing to do.

He shook the hand gravely but gently. 'And what brings you here this time?'

'I was hoping – I came to see Mr – I mean – Sir Roger Lambert.'

'You're out of luck, I'm afraid, Miss Carr. I happen to know that Sir Roger left the House an hour ago. I saw him at lunch. He is travelling to Manchester. He has a case which opens there tomorrow.' Whitby saw the disappointment spring to her face and he added quickly: 'Perhaps there is something I can do?'

'No, no,' she muttered. 'Thank you for asking.' The surprise of meeting him had sharpened the pressure on her bladder and she was desperate to get away. 'I'd better be going.'

'Nothing of the sort!' he said sternly. 'I won't hear of it. Since you are here, you must let me take you to tea.'

'I couldn't,' she said. The thought of more delay, of drinking tea, terrified her. If I don't go soon, she thought, I shall either wet my drawers or bust.

'I insist,' said Whitby, taking her arm. 'I will not take no for an answer. We'll have tea on the terrace and you shall tell me all about yourself.'

It's now or never, thought Rosie. But how could she ask? What was it that ladies said to gentlemen when they were in her predicament?

'I can't,' she said, and the next words were forced out by sheer desperation: 'I want to – I mean I've got to – ' She stopped again, unable to put her tongue to the word *lavatory* in such company and wishing with all her heart that she was back at The Winged Horse where you could tell almost anyone that you wanted to water the cabbages, or pick a sweet pea, without any feeling of embarrassment.

He came to her rescue once again, just as if he had read her mind. With perfect politeness and no hint of amusement he steered her towards one of the archways and said: 'Through here. I daresay you'd like to wash your hands before tea? I'll show you where on the way.'

She didn't dare tell him that she needed to do more than wash her hands. But at least, she thought, a washroom is better than nothing and with any luck there might be a WC there as well as a washbasin. Only let it not be too far away, she prayed, please God get me there quickly or I shall make a blooming disgrace of myself!

She need have had no fears of the washroom. It was a splendid place, containing not only a washbasin but a magnificent WC with a polished mahogany seat and a pan discreetly decorated with pink roses. Relieved at last, both physically and mentally, Rosie now applied herself to the problem of getting away from the persistent Mr Whitby.

It was not that she did not like him. He was handsome and distinguished and courteous, all those things, and there was a laughing impudence in those startling blue eyes that intrigued her. But she had not come all this way to take tea with a good-looking beau: she had come to seek aid for Tommo, and that was still her chief purpose. Sir Roger Lambert had told her that if she needed help, she should come to him. Well, he wasn't around, that avenue was closed. It was a disappointment but she was not going to allow herself to be beaten. The picture of Tommo in that bleak detention room with his head in his hands was still sharp in her mind. She decided to say a polite farewell and thank-you to Mr Whitby and get back as soon as possible to see Mr Crooks. He would surely know what to do.

Russell Whitby, however, was not to be shaken off. He took her arm as soon as she emerged from the ladies room and led her relentlessly towards the terrace, turning her protests aside as if he hadn't heard them. Rosie, aware of people watching, and of the surroundings, dared not raised her voice or argue too strongly and, in the end, she gave herself up to the inevitable.

3

The weather had turned fine and mild and the terrace of the House of Commons was crowded with MPs and their guests. Whitby and Rosie waited by the balustrade until a table became vacant, the Thames gliding smoothly below them, a convoy of barges making slow sturdy progress downstream, a pleasure-craft crammed with sightseers chugging past. Some of the people on board waved at the crowded terrace and Rosie was tempted to wave back but she decided that, in the circumstances, this would not be fitting.

When they were seated at last Whitby ordered tea for two and, over-riding her objections, a dish of strawberries and cream and a selection of cakes for Rosie. He excused his own abstinence on the grounds that he had eaten rather too much at lunch. One of the few lessons she had learned from her mother was that it was bad manners to talk and eat at the same time and she had some difficulty in coping with the food and answering his occasional question.

She managed that reasonably well but almost fell into error with a delicious-looking chocolate eclair: just as she was about to pick it up and ease it into her mouth she saw that a lady at a nearby table was eating her eclair with a funny little fork. Another of her mother's lessons in social behaviour held that fingers were made before forks, but Rosie doubted her mother had ever been to tea at the Houses of Parliament and, playing for safety, she used the fork. She ate one more cake out of politeness, a little oblong thing covered in pink icing, and then, dabbing at her lips with the napkin (as the lady nearby had done) she pronounced herself finished.

'Thanks ever so, Mr Whitby. That was lovely.'

'Nothing more I can get you?'

'Crikey, no. I'll burst if I eat any more.' This was not entirely true but in Rosie's circle it was polite for visitors to express satisfaction with the food offered by insisting that they could take no more.

'Do you smoke. Would you like a cigarette?' The late afternoon sun glinted on the slim gold case he took from his vest pocket. Rosie shook her head vigorously, shocked by the suggestion. The only women she had ever seen smoking in public were the prostitutes who hovered in the doorways of Fortune Street and the High Road. What kind of a girl did he think she was?

'You don't mind if I have one?' he asked with a smile.

'No. I mean, no, of course not.'

He lit up and a plume of bluish smoke curled on the air between them. Rosie's initial nervousness had almost passed and, sitting back, she began to take more interest in her surroundings. There were several ladies there, all of whom she defined mentally as posh, sitting with men who, by their clothes and manners, were clearly toffs. It was all a thousand miles away from The Winged Horse and millions of miles away from the dark alleys of The Compo. Did these people understand how the poor lived? Was it possible for them to do so? And if they didn't how could they make laws that would be fair to all?

She became aware then of a fall in the buzz of conversation: some people had lowered their voices to a whisper and were directing the attention of their companions towards a bearded man in a baggy tweed suit who had just come out on to the terrace. He was in earnest conversation with a tall, solemn-looking man who had a cloth cap clutched in his hands. Their clothes and something in their bearing marked them out from most of the other men on the terrace; had she seen them in the bar of The Winged Horse Rosie would not have surprised. And it was quite clear that the bearded man in particular was the object of some interest. The ladies present were, of course, far too polite to stare openly but, when he had passed by, their faces bore the look of people who had just seen a man-eating tiger and they fell at once into quick, whispered conversation.

As the pair came near to Rosie's table, the bearded man chanced to look towards her. He paused for a moment, staring at her with open admiration. With his white hair and beard and sharp yet kindly eyes he made Rosie think of a sketch she had once seen, depicting an Old Testament prophet. He moved closer and looked down at her with a mischievous smile on his face. She smiled back, responding to the glowing warmth of his personality.

'Well, well,' he said in a broad Scots accent. 'You're a bonnie wee lassie, no doubt of that, but it's my duty to tell ye that you're keeping awful bad company.'

He softened the remark by dropping a friendly hand on Whitby's shoulder, then, with a nod, he rejoined his companion and moved on.

'What did he mean by that?' whispered Rosie.

'Just a joke,' said Whitby. 'He and I are always having a jab at each other. Actually, we're good friends. I admire him very much.'

'Who is he?'

'You don't know?'

'I wouldn't ask if I did.'

'That is Keir Hardie. James Keir Hardie, MP. The famous

220

firebrand. Or notorious, depending on your point of view.'
He spoke as if the name would be instantly recognisable but
it meant nothing to Rosie.

'Never heard of him,' she said. 'Is he in that Labour
lot?'

Whitby smiled. 'Yes. He's in that Labour lot, as you put
it.'

'And what about you?'

'No. I'm a Liberal.'

Rosie frowned. 'You're Liberal and he's Labour?'

'That's right.'

'But you just said – you just said that you – '

'That I admired him?'

'That's what you said.'

'Isn't it possible to admire someone without agreeing with
everything he stands for? I admire Hardie because he has
principles and he stands by them, no matter what the cost.
And because he has guts. He fought his way up from
nothing, from poverty. Me, I went to college, university, I
had all the advantages. He started with nothing, he taught
himself by candlelight.'

Rosie looked with new respect towards the sturdy white-
bearded figure. She thought of her visit to Miss Jones, of her
own terrible ignorance. It could be done then! Here was the
living proof, a man who had begun with nothing but determination and who was now a Member of Parliament and a
respected leader. If he could do it, so could she!

In that instant, an ambition was born: not directed towards
Parliament or politics because they were incomprehensible to
Rosie, nor towards being a lady like those around her on the
terrace because that was even more incomprehensible, but
simply an ambition to fulfil herself as a human being. She did
not fully understand it, nor would she have been able to put
the notion into words, but she was gripped by a feeling that
there was another person sleeping in her body, another and
better Rosie Carr, and that it was her duty to wake and
release her.

And for a moment, for a lovely moment, she was overwhelmed by the same rushing sense of excitement, of free-

dom, that she felt in her dreams when she was astride Pegasus, the winged horse, riding beneath the gleaming stars.

4

'I have to go,' said Rosie, 'I really do have to get back.' The five o'clock chimes of Big Ben had just struck, bringing her back to the present and to the problem of Tommo.

'You've been sitting there, as silent as a statue, for the past three minutes. Now you say you have to leave. Why don't you tell me about it?' said Whitby. 'You never know, perhaps I may be able to help.'

'Tell you about what?' asked Rosie defensively.

'Whatever's troubling you. People usually come to see a Member of Parliament when they have a problem. Is that why you wanted to see Sir Roger – because you have a problem?'

'Sort of,' she conceded.

'I'm an MP,' he said, spreading his hands. 'Won't I do?'

'You're not a what-do-you-call-it, a lawyer, are you?'

'Ah!' he said. 'You need legal advice, do you?'

'Not me,' she said. 'A friend of mine.'

'Then tell me about this friend,' said Whitby. 'I shan't let you leave until you do.'

And so, hesitantly at first but more quickly as she gained in confidence, Rosie told Whitby the story. She was afraid that he might be bored, but he listened keenly, his face cupped in his hands, his keen eyes looking into hers, prompting her gently when she faltered. When she had finished he said quietly:

'Hmph. It's a rotten mess.'

'Yes.'

'And you came all this way to get help for this – this Tommo?'

'It's the only thing I could think of.'

He nodded, then put out a hand and rested it on hers. 'Would you mind – would you mind if I asked you a very personal question?'

'I don't know. I mean, I don't know till you ask it, do I?'

Under the cool weight of his hand she felt her heart quicken, as with excitement.

'Is he your sweetheart?'

'Tommo?' She smiled, making light of her answer. 'Lor, no. He'd like to be, I think, but that's as far as it goes.' More seriously, she added: 'I like him, that's all. He's quite a card. Always good for a laugh.'

'Just a friend?'

'You could say that.'

'I'll tell you something, Miss Carr,' he said. 'He's lucky to have a friend like you. Any man would count himself so.' She felt a pressure from his hand and then, abruptly, he rose to his feet.

'Stay here!' he commanded. 'Don't go away. I will be back in a few minutes!'

He was gone before she could say anything. She watched him stride away, tall and handsome, nodding to fellow-members here and there. He was checked at one table by a middle-aged man and, looking towards Rosie they held a brief, smiling conversation. She blushed, knowing that they were talking about her, and looked down, pretending to brush some crumbs from her skirt. When she looked up again, Whitby was gone.

Sitting there in the mellow sunshine, waiting, she realised how little she knew about him. Oh, he had been quite clever, she saw that now: he had asked all the questions, about her work, her background, her friends, and she had provided all the answers, artlessly and truthfully. All she knew of him was that he was a Member of Parliament, a gentleman clearly, and something called a Liberal. Her experience with men of his class was limited to her brief knowledge of Frank Lambert, but the two men were so different that this provided no yardstick of measurement. Frank, so serious, quiet, dedicated, carrying the ills of the world on his thin shoulders: Whitby, glowing with health, impudent in his humour, untroubled – or so it seemed – by any sort of problem. In a sense, she thought, with a sudden flash of intuition, there is a lot of Tommo in Whitby – both seemed to have the same quick liveliness, the same devil-may-care attitude to life. Except that there had been little liveliness in poor Tommo when she had last seen him!

Whitby came back, moving with the same long elegant stride. He stood over her, smiling, and held out an imperious hand.

'Come along, young lady. We're going.'

'Hold on!' said Rosie, pulling back. 'I'd like to know where.'

'My rooms,' he said teasingly.

'Ha!' she snorted. 'Chance would be a fine thing!'

'Look,' he said. 'I have spoken by telephone to a friend of mine. I caught him just as he was leaving his office. He is a solicitor. He has agreed to meet you at my rooms in Lord North Street in fifteen minutes to discuss your friend's problem. Now, will you come?'

'Straight up?' she asked. 'You're not having me on?'

'Cross my heart,' he replied.

As they left the terrace, the middle-aged man who had engaged Whitby in conversation a few minutes before, smiled and nodded at Rosie, rising a little from his seat to do so.

'He's quite taken with you,' Whitby murmured when they had gone past. 'He said you could be Gertie Millar's twin sister.'

'Me? Like Gertie Millar?' said Rosie scornfully. 'He wants his eyes tested!' She had seen postcard photographs of the famous actress, the Queen of the Gaiety Theatre, and she could not believe that she bore the slightest resemblance to such a blazing beauty.

Whitby paused for a moment, taking Rosie by the shoulders and studying her face. 'There is a likeness,' he pronounced solemnly. 'Not a striking one, but it is there. In the eyes, most of all, perhaps.'

'You'll let me know when you've finished, won't you?' said Rosie with a smile.

'And there, when you smile!' he cried. 'Definitely.' He put a hand briefly to her cheek and added, half-mocking, half-serious: 'Oh, yes. I am afraid you will have to face the cruel truth, Miss Carr. You are quite a beauty!'

'Right!' said Rosie. 'Now you've got that off your chest, perhaps we can get on?'

She spoke lightly, dismissively, but in the same moment her heart seemed to expand and quicken its beat and with it came the extraordinary feeling – so sharp that it became a mental image – that the linnet she had bought and released outside the pub, all that time ago, was in there somewhere, caged in her body, beating its wings in a frantic effort to get out.

The moment passed and the practical Rosie came back again. Watch it, girl, she chided herself, watch your step. Don't go getting all fanciful. She smiled as she remembered Tommo's warning.

When a girl goes out with a gent, she should keep one hand on her purse and the other on her ha'penny.

5

'What is your friend's full name?' asked Mr Bernstein. He was a small, neat, cherubic-looking man, beardless and almost bald, with sharp, fierce black eyes that glowed like anthracite. Rosie thought him rather young to be a solicitor, and certainly rather young to be so bald.

She had to think for an instant before she replied. With her, and most of the people in the pub and the market, Tommo had always been just that. Tommo or Tommo the Toff. Nobody seemed to bother with his actual name. Then she remembered.

'Thompson,' she replied. 'Thomas Thompson. We call him Tommo for short, like.'

She took a cautious sip of the sherry that Pickford, Whitby's elderly manservant, had served.

Mr Bernstein nodded and made a note in a small leather-bound book, clearing his throat as he did so. Rosie noted that he made this odd rasping sound quite a lot and thought that it must be very irritating to live with.

'Where is he being held?' asked Mr Bernstein.

'At Tottenham police station.'

This information went into the book, the throat was being cleared again, and there followed what seemed to be a long silence. Then the black eyes studied her.

'Do you believe Mr Thompson to be innocent of the charge, Miss Carr?'

'Well.' Rosie hesitated and glanced at Whitby who was sitting hunched up in a big brown leather armchair, facing her. He gave an encouraging smile and she continued: 'I don't know, to tell the honest truth. I mean, he's a bit of a card like, but he's not a crook. He's never been in trouble before.'

'You're sure of that?'

'Yes. I mean, I've never heard anything against him, nothing like that. If he has done wrong, I'm sure he didn't know he was doing it.' She paused, realising that she had not spoken entirely honestly. 'I mean, what I mean is, that sometimes Tommo doesn't think. He does things on the spur of the moment, if you know what I mean.'

'Yes. I think I do see, Miss Carr.' Mr Bernstein turned to his book again and made another entry. Then he closed it with an air of finality and studied his sherry for a moment, as though he were suspicious of it. Satisfied with the inspection, he drank half of it, set the glass down carefully and dabbed at his full lips with a silk handkerchief.

'Well, Miss Carr, I'm sure I don't have to tell you that this is a very serious business. The law takes a severe view of the crime of receiving stolen property. I would be failing in my duty if I left you in any doubt of that.'

'How serious?' asked Whitby.

'Under the Larceny Act of 1861, a person found guilty of receiving may be liable to a term of penal servitude not exceeding fourteen years. If the guilty person is a male, aged over sixteen, the court may also order that he be whipped.'

'Oh, my God!' Rosie felt as if the blood had drained from her body. She looked from Whitby to the solicitor and back again in terror. The crack of a whip seemed to scream in her head. Whitby was on his feet at once.

'Are you all right?'

She looked at him mutely, her eyes flooding with tears, gripping the hand he held out to her as if it were a life-line.

'Is it really as bad as all that, Oscar?' asked Whitby.

'Until I've investigated further, I can't say,' replied Mr Bernstein. 'I'm sorry to distress you, Miss Carr, but I think it best that you should realise the serious nature of the alleged offence and the possible consequences.'

'Yes,' whispered Rosie. 'I'm obliged. I'm sorry – I didn't mean to – '

'Goodness, there is no need to apologise. I understand only too well what a shock this must have been.'

'It will kill him. Prison will kill him.' She spoke half to herself, her head filled with the image of Tommo sitting on the edge of the bunk in the detention room, his head in his hands. Tommo the Toff, the flamboyant Tommo who loved life so much, wearing convict clothes, his hair shaved to the skull, shut away in a prison cell year after year! He would go mad, or die!

'Now,' said Mr Bernstein, 'I want you to listen to me, Miss Carr. As I said, I have told you the worst, because I do not believe that one should encourage false hopes. It is better to steel oneself to expect the worst – and if the worst does not happen, so much the better. So let us – without hoping for too much – let us consider the other possibilities.'

Rosie realised that she was still clinging to Whitby's hand. She eased away, giving him a faint smile of thanks and, sitting on the edge of the sofa, she turned all her attention on Mr Bernstein.

'First,' he said, 'first, I think we may put the whipping out of our minds. It is rare, very rare, in these days, for a court to add whipping to a custodial sentence. Not unknown, but rare.' The sigh of relief from Rosie could have been heard in the next room and he paused before continuing: 'Second, from what you have told me, it is possible that we may be able so to arrange matters that Mr Thompson will be charged with the less serious offence of misdemeanour.'

'What's that?' asked Rosie.

'It is a little complicated. In essence, it means that there are mitigating circumstances.'

'Mitigating?'

'How can I explain? A man may receive stolen goods, say, but he is able to prove that he did not know that they were stolen.'

'Then he is innocent?'

'Not in the eyes of the law, no. The law, in its wisdom, expects that when a man buys goods he should take reasonable care to ascertain that those goods were not dishonestly acquired. If he fails to do so, then he may be charged with a misdemeanour under the Act of 1861.'

Rosie dared not ask the question that hammered in her head. Whitby, who was now standing behind her, framed it for her.

'What is the penalty for a misdemeanour of that sort?'

'Seven years. Up to seven years.'

'But that's terrible!' cried Rosie. 'Seven years! Seven years for a mistake! Oh, it's cruel, cruel.'

Mr Bernstein waited a moment. 'There is, of course, a third possibility. So far we have proceeded on the assumption that your friend is guilty and will be found so. That, of course, is entirely wrong. We must presume innocence and conduct our defence on that basis, unless overwhelming evidence prompts us to change the plea or if Mr Thompson admits guilt and decides so to plead.'

There was a mist in Rosie's head now and she could not see her way through what Mr Bernstein had said. Only one word made a connection – innocence. Innocence. And she vaguely grasped that she was not alone any more, that Mr Bernstein was taking over. In fact, before she could speak, he drained his sherry glass and rose to his feet, smiling.

'And now,' he said, 'I must make my way to Tottenham Police Station to see our client, and arrange, if possible, for his release on bail.'

He beamed his cherub smile down at her and, for a moment, she had the illusion that, despite his frock coat and winged collar, this little man was an angel of mercy. Choked for words, shaking her head, she stood and embraced him.

'Well, thank you, Miss Carr,' he said when he had managed to disengage. 'That was most satisfactory.' He straightened his cravat. 'We will keep in touch through Mr Whitby.'

'Wait!' He was almost at the door when she called and turned in surprise.

'Yes?'

'I – I forgot. You see, Tommo – Mr Thompson – he hasn't got any – I mean – he's broke. Stony.' She reached for her handbag. 'I brought a bit with me. Not much. I mean, you'll want paying and that.'

'I don't think we need worry about money at this stage, Miss Carr,' said Mr Bernstein gently. 'We will consider the matter after the case has been concluded.'

'But we – I mean – Mr Thompson – he won't be able – '

'Let us concern ourselves with that when the time comes, eh, Miss Carr? One problem at a time.'

'There's something else,' she said hesitantly.

'Yes?'

'When you see him, I'd be obliged if you didn't say anything about me. I mean, I wouldn't want him to know I was – sort of – you know – involved like.'

Mr Bernstein hesitated and Whitby interposed, quickly. 'I'm sure Mr Bernstein can arrange that.'

'Thanks ever so,' said Rosie.

She could hear him clearing his throat on the stairs as Whitby showed him to the front door. Like a released spring, the tension went from her body; she could feel the sweat on her forehead, the heat between her breasts, and yet she began to shiver uncontrollably as with a fever. And then the tears came and, with the tears, great heaving sobs of relief.

Whitby found her thus when he returned. Without a word, he poured a brandy and brought it to her, but, without meaning to do so, she pushed his arm aside and the glass fell from his hand on to the table and broke.

She paused in her weeping, looking down in dismay at the shards of glass and the dark pool of brandy. When she looked at him again he was smiling and, crying again, desperate for comfort, she went to him. He put his arms around her and held her until she was still.

When she lifted her head from his shoulder at last, he was still smiling. He kissed her, very gently at first, and she felt a warmth in her flesh, as if her blood had begun to flow once more.

And because, at that moment, she needed such warmth, because she was tired of fighting, because she was grateful to him and, most of all, because he was kind and gentle and he was *there*, she responded with an eagerness that surprised them both when he kissed her again.

Yet even as this happened, even as she felt herself drifting deliciously away, the little imp of mischief that lived in Rosie and never left her alone for long, was jumping around in her head remarking on the softness of Mr Whitby's beard and how much it tickled!

6

It was gone half-past ten when Whitby drove her back to Tottenham. He had begged her to stay longer, to stay the night, but she had insisted on going back to The Winged Horse. His motor-car, a long shining brute of a machine, had no roof or hood and, since the night was chill, he put one of his coats over her shoulders and loaned her a scarf which she put around her hair and tied under her chin.

She was silent on the journey, trying to sort out the turmoil in her head. The extraordinary feature of this extraordinary evening was that she felt no guilt. A little fear, perhaps, crouching like a mouse in the shadows of her mind, but she would come back to that later. And there was sadness there too, for, in the background, the stern everyday voice of Rosie Carr was telling her that it had been a brief fairyland interlude, and that it was nearing its end. She put this thought aside for the moment also, and, closing her eyes, gave herself up to the feeling of glowing, purring happiness that warmed her whole being.

It was wrong, all wrong, she knew, and it only proved that she was a bad girl, that she had bad blood in her, but she had enjoyed the act of love and given herself to it utterly, blissfully. There had been a little pain at first but not too much and, in a way, it had all been part of the flowing ecstacy.

He had carried her into the bedroom to the big bed, and the first time had been too quick and urgent perhaps, their hunger for each other too desperate for restraint. But after this, he had undressed her with gentle, trembling hands and they had lain naked together, talking in low voices while his fingers circled and smoothed their way over her breasts and thighs and touched the secret places of her body.

Oh, it had been lovely! And it had all felt so natural as, shyly to begin with but then with growing confidence, she had returned his caresses and felt him surge and quiver beneath her touch. The second time was perfect: the pleasure and excitement of it still tingled her flesh. He entered her slowly, with great tenderness, and lay inside her for a long time, loving her gently, murmuring sweet half-heard words, the rhythm mounting little by little, bringing her closer and closer to consummation, yet holding back and prolonging the delight until she felt that her body would explode with the exquisite pleasure of it all. Her senses were urging her upwards, becoming more clamorous, and for a few desperate moments it seemed that the last pinnacle of fulfilment would be denied her. She locked herself against him, fearful that he would draw away, rocking her body beneath his, feeling his strong urgent thrusts deep inside, until the climax came at last, shattering as a star-burst.

Oh, yes, it had been lovely, lovely. And afterwards, after they had lain in each other's arms and talked and kissed and talked some more, eagerly, as if they were discovering each other – after this, he had shown her into the bathroom, a real bathroom with its own WC and a long white bath-tub that was actually fixed to the floor and had taps of gleaming brass which provided hot and cold water!

The Winged Horse had no such luxury. Rosie had heard of bathrooms but she had never seen or been in one. One of her duties at the pub was to bring in the tin bath which hung on the wall of the shed in the yard after the pub had closed and fill it with hot water from the copper, ready for use, first by The Missus and then, if he felt in the mood, by The

Guv'nor. On Saturday mornings, when she came down, her first task was to bale out the cold scummy water, bucketful by bucketful, pour it down the kitchen sink and then drag the bath into the yard where she tipped out the last few inches of water and put the bath back in the shed until the next time. It was a job she loathed.

Rosie took a bath when she could, on some other night, wedging a chair under the handle of the door as a precaution against any sudden intrusion by The Guv'nor but, for the most part, she carried hot water to her room two or three times a week, stripped naked and washed herself all over. She felt safer from The Guv'nor there and it was less exhausting than bringing in the bath.

She had stretched out in Whitby's bath, her body glowing in the steaming water, wondering if all this was truly happening to Rosie Carr. She stayed so long that Whitby, wearing a long brocaded dressing-gown, had come in to see how she was getting on. The astonishing thing was that she had no feelings of shyness or embarrassment with him: he sat on the cork-covered stool and they talked some more, and it had all seemed deliciously intimate but perfectly natural.

There was no sign of Pickford, the man-servant, and Whitby brought some ham-sandwiches and a pot of coffee into the sitting-room. Rosie guessed that he had made the sandwiches himself, for they were thick clumsy things, the bread hacked from the loaf, the ham hacked in thick chunks from the bone. And she really didn't like coffee, she wasn't used to it, and would have preferred tea. Still, it didn't matter, nothing mattered, except that she knew that she would soon have to go home and that it would all be over.

And now it is over, she thought, as the motor-car moved into territory that she recognised. The dreaming Rosie retreated, the everyday Rosie stepped forward in her place and asked Whitby to pull up some distance away from The Winged Horse.

'I'll walk the rest,' she said.

'I'll take you to the door,' he protested.

'And set all the tongues wagging? No, thank you.'

'When will I see you again?' He took her arm and pulled her closer.

'I don't know,' she said.

'Tomorrow?'

'Don't be daft! Some of us have to work, you know!'

'When, then? When? The weekend?'

'I'm working this weekend.'

'I've got to see you!'

'Perhaps it would be better if you didn't.'

'What are you talking about? What do you mean?' The grip on her arm tightened.

'Oh, use your loaf!' she said. 'You know what I mean. I like you, I like you a lot, otherwise – well, it wouldn't have happened. Don't run off with the idea that I carry on like that as a regular habit.'

'I know,' he said, 'I knew it was the first time. I suppose I ought to say I'm sorry.'

She put a finger to his lips. 'You'll do nothing of the sort! I'm a grown girl, not a baby. I had a lovely time, honest, I'm not just saying that, and I don't regret a minute of it. But all good things must come to an end, isn't that what they say? I mean, be sensible, love. I haven't just come up with the milk. It might have been the first time for me, but I'm bloody sure it wasn't for you. Was it?'

'No,' he admitted. 'But there's never been anyone like you, Rosie. And never will be.'

'Codswallop!' she said bluntly. 'You don't believe that any more than I do. Face facts. There's no future in it, not for you, not for me. Best thing is to forget it – wipe the slate. Go home, get on that telephone-thing of yours, and speak to one of your lady-friends. Ask one of them to join you for the weekend – someone more in your class.'

'Don't talk like that!' he said bitterly.

'What other way is there to talk?' she replied. 'It's the truth. We run on different rails, you and me, different lines. It was pure accident that we met.' She paused and sighed. 'So, we'll stick this evening in our memory book, kiss good-bye, and that will be that. Bob's your uncle, as they say.'

'You mean it?'

'I haven't been talking for the sake of my health, have I?'

'And you really think you'll get rid of me so easily?'

'I'll have a damned good try,' she said, smiling. She pulled her hand away. 'Well, that's your lot, Rosie. On your way!' She kissed his cheek quickly. 'Ta for everything. For Tommo and – well, everything. And tell that Mr Bernstein not to worry, I'll find the money to pay him somehow.'

'Bye, Rosie, darling,' said Whitby. 'I'll be seeing you.'

'You'll be lucky!' Rosie said. 'Bye, love.' She blew him a kiss and ran off into the night.

They were just turning out at The Winged Horse: little groups of people, their faces yellow in the lamplight, lingered outside the pub, prolonging the evening. As Rosie came into view, a shout of welcome went up.

'Here she comes!'

Tommo came running forward, picked Rosie up and swung her round. 'Rosie! I'm out! Bail! I got bail!'

'All right, Tommo,' she cried. 'All right. It's lovely to see you. Now stop larking around and tell me what happened.'

'A bloody miracle, that's what happened,' he said. 'This geezer turned up, Mr Bernstein. He's a big solicitor from up West. He worked the oracle, had the rozzers feeding out of his hand.' He clicked his fingers. 'Fixed bail like that. And he's going to take on my case – I tell you, it's a bloody miracle.'

'Did he say – I mean – how did he know about you?' Rosie waited fearfully for the answer.

'Oh, he said something about working for a Legal Society. A society that helps the poor when they're in trouble. Fair enough – I'm poor and I'm in dead trouble, right? And I tell you something else, Rosie. It won't cost me a brass farthing! This society pays the lot, puts up the bail, everything! What do you think of that?'

'I think you're bloody lucky,' she said.

Whitby, she thought. There was no society. Whitby had put Mr Bernstein up to it, he was footing the bill. What a fool she'd been not to realise that from the beginning, what an idiot! And there crossed her mind the bitter thought that what had happened in the big bed had been his way of

234

exacting payment. She felt cold inside, as if a shadow had fallen across the glowing memory of the evening.

She heard Tommo say: 'What are you doing with that thing round your head?' and realised that she was still wearing Whitby's scarf. She pulled the knot undone, removed the scarf and shook her hair free, but she made no attempt to answer his question.

'I'm ever so glad for you, Tommo,' she said. 'I'm sure it will all work out. I'll see you around anyway. I'm tired, I'm going to turn in.'

'You can't go yet, Rosie. I want to celebrate.'

'Another time, Tommo. 'Night.'

Later, in her room, she folded the scarf neatly and put it away in the box with her other possessions. Strictly speaking, it did not belong to her, but it was unlikely that she would ever meet Whitby again and be able to return it.

And, in a way, she thought, it is mine. It represents a part of Rosie Carr's life like all the other things – the rose from Major Pauley, the necklace of shells, her mother's purse and wedding ring. The scarf would remind her of this night.

Just before she fell asleep, another thought occurred to her. You're not a virgin any more, Rosie, she told herself, you've been broken. No man will want to marry you now.

Oddly enough, the thought did not trouble her. For the time being, at least, she was off men and would not care if she never went out with another man again!

CHAPTER TWELVE

1

'You're making excellent progress, Rosie,' said Miss Jones. 'It's obvious that you have an aptitude for words.'

Rosie did not know what aptitude meant, but she guessed that it was a good thing. She had been calling on Miss Jones for a fortnight, three times each week, and was now on her sixth lesson. It had been easier than she had feared and now that the barriers were down, she was passionately eager to make progress. Each night, before sleeping, she toiled over the tasks Miss Jones had set her: when weariness tempted her to the bed instead of the table, she remembered the man she had met in the lobby of The House of Commons, James Keir Hardie. Rosie had learned something more about Hardie from Russell Whitby, something that astonished and inspired her. Not only had he educated himself by candle-light after a day's work, but down in the pit, in the blackness of the pit, he had begun to learn a form of writing called short-hand, marking the outlines on the coal face with chalk! She told herself once again that she would match his example and pull herself out of ignorance whatever the cost.

The alphabet had come fairly quickly and Rosie was already on to words. She set herself a stern target: each day ten new words had to be learned and written down at least ten times. The writing was harder than the reading. Her quick mind absorbed the words without too much difficulty; APPLE, BALL, CAT, DOG, EGG, FIRE, GOAT, HEN, INK, JUG – and so on, all the way down the alphabet (although she had problems with X), she was able to read the words aloud from the book and there were pictures to help her. But writing them down was a slow, troublesome process and, quite often, she would burst into tears of frustration as her unpractised fingers clumsily copied the letters.

When she began to join words together to make what Miss Jones called sentences, there were further difficulties. She found it hard to understand words like AND and THE. J for JANE was simple: there was a picture of a little girl in the reading book and Rosie understood that Jane was her name. Little Jane, wearing her sun-bonnet, was being taken for a walk in the park by her nurse. Rosie had seen such uniformed nursemaids before, on her occasional excursions to London, and so it wasn't difficult to comprehend N for NANNY.

You could see a little girl and you could see a nanny, they existed and, in certain circumstances, you could even touch them. But you couldn't see or touch an AND or a THE. There were no pictures of these words in her book, and no satisfactory explanation of why the combination of A and N and D or T and H and E should make up a certain word. When she wrote the phrase JANE AND NANNY it didn't look right somehow. The AND looked wrong. It got harder too, as she began to realise that there were dozens of words which did not represent any particular objects or people. D for DOG presented no problem: but she thought it very peculiar when she wrote I LIKE THE DOG on her slate.

'Don't try to understand everything at once, dear,' Miss Jones told her. 'Some words are joining words, some words describe things and feelings. It will become clear as you go along. Until then, you must be patient and learn to take certain words on trust.'

For the most part, however, Rosie was thrilled by this new and wonderful adventure. Miss Jones was a good teacher and she sensed from the beginning that in Rosie she had a pupil of sensitivity and imagination. She encouraged her to feel the beauty of language and, years later, Rosie was often to hear the voice of Miss Jones in her head when her eye lit on a particular word.

'V. Look at it, Rosie. V. So simple, just two strokes. Down – up! But what a beautiful sound it makes when you say it! Vee! Vee! And all the lovely words that begin with V. Violin.

Violets. Vermillion. Velvet. Verdant. Vine. Vision. Oh, I think that V is the most beautiful letter in the alphabet, the loveliest letter of all.'

Rosie was quite won over by this approach although, in those later years, the practical side of her nature was apt to comment that V could not be granted a certificate of complete innocence. It was not all V for Violets and V for Violins. V also led the way with such words as Villian, Vandal, Violence and Virus.

Towards the end of each hour-long lesson, Miss Jones would tell Rosie to put away her slate and then spend five minutes reading aloud from her favourite poet, Lord Alfred Tennyson. Rosie loved these short sessions: they gave her a love of poetry which was to endure all her life. Over the years she had compensated for, and covered up, her lack of literacy by developing a good memory: in Chapel, for instance, she had learned by heart the words of dozens of hymns. Now bits and pieces of the poems she heard stuck in her mind and she recited them silently to herself as she went about her work. She loved the story of the bare-foot beggar maid who stood before the great King Cophetua. It rang in her head for days.

> As shines the moon in clouded skies,
> She in her poor attire was seen:
> One praised her ankles, one her eyes,
> One her dark hair and lovesome mien.
> So sweet a face, such angel grace,
> In all that land had never been:
> Cophetua swore a royal oath:
> 'This beggar maid shall be my Queen!'

Rosie, picturing this dramatic scene, could not help wondering if the king had kept his royal oath and, that being so, if the beggar maid had enjoyed being his queen. It was her general view that, on the whole, queens led rather dull lives, since they were largely confined to their palaces and only seen in public on special occasions. Did the Queen of England ever slip out of the back door to visit a music-hall or enjoy a knees-up in a pub? Highly unlikely, thought Rosie, the poor thing would be recognised instantly and surrounded by admiring crowds!

2

On this afternoon, at the end of the sixth lesson, Miss Jones, reading 'The Lady of Shalott', succeeded in reducing her pupil to tears. In an odd way, the Lancelot of the poem made Rosie think of Russell Whitby, although she could not reason out why this should be, nor why the thought should make her weep.

She was reminded, then, of the letter. His letter. The postman had dropped it on the bar-counter some four days ago, commenting as he did so:

'Oi, oi! One for you, Rosie. What have you been up to girl? That's from Parliament, that is. See that there crest on the back of the envelope? Parliamentary crest, that is!'

'What of it?' asked Rosie. It was the first letter she had ever received, but she was determined not to show her excitement.

'Must be important,' said the postman and waited, hoping perhaps that Rosie would reveal all.

'That's my business,' Rosie said. 'It's for you to deliver and me to read, and that's the top and bottom of it!' And, defiantly, she slid it down the front of her blouse.

Luckily neither The Missus nor The Guv'nor were there to ask awkward questions and Rosie was able to examine the letter in peace in her room later that day. If it was from Parliament, she reasoned that it could have come only from one of two people: Frank's father, Sir Roger Lambert, or Russell Whitby. She was unable to make head or tail of the main body of the short note but her knowledge of letters was sufficiently advanced for her to make out the R and the W of the final signature. Russell Whitby!

She felt her heart-beat quicken and immediately scolded herself for this reaction. You sent him packing, girl, she told herself, so what are you getting all excited about?

Rosie carried the letter around with her for the next two days. It gave her an odd sensation to feel it there, tucked into the top of her corset, nestling against her breasts, reviving not only the memories but the urges of that evening with Whitby. She was desperate to know what he had written, but she was caught in a trap of her own making: there was no-one in her immediate circle to whom she dare go and ask for help, admit that she could not read. The only possible person was Miss Jones (Rosie could not bring herself to think of her teacher as Maggie) and even here there was a problem. Suppose the letter contained an indiscreet reference to that evening? Suppose there were other things in it – endearments, an invitation – things that she would not want another person to see or hear?

Now, facing Miss Jones, the letter seemed to be burning her flesh and on an impulse she drew it out. Miss Jones had turned back to her crowded untidy desk and did not see what had happened.

'Well, don't stand around here, Rosie,' she said briskly. 'I've got work to do if you haven't. I'll see you next week.'

Rosie was turning away, the letter was on the way back to its resting-place, when Miss Jones swung round and saw the movement. 'What's the matter?' she asked. 'What have you got there?'

'Nothing. It's all right.'

'Stuff! It's not all right. What is that – a letter?'

'Yes.'

'Then why didn't you say so, for heaven's sake! A letter – and you want me to read it for you?'

'Please.'

'I can't read it while you hang on to it, can I? Hand it over now, quick, sharp!'

There was a long heavy silence as Miss Jones studied the letter. In Rosie's ears, the tick of the old clock on the mantelshelf sounded like a heartbeat. Miss Jones sniffed and looked up.

'Do you know who this is from?'

'Mr Whitby? A man called Russell Whitby.'

'Hmph. Is he a friend of yours?'

'Sort of. I've met him a couple of times.'

'I see. Well, he wants to see you again. That is more or less what he writes.' Miss Jones paused, poising herself as she did when about to read a poem.

> Dear Rosie,
>   I have resisted the temptation to
> call upon you at your place of employment
> for fear of causing you embarrassment but
> I simply must see you again. Please do not
> refuse. I will wait for you next Sunday at
> 12 noon by Cleopatra's Needle on the Embank-
> ment. If this is not convenient because of
> your duties, I will be there at the same time
> the following Sunday. Do come. I have such
> a lot I wish to say to you.
>   Yours truly,
>   Russell Whitby.

3

Miss Jones folded the letter and handed it back to Rosie with a thin smile. For a fleeting moment, Rosie wondered if Miss Jones had a beau, or whether the smile reflected jealousy.

'Well, he seems very anxious to meet you again,' said Miss Jones.

'Yes,' Rosie nodded.

'He is a very bright young man. One of the coming men in politics, or so they say.'

'Do you know him?' Rosie asked.

'I met him once, a couple of years back, at a function in the House of Commons. And he supports the Workers' Educational Association. I also met – ' Miss Jones closed her mouth suddenly, checking whatever she had been about to say. Instead, she added: 'He is a very personable young man.'

'Yes,' said Rosie, rising from her chair. 'Well, I'd better get a wiggle on. See you next week?'

'What? Oh, yes. Next week.' Miss Jones was chewing the end of a much-bitten pencil, seemingly preoccupied with her own thoughts. Rosie was at the door when she spoke again:

'Rosie.'

'Yes?'

'Look, it is no affair of mine,' Miss Jones got up and came round to Rosie. For the first time in their relationship she seemed to have difficulty in putting her tongue to words. 'You must tell me to mind my own business if that is how you feel. But we are friends, I hope?'

'Of course,' said Rosie. Oh, lor, she thought with dread, she's going to read me the Riot Act about Russell Whitby, tell me not to play with fire and all that tosh!

'Well,' said Miss Jones, 'on that basis, I think you ought to know, that is if you don't know already, that Mr Whitby is married. I met his wife at the function I mentioned. A charming woman.' An odd wistful note entered her voice as she continued: 'It's my experience that most handsome men are married. At anyrate, it is always best to proceed on that assumption. Well, there it is. I've told you. Did you know?'

Rosie found herself lying, and blushing as she did so. 'Yes. Mr Whitby told me.'

'Good,' said Miss Jones. 'No bones broken then. You're a big girl, you know what you are doing and won't want any lectures from an old stick like me. Next week, then?'

'Yes. Thank you.'

Outside in the street, Rosie sat on the low front wall of a nearby house to gather herself. God, what a bloody mug she was, what a bloody innocent! She had wondered briefly if Whitby were married but, seeing not the slightest sign of feminine occupation in his rooms, she had put the thought from her mind. How right she had been to give him his marching orders! He was a bastard, a sod of the first water! His kind were all the same! Because she worked for a living in a pub, because she wasn't in his class, he had considered her fair game. As for wanting to see her again, well, he could go and fly his kite. If he needed a fancy woman, he could go and look somewhere else. There were plenty to choose from!

She began to walk back to the pub. That's that, she told herself. You live and learn. Perhaps next time you won't be so eager, my girl, perhaps you'll be more careful!

And then, as the anger dwindled and died, another voice took over. What the dickens are you going on about, she asked herself. So he is married – what difference does that make? You wouldn't have wed him if he'd been free and if he had gone on his bended knees to ask you! You more or less told him that, when you said you wouldn't see him any more. So stop feeling like a martyr. You had a good time, a lovely time, no-one was hurt. Chalk it up to experience and get on with living your life!

As if to emphasise this resolution she took out the letter, tore it into pieces and dropped these down the slit of a drain-cover. Walking on, she felt a sudden twinge of regret and wished that she could call back the letter. The truth was that no man had captured her imagination or engaged her emotions to the same degree as Whitby. Was she in love with him? She had missed him, thought of him often and, if Miss Jones had not spoken, she would have gone to the Embankment to meet him. And, from his letter, it looked as if he felt the same way. It was either love or something very near it.

The sterner voice cut through these sentiments once more. You're getting all fanciful again, girl! If that's the way you're going to carry on, it's just as well that it is all over! Just get it into your head once and for all – there is no bloody King Cophetua and no bloody Sir Lancelot for you! That rubbish is for poetry and stories, you live in real life!

4

By the time she reached Fortune Street, Rosie had argued herself out of depression and anger and had quite recovered her spirits. She felt hungry suddenly and, walking on down the High Street, she went into Coltman's, the butchers and ordered a hot penny saveloy sausage and a half-pennyworth of pease pudding. Mr Coltman was as famous for these delicacies as he was for his cuts of meat. The saveloys and the pease pudding were kept in steaming trays in the shop-window and, if you wished to eat on the premises, there was a long counter down one side of the shop, furnished with stools.

Rosie chose a place near the doorway and as she sat down with her plate, she heard a familiar voice:

'Oi, Oi! All right for some! Don't they feed you up at the pub then?'

She turned, surprised but pleased, to see Tommo smiling down at her: as she did so, he swept off his curly-brimmed bowler and made an extravagant bow.

'Me Lady! Would you do me a kind favour?'

'What?'

'Would you allow a humble admirer to ping the elastic in your drawers?'

'Give over!' said Rosie with mock dignity. 'Have a saveloy instead. My treat.'

'That,' said Tommo, pulling up a stool, 'that is the best offer I've had from a lady all day!'

'Same again, Mr C,' called Rosie. 'One girl-and-boy and a ha'porth of pease pud.'

'Coming up,' said Mr Coltman.

'You are looking a treat, Rosie,' Tommo said. 'A sight for sore eyes. Better than a drowned policeman!'

'You're looking pretty chipper yourself, Tommo.'

'It goes well, Rosie love, it goes well. That Mr Bernstein I told you about is a flaming miracle. He's got the rozzers running round in circles. They've reduced the charge to misdemeanour for starters. Already that's better. Naturally, we're pleading not guilty and the way Mr Bernstein is going, I've got no worries.'

'Don't count your chickens, Tommo.'

'I tell you, he's a marvel. To look at, he's nothing more than two-pennorth of scrag end, but I tell you, when he gets going he's like a steam-engine in trousers!'

'Well, let's hope it works out,' said Rosie.

Tommo leaned towards her. 'When this is all over, Rosie girl, when I'm all free and clear, I want a word with you.'

'Oh? What about?'

'I'll tell you then.'

'No. Tell me now.'

'Well,' said Tommo, 'I reckon it's time you and me stopped mucking about.'

'I'm sure I don't know what you mean,' said Rosie primly.

'Give over, Rosie,' said Tommo. 'You know very well what I mean. It's time we stopped all this bloody fandangle. Stopped it dead. I reckon we should chuck the handle in after the hammer.'

'You've lost me,' said Rosie.

'Get wed. Hitched. Four legs in a bed. You know what I mean!' He spiked the saveloy that Mr Coltman had put before him, took a bite from it, and immediately exploded in agony.

'Christ, that's bloody hot!'

'It came from a hot place,' said Rosie.

'Well, what do you say?' asked Tommo, when he had recovered.

'I'd say that you've got the table-manners of a pig,' Rosie said calmly.

'No. I don't mean that!' he said indignantly. 'I mean – about you and me.'

'I've had better offers.'

'From who?' he said angrily. 'From that cooper, Roberts? Stan Roberts? You'd never marry him!'

'I might,' she said. 'Only he hasn't asked me.'

'Who then?'

'Don't blow your thatch, Tommo. Nobody's asked me. I was pulling your leg.'

'Then how about it?' said Tommo, and blew on his saveloy to cool it.

'Have you always been so romantic,' asked Rosie coldly, 'or did you have to take lessons?'

'What?'

'Never mind.'

'Look, Rosie,' said Tommo uncomfortably, 'you know how I feel.'

'No,' said Rosie, 'how do you feel? With your hands?'

'About you! Christ, you're a tantalising cow! I mean how I feel about you!'

'Tell me,' Rosie said quietly. 'And while you're about it,

you can tell me what brought this rush of blood to your head.'

There was a pause while Tommo chewed and gulped down a mouthful of saveloy. He looked at her, perplexed and frowning. 'What do you want me to say, for Gawd's sake?'

'If you don't know, I'm not going to tell you,' she answered.

'Well,' he said. 'I mean, well, I been thinking lately. A lot. Thinking. Time I settled down like, know what I mean? So I thought – how about Rosie?'

'Nobody else would have you, that what you mean?'

'There's nobody else I want,' he said.

'Oh, Tommo.' Rosie smiled and shook her head, knowing what an effort those words had cost him, knowing that they were the nearest thing to a declaration of love she would ever hear from his lips. He was a good man, weak in many ways, a man whose dreams were always slightly beyond his reach, but a good man at heart. He had need of her and she was very fond of him, she could do a lot worse.

'Well?' he asked.

'And suppose they send you to prison? What kind of husband will that make you?'

'I told you Rosie, we've got that licked. There's about as much chance of me going to chokey as there is of a chicken laying a square egg! So – what do you say, girl?'

'We'll see, Tommo,' she said gently, patting his hand. 'Let's wait and see, eh? I don't know whether I'm ready for the marriage stakes just yet.'

5

By the following Monday, the little mouse of fear in the back of Rosie's head began to stir. According to her reckoning she was was least three days late with her period, possibly four. It was worrying, because what she always called 'the monthlies' or 'the visitor' usually arrived promptly: she could not remember a time when she had been more than a day overdue.

The fear grew as Monday passed and Tuesday came with no change. Rosie could not tell whether the slight nausea she felt on waking was due to her growing fear or to something else. She went through her duties at the pub in a kind of daze, her mind filled with one thought only and behind that thought a dark and swelling terror.

Oh, God, she prayed, don't let it happen, don't let it happen to me!

She had seen other girls who had fallen, young unmarried girls with babies. For the most part they were sad-faced creatures, looked upon with scorn or a passing pity by the local community, and forced to turn for help to the hard unforgiving face of charity or to parents who were already hard put to help themselves. One whom she knew reasonably well, a girl called Minnie Prior, lived in a damp and miserable room scraping a living as best she could by charring for people who did not mind her taking the baby to work. Minnie had pride, but no future. Men who would look at, let alone marry, a girl with another man's baby were as rare as rain in the desert.

Many such girls were forced into prostitution simply to survive. Again, she had before her the example of one of the women who plied their trade near The Winged Horse. Her name was Vicky and, according to the local gossip, she had come from a respectable family on the Isle of Wight. There were some who said that her father was a minister in the Church of England. Minister or not, he had turned her away in disgust and she had found her way, by stages, and without any plan, to North London. She was a strange, dark-eyed creature, rapidly losing her looks, who drowned her plentiful sorrows in gin when she could, and who was known to entertain clients in the same room and on the same bed where her little boy slept.

Oh, God, don't let it happen, don't let it happen to me!

There were moments when Rosie railed at men, as thousands of women in her plight had done before her. How easy it was for them! They could take their bloody pleasure and forget it afterwards! There were things, things they could use, but how many bothered? No, they just enjoyed them-

247

selves without a thought for the girl and the consequences. As for Mr-bloody-Whitby, she cursed him and she cursed the seed he had planted in her body, the little invader that threatened her whole life.

There were other moments when she thought bitterly of her own background. The bad blood had come out, and she was being punished for it. Was she about to repeat the pattern of her mother's life, moving from lover to lover with a child clinging to her skirts?

Oh, God, dear God, don't let it happen, please don't let it happen to me! Help me this once, just this once, and I'll never sin again! I'll be a good girl, I promise, I promise, I promise.'

By Thursday, fear had been joined by its darker brother, desperation. Rosie lit a fire under a copperful of water and, when the pub had closed for the night, she dragged in the tin bath. The Missus came in as she was making her preparations and, with a note of curiosity in her voice, begged leave to know what was going on.

'I've got a bit of a chill,' Rosie said. 'I thought if I took a hot bath it might help to sweat it out.'

'You need something!' The Missus said curtly. 'You've been in a doze for the last couple of days. Like a tit in a trance. But next time you want to take a bath in the middle of the week, you might consider asking my permission. I know I'm only the dishrag here, I know you do as you please, but it does happen to be my wood and coke you're burning, not to mention the use of the soap and water!'

With this ritual reproof, The Missus went to bed. Rosie waited at the foot of the stairs until she heard the tell-tale squeal of the spring on the double bed which told her that The Missus was safely settled for the night and then filled the bath with scalding water. She had heard somewhere that the water had to be almost too hot to bear. For good measure (for she had heard also that this was part of the treatment) she swallowed a stiff dose of castor-oil. Her stomach revolted against the fishy liquid and it was as much as she could do to keep it down: she sat for awhile, fighting the nausea, her stomach churning, hoping against all the dictates of reason that this was a good sign.

It was agony to lower herself into the water. The heat screamed at her body until it seemed as if the blood was on fire and sweat streamed from her face. She lay there, her eyes closed, her teeth gritted, gripping the sides of the bath, praying that it would work, praying once more for help. As the worst of the heat went out of the water and the steam faded, she saw that her flesh had gone a deep pink. Had it worked? She wasn't sure but she had an idea that, if she had been successful, there would be signs of blood in the water, but there were none. She consoled herself with the thought that perhaps it was too early to expect results.

As she clambered from the bath she felt a sudden pain in her stomach, a pain so sharp that it doubled her up in agony. Again, hope had a moment's holiday and then, as her stomach rumbled ominously she realised what it was. The bloody castor-oil was working, though not in the way she had intended! She threw on some clothes and made a frantic dash for the lavatory outside in the yard, the wooden hut marked down for the use of staff.

Two hours passed before an exhausted Rosie could haul herself off to bed, two hours filled with frequent visits to the yard. Before lying down she spread an old towel over the lower part of the bottom sheet just in case the treatment worked and her reluctant period turned up at last, then, almost dropping with fatigue, she slept.

6

She was awakened by a voice shouting her name, by a rough hand shaking her shoulder, and looked up into the angry face of The Missus.

'Do you know what time it is, girl!'

Rosie struggled up out of sleep, looking at the intruder with dreary eyes.

'It is nigh on eight o'clock! Mr Quorn has been waiting for his breakfast this past half-hour. What's come over you, for heaven's sake? You've never done this before. Whatever else, you've always been reliable. I've always given you full credit for that. Now what am I to think?'

Rosie stared at The Missus uncomprehendingly throughout this tirade, trying to listen over the painful hammering in her head.

'Don't move, will you! Don't let me disturb you!' cried The Missus, growing more angry by the minute.

'I'm sorry.' Rosie pulled herself out of bed and the motion of doing so set the hammering going with renewed fury.

'Good!' said The Missus with heavy sarcasm. 'Thank you. Much obliged, I'm sure.'

'I'll be down directly,' mumbled Rosie.

The Missus marched to the door, then turned and said: 'You'd better start pulling your socks up, my girl. If this morning is anything to go by – not to mention the past two days – you'll be looking for another place.' She took a step back into the room and lowered her voice. 'I'll tell you something, Rosie, something for your own good. Mr Quorn has been at me for weeks, months, to get rid of you. Why, I don't know. You must have done something to get up his nose. But I've always stood up for you. You've been loyal and hard-working and it is not in my nature to abuse that. I am not a vindictive woman, as you well know and others can confirm. But there is a limit. If you go on like this, I shan't have a leg to stand on. Do you understand what I am saying?'

'Yes, ma'am.' Rosie nodded. 'It's this chill. I'll be all right as soon as I get moving.' She stood up, steadying herself on the bedpost.

Frowning, The Missus moved closer and there was a marked softening of her tone as she asked: 'Are you all right, Rosie?'

'Yes. Truly.'

'Hmph. Let me look at you.' The Missus lifted Rosie's head and studied her face. 'Hmph, you don't look all right to me. You look like death warmed over. You're sure there's nothing wrong?'

'No, no, really and truly.' Rosie was beginning to become alarmed by this persistent questioning. The last thing she needed just now was to lose her job at the pub and that would most certainly happen if The Missus even guessed at the cause of her distress. In a couple of months or so, when she began to show (the thought stabbed her body like a knife), The Missus, pressed by The Guv'nor, would have no option but to turn her out. And where on earth would she go then? She had to hang on, she needed time.

'All right then,' said The Missus. 'Don't moon about up here, feeling sorry for yourself. Other people have chills, you know, you are not the only one. You won't find me giving in to aches and pains. Best cure for a chill is to work it off. I'll expect you downstairs in five minutes.'

As soon as the door had closed, Rosie pulled back the cover and examined the towel. There was no stain, no tell-tale hint of blood. Her heart sank and the despair came back, freezing her blood. It had all been for nothing then, all that agony for nothing!

7

By the time Sunday came, Rosie had reached a decision. It was her day off and, wearing her best costume, she set off in bright sunshine for London to meet Russell Whitby. In his letter he had said that he would wait on the Embankment at noon on two consecutive Sundays; she had let the first one go by, determined to hold to her pronouncement that she would not see him again. Since then her circumstances had altered dramatically and she saw this meeting as her last hope.

There was still no sign of her period and she had resigned herself to the inevitable. She was pregnant, and that was that. In the last couple of days she had taken a cooler look at the situation, weighing up all the possibilities. The fear and desperation were still there and capable of bringing her out in a hot sweat when she thought about the future, but she had succeeded to some extent in bringing her emotions under control. She had forced herself to concentrate on the present, on her daily tasks, and found that this helped her not only to keep the fear at a distance but to think more clearly in general.

So she had come to the conclusion that she would have to

go and meet Russell Whitby and seek his help. Her anger at his part in the affair had now resolved itself into a deep bitterness: they had both acted irresponsibly perhaps but she could not help feeling that the greater share of blame rested on his shoulders. With his vastly wider experience he must have been awake of the risk he had taken and the consequences for her.

Even so, what point was there in apportioning blame? The thing was done now, the consequences were upon her, and blame was a useless thing. Yes, he must be made to pay, to carry his share of the responsibility, but she must be careful not to let her bitterness overflow, to allow an angry tongue to drive him away. She needed his help, she needed it desperately and, if necessary, she was prepared to plead for it. This was no time for pride. Pride, she thought wryly, is for married women or unpregnant girls.

At Charing Cross she asked a policeman the way to the Embankment and Cleopatra's Needle and, for good measure, requested to know the time. He was young and fresh-faced, and smiled at her appreciatively as he responded, but she scarcely noticed him. She was relieved to learn that it was only 11.45 a.m.: she had time in hand. As she thanked the policeman and moved away a heavily-pregnant young woman walked past, sweating profusely in the dusty heat. It's strange, Rosie thought, but in the last few days she had seen more pregnant women than ever before: were there more about or was it simply that, because of her own condition, she had begun to notice them more? And she wondered enviously if the young woman was married.

She waited for an hour, looking down at the rippling water of the river or scanning the roadway for a sign of Whitby or his motor-car. With each passing minute, the stone she had carried in her heart for almost a week grew heavier and colder. Big Ben chimed one o'clock. Perhaps she had mistaken the time? She decided to give him five more minutes, then another five, then five more. At a quarter past one she realised that it was hopeless. Still, she hung on for another fifteen minutes staring down at the river and thinking that, if all else failed, there was one way out, wondering what it would be like to drown. She could never take a knife to herself, the pain and the blood would be too much to take: but the water seemed to be cool and inviting, even friendly, as if it were opening its arms to her.

A family, husband, wife and two children, drew near, laughing together. Rosie turned to watch them, thinking how odd it was that almost everyone seemed to be in happy holiday mood this day. The pretty young wife glanced at Rosie as they went past and, for a moment, their eyes met. It was probably imagination, but Rosie thought she saw concern and sympathy in the other girl's eyes; it lasted only a instant, then she smiled at Rosie and passed on. Had she guessed? Had some feminine instinct told her?

The tiny incident changed the direction of Rosie's thoughts. If Russell Whitby would not come to her, she would go to him! She remembered that his rooms were in Lord North Street and felt sure that she would recognise the house again if she saw it. And Lord North Street was only a few minutes walk away from where she had been waiting.

A policeman in Parliament Square gave her further directions and she walked on, hurrying a little now as her hopes see-sawed upwards once more. Had he simply forgotten the arrangement to meet? That was unlikely, she thought: it was far more probable that he had turned up on the previous Sunday, and, having been disappointed, decided that he would waste no more time on her. After all, she told herself, he is a Member of Parliament, a busy and important man. You could hardly expect such a person to spend his time chasing after a barmaid, an uneducated skivvy.

By the time she reached Lord North Street, Rosie had quite forgiven Whitby for his failure to turn up for the appointment and convinced herself that he would be delighted to see her. She imagined his surprised smile of welcome when he opened the door and saw her standing there.

But which was the house? Was it on the left or the right? She remembered quite clearly that boxes of flowering geraniums stood on either side of the approach to the front door, but geraniums appeared to be popular in Lord North

253

Street and at least a dozen houses boasted a similar display. A milkman who was making deliveries in the street and who had an eye for a pretty girl, noticed her rather lost appearance and came to her rescue.

'Russell Whitby?' he said in response to her enquiry and gave her a curious look. 'Well, that's his house, over there. Number 12. Leastways, I suppose you could say it was his house.'

'You mean – he's moved?' she asked sharply.

'Oh, yes, he's moved all right, in a manner of speaking.' He frowned at her and added ponderously: 'Oh, come on, miss. You must have read about it. It was all over the papers.'

'What? What was in the papers?' A sudden fear gripped her, icicle fingers squeezing her heart; she saw the drawn blinds at Number 12 and knew the man's answer before he made it.

'Dead,' he said. 'Dead as a doornail. Killed when he was out hunting last Wednesday. Mind you, he was a mad bugger, they say he asked for it. Fell at some big jump and the horse rolled over on him. Killed him stone-bonker dead. Best thing, some say. If he'd lived, he'd very likely been a cripple.'

Rosie stared at the man. His face looked oddly distorted, his voice came to her like a distant echo. She swayed, murmured something incomprehensible and the astonished milkman caught her in his arms as she fainted and fell against him.

CHAPTER THIRTEEN

1

Rosie did not know how she found the strength to get back to Tottenham on the calamitous Sunday. She walked all the way, trudging mile after heavy mile as though her shoes were soled with lead. All she knew was that she had to be alone, that to sit on a bus or tram close to other people, to have to meet their eyes, would have been impossible.

For the time being, her own problems were pushed to the back of her mind and all her thoughts were concentrated on Russell Whitby. She was appalled by the enormity of his death, by the sheer waste of such a young and vibrant personality. What made it all the more unbelievable to her was the manner of his dying. Hunting! Chasing a bloody fox! He had died for nothing, for no good reason, he had thrown his life away!

Her senses were haunted by the memory of those clear, sparkling blue eyes, of that extraordinarily fair hair, of his teasing laughter, of the warm masculine scent of his body. Gone, all gone! Was he already buried, she wondered and, with a shiver, imagined him lying stiff and cold in underground darkness. There was heaven to be reckoned with, of course, but despite her Chapel connections Rosie had no great faith in the hereafter. It seemed to her that death was too final, too conclusive to leave much hope of heaven. She sensed that the whole idea was little more than a cruel device to persuade people, especially poor people, to accept today's hunger and misery without complaint on the understanding that tomorrow would be better. Rosie felt certain that God was far too sensible and just to indulge in such trickery.

By degrees, as her mind adjusted to the shattering loss of Whitby, she came back to her own problems. She was now far worse off than when she had started out that morning. There was no-one now to whom she could turn, no-one. She could not burden Mr Crooks or his family with her shame, nor could she seek help from Tommo or Stan Roberts. The mere thought of their finding out filled her with horror. But how was she to manage? How? She would in time lose her place at the pub and she would have nowhere to go. Her savings would just about allow her to move away to another district and take a small room for a few weeks. Even that would be difficult, for there were not many landladies who were prepared to take in pregnant unmarried girls and, even if she struck lucky, how would she cope when her money ran out? She knew next to nothing about having a baby – where would she have it and who would help her?

'Hiya, Rosie! Too proud to speak to your mates, are you?'

Rosie wrenched herself back to the present and turning, saw Big Bess smiling at her.

'Hello, Bess,' she said. 'Sorry, I didn't see you.'

'Not surprised. You were miles away, girl.' Big Bess came closer and wrinkled her face in concern. 'Blime old Reilly, Rosie, what have you been doing to yourself? You look like a bit of boiled rag!'

'I've been walking.' A wave of exhaustion swept over Rosie as she spoke and she staggered a little.

'Steady, girl! Easy does it!' Bess put out a huge hand and took Rosie's arm. 'Walking, is it? Where you walked from then?'

'London. The West End.'

'You want your brains dusted, girl!' said Bess in disgust. 'Here, you'd better come back with me and have a cuppa. I'm just round the corner. No argument now! You had any dinner?'

'No.'

'Anything to eat?'

'I had a bit of breakfast.'

'Nothing since then? Your guts must be fairly on the rumble. Look, I just popped out to get some muffins for tea.

Bloke will be along in a minute. How about that, eh? A couple of hot muffins, a cup of char and put your feet up. How does that strike?'

'Lovely, Bess. Ta ever so.'

A hand-bell sounded in the distance and Bess released Rosie's arm. 'That's the muffin-man. Hold on here a minute, ducks. And don't fall down till I get back.'

As Bess bustled away Rosie leaned against a shop-front, trying to gather herself. You've got to be careful Rosie, she warned herself. If you go back to the pub looking like death warmed over you'll be in dead trouble. You'll get your marching orders as sure as eggs are eggs and then where will you be? You've got to pull yourself together.

2

Ten minutes later, Rosie was sitting in Big Bess's kitchen supping tea and sinking her teeth gratefully into toasted muffins that fairly oozed with butter. She had not been to Bess's home before and was surprised to see how clean and precisely neat it was; such order somehow did not chime with Bess's boisterous, slap-happy manner. The faint salty smell of shellfish floated on the air as a reminder of Bess's daily occupation but Rosie did not find it unpleasant.

A little old man, round and gnarled as a walnut, sat in a worn leather armchair by the fire, toasting the muffins with a long wire fork. From time to time he sent quick delighted smiles and rippling chuckles in their direction, as though he were hugely enjoying himself.

Bess had introduced him as her father. 'Not a bad old stick. Deaf as a post. Can't hear a dicky-bird. Look, I'll show you.' She advanced on the old man and stretched her formidable lungs in a bellow that must have reached the street outside.

'You're a stupid old sod, right?' He nodded eagerly. 'How'd you like me to cut your cotton off?' Again the eager nod. 'Don't you reckon I ought to pack you off to the whore-house?' He nodded with even greater enthusiasm and chuckled hoarsely.

'It's a shame to tease the poor old feller,' said Rosie.

'Oh, he don't mind,' Bess said. 'Can't hear – thinks I'm playing a game. He's ninety-two, you know, or so he reckons. Worked on the stall up to six years ago. Ah, he's no trouble. Only thing's the fire. Fancy having a fire in this weather, eh? But the old man likes a bit of fire so I light it for him. Why not, eh? He hasn't got much to enjoy, has he?'

Her rough tenderness towards the old man touched Rosie: she had always suspected that the big woman's bark was worse than her bite and she found herself warming towards her. She found herself warming up in other ways too, for the internal heat generated by the hot tea and muffins, combined with the heat of the fire, brought a flush to her face and sweat to her forehead. Bess was in much the same way, for she said:

'Here, Rosie, bring your tea out to the back-yard. It's like a bloody oven in here. We'll leave the old man to sweat in peace.'

He sent a smile and a chuckle after them as Bess led the way to the yard. A heap of empty fish boxes and crates littered one corner, but just before the back door a small area had been cleared of rubbish and furnished with two wicker-work chairs and an upturned box for use as a table. At the end of the yard a few flowers struggled for survival in the only bit of earth that had not been paved over. From a nearby yard an unseen neighbour provided a musical background on a mouth-organ. After they had settled, Bess said:

'That's better. Nice bit of fresh air.'

'What's that for?' asked Rosie, pointing to a basket filled with pebbles that stood by Bess's chair.

'You'll soon see!' Bess replied and, as if on cue, a cat appeared on the top of one of the side fences. Bess scooped up a pebble and threw it at the cat, registering a near miss as the stone clattered against the fence and the startled animal made a leap to safety.

'It's the smell of fish,' said Bess. 'Brings the cats for miles around. I pelt the buggers but they still keep coming. I've had as many as a dozen sitting on that fence, watching me, daring me to throw.' She smiled and sighed. 'Well, never mind the cats. What's your trouble, eh?'

'Trouble? No trouble that I can think of,' said Rosie.

'Leave over, girl,' said Bess severely. 'I didn't come up with the milk this morning. I've been watching you this past week. You're not the same girl. What's the matter? Have you got one up the spout – is that the trouble?'

'What?' Rosie stared at Bess white-faced. God, dear God, had she made it so obvious?

'No need to look so shocked,' said Bess. 'You wouldn't be the first girl to get herself in the club and you won't be the last, by a long chalk.'

'Does it show?' whispered Rosie, looking down at her stomach.

'Not there, it doesn't,' Bess said. 'Tell the truth, I was guessing. Not far out, was I? It does show a bit, you know. I've seen enough girls in trouble to read the signs. It shows in the face, in the eyes.' She added, without emotion, as if she simply wanted to establish her credentials. 'I had a kid once, you know. Died of the dip when he was five. Diphtheria. That's a killer. Then I lost my old man a year later. He worked in a brewery. Got killed when some ropes broke and he was crushed under the big casks.' She smiled wryly: 'I always said the drink would kill him.'

'I don't know what to do,' said Rosie in a small voice.

'Well,' said Bess plainly, 'it takes two to make a baby. Find the bloody man and tell the bugger he'll have to wed you.'

'I can't,' replied Rosie and she told Bess the whole story pouring the words out with relief. Just to talk about it, to share the secret with someone, seemed to lighten the burden. Apart from pitching the odd pebble at an intrusive cat, Bess listened intently. When Rosie had finished, Bess nodded two or three times:

'Funny, y'know. I could have sworn you were going to say it was Tommo. He'd have you, you know, he'd have you like a shot. Always fancied you he has.'

'He asked me to marry him,' Rosie said. 'A week or so back – in his roundabout way. You know Tommo.'

'What did you say? You didn't turn him down?'

'No. Not straight out. I told him we'd have to wait and see.'

'There you are then,' said Bess, 'there's your answer.'

'He wouldn't have me now. Not in this state.'

'He doesn't have to know, does he?' said Bess calmly.

'How'd you mean?'

'Wake up, Rosie. You're usually bright as a brass button. Look, you go to Tommo. You tell him you've thought it over. You've decided to accept his offer. You don't want a long engagement – you'd like to get wed within the next week or so. Then, after the first week, you tell him you've got a bun in the oven.'

'I couldn't!' Rosie stared at Bess, her eyes wide with shock. 'Why not?'

'It wouldn't be fair, it wouldn't be right.'

'That's a load of swosh if ever I heard it!' said Bess. 'Who's talking about being fair? Was that MP geezer fair to you when he put you in the family way? No, girl, all men are the same, they don't care. A man can stick his poker in a hundred different fires and no-one thinks the worse of him. But let a girl carry on the same way, let her slip up like you, and the whole world is up in arms. And so we have to be cunning, don't we? We have to use our brains. It's the only weapon we've got. If some poor bloke gets lumbered with another bloke's kid, that's just too bad. That's nothing compared to what the bastards do to us.'

'I couldn't do it,' Rosie said, 'I wouldn't have the nerve to do it.' But in spite of her words, her mind was already biting on the idea, and a little desperate hope was flaring in her heart.

'I thought you liked Tommo?' Bess said.

'I do. I like him a lot.'

'Then I'm buggered if I know what you're waiting for.'

'He's got this case hanging over him. Comes up in a couple of weeks. I reckon he's got enough on his plate without taking on my troubles.'

'Get away! All the more reason for you to move in smartish before they send him to chokey. You're too bloody senti-mental, that's your trouble, Rosie. Girl in your position can't afford sentiment.'

'You don't think they'll send Tommo to prison?' A new

260

and terrible thought struck Rosie. With the death of Whitby it was probable that the finance for his lawyers would dry up. What would happen to poor Tommo if there was no-one to defend him? She heard Bess answer her question as from a distance:

'I'll lay odds they put him down for at least two years.'

No, thought Rosie, no, no, no! I can't take any more, I just can't take any more. It seemed to her as if her whole world were crumbling: the life that only a few weeks before had appeared to be so solid and permanent was falling apart, piece by piece, person by person.

'If I were you,' Bess said, 'I'd get hold of Tommo right away. The sooner the better.'

The mouth-organist began to play the song 'When You Come to the End of a Perfect Day'. Rosie had learned it a few weeks before to play in the pub and she listened now, thinking sadly about her own day. Then, with a confidence that she was a long way from feeling, she said:

'No, Bess. Ta all the same. But I couldn't do that to Tommo. Nor to anyone else come to that. No. Tommo's got his own troubles without having to contend with mine. I got myself into this mess and I'll have to drag myself out of it somehow.'

'Your funeral,' Bess said cryptically. Then, after a pause, and in a matter-of-fact voice, as if she were talking about the weather, she asked: 'Do you want to try Kate?'

'Kate? Who's she?'

'Woman I know of. Never met her myself, but I've heard of her. Have you got five quid?'

'Yes.'

'She'll get rid of it for a fiver. That used to be her price any road.'

'Oh, my gawd!' Rosie stared at Bess in disbelief. The see-saw within tilted once again and she felt yet another surge of hope. 'You're not having me on?'

'Why would I want to do that?'

'What does she do exactly?'

'You'll have to find that out for yourself.'

'She's done it for other girls?'

'Quite a few that I know of, yes.'

'And it works? I mean, what she does?'

'Well, she seems to have plenty of customers.'

'Could you take me to her?' asked Rosie eagerly.

'Now look, Rosie,' Bess said seriously. 'You are sure about this?'

'Please, Bess, please. I'm desperate.'

'It's not legal, you know that? You'll be breaking the law and so will she.'

'I don't care if she don't.'

'All right. But you've got to be dead careful, understand? Not a word to anyone.'

'Oh, Bess!' Rosie got up and flung her arms around the big woman. The pent-up tears came freely now. 'Oh, Bess, thank you! Thank you! You're a wonder, a real wonder.'

'I know,' said Bess. 'I surprise myself sometimes.' Then she took Rosie's face in her great hands and added, very gently: 'Little Rosie. I remember when you first came to the pub. A skinny kid. You hadn't had much of a life before that and you haven't had much since. When God was dishing out luck you must have been out in the back-shed. I hope you're doing the right thing about this baby, that's all I hope. In a way, I wish I hadn't mentioned Kate. I reckon you'd be better to go to Tommo.'

'No, Bess. Please!' Rosie pleaded.

'All right.' Bess sighed and said: 'I'll take you some time this week.'

3

Rosie spent the next three days in a state of mental confusion that was far worse than anything she had known before. She was made angry and frustrated by her inability to think clearly and act decisively.

On Sunday, she had seen the woman called Kate as the answer to all her problems, as the only possible release from her present agonies. But no sooner had she left Big Bess than the doubts began to appear like cracks in the ice that grow and splinter in all directions; then came fear as her imagination conjured up dark and bloody pictures, pictures in which she lay naked on a stinking mattress in a dank cellar while an old crone named Kate advanced upon her with fearsome instruments . . .

As if all this were not enough, she began for the first time to think of the tiny creature growing in her womb in odd, personal terms: in her mind's eye she kept seeing a little boy with the corn-coloured hair and impudent blue eyes of his father. The image wrenched at her heart and guilt came in to join fear and desperation . . .

In the event, the reality – on the surface at least – was much less frightening than her worst imaginings. A neat little draper's shop in a road just off Morning Lane in Hackney. A small handsome fresh-looking woman aged about thirty-five, with shining dark hair pinned in a bun, gentle brown eyes and a kindly manner. Such were Kate's establishment and Kate herself. Reassuring, not at all alarming.

The shop, of course, was a cover for what went on in the upper back room and it served that purpose well. It was the most natural thing in the world for women to patronise the place: it gave Kate a chance to sum them up and to estimate their reliability, something for which she had an unerring eye: and there was a back entrance, leading to an alley, which could be used in case of need.

A few minutes were spent in a ritual inspection of the stock and the purchase of some hat ribbons. Kate stood behind the counter, watching them benignly, smiling whenever Rosie caught her eye. Rosie was puzzled, wondering how on earth they could approach the real point of this visit. Excuse me for troubling you but I'm going to have a baby. Could you get rid of it for me, and how much do you charge? It couldn't possibly be like that surely. But how?

Bess solved the problem quite easily. As Rosie was paying for the ribbons she asked Kate: 'I think you know a mate of mine. A Mrs Wandle. Minnie Wandle.'

'Minnie!' Kate smiled. 'Oh, yes. How is she? Haven't seen her for ages. How is she?'

'Fit as a flea at a picnic,' Bess said. 'She sent her regards.'

'And you give her mine in return when you see her,' said Kate. 'Well, well, so you are friends of Minnie Wandle. Fancy. You should have said before. Any friend of Minnie is a friend of mine. Is there anything more I can do for you?'

It was as simple as that. Within minutes Kate's sister was summoned from the back to take charge of the shop and Rosie ascended a flight of linoleum-covered stairs to an upper back room. She was in real fear now and might have fled in panic but for the comforting presence of Bess.

The back-room did not live up to the promise of the shop below. The lower panes of the window had been painted a dark bottle green, cutting down the light and giving an odd cave-like chill to the room. A single bed with a black iron headrail stood against one wall with a folded grey blanket and an uncovered striped pillow lying on its stained mattress. Two or three bits of old carpet tried without success to cover the floor. A pair of wooden chairs. A wash-stand in which there stood a chipped pitcher and bowl. On the ceiling, dampness had stamped a dark stain that, to Rosie's eye, had the outline of a great hump-backed animal. Stacks of cardboard boxes against one wall gave support to Kate's claim that this was both stockroom and restroom.

Kate herself seemed to have changed on the climb upwards. The smile was still there but it seemed less natural, more forced: her voice took on a strange sneering tone and the gentle eyes grew sharp and calculating. She frightened Rosie and the girl had to clench her hands into tight fists to stop from trembling.

'Well,' said Kate, shaking her head. 'You girls. I don't know. You never learn, do you? Where you'd be without me, I do not know, I do not know. A girl's best friend, that's me, I reckon, eh? What do you say, eh?'

In truth, Rosie did not know what to say, but she murmured a polite yes.

'Mind you,' said Kate, 'you've got the looks. I'll say that, you've got the looks. I can understand the fellers hanging their hat up to you. You're quite a beauty. And you know it, eh? I bet you know it.' She smiled and touched Rosie's face. Her hand was quite tiny, almost doll-like. 'Nice skin. Lovely skin. Wish I had skin like that.' And quite suddenly, changing tack and tone, she added: 'It'll cost you. Might as well get that clear from the off. It'll cost you.'

'How much?' asked Bess.

'Ten quid.'

'I heard – ' Bess began, but Kate cut across her.

'Don't know what you heard, mate, but it's a tenner. No argument. Ten quid. Extra if I supply the gin, but you're welcome to bring your own. She'll need a drop of something. Well? If you don't like the price, you can turn round and go back where you came from and no hard feelings. What do you say?'

'Have you got that much, Rosie?' asked Bess.

'I brought six pounds ten,' said Rosie.

'No,' Kate said firmly.

'I'll make it up. It'll be all right,' Bess said.

'Good. Don't think I'm greedy, but I've got my expenses, you know. And I run the risk. Now, let's get down to it. First, how far gone are you, girl?'

'About two to three weeks,' said Rosie in a whisper.

'Is that all?' Kate said scornfully. 'Oh, my gawd! You girls! You miss one period and you get into a mad panic!'

'I know I'm – I'm sure – ' muttered Rosie, conscious that she was blushing deeply.

'You're sure you're pregnant. All right, all right! I don't doubt it. But I can't do anything for you.'

Rosie simply stood staring at Kate, wondering why she felt as if a great stone had been lifted from her heart.

'What do you mean?' Bess demanded.

'It's too early, that's what I mean,' said Kate. 'Too early for me to do anything. You'll have to bring her back when she's about two months. No good looking like that! I could take your money and go through the motions but that is not my style. Come back in six weeks.'

Bess sighed. 'Sorry, Rosie. Wasted journey.'

'Not your fault,' said Rosie, still floating on a wave of relief and desperate to leave this fearful place. 'Let's get back.'

'Wait,' said Kate. 'Since you're here, I might as well run the rule over you, see that all the parts are in order, as they

265

say.' She turned to Bess. 'Would you wait outside a minute, please? There's chair on the landing.'

The fear began to steal back to Rosie as Bess went out and the door closed behind her.

'Right,' said Kate briskly. 'No need to look like a scared rabbit. This won't take a minute and it won't hurt. Now, take your drawers off, lift up your skirt and petticoats, and lie on that bed.' And as Rosie hesitated she clapped her hands and added: 'Come on now! Sharp's the word and quick's the action.'

Kate spread the blanket over the bed and a trembling Rosie lay down as bidden, her skirt and petticoats tucked up almost to her chin. She was afraid but stronger even than the fear was the deep sweating sense of shame. She bit back a cry as those tiny hands parted her legs and eased her open. The hump-backed animal on the celing leered down at her and an echo of terror from that night in Brown's Alley rang in her head. She closed her eyes trying to shut out even the thought of what was happening.

The pain and the probing stopped, a hand slapped the side of her bottom and Kate's voice said: 'All done. Nothing wrong with your works, dearie, not that I can see. Come back in six weeks and we'll perform the oracle. That'll give you six weeks to have some fun, eh? You can let yourself go – no risks. Lovely, eh?' Her voice broke into a low tittering cackle.

Rosie stared at the woman. It was as much as she could do to stop the vomit rising from her stomach.

4

The clear light outside. The warmth of the sunshine. The clatter of great horses, the rattle of chains as a dray went by loaded with barrels of Ben Truman beer. A coster with a basket of kippers on his head swinging briskly along the pavement to the cry of:

'They're luverlee! All fresh and luverlee! Kippers! Kippers! Two pair a penny! Luverlee fresh kippers!'

Outside Kate's shop, Rosie stood and drunk it all in. She

felt a sense of release so great that her whole body seemed to be rippling with happiness. It was like escaping out of a dark tunnel into light, like waking from a nightmare, like riding Pegasus, like watching a linnet fly free. It was like coming back to life!

'You all right, Rosie?' asked Bess.

Rosie gave her a radiant smile. 'Oh, Bess, I feel wonderful! I've never felt better in my whole entire life!'

'Pity about today,' said Bess. 'Wasted journey. But I'll come back with you when it's time.'

'Oh, no,' said Rosie. 'I'm not coming back. I wouldn't come back here if you paid me in diamonds!' She took Bess's arm and hugged herself up to the big woman.

'I'm going to have my baby, Bess. I'm not going to let anyone take it away from me.'

'Blimey, what brought this on?'

'It's all clear now, Bess, all clear in my head. I know what I'm doing, truly.'

'How will you manage? Have you thought of that?'

'I don't know and what's more I don't care! I really don't care! I'll manage somehow. I've survived so far and I'll go on surviving. People can think what they like and say what they like. I don't care. I'm going to have my baby and nobody is going to stop me!'

5

On the night before his trial, Tommo was in sombre mood. He tried hard to maintain an optimistic front but his banter lacked conviction: it was obvious to Rosie that, inside, this man was deeply afraid. Sensing his need for company, Rosie waited until the Quorns had gone to bed and then let Tommo into the kitchen by the back door.

'You'll have to keep your voice down,' she warned. 'The Missus will have my guts for garters if she finds me entertaining young men in her kitchen.'

'Ta, Rosie,' he said.

'Cuppa tea? And a bacon sandwich?'

'Tea – lovely. No sandwich, not hungry.' He watched as she moved around the kitchen. 'You're looking fair, Rosie, very fair.'

'Thank you, sir.' She dropped him a little teasing curtsey, then added more seriously: 'And what about you, Tommo? How are things?'

'Oh, couldn't be better, straight up.'

'Is that Mr Bernstein still handling things for you?'

'Yeh, oh yeh. Don't know what I'd have done without him. And he's hired this-what-they-call-a-barrister to speak up for me.'

'Tommo,' said Rosie, 'tell me the truth. No malarkey. What do they reckon your chances áre?'

'Of what?'

'Getting off, of course.'

'About fifty-fifty.'

'As bad as that!' Rosie was shocked and she showed it.

'These lawyer blokes always look on the black side,' said Tommo, trying to sound cheerful. 'Trouble is the judge. According to Mr Bernstein we've drawn a bad card there. They've landed us with a real bastard.'

Rosie made the tea and lined up the cups in a heavy silence. Then Tommo said:

'Did you think about what I said?'

'You say so many things. What in particular?'

'When we talked in Coltman's. About us getting spliced. If I come out of this trial free and clear, how about it, Rosie?'

Rosie thought for a moment and then said, very gently: 'It doesn't matter to me if you are free and clear, Tommo, or if they send you to prison.'

'Thank you,' he said wryly, 'thank you very much.'

'You know what I mean,' she said. 'Of course, I don't want you to go down, but if you do it won't alter my feelings for you. What kind of girl would I be if I changed because of that? I'll be your friend, Tommo, whatever happens.'

'Friends!' he said scornfully. 'Who's talking about bloody friendship!'

'That's as far as it can go, Tommo,' she said.

'Why? Is it that copper?'

'Stan Roberts. No. I haven't seen him for weeks. I think he's given me up as a bad job.'

'Then who?'

She poured the tea and passed him a cup before replying. 'There was someone if you must know. Didn't last long. It's all over now.' She added calmly: 'Help yourself to sugar.'

'Who was he?'

'I don't think that's any concern of yours. It was no-one local, if that's what's worrying you.'

He chewed on this for awhile. 'And it's all over?'

'Yes.'

'What happened?'

'He's dead. An accident.' She felt the pain of the words even as she said them. 'And I couldn't marry you, Tommo, even if I wanted to, because I'm going to have a baby.'

He looked at her in astonishment, his mouth sagging open.

'It's the truth,' she said. 'Better I tell you straight. Don't want you hearing it from someone else. Big Bess is the only other one round here who knows. I'd like you to keep it to yourself for the time being.'

'Whose is it? This dead feller's?'

'Yes.'

'Well, there's a nice turn-up for the book!' he said cruelly. 'Little Rosie Carr in the pudding-club! Rosie Carr, the famous prick-teaser, has been caught! Rosie's going to have a little bastard!'

'That'll do, Tommo!' she said quickly.

'Don't tell me what to do!' he said. 'A right little cow you turned out to be, a right little whore!'

'I've been with one man, Tommo,' she said. 'How many women have you had? A dozen – fifty! Don't sit in judgment on me – it doesn't become you!'

'That's different,' he said. 'It's different for a man.'

'Oh, yes,' she said. 'I found that out the hard way. It's different for men. They don't have to face the consequences, they can get away with it. If I sleep with one man, they call me a whore. If you sleep with a dozen girls they call you a bit of a lad. Oh, it's different all right.'

'I didn't mean – ' he said.

'You said it and you meant it. I hoped for better from you, Tommo, that's all. Not pity, I don't need that. And I don't expect you to understand. It's just – well – I hoped for something better.'

He took a slow sip of tea and made a face. 'Where did you learn to make tea – from the Arabs?'

'What's wrong with it?'

'Nothing. I like it thick and strong.' Then he said: 'Sorry, Rosie.'

'I told you, I don't need pity.'

'No. I mean about flying off the handle. You took me by surprise. I – I take back what I said.'

'That's all right, Tommo. Sticks and stones can break your bones but words can never hurt – isn't that what they say?'

6

The next conversation they had together was in a cell under the court. It was Tuesday afternoon and Tommo had just been sentenced to twelve months imprisonment with hard labour. Mr Bernstein, who said that given the harsh reputation of the judge Tommo could count himself lucky, used his influence to get Rosie five minutes alone with the prisoner. Rosie couldn't see anything remotely lucky about a year's hard labour but she accepted Mr Bernstein's intervention gratefully and thanked him for his efforts on Tommo's behalf. He made no mention of payment for his services or for those of the barrister and she did not press the matter, reasoning that both she and Tommo had enough problems. She was relieved that Mr Bernstein made no reference to Russell Whitby.

Despite her determination to hide her feelings, she wept when she went into Tommo. He looked small and alone in the stark cell and her heart went out to him. He was near to tears too as he held her close: the silence heaved around them and it was a long time before it was broken.

'Don't cry, Rosie love,' he said at last. 'Could have been

worse. If I keep my nose clean, I'll ger remission – be out in a few months.'

'I could kill that judge!' she said viciously.

'Listen,' he said, 'I've been thinking. When you get near your time you'll have to leave the pub. You'll need a room. Rooms cost money. Well, you know my barrow? It's in the yard at Compton Road. If you sold that, it will bring in a few quid. And there's – '

She cut him off. 'Tommo, love, I'm all right. Big Bess says I can go to her place when I'm ready. I can help with her father and do a bit around the house. Then, after the baby's born, I'll get a job. I reckon they'd take me on at The Bunch of Grapes playing the joanna in the evenings. Besides, you're going to need that barrow when you come out. Mind, I'm grateful. It's ever so good of you to offer.'

'There's another thing,' he said.

'What?'

'If anybody asks about the baby, tell them it's mine.'

'Tommo!'

'I mean it. Say it's mine and that I'm going to put things straight when I come out.'

'Tommo, oh, Tommo. I couldn't.' Her eyes filled with tears again. 'I couldn't lumber you with that.'

'Who's talking about lumber? The way I work it out is this: I'm in trouble and you're in trouble, so we start even. Right?'

'In a way,' she said reluctantly.

'Besides, it will give me something to hold on to while I'm inside, something to look forward to. You – and a little ankle-biter. When I get out, we'll get hitched, start up afresh, have a handful of kids, and make our bloody fortune while we're about it.'

Keys began to rattle in the lock and he said desperately: 'What do you say, Rosie? What do you say?'

She reached up and kissed him. 'We'll see, Tommo, love. We'll see.'

'You'll think about it?'

'I promise.'

'You'll have to go now, miss,' said the court jailer.

'You'll come and see me, Rosie?' asked Tommo.

'Try and stop me,' she said.

'And you'll write? I'm allowed one letter a month, I think. Maybe more.'

'Yes, Tommo. I'll write,' she said.

7

That night Rosie lit a candle, got out her slate and books and began to pick up her studies again.

THIS IS A DOG. THE DOG HAS A BONE. THIS IS A CAT. THE CAT HAS A MOUSE. THIS IS JOHN. THIS IS MARY. MARY HAS A DOLL . . .

She had to learn and learn fast, so that she could keep her promise to write to Tommo. And I can't even write his name yet, she thought. She tried the letters on her slate.

T-O-M-O.

It didn't look right. In any case, she couldn't write to him as Tommo when his real name was Thomas. Thomas? How did that go? The pencil squeaked on the slate.

T-O-M-A-S.

She smiled. That looked better. A light wind rattled the pub sign and it sounded as if the winged horse were applauding her efforts. Or was he simply reminding her that she had been neglecting him of late?

She went to the window and looked down at the restless sign. 'Sorry, Pegasus. No more rides.' She patted her stomach. 'Got someone else to think of now.' The sign swung a little as if the winged horse was nodding his understanding of the situation. Rosie sighed. Suddenly she felt quite old.

It was hardly surprising, she told herself. After all, in a few weeks' time she would be nineteen.